GARBAGE Angel

GARBAGE Angel

Sarah's Story

CLYDE WHITE

Oma Publishing Company
Seguin, Texas

OMA PUBLISHING COMPANY
325 River Springs Drive, Suite 100
Seguin, Texas 78155-0179

The characters and events depicted in this book are fictitious. Any resemblance to any persons, living or dead, is coincidental. The town of Cibolo Falls is fictitious as well, and may or may not be based on many other cities and towns in Texas.

Book designed by Budget Book Design
Cover designed by Suzanne White
Author photo by CE Something Different Inc.
Front and back photos by Suzanne S. White
Earth photos provided by National Aeronautics and Space Association

Back and front hand photos modeled by Aaryn and Christine Gray
Manufactured in the United States of America by RJ Communications
Library of Congress Cataloging-in-Publication Data
White, Clyde
GARBAGE Angel: Sarah's Story / Clyde White

ISBN 0-9747175-0-9

1. Fiction—Texas 2. Ecology—World 4. Spiritual
I. Title
2004098796 2005

Dedication

This novel is dedicated to Sarah, now deceased, who had the original story idea and encouraged me to write it.

This novel is also dedicated to you, the reader, for without you there would be no need for novels. There is a saying that you are right where you are supposed to be in this space and time. I am glad you are including this novel in your present space, your present time and your present circumstance. It is no accident that brought us together. Please read with openness and, of course, understanding, because Sarah McPhee is, indeed, us.

SPECIAL THANKS

A special thanks for the support and help of my wife, Suzanne, who suffers my craziness when I write, and does all those things I can't—computer guru, editor, cover photography and design, sounding board, and devil's advocate.

Thanks to Bridget Richmond, a special lady, for sharing her wisdom concerning all matters spiritual. Thanks to my editors, Patricia Meyer, Suzanne White and Lynn Park. They each played a major part in different phases of manuscript development.

COMMENTS

Please send your comments about this novel by visiting our website at *www.omapublishing.com*. Enclose your e-mail address for Spook's Newsletter and news of forthcoming books on the continuing saga of Sarah McPhee, including Spook's complete journal.

Oma Publishing Company
323 River Springs Drive, Suite 100
Seguin, Texas 78155-0179

Author's Note

Although Eastern spiritual beliefs and practices have always held truth to a few Westerners, the masses weren't introduced to them until the late sixties. Before then, if you wanted to gain more knowledge about your spiritual side, there was very little information at your local library or bookseller. Now there are aisles of books.

The belief that we are all spiritual beings and exist in a dimension other than our conscious sensory-based level is growing stronger. Those who are gifted with paranormal or psychic ability provide us with a peek through the window to that unseen spiritual realm. However, do you really want to listen to those that claim wisdom about all that's going on behind our conscious senses? Some of today's religions say no. Many of our scientists say no; if it doesn't register on our earthly sensory screen and it can't be proven in black and white by usual accepted scientific principles, then it just isn't so.

So what do you do when one of these soothsayers, a psychic, or a convenient angel, shows up on your porch with "insight" to share? Do you send him packing or hear him out with caution and perhaps heed his message? It could happen to you.

It is happening to Sarah McPhee. Should she listen?

Although this is Sarah's story, it is also a message about the relationship of individual spirit to the collective. The tale reminds us that we are all in this together, spiritually connected, and what affects one affects all. A spark of life—a spark of love—is infused in everyone and everything on the planet. If even one little spark is lost, we all lose.

CHAPTER 1

"Cornmeal."

"Cornmeal?"

Ralph Coggins was agitated. "Did I stutter? It's cornmeal. Yellow cornmeal. You know, as in cornbread." He stuffed the bulging Ziploc bag into his backpack.

"Sure, Ralph." Sarah McPhee eyed her friend suspiciously. "Cornmeal. I would know it anywhere. Now, give me a hint—just a little one: what the hell are we going to do with it?"

"It's for the spirits." Ralph enjoyed the banter with his best, however lately moody, friend. As he waited for her response, he glanced around the fairground. He loved the smell of hotdogs, popcorn, and fried foods, even mixed with the peculiar odor of the dusty air. Thousands of carnival lights bounced off the low overcast sky and gave a strange glow that would help light their trek to the bridge. The clash of laughter, the nearby merry-go-round calliope, and an assortment of rock music from the distant midway tugged at him to forget their plans and check out the carnival.

Donnie, JB, and Smiley approached together. All wore backpacks and had their arms loaded with soft drinks, hotdogs, popcorn, and other snacks. Ralph was relieved that everyone had showed on time.

Sarah greeted her friends, then prodded Ralph, "Come on. Just tell me in five easy words what it's for. Is that too hard for you?"

"Hey, guys." Ralph flashed a wave to the newcomers. "All right, already," he snapped as he turned back toward Sarah. "Let's see if I can make this simple for you." He counted on his fingers as he enunciated each word: "To keep away the evil spirits." He lacked one finger so he flipped the middle finger of the other hand at Sarah and grinned. "So, it's six, but who's counting."

Sarah glared at him.

Smiley picked up on Sarah's irritation—something that seemed to happen quite often the last few weeks. A tall and lanky kid, Smiley was everyone's favorite. His long, stringy hair covered his forehead and draped to his shoulders. His upturned mouth and the natural creases and dimples of his face projected a permanent smile, and when he did actually smile, his whole face lit up. His real name was George—George Shirley Schultz. Of course, when he spoke, he spoke with a smile.

He towered over Ralph as he clutched his snacks to his chest with one arm and lightly punched Ralph in the shoulder with his free fist. "To keep away what evil spirits, Short Stuff?"

"He says he's going to keep them away with cornmeal," Sarah said.

"Uh-huh, cornmeal." Smiley nodded as he glared down at his friend. "So, I betcha you're just aching to tell us exactly what you're getting us into, aren't you, my man?"

Smiley backed away as Juanita Beatrice Martinez, better known as JB, jumped right in the fray, a menacing glare in her dark eyes. "Yeah, *amigo*. You said this was going to be fun. What was it? Let me see? Now I remember: we're going to communicate with some spooks to gain enlightenment, or some other of your shit. That's what you said. Now you say you're going to have to protect us from bad spirits. And you're going to protect us with cornmeal, Ralph? What are you, some kind of idiot?"

Donnie Rimkus took a heavy step toward Ralph and fixed him with an intense stare. Unfazed, Ralph methodically buttoned his coat up to his chin and pulled the collar up around his neck to protect him from the unseasonably chilly wind of late spring. "So, what's the story, Ralph, old friend, old pal, old buddy?" Donnie demanded. "Lay it on us doofus."

Ralph ignored Donnie. He turned to JB and whispered, "Don't call the spirits spooks. They don't like to be called spooks and they might turn on us. Especially the evil ones."

JB countered, "Ralph, you're full of it. Sometimes I wonder why we keep putting up with you and your dumb ideas. This séance crap is crazy and it'll probably get us in trouble. Then it's *y se acabo.* Over for you, dude."

The group watched Ralph laugh and turn a little circle on his toes. With a toss of his head he flipped a lock of hair out of his eyes, and then reached up to straighten his black-rimmed glasses. "Come on, guys. Would I, Ralph Coggins, lead you in the wrong direction? No. Would I, your greatest friend, do anything—I mean, anything at all—to lose your trust? That's a no."

"Yeah, Ralph, you would," Smiley said, slowly shaking his head. "Like about once a week."

"Look, the cornmeal is just to be careful. It's something you're supposed to do when messing with…uh…meeting with those in the spirit world, I mean, realm. It's the same for the tobacco. When you meet the spirits, you give—"

"Now hold it, dawg," Smiley interrupted, his lips set in an unintentional smile. "Tobacco? You brought 'em tobacco?"

"It's a gift. Cool, huh? You know me. I think of everything. Anything that can happen with the spirits, I'm ready. So, don't worry about it. I've got everything under control. You know me; I'm the main man."

Ralph noticed Donnie wring his hands. He knew that Donnie was about to unload. "Yeah, right, Ralph. You don't remember too good. Like, how many times have you told us that everything is cool, and then it blows up in your face—and ours, too? We oughta take away those crazy books he reads. That's where he got the idea for us to make all that money selling plastic milk carriers that we got caught stealing behind the grocery store. If Smiley hadn't talked him out of it, the manager would have called the police."

Ralph shook his head. "Wrong. You can't blame it on my books this time. I found this cool site on the internet."

"Whatever," Donnie retorted. "I think all this spirit stuff sucks, anyway."

Before Ralph could respond, Sarah plunged in, her words right to the point: "Donnie's right. This whole scene is too weird. We're not going to meet any spirits tonight and you know it. All you're going to do it get me in more trouble."

Ralph gestured with a hand to interrupt. "Come on, Sarah. I—"

"Come on, nothing," she shot back. She knew she was overreacting and letting Ralph get to her. "Look, my mom and dad are already on my case. And if we get caught at South Park after closing hours, Chief Sheck is going to send us to Juvy, for sure. He helped me get off last time, but he said I only get that one chance. One chance. Do you get it?"

"Wait a minute. Listen—"

"No, you listen," Sarah pushed on, her voice sharp and edgy. "My mom also said that I'd rot in jail if I get picked up for anything. She isn't going to bail me out again. That's what she said—'rot in jail.'" She planted her hands firmly on her hips and learned forward. "Will your mom and dad bail me out if you get me busted?"

Sarah's unusual outburst took the group by surprise, and others nearby turned to see what was all the commotion. Flustered by Sarah's tirade, Ralph held his hands out. "Hey, cool it. We aren't going to get in trouble. If I thought there was any way we would get caught, I wouldn't go. I've already checked it out. All the police officers are on duty here at the carnival. There's no way they'll be patrolling South Park. Even if they did, we'd see them coming. They'd never find us under the bridge."

Ralph studied Sarah. Her silence unnerved him. "So, what's your problem, anyway? Ever since you got picked up with your dumb-ass cousin, Rodney, you've had this shitty 'tude. You've been acting like a bitch. Just cool it, okay?"

"Yeah, Ralph!" Sarah shouted. "I'm the little crazy bitch, put here to make you miserable. And don't you forget it!"

"All right, guys. Enough. Quit badmouthing each other." JB stepped in. "We're friends, remember?"

"That's easy for you to say," Ralph retorted. "She isn't always putting you down."

"Poor thing," Sarah said over her shoulder as she turned and walked toward the food booths.

Sarah felt bad about her reactions. She had been irritated with everyone for over a month. Everything seemed backward and out of sorts. Her parents had grounded her and were always on her case about one thing or another. She never felt happy any more.

Strong in athletics, Sarah had developed a tomboyish style. She had a square, determined chin and a wide mouth that magnified her smile, and medium-cut straight, sandy-brown hair that fell in short bangs across her forehead. JB insisted she use a little lip-gloss and eye shadow to highlight her brown eyes, and blush to illuminate her high cheekbones.

Smiley watched her disappear in the crowd. "Dang, she sure does have her panties in a twist. What's her problem?" he groaned. "She goes batty over everything."

JB replied, "Yeah, I know. She's been PO'd ever since the Weyland party. She can't understand why no one believes what happened—especially her mom and dad."

"What's the big deal? They eventually got her off," Donnie asked, his mouth full of hotdog.

"Yeah, her dad knows Chief Sheck. But her mom still gets hyper over the whole thing. Sarah says her mom just keeps ragging her about it, saying she can't think for herself."

"Bummer," said Donnie.

"Right, Sarah said she'd run away if she had a place to go."

Ralph, silent for too long, spoke up. "Well, okay, but that don't give her any right to dis me. That's not cool."

"Aw, come on, Ralph," JB coaxed. "She needs our help. We've got to support her 'till her mom gets a grip."

Ralph considered what JB said. "Umm…okay. I guess since she's so against going, let's just forget it and check out the carnival."

As Sarah bought some snacks she began to feel bad about the way she had treated Ralph. He always stood up for her and didn't deserve her grief. Her guilt demanded that she make peace. She returned with two lemonades, a couple of hotdogs, and Ralph's favorite, cotton candy. She held out half to Ralph with a meek smile. "Sorry, Ralph. I've been acting shitty lately. Maybe if I feed you, you'll forget it. I don't mean to be a screamer. It's just that I—"

"Hey, make my day," Ralph took half the snacks from Sarah. "I'll forget anything for cotton candy." He plucked off a bit and stuffed it into his mouth.

"We've decided not to go, Sarah. We'll go another time," JB said.

"Oh, no," Sarah insisted. "It's okay. I really want to go. Ralph's right. It'll be fun." She poked Ralph in the ribs. "And maybe the ghosts can help me get my shit together. You think the spirits care if I call 'em ghosts?"

"Great!" Ralph ignored the question. "What do you think, guys? Wanna go? The spirits are waiting."

Everyone nodded their approval. They got their flashlights from their packs and started the half-mile walk through the woods to South Park. Their lights played creepily off the hanging moss of the oak trees.

Ralph was shorter than the girls, and the boys towered over him. Pencil-thin, he weighed only ninety-five pounds. Since grade school he had been the habitual butt of skinny, shrimp, and four-eyes jokes from most of the boys his age. Like Smiley and Donnie, he wasn't active in sports as most of the other boys were, so they somehow came together as a group. As far as they were concerned, their little group was made up of the only good guys on campus. Though they didn't have an official leader, if a vote were taken, Ralph would get the most without anyone being able to give a reason why.

Sarah and JB took Ralph as he was and, despite his not being "a great male specimen"—a secret they kept to themselves—they enjoyed his being around, particularly the comedy that he provided. Despite his own inexperience, he was willing to offer candid and humorous male insight into questions arising from their growing interest in certain guys in town.

After about fifteen minutes of working their way through the woods, they arrived at their favorite spot on the Guadalupe River, beneath the highest bridge in Cibolo County. Ralph dropped his pack and instructed everyone to gather firewood and some of the bits of paper that littered the whole area. They cleared a small area of grass near the top of the embankment where the end of the bridge connected, just below where they were to hold the séance. He stacked the wood with the smaller branches on the bottom, arranged over the litter. He pulled out a cigarette lighter and blicked it. The paper flared up and started burning the smaller branches; they in turn caught the larger branches on fire.

"Yo, dawg," it was Smiley. "You said we would hide if the law showed up. Gonna be pretty hard to hide with that fire. Why don't we just send up a flare?"

"Don't worry about it. We'll be okay. We need the fire to invite the spirits into the circle. After the séance is over, we can warm up before heading back to the carnival."

"What do you mean, circle? What circle?" JB asked as she edged closer to the growing fire, rubbing her hands together over it. The breeze swirled and shifted the smoke into her eyes. She rubbed her eyes and moved over a step to escape the smoke.

"The circle is very important. Just wait. Okay?"

"Okay, Ralph. I'm cool," she replied with another long shiver. "No, I'm not cool; I'm *mucho frio*. Let's get started. My parents are picking me up at ten-thirty at the fairgrounds front gate. I don't think we have time to screw around if this so-called ceremony is going to take very long."

Sarah followed, "Mine too. My dad said if I wasn't there at exactly ten-thirty, he was leaving without me. That means I can't even be one minute late. Mom is just looking for a reason to ground me again."

"All right, I get the message. We'll hurry, about as much as you can hurry these things," Ralph answered, his voice raising an octave as it usually did when he got excited. "As soon as we get JB's butt warm we'll get started."

Donnie sprawled his large frame on the grass in front of the fire. The light from the flame danced over his face. "Why don't I just hang out right here, so I can keep warm?"

"No way, dude. You gotta sit inside the circle, but we'll give you a spot close to the fire."

"Asshole," Donnie muttered as Ralph gestured for the group to follow as he moved up the incline a few feet to the very top where the bridge joined the upper bank. Unlike the angular Smiley, Donnie was more than a bit rotund. His weight struggled to break free from a coat that was obviously too small, and it was difficult to tell where his neck left off and his head started. If an observer could get past the bulbous nose that dominated the meaty features of his face, he would find compelling blue eyes. His hair was probably blond like his parent's, but it was hard to tell because he kept it shaved, revealing two small scars on top of his head. It would be easy to mistake him for an adolescent professional wrestler. As he struggled to get to his feet, he reminded himself of what his mother had said, that he had to exercise more and quit eating the very foods he ate tonight.

The group had to stoop over to keep their heads from touching the bottom of the bridge's steel girders. All flashlights were on Ralph as they watched him open his pack and remove the Ziploc of corn-meal. He sprinkled the cornmeal in a line to make a large circle and instructed his friends to sit just inside the circle, facing the middle, close enough so they would later be able to hold hands in a complete circle just inside the cornmeal line. Donnie complained when he didn't get the promised spot closest to the fire; he was ignored.

"The cornmeal will protect us from any evil spirits that wanna come to the party," Ralph announced softly with an odd reverence to his voice. "All we have to do is stay in the circle while the séance is going on."

JB exaggerated a nod to irritate Ralph. "So, only the good spooks—oh, sorry—good spirits can come in the circle with us. That's nice to know, Ralph. Good in, bad out."

All except Ralph giggled nervously. "That brings up a problem for me," Smiley said softly. "How do the spirits know if they are good or bad? I mean, who decides whether a spirit is good or bad? Who chooses?"

Ralph stopped rummaging through his pack as he and the others pondered this important question. Donnie deadpanned, "Probably the good decide." Even Ralph laughed.

Ralph continued his pack search. He retrieved a pouch of roll-your-own tobacco along with a packet of cigarette paper and placed them in the middle of the circle. This brought the lingering giggles to a halt. He knew he had the group's full attention and with all the flashlights trained on the pouch, he announced, "This is a peace offering. Whenever you meet with the spirits you should always bring a gift that the spirits can use. And their favorite is tobacco."

"Why didn't you just bring a pack of real cigarettes and save the spirits some trouble rolling their own?" JB asked. "And what if you cause the spirits to get cancer?"

Donnie chimed in. "Hey, I wonder if spirits even get sick?"

"They will if Ralph keeps bringing them tobacco to smoke," Smiley chortled.

"Okay, guys, knock it off," Ralph pleaded. "If you don't get serious, the spirits will never show up. You have to have a little rev…rev—"

"Reverence, Ralph," Sarah assisted, until now content to be silent and enjoy being out of the house on her own for the first time in weeks.

"Yeah, that," Ralph nodded as he pointed at his friend. "Reverence is necessary to bring the spirits out into the open."

The group again trained their lights on the pack as Ralph brought out a bundle of long church candles. "Uh-oh, *vela femeninos*," JB mumbled, hardly moving her lips. "What're you gonna do with those, Ralphy-boy?"

Ralph began to stand the candles in a circle surrounding the tobacco, just in front of the seated group. "There are seven of them. When I light them, that will make a good…uh…environment—yeah, environment—for the spirits to join us. Then all we have to do is call to them and they'll come."

"Why seven?"

"There is one candle for each chakra of our bodies. Seven chakras, seven candles."

"Chakra? What the hell or you talking about?" Sarah asked. "Are you making this up?"

"Power centers, my dear. Ralph always speaks the truth. Each one of us has seven power centers or chakras in a row from the top of our heads down to our asses. Our bodies exchange energy with the spirit world through each one. So, we have one candle for each chakra, reminding the spirits that we know what we're doing here."

"Ralph, you're full of shit," Smiley countered.

"Laugh not, ye *stupidos*. You guys will never learn." The group watched Ralph cup his hand around each candle flame to ward off the wind until it was well lit. "Sooner or later you'll realize that I'm the master."

The breeze picked up and blew out several of the candles just as he had completed the circle. He relit them as he instructed: "Okay, now turn off the flashlights and I'll sit with you in the circle. They watched Ralph sit down and cross his legs. He learned toward Sarah on his right, reached out and took her cold hand, He gestured for Donnie's beefy hand on his left. The others followed his lead, all holding hands in a complete circle.

The smoke from the fire escaped the breeze and hovered between the girders, causing the fire and the candles' flickering light to reflect eerily off the bottom of the bridge. They sat in silence as they listened to the occasional overhead popping of cars passing over the bridge's expansion joints.

Ralph whispered, "Now, brothers and sisters—"

He stopped as Smiley snickered, bringing giggles from the others. Ralph shot Smiley a menacing glance. "Now let's get serious and don't laugh or say anything about what's going on. It might offend the spirits and they won't show up. When they speak or show themselves, don't be afraid of them, and let me do the talking unless they ask you to, or they ask you a question—whatever."

He made an exaggerated attempt to clear his throat, signifying to the circle it was time to get down to the business of spirit communication. "Okay, guys, let's close our eyes. Only open them when the spirits come forward." He looked around the circle to make sure they all complied. He didn't want any screw ups. This had to be perfect.

He spoke with renewed reverence, however nervously: "Spirit friends, out there, uh, here with us. Please hear me now—my plea. I hope and trust that you find us worthy of your presence."

Ralph paused as he searched for what to say next. Donnie turned his head toward Ralph and opened one eye to see why he hesitated. Something appeared different. Something was wrong. He opened both eyes and looked beyond the circle.

Ralph continued, "So that you might honor us by sharing your wisdom and—"

"Shit!" Donnie shouted. He released both Ralph and JB's hands and struggled to his feet, bumping his head on the bridge girder. "Look!"

He answered on the fourth ring: "Pizza Shack. Bob McPhee here. May I help you?"

"Bob. Donald Sheck."

"Chief. How's it going?"

"Well, I'm doing okay, but I think you have a little problem."

Bob didn't want to hear what was coming. He checked his watch. It was five minutes until ten. "Sarah?"

"Yeah. Caught her and a few of her chums at South Park after closing."

Bob felt a wave of relief. It certainly could have been worse. "Well, dammit. She was supposed to be at the carnival. I swear, I'm going to have to keep her locked up to keep her out of trouble."

"There's more, Bob. They accidentally set about a half-acre on fire. The wind scattered their campfire. The fire department sent out two units."

"Any major damage?" Bob tried to remain calm, despite his growing anger with his daughter and at himself for urging her mom to let her go to the carnival without adult supervision. For the second time in a month, the police chief had to deliver bad news about Sarah.

"No, just grass, but there's more you need to know. It seems they were in the midst of some type of ceremony under the bridge. They had made a circle of sorts with a grainy substance on the ground and inside they had lit some candles. Looked a bit weird to me."

"Well, that's great, just great," Bob muttered under his breath, but loud enough for Sheck to hear. "What do I need to do, Donald?"

"First off, you best come down here and pick her up. We can discuss where this is headed after you get here."

"You know, last time she screwed up, we talked about letting her spend the night in jail. Maybe now would be a good time to shock some sense into her?"

"I agree, but we have only one holding cell for women available, and a couple of crazies already have reservations for the night. I don't think you want Sarah spending five minutes alone with either one of them, if you get my drift."

"All right, I'll be right there. Thanks."

"Glad to help. I'll have to write up a report for the city attorney, but I'll do what I can. She's a good kid. Even after she got mixed up in that Weyland deal, she acted just as I would want my daughter to act."

"Thanks, Chief. I'll be there in thirty minutes."

Bob told his wife, Barbara, of the trouble, and listened to her tirade about the lifelong punishment her daughter was about to receive. She eventually settled down and they decided it best that she stay at the family-owned Pizza Shack until closing while Bob handled the problem at the police station.

He arrived at the station about the same time as the other parents. After introductions with the chief, they met as a group in his office without the kids who, much to their horror and embarrassment, were in a holding cell.

A young officer scrambled to find enough chairs for the eight parents crammed into the small office. After the officer completed his mission, the chief released him with instructions to close the door behind him.

Bob watched Chief Donald Sheck lean back in his chair and unconsciously nibble at the hairs of his mustache. He saw a man in his early forties, lean and trim in a snug-fitting khaki uniform. He had leathery tanned skin and windblown curly brown hair that had a touch of gray at the temples. His profile was rugged, but compassionate brown eyes revealed a man that could be fair and trusted.

"As the kids tell it, they left the carnival just after dark, walked over to South Park, and then built a fire. The wind picked up and the nearby grass caught fire. By the time they reacted, it was too late—the fire was out of hand. A passerby on the highway called the fire department, who in turn called us. They responded with two crews and extinguished the fire in minutes.

"It's our policy when someone is caught in the park after hours, if they're not up to any particular mischief, we run them off after taking their names and addresses. If they're caught a second time, they're fined. Unfortunately, because of the fire, this will likely fall in the lap of Assistant City Attorney Joyce Mueller. She's a nice lady, but she may very well want to bring the kids before the judge to decide punishment."

"Do the kids have to stay here until a decision is made by Ms. Mueller?" Mrs. Martinez, JB's mother, asked nervously.

"If it was a serious crime, no doubt they would have had to wait until tomorrow for arraignment, but in situations such as this, because we're such a close-knit group, she and the judge have no problem with my releasing your kids to you on your own recognizance, if you agree to accompany them back if necessary. I really don't think your kids are going to skip out on us.

"One more thing I believe you need to know. The kids were having some type of ceremony with candles and such. They said that they were having a séance, but the fire interrupted. I will have to include that in my report, but I will downplay it, because I feel it was just teenage craziness and they meant no harm. I suggest that you get with your kids and see what was going on. That's about it, folks. Questions?"

Bob broke the silence. "Chief Sheck, whatever happens, I think I speak for all of us when I say, I appreciate your situation and also your help. We'll do what's necessary to get this taken care of. Of course, our main concern is the kids. We want to protect them, but again, we want to see that this never happens again. I think I know you well enough from past experience that you have our best interest at heart. Again, thanks for that."

Sheck nodded his thanks with a thin smile. "Any more comments or questions? Okay, in a short while my clerk will have some papers for you to fill out in order for us to release your kids. You'll be notified in a few days what action will be taken. You folks seem to have some good kids. I sure would be disappointed if I had to make another trip up here tonight because some parent executed an offspring because of this trouble."

The parents signed the release papers and retreated to the front steps of the police station to wait for their kids. They discussed group punishment and decided to hold off until after Ms. Mueller's decision. About thirty minutes later the kids came out the front door of the police station and followed their parents to their cars. Sarah got in the front seat beside her father and dropped her pack on the floor. She fully expected the worst.

"Hello."

"Hi," she answered as she looked straight ahead.

"How was the carnival?"

She didn't answer. The remainder of the ride was in silence; however she knew that it wasn't going to last long. Her mom would see to it.

When they arrived home, Sarah closed the car door and walked up the sidewalk to the front door. Her dad followed close behind. It entered her mind that this would be the perfect time to bolt and run away. But where would she go? All her friends were in the same mess she was; they certainly wouldn't take her in. That's crazy, she thought. They couldn't take her in even if they weren't involved. She opened the door to find her mom, still dressed in her red and white plaid Pizza Shack uniform. She stood in the middle of the living room. Sarah could see her mother's rage, and resigned to the fact that there was no way she was going to get out of this. She wanted to rebel: "*No, ma'am, I don't want you to take my order.*" However, she thought it would be better if she kept her mouth shut and took her punishment, whatever it might be. Was there any other choice? Following her mother's pointed finger, she sat down on the sofa and folded her arms across her chest in feeble protest.

Bob closed the front door and crossed the room. He stood with his hands in his front pockets as he and Sarah watched Barbara pace back and forth as if she didn't know what to say. They waited for the expected rage.

"Well, I guess four weeks' grounding wasn't enough. Your first night off the leash and you try to burn down South Park. What were you thinking? Not only do you build a fire in a windstorm, you break into the park after hours, when you're obviously not supposed to be there. You go from one problem to the next. If the chief wasn't a friend of your father, they would have charged you with drinking as a minor a month ago. And now you—"

"I wasn't drinking, and you know it!" Sarah blurted out.

Barbara glared at her daughter and declared through a clinched jaw, "We've been through this. If you had any sense at all, you would have left the party the minute you saw that the others were drinking."

"I told you, I begged Rodney to leave, but he said there wasn't any problem."

"Then you should have just walked out and called us to come get you. You should've never been with Rodney to start with. Then you wouldn't have been arrested with the rest of them."

Sarah gaped at her mom. "I don't…Mom, you gave me permission to go with him. You know that he's a druggie and drunk, but you said it's okay. Now you say that I shouldn't have been with him. That's not fair, and you know it."

"No matter if I gave you permission or not; it's up to you to make the right decision in any situation. And you've shown that you can't. You are just not using common sense—and tonight proves it."

Sarah fixed her mom with the best glare she could muster. She knew that no matter what she said, it would do no good. She pushed on, her voice quivering, "I should've left the party. I didn't. That was a mistake. But I wasn't drinking, and you've been punishing me ever since for something I didn't do. And it's not fair. Everyone thinks I'm a drunk, but I'm not. I'm—"

Sarah stopped short, her shoulders slumped in defeat. She turned toward her dad in a plea for help. She received none, so she fixed narrowed eyes on her mom and waited. When her mom's frosty silence continued, she released a long breath and continued calmly:

"Yes, I was at the park. We broke in. We started a fire to keep warm and the wind spread it to the grass. We tried to put it out, but it was too much. It was my fault, and I will take the punishment. If there is a fine, I'll pay for it out of my Pizza Shack wages."

Barbara's piercing green eyes studied Sarah. Her daughter glared back, determined that she was not going to allow her mom to intimidate her as she had done the last four weeks. She would take her punishment, but she would fight back and if that didn't work, she would leave home and live with her grandmother if necessary.

Barbara took a quick look at her husband, then spoke to her daughter, her voice firm and final: "You bet you'll take your punishment…and pay the fines. No daughter of mine will now or ever wiggle her way out of what's coming to her. I'll see to it. And you can bet, whatever the punishment, it will be nothing compared to what you get from me…from us."

Barbara was scared. She had seen mothers and daughters turn against each other over what seemed to be minor misunderstandings or differences of opinion, but she had always said that it wouldn't happen to her and her daughter—she would not let it. Now it was happening, and as much as she tried to be fair, the division between them seemed to be widening. However, basic conduct and discipline had to be maintained. If that ruined their relationship, so be it.

"I'm not going to stand for these continual scrapes with the law. They will end here and now, or you'll be grounded forever." She nodded sharply, her face taut. "Do you understand?"

Sarah blinked, but held fast, looking intently into her mom's eyes. "Yes."

Barbara turned toward Bob, who shrugged his helplessness. Sarah hoped he would be more reasonable, but knew he always held back and let Barbara take the lead. He finally spoke up. "I think there's more that we need to discuss. Sheck told me that they found some candles. It looked like there might have been some sort of ceremony. What were you guys doing with candles?"

"What? You're kidding!" Barbara broke in and took an abrupt step toward her daughter, her jaw tense and face reddened. "All right, Sarah. What gives?"

"We were going to have a séance."

"A séance?" Barbara repeated. She studied her daughter pensively. "Don't tell me you believe in all that spirit stuff."

"I don't know. I guess maybe there are spirits, ghosts, whatever."

"You must believe in spirits or you wouldn't be having a séance."

Sarah tried to disguise her annoyance, but failed. "We were just looking for something to do, Mom. We weren't hurting anybody. What difference does it make anyway?"

"Well, it certainly makes a difference when you set fire to the park in the process."

Sarah kept quiet and watched the corner of her father's mouth turn up in a little smile. She wished her mother would lighten up a bit as well.

Barbara continued. "You and your little gang had better think twice about this séance nonsense in the future. It's nothing but mumbo jumbo. So, forget it. Find some harmless entertainment. Something that won't get you in trouble."

"Yes, ma'am."

Sarah watched her mom frown and curl her mouth. She wondered how much longer she was going to be bashed. Much to Sarah's relief, Barbara asked her husband, "Where do we go from here? Have they decided about fines, punishment?"

"Well, Donald thinks that since there was a fire involved, the city attorney might take it before the judge. Maybe not. They're going to let us know in a few days."

"Well, that's just great," Barbara replied under her breath. "So what'll we do now?"

"Wait."

"Okay. We wait," she nodded positively. "Now, you…" she turned her attention toward Sarah, "I have no idea what kind of punishment you're going to get from us. We'll wait and see what the city decides first. In the meantime, you're grounded until further notice. Since you won't have anything else to do, we'll increase your hours selling pizza. That way you'll have the bucks to pay any fines. Any questions so far?"

Sarah crossed her arms and rolled her eyes. She finally answered, her tone and manner heavy with sarcasm: "No, ma'am. No questions."

Barbara ignored the insolence, surprising Sarah. "Also, starting now, you're going to spend more time hitting the books. I don't want any more of your teachers calling about your shoddy or nonexistent class work. You used to be an A student. Now, in the past month, you've become a nonstudent. That changes here and now. Understand?"

"Yes, ma'am. Anything you say," Sarah replied flippantly, egging on her mom's fury.

Bob could see Barbara's anger and watched for the explosion that he felt was sure to come. She turned away as if giving up the fight. Before he could speak, Barbara turned back and faced her daughter. Sarah watched her mom and waited for the tirade to continue.

Sarah became unnerved by her mom's stare and shrugged for comment.

Barbara released a long breath of tension and said softly, "Sarah, I realize I've—we've—been hard on you the past few weeks but you must understand that we just want you to do well. And, of course, we want you to stay out of trouble. I don't like having to discipline you and I don't want you to be unhappy. However, a—"

Sarah watched as her mom's eyes teared up. "Sarah, sweetheart, I love you."

Bob waited to see if Barbara had more to say. When it was apparent she was through, he said firmly to Sarah:

"Okay, being that tomorrow is Saturday, we'll need you for two shifts—the first and third. Get your butt in gear and be on time."

"Yes, sir. Anything else?" she asked as she stood up. She looked to both her mom and her dad. Dismissed, she quickly retreated up the stairs to the welcome solitude of her bedroom.

Journal Note

"You are created in the image of God. In essence, you, as an individual here on Earth, are the physical expression of the loving spirit of God. Your spirit is merely an extension of God's spirit, as is the spirit of all others that have been placed on Earth by God. The plants, the animals, the water you drink, the ground you walk on, and the air you breathe are all a physical extension and expression of God's spirit."

CHAPTER 2

The Courthouse had long seen its better days and was under, it seemed to those who worked there, constant remodeling and repair. The faint odor of dust layering the furniture permeated the air along with the aroma of coffee and *carne guisada* tacos from the snack bar. The halls were cluttered with workers and scaffolding that had to be negotiated by the constant stream of clerks, lawyers, and visitors. The courtrooms and other offices, even behind closed doors, were unable to escape the distant hammering and other construction noises. In musty Courtroom 3, the eight tall windows were open, adding the sound of traffic from two floors below.

"Municipal Court, in and for the City of Cibolo Falls, Texas, Judge John Abbot presiding. All rise."

There was a light rumble of feet on the wooden floors and creaking of the bench seats as the three dozen spectators and accused alike scrambled to their feet. The judge emerged out of a side door and took his place on the bench. He acknowledged the court clerk, two C. F. police officers, and several attorneys with a nod.

He reviewed the caseload and then announced, "Well, it looks like we have a full morning ahead. We'd as well get on with it. First case, please."

Judge Abbot watched the court clerk motion for the kids and a prearranged one parent each to come before the bench. They came meekly forward and stood before the judge as Assistant City Attorney Joyce Mueller joined them.

"Your Honor," Ms. Mueller declared as she checked the legal pad she was holding, "we have five local 13- and14-year-olds—Juanita Martinez, Ralph Coggins, George Shultz, Sarah McPhee, and Donnie Rimkus—all presently students at C. F. Junior High School. They are charged with breaking Cibolo Falls City Ordinance 1371b, being in a park after posted hours last Friday night. They are also charged with a Class C misdemeanor, starting a grass fire in the park."

Judge Abbot peered down at each of the kids and their parents, and then back toward Mueller. "Do the defendants have legal council?"

"No, they don't. They have elected to plead guilty." She made a point of clearing her throat. "And put themselves at the mercy of the court."

"And hope the judge is in a good mood, I presume," he remarked as reviewed the report in front of him. "Is Chief Sheck in attendance this morning?"

"Here, Judge," Sheck called out as he stood up from a seat in the back row. Everyone turned to see him walk up the center isle to join the defendants and their parents; the noise from his boots on the hardwood floor echoed off the walls.

"Chief, I see that you wrote and signed off on this report. Were you the arresting officer?"

"Yes, sir. I was at the station when the fire was reported. Since we were short-handed, I decided to ride out and see what the situation was. The fire department had just put out the fire and were fixing to call the police department when I arrived."

"The kids who started the fire were still there?"

"The firemen had suggested that the kids hang around until I got there, to avoid additional trouble. They readily complied."

"The kids gave you their full cooperation?"

"Yes, sir."

"And what's your take on this 'crime'?"

"You know, Judge, if they were mine, I'd have their hides, if you know what I mean. However, having said that, I don't know. Being it's their first offense and their having given both the police and firemen their complete cooperation, I feel for them and their parents. Bottom line, the fire was a stupid accident, but they should've never been there in the first place."

"So, what are you suggesting, Chief?"

Sheck grinned. "Well, Judge, I think it would be a little harsh if you gave them two years of hard labor."

The judge smiled and there were several snickers from the courtroom. "Thanks for your help, Chief. I think that's all I need." Sheck turned to walk back to his seat when the judge stopped him. "Oh, Chief, one more thing. Yesterday morning in the Crime Blotter section of the newspaper, there was a blurb about the fire at the park. It mentioned that, before the fire, there had been some kind of ceremony akin to witchcraft. You mention it in your report, but don't go into detail. What can you tell me about it?"

"I dismissed it as young teenage craziness. I really don't put any importance on it. Those kids were not practicing witchcraft for sure. I think that reporter was just looking for something to spice up the report."

"What was the reporter doing there?"

"Looking for some action, I guess. He picked up the fire call on his scanner. He was already there when I arrived. The firemen showed him the candles."

The Judge stared quizzically at Sheck. "You're sure about this? I certainly don't want to dismiss this if there's any chance of it growing into goat-killing or something."

"They are good kids, your honor. They aren't witches or warlocks. Trust me."

"Dismissed, Donald."

Chief Sheck returned to his seat as the judge again gazed at the kids. Without taking his eyes off of them, he asked, "Ms. Mueller, do you have a recommendation for the court?"

"Fines, court costs, and the cost of fire damage. And probation, your honor."

"What about the fire department?"

"Unlike the EMS, the fire department doesn't charge for manpower and equipment at this time."

"Okay, Joyce. Thanks." Judge Abbot turned his attention to the kids. Ralph wanted to hide as he watched the judge fold his hands in front of him and stare down to study each kid. In his twenty years on the bench the judge had plenty of youthful trouble-makers stand before him, charged with crimes both large and small, but these just didn't seem to fit the bill.

"Well, folks," he said firmly, "you messed up. Now you're here in front of me to answer for what you did. But I'm the least of your problems. Your parents are here. They are upset and don't want to be here. You have to answer to them everyday. You know what that means? Every day for a long time you had better act right and have the right answers, because they don't want to come back here again.

"Now, which one of you is Ralph?" he asked.

Ralph's body slumped and his head dropped. "I am, sir," he answered meekly. He wondered if they could see his heart pounding.

"Speak up, son. There are a lot of people in this room who came just to hear what you have to say. You wouldn't want to disappoint them, would you?"

Ralph looked up, pointing his chin directly at the judge, and croaked, "No, sir."

"That's better. Now, this police report tells me that perhaps you are the leader of this little band. Is that true?

"I believe that—" Ralph took a quick peek at his friends and was resigned to defeat: "Maybe I was until Friday night. It was my idea to go to the park. If you want to throw...well, I think if anyone gets punished, it should be me. It was all my fault."

"You're saying that you're guilty, and I should let the others go; is that correct?"

"I'm guilty. They aren't." He felt much better having taken the blame, which he truly felt was his.

"Do you want to say anything else?"

"Well, I'm sorry. I screw...messed up. I apologize to my friends, to Mom and Dad, and everybody."

"What about the candles?"

"We went to the park to have a séance. The candles were a part of that."

"Have you ever had a séance before?"

"No, sir."

"Then how do you know what to do when you have your first séance?"

"I found it on the Internet."

"Well, I assume it worked. You get visited by some spirits?"

"No, sir. No spirits showed up."

"You going to have another séance—to try again?"

Ralph hazarded a wry grin. "No. One was a little more trouble than I wanted."

"Good decision."

The judge nodded at Ralph and consulted the report. "Juanita Martinez?"

"Yes, Judge," she said, taking a half-step forward.

"Guilty or not guilty?"

"Guilty" she answered. She could actually feel her knees shaking. She willed them to stop before anyone saw them.

"Ralph says you're not guilty?"

"We've all talked—me and the others—and we agree that Ralph is crazy, uh, has some crazy ideas, but we did follow him. We didn't have to. We all are just as guilty."

"Now we have Sarah McPhee. What say you?"

Sarah looked directly at Judge Abbot. "I'm guilty," she squeaked.

"George Shultz?"

"Guilty, sir."

"Mr. Donnie Rimkus, do you go along with the others?"

Donnie nodded and said, "Guilty."

"So, where do we go from here, Donnie?" the judge asked firmly.

He dropped his head in dismay. "I guess you maybe put us in jail, or make us pay some money to—you know—for fines or something. Whatever." He looked up at the judge; a beefy grin crossed his face. "If I was the judge, I'd probably let us go?" Chuckles arose around the courtroom. His father, standing next to him, shook his head in embarrassment.

The judge stared seriously for a long moment at Donnie and then smiled. "Well, you've talked me into it. I'm going to let you go, but there are several conditions that must be met—all of them. First, court costs are one hundred dollars each. Fines, damage to the park, fifty dollars each. Being in the park after hours, one hundred dollars each. That totals 250 dollars for each of you. Your parents may pay this now, but I want proof of some sort, thirty days from today, that you paid them back. These fines are your responsibility."

He consulted Sheck's report, then continued, his voice stern: "There's more. Each of you is on probation for six months. If any of you get in trouble again during that time, I will reconsider this sentence, and I guarantee, you won't like it. And Ralph, no more séances, chicken killings, or anything that closely resembles it. Understand?"

Ralph nodded as did his cohorts.

"Last, but I assure you, not least: in the next thirty days, each of you will spend fifteen hours in community service to pay back the City of Cibolo Falls for your misdeeds. I want each of you to get out there and clean up the litter that is everywhere you look. Pick it up and carry it home with you. Have garbage pick-up service collect it or have someone take it to the dump. I want time spent documented, meaning keep a record. At the end of the thirty days, deliver the proof of time spent picking up litter, and the proof that you paid back your parents to my secretary. She will notify me that you have done so. If any of you think I might forget about this—don't. I will have you spend time in Juvenile Detention."

Ralph knew they were about off the hook as he saw the judge spread his hands. "Questions?"

Five kids shook their heads.

"Are you sure? I will not accept, later, an excuse that you didn't understand."

Still no reply. "All right, get out of my courtroom, and don't return. I don't forget a face. Understand, Ralph?"

"You'll never see me again, Judge." Ralph grinned his relief.

After school on Wednesday, Sarah and JB trudged along Welshire Street, serving their first litter duty. Sarah kept a keen eye on passing traffic, hoping for invisibility. Being seen was just fine with JB and she couldn't resist teasing her friend: "The only difference between you and a convict on a work gang is that you aren't wearing a prison uniform."

Sarah really didn't care if she actually picked up litter or not. She would put in her thirty minutes a day and keep a record to satisfy Judge Abbot, but he didn't say exactly how much garbage she had to collect. She had many things on her mind and litter really wasn't one of them.

JB watched Sarah and wondered if she was ever going to let go of the anger she held toward her mom. JB had tried on several occasions to talk to Sarah about it.

"Look," JB blurted out, "so you got grounded for six weeks. Just do it and get it over with."

"Yeah, that's easy for you to say," Sarah retorted, her mouth and jaw tight and grim. "You only got two weeks. How fair is that?"

JB watched Sarah twist and gather her garbage sack into a ball and pitch it down the street in front of her. It didn't go far because she had put very little in it in over ten minutes. "And Ralph. Wow-wee, he got off without any punishment at all. He got us into that mess and his parents probably patted him on the back. That's shitty, JB, and you know it."

"So, tell your mom what you think. Maybe she'll give in."

"In my dreams," Sarah countered. She stopped, bent over, and picked up the sack, slung it over her shoulder, and turned to face JB. "Last night she was ragging me again, so I told her to leave me alone. When I said that Ralph didn't even get grounded, she really got pissed off. She said that if Ralph was her son, he would have gotten six months, so I should be happy if I only got six weeks."

"Damn, she is kind of bitchy, isn't she?"

"I thought for a minute she was going to throw me out of the house when I said that I was very happy—so happy that there just weren't words to describe it. And my happiness was all because of her."

JB giggled. "Uh-oh, bad news. What did she say?"

"Let me see if I can get this straight. Mom said, 'One more word out of you, young lady, and you will get six months, or maybe six years.' Damn, I hate being called 'young lady.'"

"So, did you?"

"Did I what?"

"Say anything else."

Sarah forced a throaty laugh. "You kidding? It was really hard not too, but I shut up and got away from her."

"Look, sweetie, maybe the time would go by faster if you just do it—pick up the garbage, okay?"

"Hey, now. A little bossy, aren't you?" Sarah replied with easy defiance. "I don't want to pick up someone else's crap. It's just not fair."

"Maybe not, but it's not going away. So just do it and make it a party. In a few weeks you can forget about cleaning up the trash." Annoyed with Sarah, JB decided it best to work alone for a while. "*Hasta luego*," she said as she veered off to the right. She looked back, hoping Sarah wasn't following. She wasn't, but she wasn't picking up litter either—she just ambled along, her garbage sack slung over her shoulder, swinging back and forth across her back.

The wind picked up. It swirled around JB and blew her long, glowing dark hair across her face. She didn't want to take the chance of being seen with her hair in a tangled mess if any boys happened by, so she dropped her sack, reached into her pants pocket, and pulled out a scrunchie. She gathered her hair into a ponytail and tied it.

She took a small compact out of her back pocket to check her make-up, again, just in case. She saw a face that she was proud of. It was somewhat irregular, yet feminine, with dark deep-set eyes and a nose that was a bit too large, inherited from a distant Mayan relative. She had a square chin and a full mouth offset with deep dimples when she smiled. And she made it a point to smile when the boys were around. The compact revealed no particular problems, so she kissed her image in the mirror and followed with a practice wink and smile. She snapped the compact shut and replaced it in her pocket.

She checked her watch and found she had ten minutes to go, so she grabbed up her sack and made her way back to where they had left their bikes. Sarah's bike was there, but she was nowhere in sight. She wondered whether she should call her on her cell phone or just wait for Sarah. She decided against both because she wanted to take a quick side trip by the football practice field. With Sarah's shitty attitude, she probably wouldn't be interesting in checking out the guys working out over there. She tied the sack on the bike's back rack and took one last look for Sarah before riding off.

Sarah walked along depressed. She had no inclination to pick up litter; her heart was not in it. And what difference did it make anyway? A hundred people could try to clean up the city and it would never happen. Everybody littered and it was impossible to clean it all up.

So, why bother. And who cared anyway?—except for Judge Abbot.

She pulled out her cell phone and looked at the time. "Oh, no, I worked ten minutes over," she muttered to herself. "Well, tomorrow I'll only work twenty minutes."

She turned to walk back to the bikes. Since her sack was practically empty, she folded it with what litter it had and stuffed it in the back of her pants. She walked slowly, not in any hurry to get home.

"You can make a difference."

"You can make a difference," came a strange male voice, hardly above a whisper.

Sarah turned and looked over her shoulder. Then she looked over the other shoulder. There was no one, no parked autos, no trees, no buildings—nothing nearby that the voice could come from.

"You can make a difference, little one."

Sarah turned in a complete circle. "Who—? What's the matter with me?" she mumbled. "Now I'm hearing things. All this crap must be getting to me. I'd better get a grip before I go psycho."

"Yes, the crap is getting to you, but you will not go crazy." The voice, even louder, had a metallic sound, much like a bell, and echoed like it was coming from a large empty room.

Sarah made another quick turn to make sure that no one was behind her. She shuddered as she felt the hair stand up on her forearms and a chill run up her back and neck. She thought of running away, but what would she be running from or to? Her alarm escalated. "Who…are you and…where are you? What do you want?"

She waited but no answer came. I am losing it, she thought. I'm hearing voices, and that's when they put you in a padded cell. I'd better get the hell out of here while I still can.

"I am a friend. I am your friend."

Sarah turned around and looked in all directions. "If you, whoever you are, are my friend, then why don't you quit playing games, and let me see you?"

"I don't have a physical body, little one. You cannot see me because I'm in another realm. I'm what you could call a spirit or ghost."

Sheer black fright swept through Sarah. She either imagined the voice or she was in big trouble. And if this spirit was real, she was powerless to protect herself if it meant to harm her. "That crazy séance must have worked! We've really screwed up now!" she exclaimed under her breath. She felt cold and clammy, and her whole body numbed in weakness. Her mind raced from one thing to another. JB, help me. Where are you? Ralph, you wanted one, now come get it. I'm sorry, Mom, I'll serve my six weeks happily. Just come get me before this thing does. Maybe a car will come by and save me? I've got to run. I've got to get away, right now.

She turned to flee, confused about which way. Where are the bikes? Her thoughts swirled in panic, demanding action, but lost in confusion.

Just run. Go. She ran, her knees rubbery and weak. She ran straight ahead, but in no particular direction. To get away was her only goal. Where she got away to didn't matter.

After several minutes, she tired. She slowed down and stopped, her breath ragged and deep. The breeze chilled her skin, moist with sweat. She shook her head to stop the dizziness, but it only made it worse. Taking several deep breaths, she felt the dizziness gradually disappear. She listened. Nothing. Questions ran through her mind looking for instant answers: *Did I really get away? Am I safe? Is it still watching me? Will it come back again?* She took an even deeper breath, and then slowly released it in an effort to calm down. *Just get out of here. Right now. Go home.*

Sarah looked around to figure out where she was—anything to tell her where they had left the bicycles. A street sign gave her the information she needed. She glanced back where she had heard the spirit and, seeing nothing, hearing nothing, quickly jogged the four blocks to the bikes. She was disappointed to find only hers. JB had already gone, and she needed someone to talk to as soon as possible. Again she looked in the direction of the spirit before mounting her bike for the short ride home.

When she got there she let herself in through the back door, thankful that her parents were both working at the Pizza Shack. She rushed upstairs and shakily called JB.

After JB heard the whole story, she said, "Okay, sweetie, write it all down the best you can, and don't leave anything out. Then we'll go over it tomorrow and decide what to do about this spirit thing, or whatever it is. And call me if anything else happens. I'll come right over."

* * *

JB stopped by the Pizza Shack with Sarah after school on Thursday. She watched and listened to Sarah's mom give Sarah a long list of do's and don'ts for the rest of the afternoon, Sarah nodded at her mom without comment and followed JB out the door.

"You're right," JB said. "Your mom is kind of controlling. Do you have to ask her when you have to pee, too?"

Sarah rolled her eyes dolefully. "She never quits. Last Saturday, she decided she didn't like the way I wait on the customers, so now I have to work in the kitchen." She grinned slyly. "But I like the kitchen, because it's easier, and I have time to talk on the phone. I just have to keep an eye on her so she doesn't catch me."

They jumped on their bikes and headed toward South Park for their half-hour of litter work. "Anything new from that spirit after we talked yesterday," JB called back to her friend, who was close behind. She was hoping Sarah would say no and she did.

"But I didn't sleep too well all night. I keep telling myself that I'm dreaming this, but I'm not. It was real. I just know it."

"Did you write it all down?"

"Yeah, there really wasn't that much." Sarah pedaled harder to keep up with JB.

When they reached the picnic area of South Park, they abandoned their bikes and picked up litter that was strewn about, under bushes and park benches, and around overfilled garbage cans. They made their way past several moms playing with their kids, and came upon a secluded picnic table. It was Sarah's idea to rest awhile, although JB knew she wanted to use her thirty minutes doing anything but picking up trash. When they sat down, Sarah handed JB the notes she had made on the spirit visit, and JB read over them.

"How do you know it's a he?" she asked, looking up from the notes.

"It just sounds like a man's voice. It's not female, for sure."

"He said, 'You can make a difference.' What do you think that means?"

"Don't know."

"Wow, this is so weird," JB responded as she again looked over the notes. "Do you think he'll come back again?"

"Yeah. Why would he come just to tell me that I can make a difference without explaining how?"

JB looked off in the distance as she considered the ridiculous situation that her friend faced. Sarah waited, hoping that JB didn't think she was crazy.

Just as Sarah became unnerved, JB spoke: "I just don't see how a ghost would talk to you, if there is such thing as a ghost."

Sarah felt abandoned. "Then you don't believe me?"

"I didn't say that. It's just...Look, let's say it's real. You know what? This guy, thing, spirit, whatever, wasn't going to hurt you. Once you got scared and ran away, there was nothing he could do, because you would've only gotten more scared. He probably didn't expect you to act that way. If you would've hung out and talked to him, he might've have told you why he was there. It seems to me, if he was going to hurt you, he would've followed you and done whatever."

"Would you have stayed, JB?"

"Are you kidding, girl? I would've outrun you."

They laughed at the thought. "Well, what do I do now?" Sarah answered, her brow drawn quizzically.

"What can you do?"

"Just wait and see what happens. I guess, if he shows up again, I'll ask him what he wants."

"Well, good luck," JB said. "I'm not talking to any ghost, good or bad. I'm just glad it's you and not me." She punched Sarah playfully on the arm and stood up. "Good luck to you, sweetie. Hey, gotta clean the park. See you later." She grabbed her garbage sack and swished off without looking back. Sarah watched her for a while, wondering if she should also get to work.

"Good afternoon to you, little one. I'm pleased that you are not going to run away."

Sarah's heart skipped a beat as she gasped in surprise. She closed her eyes and willed herself to be calm, reminding herself that this spirit didn't hurt her before and hopefully wouldn't this time either. She opened her eyes to call out to JB, but she was nowhere to be seen. As she looked straight ahead, her heart pounded faster and the tingling returned to her neck.

"Of course I will not hurt you."

"I didn't say that," Sarah forced, her voice sounding distant to her.

"Ah, so you did not, but you did think it, did you not?"

"Yes, I did think that I hope you aren't going to hurt me, and I also think that you want to be my friend, maybe." Casper the friendly ghost crossed her mind.

She heard a soft laugh. *"I would hope that I am better looking than Casper."*

"I wouldn't know unless I saw you. Do you know everything that I'm thinking?" She asked, her fear eased a little.

"Yes, if you wish, you need not even talk to me. Just think and I will receive your projection."

Yeah, right. Let's see. My name is Sarah. Do you know my last name? she thought as clearly as she could.

"Yeah, right. Let's see. Your name is Sarah McPhee."

"Wow!" Sarah exclaimed, her fear diminished a little more.

"I must tell you, it was not my intention to frighten you yesterday. I overestimated my ability to charm. I have been out of practice of late."

"And I shouldn't have run away. I was really scared."

"I know. I was running right alongside of you. Your friend JB was correct: I felt that I could not say anything to calm you down. You would have grown even more frightened."

"You were listening to JB and me talk?"

"Yes, and on the phone, yesterday."

Sarah mulled over it all. She wondered if she wanted anyone or anything listening in on her every thought, as she knew he was at this very moment. Well, it was happening, whether she liked it or not. She'd have to make the best of it if she wanted to continue. She hadn't decided that yet for sure. She needed more information.

"Did Ralph bring you here with the séance?"

"No, he did not. However, other spirits and I were in attendance. It was amusing and fun for us. It has been my plan to come forward for a long while. The time had to be right for you to accept me. It is now that time, if you so choose."

Do I get to choose? Sarah pondered. Do you have a name?

"My name will be whatever you wish to call me."

"Hey, that's cool, but I don't know what to call you. I can't think of a name."

"In honor of Ralph, who thought the spirits would be insulted if they were called spooks, maybe you should call me Spook."

Sarah giggled and it struck her that she hadn't really felt this good in several weeks.

"Perhaps it is time that you lighten up and have fun for a change. Laughter is good for you."

She smiled. All the fear had melted away. She still was cautious about Spook, but she was no longer afraid. This was very strange, and she didn't know where it was going or even if she really wanted to go; however, right now she enjoyed it.

"Good. You have no reason to be afraid. And I promise you, you will not be forced to go anywhere you don't truly want to go. I will also leave any time you feel that I am not of value to you or that I am harming you in any way."

Sarah stood up, then climbed on top of the table, and sat with her legs crossed. She projected: So, you are going to stay with me?

"I will always be nearby if that is your wish. I do have other spirit obligations that I need to attend to, but I will never be far away. You will only need to say or project my name three times. Spook, Spook, Spook. That has a nice ring to it, don't you think?"

"Why are you here and why did you pick me to talk to?"

"You chose me. Although you were not aware of it, you chose me to guide you in days to come on a very important mission. We will talk about this mission soon, but right now I am going to leave so that you won't be late returning home. It would not be desirable to make your mother angry at this time."

"What's the mission? Will it be fun? When will—?"

"You're excitement is appreciated, but we will have to discuss the mission later, after you know me better."

"Should I tell my parents about you?"

"If you desire, but it would not be wise right now. Soon, things will happen and, at that time, you will surely tell them. We don't wish to hide things from them, but right now they would not understand."

"How about, Ralph, JB, and the other guys?"

"Yes, but you must tell them it is a secret among friends at this time. They must tell no one outside of your group of friends. We will have many discussions about the part your friends will play in your mission, as well as other matters."

"Will they be able to hear you and talk to you?"

"They will not. Because I exist on the spiritual level, I am limited to what I can do on your level, the physical level. I will not be able to talk

to others, except in very special instances. Of course, I will always listen."

"Can you do stuff, I mean, can you, like, maybe move a chair or something, if you wanted to?"

"I am not able to react on your level to change physical things. That is partly the reason for my relationship with you. If I need to throw a rock, I cannot do that. But perhaps I can ask you to. I am able to manipulate a few minor things on your level, but this is usually very difficult for me and involves a lot of spiritual energy. We will talk about these matters many, many times."

"Then you promise that you're coming back?"

"I will be back if you want me to come back."

"I do."

"Then it is good-bye until the next time. JB is now returning. Perhaps you have some big news to tell her."

Immediately Sarah sensed that Spook was gone. She felt good, better than she had in weeks. *Is this true? Do I have my own spirit friend? Or is this some crazy dream that I am going to wake up from? Only time would tell.* Tears came to her eyes as JB approached.

When JB spied Sarah's empty garbage sack she shook her head in annoyance. She was about to rag on her about it when she saw the tears and a depth to Sarah's smile that had been missing for way too long. JB's face split into a wide grin of surprise. "Tell me. He came back, didn't he?"

By midmorning the following day, Friday, the news had not only spread to the other three best friends, it had filtered to the next level of friends and acquaintances. There was a mixture of belief, disbelief, and wait-and-see among the eighteen who knew. Everyone, however, wanted to know, word-by-word, what the spirit supposedly had said to Sarah. The buzz among the small group was that Spook wanted to guide them on some important mission in which all who wanted could get involved.

Sarah felt uncomfortable with all the attention she received, and even more unsettled that most kids didn't believe she had actually talked to a spirit. A few even made fun of her, saying that she was making up the whole thing. Their attitude became, prove it or shut up about it.

"Spook. Spook. Spook," Sarah called as she sat on her bed after school, new journal and pencil in hand. She was a bit nervous about this first effort to contact the spirit and still a bit apprehensive about the whole relationship. "Spook. Spook. Spook." She waited. She closed her eyes and after about three minutes she observed a hazy white cloud in her vision, although her eyes were still closed. The cloud drifted away, followed by a soft humming sound. Suddenly the voice of Spook echoed forth as if coming from a long hollow shaft:

"Greetings, little one. It appears that you have had a very interesting day. There is excitement as well as doubt among the friends. That is to be expected."

"Yes, there is doubt. As you probably already know, Jody said, 'If I can't see it, I don't believe it.'"

"Yes, he, as well as many others, will not have the, shall I say, enthusiasm to participate in your first mission unless they have some visual confirmation of my presence. They will need proof that you and I indeed communicate. Perhaps we will have to conjure up some harmless energy, a bit of magic, for those doubters. I may have to drastically reroute my resources to accomplish this, but I think it can be done. It is most unusual for spirits such as myself, so I'll have to practice."

"When are you going to tell me about my first mission? Is there something that you want us to do?"

"No, I do not want you to do anything. It is what you want to do that is important. I will never ask that you do anything. I may suggest or strongly recommend a certain direction that you may take, but it is always your decision whether you follow my directive. You will never, never be criticized or punished for ignoring or declining any suggestions I make."

"But, if you tell me something, it's because you believe it's right. If I don't do it, I will not be doing something that is right, so my decision is wrong."

Spook hollowly laughed. *"Well said, little one, and at a later time we will discuss right and wrong action. But, for now, you do not understand my purpose in communicating with you. I am only here to serve you. I will teach you, I will guide you, and I will help you in any way I can. That is the quickest way you can improve yourself and accomplish what you have chosen to do. However, when I guide or counsel you, you have the option of choosing only what you feel is good for you at that particular time. You will be thought of no more or less, no matter what you choose. It is always your decision. And what you choose will always be what you need at the time."*

Sarah thought over what Spook said. "I haven't chosen to do anything, have I?"

"Yes, you have chosen a great amount, but it is not yet on your list of things to do right now. It is not on your conscious screen. It is subconscious."

Sarah got off the bed. Puzzled, she wandered around the room. "I'm sorry. I don't know what you mean."

"Think of it this way: you have all this information on your computer hard-drive. Some of it, you do not even know it is there, but it is. Then some day when you need this information, you merely call up a certain file on the screen. It leaves the subconscious level and becomes conscious."

"The subconscious level is...?"

When it was apparent that she was not going to continue, Spook answered. *"The subconscious level is just an unseen part of you on the God level."*

Even more confused, she tried to make sense of what Spook said. It was a long time before she asked, "Part of me is on the God level?"

"Yes, actually the largest part of you is on the God level. All unseen, but there nonetheless. You could also call this the spirit level. That is where I exist."

Her mind struggled in confusion. "I don't...if a part of me is on the spirit or God level, then I am like you in a way. I'm a spirit?'

"Or God."

Her head swirled with questions. She sat down on the bed. For a long while she refused to think about the next step. This is crazy. If what Spook says is true, then—

He finished her thought. *"You are God."*

Sarah sat in disbelief, thrilled and frightened at the possibility of this being true. "No," she blurted. "This can't be. I can't be God. Why me? You're joking with me, aren't you? Why would I be...God, when there are so many others that could—?"

"Let me be more clear," Spook cut in. *"Everyone and everything on the physical level—on Earth—is connected on the spiritual or God level. It is kind of like we are all of the same spirit or God, therefore, we are all God. It is not just you; everyone and everything is God. We are all God."*

"Oh, I see," Sarah answered with a trace of a smile. "Yeah, that's cool. We are all God. Yes, I like that. I can believe that."

"Of course you can. Now, think about it: if you are God, then you should always act like it. You should always treat people and things around you as God would, with love and respect, as if they are God, which they are. Does that not change your attitude toward everything?"

Sarah's eyes teared up. She smiled her approval as a genuine peacefulness and satisfaction spread through her whole being. Spook was right because it felt so right. She was filled with pure love for everyone and everything, and was charged with an excitement and desire to do things for herself and others that she had never felt before. She wondered if this was how God felt?

"That is how God feels," said Spook. *"You must always remember the feeling, because sometimes it will fade. When it does, you can bring it back by remembering you are God."*

There was silence for several minutes before Sarah renewed her smile. "You know what? I can't wait to get out there and do the job that Judge Abbot asked us to do. It's time to clean up this town."

"Yes, it is, little one, and have some fun doing it. And by the way, cleaning up Cibolo Falls is your first mission, if you choose it as such. Of course, you will need to enlist the help of the doubters. Do you think you can get all those that have heard about me to meet at the river tomorrow morning, during your Saturday litter time?"

Before Sarah started her homework, she called Ralph to get him to set up a meeting with everyone the next morning. She also asked if he'd join her and JB later for litter duty. She finished her schoolwork and hopped on her bike to meet them downtown.

Ralph and JB watched as Sarah filled her plastic garbage sack to the top. They knew She had had an earlier session with Spook, but she hadn't let them in on what they'd talked about. She promised to tell them the whole story at the river meeting the following day. They were already well aware, however, that Sarah had changed.

Later when she arrived on her bike at the Pizza Shack for her Friday night kitchen shift, she found her mom and dad behind the cashier's counter working on the books. Both nodded their hello as they wondered just how bad Sarah's usual foul attitude would be.

"Hi, Mom, Dad," she said as she grabbed an apron out of the

cabinet. "How's your day been?"

Barbara, caught off guard, wondered if that was truly Sarah or someone that just looked like her. Bob's jaw dropped in surprise.

Sarah didn't wait for an answer. She slung the apron over her shoulder and pushed open the kitchen door. Before she passed through, she looked back and added, "I love you guys."

Her parents stared at the swinging door.

Saturday morning, the nineteen friends met under the bridge for what they were told would be the details of their first mission as suggested by Spook through Sarah. The blackish area of the fire was in stark contrast to the surrounding area that was still brown with last summer's dead grass, mixed with an equal amount of spring's new green growth. Ralph and the others responsible took some good-natured dissing about the fire.

When Sarah's time came, she stood before the group unsure as to how her message would be received. "Okay, guys. I know you aren't going to believe this, but you really need to know. Yesterday, I got some more information from Spook…"

She felt uneasy about sharing Spook's message. She knew that most wouldn't believe her. She was right. About two-thirds of the group were highly skeptical and laughed off the idea that they were God. And most wanted proof that Spook existed before they would believe anything he supposedly said. A like number could care less about joining her in the clean-up mission. They called it a waste of time and impossible to do without more help—much more help.

Sarah became discouraged when Smiley and Donnie left the discussion and walked down toward the river. She needed to do something fast, but she had no idea how to get them to believe that Spook did exist and communicated with her. She expected help from Spook, however she had no sign that he was even around. There had been no response when she attempted to reach him.

Ralph edged up to her and whispered, "Gut time, Sarah. You better say something that the guys will believe or you're going to loose them, mucho-quicko."

"I will, Ralph. I'll think of something. I just need a—"

"Hey!" Smiley shouted from the river! "Come down here! You gotta see this!"

Everyone turned to see Donnie and Smiley wave from the bank. They headed for the river. When they reached the water's edge, they stopped to find Smiley and Donnie standing on a ledge about two feet above the calm water of the Guadalupe River.

They both smiled at Sarah as the puzzled others looked on. "This is really weird," Donnie announced, enjoying the spotlight. "Sarah, come look."

Baffled by his excitement, she glanced at Smiley, who motioned with one hand toward the water. "Just look," he urged.

Smiley watched Sarah approach the edge and look down into the water. He knew that she was going to be surprised. She saw her reflection on the water's surface. *Wait a minute, that's not right.* She looked closer. It was her all right, but it was not really a reflection. It was an image on the surface of the water. Her image smiled and picked up a paper cup off the ground, then dropped it into a plastic sack. On the sack in large white lettering were the words *CLEAN UP YOUR EARTH*. The whole scene lasted no more than ten seconds, then immediately repeated, as if on video tape.

Sarah watched the scene play through five times before turning away. There was no doubt that the image was of her. Spook had not only come through as he said he would; he came through huge.

She got it together and turned toward Donnie. "What did you see?"

"You," he answered with an all-knowing grin.

"And you?" she asked Smiley.

Smiley increased his grin. "Sorry I didn't believe you about Spook. I do now. It was you I saw on the water."

Sarah turned toward the others with an air of calm and self-confidence. "You wanted proof. Spook has sent you a message." She turned to Ralph and said, "Check it out."

Sarah watched Ralph and the others push toward the water, shoulder to shoulder. The ones in the back urged those at the water's edge to hurry up. All turned away from the image amazed. There was no longer any doubt about Sarah's relationship with Spook, and all became excited. What started as a grassfire suddenly turned into a mission to clean up the town.

Sarah, Smiley, Ralph, JB, and Donnie—the original five—walked back up the hill astonished at what they had seen. Things were sure to change because of Spook. With school out in two weeks, this summer would be exciting and fun. They had a job to do, if even a small one, and according to Sarah, it was sure to grow into other very important missions.

Ralph, the nonstop organizer, took over as the group gathered around. "Look, guys," he announced, "I don't think you need any more proof about Spook being real. So, let's get together and do what he tells us to do. It's obvious that he wants us to help clean up the earth. Let's really make a difference, and it starts by our acting like the Gods that we are.

"And the first thing we'll do is start making a difference in Cibolo Falls, by cleaning up the place. Is anybody still against us doing this?"

All eighteen of those present agreed to take part and JB gestured with a flick of the hand that she had something to say. Ralph nodded for her to go ahead. "There aren't enough of us to do much. We've got to get others interested. We have them all in one place at school, but with school being out so soon, we might not have another chance. Let's do something quick, before they get away. *Comprende?*"

"Beautiful, JB!" Ralph exclaimed. "Anybody have an idea what we can do?" When there were no takers, he nodded, "We'll come up with something. Also, by the end of next week, we'll try to get organized with some rules and stuff about what we're trying to do, and all that. We also need to come up with a name, if you know what I mean. You guys think about all that and give me a call if you think of anything brilliant."

He turned toward Sarah. "Want to add anything?"

"Well, we need to set up a time for our next meeting. With some of us grounded, maybe we should wait for another two weeks, until after school's out. That'll also give us more time to get organized."

"Any others?"

"Should we tell anybody about what happened here today?" It was Smiley.

Ralph looked to Sarah for help.

"Whatever," they both said at the same time. Everyone laughed.

Journal Note

"Life is a learning experience. No matter how insignificant, everything that happens is for a specific purpose. In each and every incident, look closely for the lesson."

CHAPTER 3

The heavier than usual applause was not so much for Sarah McPhee as it was because she was the recipient of the final student award, bringing summer vacation even closer. Without visible emotion she bounded up the narrow steps and across the stage. From behind the lectern her basketball coach smiled and shook Sarah's hand, and presented her the small trophy honoring Cibolo Falls Junior High's female athlete of the year. Sarah accepted the trophy and started back across the stage to renewed applause.

She stopped mid-stage and raised her right hand, palm out and fingers spread. She had something to say to her 462 surprised classmates. The applause came to an abrupt halt as Sarah stood stoically before her peers in silence. Her eyes searched the auditorium for those eighteen who awkwardly scrambled to their feet and raised their right hands just as Sarah had raised hers. Whispers rippled through the student body.

Sarah felt a wave of regret but knew it was too late to back out. Her hand closed in a fist, she heard her words, meek but loud enough for all the students to hear: "I am God."

Right on cue, the band of eighteen followed her lead. "I am God," they chimed in guarded unison, bringing stifled snickers and giggles from across the assembly.

Sarah called out, her voice firm and confident, "I am God!" Her friends repeated with assurance. Teachers and administrators exchanged inquiring glances, each leaving it up to the others to step in and stop the nonsense. Some looked to the rear of the auditorium for reaction from the assistant principal.

The third time, louder and more forceful, ended Sarah's salute as she dropped her hand and left the stage. Her footsteps on the stage steps and tile floor echoed throughout the strangely quiet auditorium. When she reached her empty seat on the aisle, she didn't bother to stop, fully aware of the beckoning finger of Blanche Nichols, the assistant principal, who loomed in the back near the doorway. Sarah dutifully followed the administrator. She usually mocked the middle-aged woman who always wore a loosely fitting, dull gray cotton dress and black grandma shoes. But this time, she remembered what Spook said about treating everyone like God. They exited into the empty hallway.

The awards assembly neared completion and Sarah counted on the mass exodus of students to save her from Ms. Nichol's wrath. It crossed her mind that she could perhaps be the one that finally caused Hatchet Woman to have a heart attack—a joke shared and passed on by students over the years. *Sorry, Spook. That's not God-like.*

As soon as the doors of the auditorium swung closed, Ms. Nichols stopped and grabbed Sarah by both shoulders. "This little outburst, Sarah McPhee, is not welcome, and I take it as an affront to my authority as the main disciplinarian of the school."

Because of her massive weight, anytime she exerted herself, mentally or physically, she perspired and her breathing became labored. This was one of those times.

"Well, just because this is the last day of school and you're moving to high school next year," she gasped, stopping to catch her breath, "don't think for a minute that you can just march up on that stage and do anything you please! Not at my school!" She paused for a labored wheeze. "Just what was the purpose of that little display?"

Intimidated, Sarah became overwhelmed. *How could I have been so stupid to think I could get away with that? But it's too late to back off now. Stand up to her, no matter what the consequences.* Sarah managed a flippant shrug but didn't answer. She turned her head away to avoid both the administrator's glare and her putrid breath as well.

The angry woman grasped Sarah's shoulder with one hand and used the other to turn Sarah's chin front and center. "Look at me when I speak to you, young lady! I want to know, here and now, what the purpose of that outburst was! 'I am God.' Who do you think you are, saying such a thing? I know your mother and father well, and I know they will be disappointed in you today." Wheeze. "Now, why did you say that?"

Unwelcome tears welled up in Sarah's eyes. *I can't let her see me like this. Stop the tears. I've got to be strong and stand up to her. Don't let her overpower me like she does everyone else.* She stuck the trophy in her back pocket, then defiantly removed the woman's beefy hands from her shoulders, and backed away a step. "I said that I am God, because I am."

"You are what?" Ms. Nichols asked, drops of perspiration beading on her forehead and cheeks.

Sarah swallowed hard, lifted her chin, and boldly met her gaze. "God. I am God. I say that because I am—I am God." She braced herself for the new wave of tongue lashing she knew was sure to follow.

The assistant principal, her shoulders lifting and falling with each breath, groped for a response. The auditorium doors flung open and the swiftest of the noisy study body burst free for the summer. With Ms. Nichols distracted, Sarah seized the opportunity to escape further wrath. She jumped in front of the oncoming students and led them toward the exit at the end of the long hall. Ms. Nichols hobbled after her.

Crimson, Ms. Nichols screamed, "Sarah McPhee! Just because school is out, don't think you're getting away with this! They'll be waiting for you next year in high school! I'll see to it!"

Sarah beamed a triumphant smile, turned for the exit, and flipped a small wave over her shoulder to the administrator. She didn't bother to look back; after all, it was summer vacation. She left the building and danced down the steps and into the school yard. In relief she shouted, "You have a good summer, Hatchet Woman!"

The students flooded out the door into the sunshine. If Sarah wanted to be God, that was fine with them. Not much else mattered but the next three months of freedom.

"Sarah, wait up!" came a shout from behind. It was JB and Ralph.

"What did Hatchet Woman have to say?" Ralph asked as he brushed back a lock of dark hair. He inadvertently knocked his heavy, dark-rimmed glasses askew. Sarah thought it was cute the way his hair always fell over his right eye.

"Did she expel you?" JB handed Sarah the backpack she had left in her auditorium seat.

Sarah thanked her and stuck the small trophy inside the pack. She stuck one arm in the strap and hoisted it over her shoulder as she turned to start her walk home. JB and Ralph fell in step beside her. "Just the usual barf. I thought I was going to pass out from her breath. No, I don't think she'll expel me. The grades are already recorded, and I'm high school's problem now. All she's interested in, anyway, is the principal's job, if she doesn't stroke-out first. Did you hear her scream?"

"Yeah, not too cool. She nearly lost it," laughed Ralph, "and the way she was huffing and puffing when we went by, I thought she was going to keel over any minute."

"Yeah," JB followed. "I always hoped she wouldn't croak while I was near her, so they wouldn't blame me. Just think, Sarah, you could've been the one to finally kill the old bitch. I can't believe you just walked away from her. She looked like she was going to explode."

Sarah spread her hands in mock innocence. "But Hatchet Woman, I thought you were through with me. After all, you turned away, ignoring me."

A car passed with several high schoolers, and a boy leaned out the window and yelled, "Hey Ralph Coggins. You good-for-nothing, shithead dork. When you gonna grow up?"

Ralph, not one to practice caution, stepped out into the street and flipped the bird. "Same to you, fella! Why don't you come back and say that?"

JB and Sarah giggled. "Who was that, Ralph?" Sarah asked as he joined them on the walk. "What would you do if they came back?"

"Run like hell, probably," Ralph laughed. "Naw, he's a homie, about two houses down from me. We're cool."

As they ducked to avoid an overhanging tree limb, JB had a disturbing thought: "Did you see that newspaper guy there for the principal's award? He not only got your picture giving the Earth Salute; he got some of us too. We're all going to be right back in big trouble if they find your ceremony interesting enough for the newspaper."

A flicker of apprehension coursed through Sarah. "Well, I guess that's what we wanted, wasn't it, to get publicity? We just got more than we asked for, and I guess we'll take whatever punishment that comes with it. We have to, now that it's over. I was really scared on that stage. I just about decided to forget it but didn't want to let you guys down."

They walked for a moment silent in their own thoughts before Ralph made a point of clearing his throat. He had something important to say.

"Yeah, what's up, Ralphy?" JB asked, tacking a syllable onto his name for emphasis, something she knew he hated.

Ralph glowered his immediate disapproval, but then smiled and cupped his hand around his mouth, pretending to keep Sarah from hearing: "Sarah's mom is going to be pissed, big-time, whenever she finds out."

Sarah appeared unperturbed. "So, what else is new? She is always looking for something to get on my case about. It might as well be this."

"Methinks you're taking your mom too lightly," Ralph retorted. "It ain't gonna be easy being God. We're all gonna have big problems; I just know it."

Sarah considered what Ralph said as they approached the street where she was to turn off toward home. She tried to ignore her building anxiety. "I guess it's like Spook says, 'Life is a learning experience. Everything that happens is for a specific purpose'."

"Yeah, right," Ralph scoffed, "that's easy for Spook to say. He ain't gonna be here when everybody comes down on us for being God."

"He'll be nearby though," countered Sarah.

JB bent over and picked up a discarded paper cup without missing a step. She stuffed it in her pack. "Are you going to tell your parents about Spook?"

The three of them stopped at Sarah's street. "I don't think so. Not right now, unless..." her voice trailed. She continued with a renewed smile: "Okay, big meeting tomorrow morning at the bridge, right?"

"Yeah, we'll be there," JB answered. "Haven't got anything else planned for the summer, except for falling madly in love with some hottie I probably don't even know yet. Ralph, want to fall in love?"

"Hey, you leave me out of your love plans. I've got better things to do than play kissy-kissy with some oversexed, love-starved woman who will want to have my babies." Ralph backed off, hands held out in front of him. "No, I'm just kidding. Seriously, with my magnetic charm, I'll have to have a lottery just to see which woman is lucky enough to hook-up with me. If you want, JB, I'll enter your name in the drawing."

"In your dreams. I don't enter anybody's drawing. They'll be waiting in line just to look at me. I'm the bomb and everyone knows it."

"Yeah, right. Now, look who's dreaming."

"Come on guys. Knock it off," Sarah interrupted sharply. "You're both beautiful. Just not to each other. Now, let's get back to tomorrow. Does everyone know?"

Ralph nodded as he playfully patted JB on the cheek. "All the regulars, plus I think we may have gained a few more fans today. Jody had planned to pass out flyers after the assembly for those interested in finding out what's going on." He laughed and punched the air with a fist. "Man, are we going to take over the world totally or what?"

"Relax, big guy," Sarah chided. "I don't think our purpose is to take over the world; just improve our little part of it."

"Aw, man, you guys never want to have any fun. I think we ought to go for it while we're on a roll," he said with the boyish wink that always made her smile. "See you in the morning, your royal *nothingness*. Remember, I'm due for execution by the dentist, so I'll be late. Say hello to your angel for me."

"Uggh. I'm glad it's you and not me," Sarah teased. "I'll try to give you a call later this evening after softball practice."

"You don't have to sell pizzas tonight?"

"Dad convinced Mom to let me off for a change."

The three said good-bye, and Sarah watched JB and Ralph walk away in animated conversation. Although deep uneasiness rose inside, she let it go and headed for home. She picked up speed and thought about running the rest of the way, but today, because of the assembly, she had worn loafers instead of her usual Nike Cross Trainers. She stopped, took off her shoes and socks, stuck them in her pack, rolled up the cuffs of her slacks, and sprinted the remaining two blocks home, The warm spring wind of the Texas hill country blew through her hair and made her feel free and powerful.

Reaching home, she let herself in through the patio door and climbed the stairs, thankful that her mom and dad were at work. Softball practice wasn't for another hour, so she had plenty of time for a short nap or perhaps information from Spook. Just in case he might make an appearance, she opened her journal to the next blank page and laid her pencil across the crease. As she lay on the bed she became aware of the same deep uneasiness she had earlier. There was a persistent nagging feeling that she just couldn't identify. She focused inward in an attempt to clarify what might be bothering her, but when no answers came, she drifted off to sleep. Soon she began dreaming about her confrontation with Ms. Nichols. This time, however, Sarah didn't fare so well.

Journal Note

"Remember, deep inside of you, if something feels right to you, you can never be wrong, no matter what others say. No task is too big for you, if you will only set out to do it. If you perceive it as a problem, change your thinking, where the problem turns into an opportunity. Do not fear it, because you will lose the power of love—your love as God."

CHAPTER 4

JB didn't stop at the South Park bridge. She rode on past, shifting to a lower gear as she pedaled as fast as she could up the slight incline of the road bordering the Guadalupe River. She stopped at the point where the road was closest to the river and laid her bike down, stripped down to her bikini, tied her hair in a ponytail with a scrunchie, and waded out up to her waist. The water was much colder than she had anticipated, but she was determined to get in this first swim of the season. She pushed off and swam out a few yards, careful to keep from getting her face wet so she wouldn't have to put on fresh makeup. She turned on her back and paddled out farther, the morning sun shining directly in her eyes. A few more yards and she turned and headed back to the bank.

The breeze was chilly. It brought a shiver and regret that she had gotten wet. She retrieved a towel from her backpack and dried, tilted her head to one side and squeezed the water out of her ponytail with both hands. She stepped into the yellow shorts that matched her bikini top, careful not to soil them with her feet, then slipped on her socks and Nike Cross Trainers.

She hopped on her bike and headed back. A favorite among her classmates who waited in the shadow of the tall bridge, she was greeted with a round of good-natured jeers for arriving late. She stuck out her tongue at the mocking group and found a seat next to Sarah. The group, sitting on their bikes or sprawled on the grass, waited to find out what had happened at the assembly the day before, anxious to be a part of anything that meant excitement.

Sarah felt the hem of JB's shorts. "Cool. These new?"

"Yeah, my mom bought them for me. I think she feels bad because I'm grounded. Sexy, huh?"

"Yeah, especially with the bikini top. With boobs like yours, you make any outfit look sexy. Maybe in the next year or so mine will perk up some."

JB grinned. "My mom says it's because I eat Wheaties for breakfast."

"Yeah, right. That's why the grocery store's always sold out."

"I order them special, by the case, so I'll have a good supply. Anything from Spook last night?"

"Just some stuff about the experiences we have and how they affect everybody. I'm really confused sometimes. When I write it down wrong in the journal, he corrects me."

"Maybe someday you're going to have to show it to the whole world, so he wants it right. Say, sweetie, looks like the group is getting a little restless. I guess maybe we'd better get started."

"So, go for it." Sarah winked.

"Hey, why me?" JB retorted, faking a pout.

"You've been Student Council president for the last two years. You're the leader. They look up to you. They'll follow you anywhere. You're—"

"Enough, already," JB interrupted. "I thought it was agreed we wouldn't have any leaders. And even if I'm supposed to lead, I've never had to sell the idea of some angel that's lost his way." JB was surprised that there were quite a few sixth and seventh graders present as well as a few more from eighth. Four or five were elementary students—probably brothers and sisters of older kids attending. "Wow, there's a lot of kids here. How many do you think?"

"Jody said about ninety. Up from our eighteen yesterday, that's not too bad."

"Oh, my God, that's really crazy. They must have heard about the image on the water," JB beamed.

"Some did. The others came because of Jody's handouts after the assembly yesterday."

"Is the image still there?"

"Yeah. Most went down to see it earlier. Spook says it will be there for a while. But only certain people will be able to see it."

"Why not everyone?"

"I asked him the same thing. He said some people just aren't ready to believe in spirits. Something about being open and, I think he said, 'receptive.' You have to be in tune with your spiritual side—like having the right vibration or something."

"Bummer. Spook's no fun at all. If everyone could see it, we could sell tickets and make a billion dollars, and everybody would know us. Just think of all the guys we could have if we were rich and famous."

"I'll tell him what you said. Maybe he'll change his mind if it'll get you some boyfriends."

"Hey, girl, I'm not greedy—just one will do."

Sarah patted her friend on the knee. "I'm sure he'll take that into consideration. Right now, we'd better get moving. I'm supposed to be on trash clean-up time, and I don't think Mom will be too happy if I'm late for my lunch shift. She might ground me for another week."

"Yeah, me too," JB replied as she used Sarah's shoulder to boost herself to her feet. "Well, here goes. I hope we get this over with before the police drop by. They might think, with this many people, we're organizing a riot or something."

"Well, aren't we?" Sarah shaded the sun from her eyes with her hand as she looked up at JB. "Good luck, sexy."

Even though she was dry, all except for her bikini top, the chill still bothered her. She went back to her bike and got a T-shirt out of her pack. She pulled it over her head and raised a hand to quiet the noisy group. It took a while for them to settle down; the only sound became the repetitive clickity-clack of cars passing over the expansion joints of the bridge above—reminding her of the séance fire. She smiled, at ease despite not knowing exactly what she was going to say. She raised her right hand, fingers spread with the palm facing the group. About twenty-five of the older kids quickly stood and also raised their right hands. The others followed, even the elementary kids. *Mob rule. I wonder what they would do if I said, let's hang the police chief?*

"All nature!" she announced as she wiggled her fingers.

"All nature!" a few of her audience repeated.

JB smiled and nodded. She closed her hand into a fist. "Whole Earth!"

"Whole Earth," about half called out. The group began to warm up to the game.

"I am God!" JB called out.

"I am God!" her peers followed; a few giggled in the process.

"I...am...God!" JB repeated louder, a significant pause between each word.

"I am God!" the kids barked back.

"I...am...God!" JB yelled out, her voice screeching out of control.

Laughter followed as the others hollered out, "I am God!" The sound echoed down the river.

JB laughed with the rest. She lowered her hand and gestured for the group to sit. "I think this God needs speech lessons."

She paused to organize her thoughts. "We're glad you came this morning, and hope you'll want to come again and again. Why? Because we have a problem, and we need your help.

"Now, before I tell you how you can help, you need to know where we get all these crazy ideas, if you haven't already heard. All this stuff comes from Sarah's guardian angel, named Spook. As proof that he's an angel, he's the one that put Sarah's image on the water. He said that not everyone will be able to see it, so, if you bring someone and they can't see it, that's the way it is. Sorry.

"Now, back to—where was I?"

"We need help," Sarah coaxed.

"*Sí. Gracias, querida,* Sarah. Most of you saw the—"

"*Querida?*" Sarah interjected.

"It means darling," JB replied with a wide grin, before getting back to the group. "Most of you saw the Earth Day program on TV a few weeks ago. Some of us even had to write a paper on it in Science class. Well, it was scary. It showed how we are trashing out where we live—the Earth. And you don't just see this stuff on Earth Day; it's on the news every night.

"Spook says that time is running out for Earth if something isn't done soon, to keep our forests from dying, the oceans from being polluted, and whole species of birds and animals from dying out. Well, I try not to believe everything that Spook says, so I checked it out on the Internet. He's right. It's really scary.

"So, who cares, anyway? It isn't my fault, is it?" JB crossed her arms over her chest and lowered her eyes. Someone stifled a cough and a youngster could be heard shouting down on the river.

"You know what? It *is* my fault. And yours. It took billions of people just like us to cause the waste, the water and air pollution, the garbage." She laid her hand on top of her head and slowly nodded: "Yeah, it's everybody's fault.

"But what can I do about it? If the government can't, or won't, do anything about it, how can I? If the big companies can't, or won't, do anything about it, how can I? If the city can't…or the mayor—?"

The sun had moved enough that JB was now in the shade of the bridge. She moved over a step, back into the sunlight. She spoke clearly: "You know, it would be a mucho big mistake if we didn't do anything about the problem because we think we can't do very much. What if…what if each one of us did some little something, everyday, to help clean up Earth, at least our little part of it? What if there were four or five thousand, just like us, doing the same? Two million? Maybe ten million all over the world?"

JB bent over, grabbed Sarah by the hand and pulled her to her feet. "*Querida,* how many?"

"One billion," Sarah declared to the group. "One billion kids, just like us, all over the world, could help clean up Earth, by spending just a few minutes everyday. We've got to do it ourselves, and we're also going to make those in our government pass better laws to help clean up the environment." JB waited for more. Sarah, with a flip of the hand, indicated she was through.

"Is that what we are going to do, Sarah?"

"Yeah, that's what we're gonna do, *Guido,*" Sarah quipped with a grin as she sat back down. "Me, you, and our ninety friends, here, are going to get it started."

"*Guido*?" JB laughed. "Think so, huh?"

"Know so," Sarah nodded with pressed lips. "It might take a while to get it going, but if we just go out and do our part, it will catch on.

First, the town, then the state. After that, who knows? But somebody has to start it, and it might as well be us. And you know what? It'll be a lot of fun."

JB looked out over the group. "Wanna do it?"

The claps and cheers that echoed off the bottom of the bridge surpassed both JB and Sarah's expectations. It had been much easier than Sarah thought it would be. The assembly and the image on the water had been the key, but JB had surprised Sarah with her dramatics in convincing the group that something needed to be done and that they were the ones to start it off.

When they settled down, JB continued:

"Okay, now everybody listen up. My number one bud, big Donnie Rimkus—don't give him any grief—is going to pass out some stuff you need to know, while I put some simple rules on you. First, we won't have any elected leaders. Second, meetings are Tuesday mornings at ten. Don't be late or you'll have to answer to Donnie. The meetings will be short, so we can hangout afterward, maybe work on our tans."

"Is that all?" came the protest from Smiley.

"Yeah, *hijo*," JB retorted. "You're not old enough to do anything else." She puckered and blew him a kiss, then winked.

Smiley flashed an alligator smile. "It doesn't hurt to try."

"Well, you can get in a little swimming. Since you're not old enough for anything else, it'll be kind of like a cold shower, if you know what I mean."

"How do you know I'm not old enough? Wanna try me?" Smiley retorted, bringing oohs, ahs, and scattered giggles from the group.

JB nodded her head and lifted a brow. "Well, I just might do that." She pointed a finger at Smiley and added, "But don't hold your breath."

Another quick wink at Smiley, then she focused on the group. "We won't have any dues or anything like that. If you want to quit, then quit. If you want to bring a friend, bring hundreds, because the more you bring, the more we can get done, and hopefully, the more friends they will bring."

"What are the meetings for?" a petite freckle-faced girl with flaming red hair asked.

"We'll give you ideas at these meetings about some of the stuff you can do to make a difference, like writing our government leaders, calling on your neighbors to help in some way. We might even march on City Hall. You know, that kind of stuff."

"Sounds like an underground revolution," came a voice from the back.

JB waited for the scattered laughter to die down. "If you get any ideas about stuff we can do, share them with us, okay?"

A hand went up from a seventh grade class leader. JB nodded for comment. "What about this 'I am God' stuff?" he asked. "Isn't that, I mean, that's crazy. It's going to make a lot of people—like they won't understand. You know, like my mom and dad. My mom would kill me if I said that." Several of the others nodded in agreement.

"Yeah, I know, and Sarah will explain the purpose of that in a minute. It's important, along with the Earth Salute and why we use it. Okay?" The kid nodded, satisfied for the moment. "Okay, any others?"

A sixth grader's hand shot up as if he was in the classroom. "Yes, Mr. Sanchez," JB pointed at the kid. "*Dar una charla, hijo.*"

"*Gracias.* Are we going to have some kind of, you know, sort of an emblem, so we'll know we're...uh...us?"

"*Bueno,*" JB responded following scattered laughter. "Got an answer, Smiley?

Leaning against his bicycle, Smiley looked like he was in orbit. It took a moment for him to come down to earth. "Oh, yeah. Sure. We're like working on a logo with either a closed or open hand, probably open, with the Earth Salute. It might have a picture of the Earth in the palm or something. When we get it done, maybe we can get T-shirts made up. It'll probably cost about fifteen bucks to get one. They'll be rad though, I'll bet."

"Thanks, guy," JB said, "and by the way, Smiley, lighten up, will you? It doesn't hurt to smile once in a while."

Everyone laughed except Smiley who tried to frown—unsuccessfully.

"Okay guys, Sarah's turn." JB announced abruptly and sat down on the grass.

Sarah stood and smiled at her peers. "Before I get into what the salute is and why we use it, I want to thank you guys for supporting me yesterday at the assembly. If you hadn't, I would've been really embarrassed. According to Spook, we're going to have some problems. I don't know what kind, but he says that's part of life—having problems to solve. It's supposed to make you better or something. Anyway, we might have to stand up for each other in the future. I will definitely stand up for you."

She rubbed her hands together in nervous anticipation. "Spook told me last night that he is real excited about what we're trying to do. He says we're all God and everything on Earth is God. But we've trashed out Earth. Which means we have trashed out ourselves. To honor God, to honor others, and to honor ourselves, and to ensure that all, as God, continue to live, we must make a big change. We must clean up our act. That's why we've started this group.

"Okay, the name we have chosen for our little, hopefully our soon-to-be big group, is *Grassroots Alliance for Reviving and Building A Greater Earth*. If you write that down, you'll see that the first letter of each word spells GARBAGE." Sarah smiled as she looked over the group. "Cool, huh? That was Ralph's idea. He'll be here later. He's at the dentist's office."

JB watched as Sarah seemed to glow as she held up her right hand, palm out. "Now that we have a name, let me tell you about the Earth Salute and what it means to us." She wiggled her little finger. "Air. The little finger represents air. Air is a spark of God's love, and *is* God. We definitely cannot do without the air we breathe. We would die."

Up went her ring finger. "Water. All the water of the Earth is the spark of God's love and creation. It is a part of the whole of God. It *is* God. Like air, we can't do without water."

Sarah held up the middle finger. "What is this?"

"The bird," Donnie called out. Laughter echoed off the bottom of the bridge.

"The middle finger is vegetation," JB answered when the group settled down.

"Right, it's not the bird," Sarah grinned at Donnie. "All plants and vegetation, including the rain forests, are God's creation. All are a spark of God, and *are* God. We can't do without them.

"Now, what is this?" she asked as she held up her pointer finger.

"All the birds, animals and fish." Smiley smiled.

"Right, George, my man." On a roll, she held up her thumb. "And this is what?"

"Us!" one called out.

"Humans!" said another.

"Man!"

"Woman, you jerk!"

Sarah laughed along with the group. When it quietened down, she said, "We, as jerks, or humans," she smiled, "are a little part of God's spirit in a physical body. We are nothing more or less than a spark of God, God's creation, or a part of God. We *are* God, as are the oceans, the trees, grass, fishes, and monkeys.

"You guys understand what I'm saying, so far?" She received a few nods, then added, "Good, because I don't know if I understand what I'm saying."

She rubbed the palm of her right hand with the fingers of her left. "The palm is the ground, the mountains, the valleys, the soil. It, like everything else, is a spark of God, and *is* God, as much as, and no less than the others."

She again held up her open hand toward the group and closed it into a fist. "The birds, bees, fishes, grass, insects, the wind, water, wart hogs, the dirt, man—they all make up what we call the Earth. They, we, are all Earth. They, we, *are* all God. None are lesser Gods or greater Gods."

Donnie rubbed his hand over his bald head. "I know a few lesser Gods. Some of those football jocks really do need help, if you want them in the greater God group. Gotta tell you, man. I ain't kidding. Everyone of them should have their 'tude dialed, if you ask me."

"I think some of them are *mucho caliente*," JB chimed in with a wide smile.

"Hey, lady, hot don't count," Donnie countered. "A fence post has more brains than most of those guys...and you'd be better off with one—at least a corner post."

More laughter. "I get this feeling that you don't care too much for football players? But I've heard that you used to play and were pretty good. What happened?" Sarah asked.

Donnie merely smiled.

Sarah thought for a moment as she figured where she left off. "Okay, let's get back to—every species of plant and animal, every drop of water or grain of sand is important to our survival. We must all live together or we'll die together. The first rule of being God is to love and treat everything on Earth as if it is God...as it really is.

"Now, does everyone agree that you *are* God?"

She noted a few nods, some frowns, much confusion and indifference.

JB watched and wondered if Sarah could overcome the negative. Sarah charged on: "You have no problem with that, because you are an individual part of God's spirit. Well, if you are God, every hour, every minute, every second of the day, why don't you act like it?"

Sarah panned the group. "It's hard already, isn't it? I'll tell you why we won't be able to act like God all the time. Because we will forget. Here we are, God as individuals on Earth, and then something happens, somebody rubs us the wrong way, and we forget that we're God. We might even come face-to-face with Donnie's football player in the hall. We're no longer loving, trusting, giving, helping, forgiving. It's all because we forgot. Right?"

"Right," a few agreed.

"Go, girl," JB added.

"Well," Jody commented, "the way I see it, God isn't under curfew, and he doesn't have to clean his room and take care of his little brother. That makes it easy to forget."

"I agree, Jody. Being grounded is enough to make me forget, but we do have a reminder. Tadaa," Sarah chimed as she held up an open hand toward her friends. She closed it and said, "We have a reminder, the Earth Salute." A hand went up near the back. "Yes," she pointed.

"Do we need to say that we are God?"

"It's up to you. I think that everyone here will know, if you give the Earth Salute, what you mean."

Sarah fixed the doubtful seventh grader with a serious look. "From your look, you still don't get it."

The student fidgeted before he answered, "I…I just can't…don't believe it. And I don't think my mom and dad will be too happy about it either. I'll just get into trouble if I go around saying I'm God."

Several kids nodded their agreement. "That's fine. You don't have to give up or change what you think. Just don't hold our beliefs against us either. That way, everybody's cool. You can still be a part of our group. And you know, if you want to quit, it's no big deal. We know we're kinda weird. But, we can still be friends."

He didn't respond. "I hope I have answered your question or doubt. Okay now, remember, each little thing you do, good or bad, might not help or cause a particular problem, but if several million are doing the same thing, sooner or later it adds up, again, good or bad. Does that make sense?"

"That's the one-little-candle thing," Smiley interjected, trying not to smile.

"Hey, don't even mention candles to me," Sarah replied as she pointed at the burned area.

Most of the group reacted positively to what she was saying. Even some that had disagreed earlier seemed to be interested. "Let's start off easy, okay? Suppose we have this as our first daily rule. Each day, let's spend at least—more if you want to—fifteen minutes doing something positive to pay back the Earth for what it is to us. It may be something simple like picking trash up off the streets, or even along the river here. Maybe you can urge your family to use fabric instead of paper towels in the kitchen so we'll have less waste.

"Jody will give you a list of the many projects you can do that will really make a difference if everyone participates. Got the lists?" she asked as she looked toward Jody. He nodded and held them up for her to see. "Good, check with our tall, blond Adonis, Jody, after we're through. But keep your hands off him, girls. He's too young.

"Later on, we'll add some more things we can do to make a difference. We'll also have some group stuff that we can do, like demonstrating. Okay?" Sarah smiled, happy that the meeting had been successful. "Anyone have any comments or questions before we quit for the day?"

"Yeah!" JB exclaimed from the side. "Look! What in the world is that?" She pointed toward the road.

The group turned to see Ralph approach on his bike, a gray plastic raincoat flapping madly in the wind, its hood pulled over his head hiding all but his chin. His knees fought to break free of the coat as they labored against the pedals. Everyone laughed when he screeched to a halt, lost his balance, and fell over the handlebars.

Well aware that he had garnered the attention of the group, Ralph jumped up and straightened the raincoat. "Hi, guys. Sorry I'm late. The dentist was having so much fun, he wouldn't let me leave."

Sarah frowned, "Okay, we give up. What's the raincoat for?"

"I'm just being prepared for when the shit comes down." Ralph shook his head in regret. "And it has." He saw a wave of alarm cross his friend's face.

Sarah's heart leaped. She knew she didn't want to hear what he had to say. She understood Ralph and his mannerisms too well to know this wasn't one of his usual jokes, so she braced herself.

Ralph reached inside the raincoat and pulled out a folded *Cibolo Falls Daily Gazette* newspaper. He opened it and held the front page up for Sarah to see. The headline read: "Cult practices run rampant at C. F. Junior High School."

An instant of confusion surged through Sarah as her eyes dropped to the picture under the headline. There she was, center stage of the Junior High auditorium with her right hand held up in the Earth Salute. The caption read, "Student leads group of followers in a rebellious affirmation."

Sarah paled as she gaped at her picture. As many as possible gathered around to get a better look as she dismally shook her head and turned away. *Cult practices? Rebellious affirmation? That's not true. How can they say that? They don't understand. This is not fair.* A wave of remorse swept through her. She felt light-headed and queasy. She needed some space, so she walked down toward the river. She found a flat grassy place, slumped down, and put her head between her knees. *How can this be happening? Other than taking a few minutes of assembly time without asking, I haven't done anything wrong. Why are they saying that?*

JB, Ralph, and Smiley joined her and sat down. Smiley hesitantly patted Sarah on the shoulder. They could only hear parts as Jody read the article to those of the group who remained up the hill.

Sarah tried to ignore the heaviness centered in her chest. "What did it say?" her voice cracked, hardly above a whisper.

Ralph was already getting to his feet. "I'll get it," he answered as he started back up the hill.

"Tell them not to leave until we can talk to them," JB called out to him.

"Right, we'd probably never see them again," Ralph answered over his shoulder. He hurried up the hill to the others. Sarah, JB, and Smiley could hear him asking the others to stay until Sarah had a chance to read the article. He returned and handed the newspaper to Sarah.

Sarah reviewed the headline. "We aren't that important," she sighed. "Even if we're some kind of crazy cult, we shouldn't be this important—not the front page. This is going to destroy us before we even get started." Defeated, she stared at her photo. "Nice picture. I'll bet Mom and Dad are really enjoying it. They're going to kill me. I know they are."

She read silently:

The group is thought to be linked to a sect of devil worshipers in Central Texas. According to Assistant Principal Blanche Nichols, the administration has had the alleged cult leader, Sarah McPhee, under close scrutiny for several months now. Ms. Nichols maintains the situation is well under control, and cult practices such as this are not tolerated under any circumstances. Ms. Nichols promised the proper punishment will be rendered to Ms. McPhee and the approximately twenty other students involved. Others are not named at this time.

As Sarah read the final paragraphs of the article she didn't bother to wipe her tears. She finished, handed the paper to Ralph, and looked out over the river in silence. There were several ducks working along the opposite bank. She wondered how they could look so peaceful when she felt so terrible.

"Geez," she sniffled. "I've been in trouble before, but nothing like this. I won't be able to explain it's all a mistake. With the newspaper, that reporter, and Hatchet Woman saying things that aren't true, who's going to listen anyway? Mom and Dad are going to be totally pissed and I know they won't even listen to my side of the story. My side isn't even believable. If I say I have an angel that talks to me, then they'll really think I've lost it."

"It'll work out," JB placated, although she wondered how it could. "I'll be back."

She stood and climbed the incline to the waiting group. She urged them to stay a while longer, then looked over the mass of bicycles, searching for Sarah's. She rummaged around in Sarah's pack on the handlebars, pulled out the large black journal, and hurried back down to Sarah, Ralph, and Smiley.

"Did you hear what they said about the article, Ralph?" Sarah wiped her tears on her sleeve.

Ralph cocked a threatening brow. "You sure you want to know?"

"Yes. If I'm going to get in trouble for being God, I'd just as soon know, right now."

Ralph's voice was ominous. "I think blasphemous pretty well sums you up, according to people at the dentist's office, at least."

Sarah cringed. "Shit," she stammered. "Did they know you were in on it?"

Ralph took off the raincoat. "Doctor Jennings asked if I knew anybody involved. He had both of his hairy hands in my mouth, so my answer was kind of mumbled. He took it as no, I guess."

Sarah felt a nauseating knot building in her stomach. She dropped her head in despair. "I guess we're through. Those that want to stay in the group won't be able to, because of their parents, and we'll probably be locked in our rooms the rest of the summer anyway."

She looked up at JB thumbing through the journal. "I guess we'd better tell the rest of the guys, thanks but no thanks, huh?"

JB studied her friend, concerned that she was about to give in to defeat. "No, not hardly. We can't give up. Not now."

Sarah looked for the ducks. They had disappeared. She wished she could also disappear. *Spook, I can't do this anymore. It's just too much for me to handle. You'll have to find someone else.* "Let's just forget it, JB. We can't do anything if people think we're evil and blasphemous."

"No, Sarah," JB repeated softly, getting a bit choked up herself. "We aren't quitting. Look, remember when Spook said there would be trouble? Well, apparently this is it. But, he also sent some other advice. It's right here." She tapped the open journal.

Sarah stared at her friend for a moment. "Okay, what does he say?" *Do I really want to hear this? There is nothing that Spook can say, right now, that's going to help us.* "His advice so far has gotten us into this mess."

JB ran her finger down the page. "Listen, you wrote this last week I think: *A problem is a lesson you give to yourself, to help you remember who you are, which is God. As long as you remember that you're a part of God, the solution will come to you. Things might be difficult for a while; however, this difficulty is only a lesson you need to learn, to make you more perfect. Remember, deep inside of you, if something feels right to you, you can never be wrong, no matter what others say."*

Sarah's panned the river. The ducks were back. She ran her fingers under her eyes to wipe the tears. "You're right, JB, as usual. I don't know how we're ever going to get out of this mess, but we'll try if you guys are willing."

She looked to her three friends to find cautious smiles and nods. "You guys are as crazy as I am. Well, let's do it," she said, lips tight and jaw set in determination. Getting to her feet, she added, "Now all we have to do is convince the others." JB, Ralph and Smiley followed her up the hill to those waiting.

Sarah stopped in front of the group and tried to put her thoughts in order. She spoke, her voice strained and cracked: "I hope you all know, that stuff in the newspaper isn't true. All we want to do is help save the Earth. Maybe what I did yesterday at school wasn't the right way to go about it, but we aren't some type of cult like the newspaper says. We are God. I believe that and will not change, no matter who calls me blasphemous.

"But my parents might lock this God in the closet for the rest of the summer." She was relieved to hear a few chuckles. "Hey, ya'll probably get grounded too.

"You know, your parents might tell you to have nothing to do with us. We understand. We might be facing the same thing. I guess you do whatever you feel you have to do. But, like I said before, this is an open group and you can quit or stay—whatever you want.

"I love you. We all love you, whatever you decide. But, I want you to remember one thing: even if someone keeps you away from our group, you are still an important part of humanity, a member of the Earth, and you need to do your part to make it better. You don't have to be a part of this 'cult group' to make a difference.

"That's it, I guess. I wish there was something I could tell you to make it easier with your parents, but...sorry. Any questions?"

The red-headed girl gestured hesitantly: "What should we tell our parents whenever they want to know what's going on?"

"I'm going to tell the truth. It sounds a whole lot better than any lie I can think of. If they don't believe the truth, then I'm really in trouble."

"What about next week? Are we going to have the meeting Tuesday morning like you planned?"

Sarah looked toward JB and Ralph for help but got none.

"I've got an idea." Despite the trouble, Jody smiled with confidence and ran his hand through has short curly blond hair. "Nearly everyone here is online. If you give me your e-mail addresses, I can let everyone know when we have news. Gotta do it sooner or later, anyway. If you're not online, I can tape a notice up under the bridge near the top, if there is a change in the meeting." He gestured toward the base of the bridge. "There's also a little ledge on the outside steel beam.

Early Tuesday morning, I can leave information there for those whose parents don't want them to meet with us. At least that way we can stay connected so everyone can participate."

"Awesome, Jody!" Sarah exclaimed.

"Right on," Jody nodded. "Once I get all the addresses, I'll send everyone's address out, so we can use instant messaging, too. E-mail me if you don't know how."

"Thanks, Jody. And everybody, if you have a cell phone, put your number on Jody's list, too. It'll be quicker to reach you by phone."

Ralph nodded. "Good idea. Why don't I give everyone my cell number, so they can call me direct?"

"Great!" Sarah called out. "Hey, everybody! Take this down! Ralph's number is 684-3200! Anytime you have a problem, call him!" She finally smiled. "In fact, why don't you call him every ten minutes! That should run up his bill and drive him crazy at the same time!"

"Thanks a lot, Sarah," Ralph deadpanned. "Glad you're feeling better."

"I'm not," she forced a grimace and raised her hand in the Earth Salute. "Thanks a lot, guys, and good luck! I think we're all going to need it."

Many gathered around to leave their information on Jody's list. Several wished Sarah, JB and Ralph luck. Nodding her appreciation of their concern, Sarah replaced the journal in her pack and pulled out a large green garbage sack.

"What are you going to do with that?" Ralph asked.

"I don't think I'm going to have time later today to please Judge Abbot. I'd better do it now, before Mom gets hold of me." As she turned toward the river, she called back over her shoulder, "I don't want to face Mom and Dad for a while anyway."

They watched as Sarah walked down to the riverbank. She stopped and looked to make sure her image was still on the surface. *I guess Spook is still on the job, even though he doesn't say anything when I need him the most.* She turned and walked down the trail along the bank, picking up bits of litter and an occasional beer or soda can.

JB watched too, touched by her friend's dedication. She whispered, "I don't blame you, Sarah. I'll bet, before this is over, you'll have to face the whole town."

Journal Note

"Nothing happens by accident. Actually you create each experience for just that—the experience. It is not good or bad. It just is. You may take the opportunity to experience it, however, you are not obligated to do so. If you choose not to, simply walk away from it."

CHAPTER 5

Sarah fidgeted as she sat at the desk in the little cubicle of an office at the Pizza Shack. She could hear her mom pace back and forth behind her, slapping the folded newspaper against her open hand. *Just get it over with, Mom. Say something.*

"I am God!" Barbara exclaimed, startling Sarah. "You've got to be kidding. Surely you didn't say that? Not in front of the whole student body and teachers, too?"

Sarah watched her father across the desk, doodling on a scratch pad.

"Well?" Barbara pressed as she tapped her daughter's shoulder with the newspaper. "Let's hear it. Tell me you didn't say, 'I am God.' Tell me this newspaper has it all wrong."

Well, here goes, thought Sarah as she turned in her chair to face her mom. "Yes, I said it, and yes, the newspaper got the story all messed up, because Hatchet...uh...Ms. Nichols wants to look good for the whole town to see."

Bob watched Barbara nod repeatedly, her eyes fixed on her daughter, her face mirroring her agitation. "Well, that's just great—just great." Barbara turned toward her husband. "See, I told you so; she did say it."

Sarah's mother was the driving force behind the McPhee family, not only in household matters but in managing the family restaurant as well. She was a trim, youthful woman of medium height, with rusty-red short-cropped hair, green eyes, and an elongated face with a few too many freckles, particularly when she spent time in the sun. In her red and white plaid Pizza Shack uniform, she looked a great deal younger than her thirty-eight years, so much that occasionally she gained the misguided attention of male customers from the local college.

She always appeared to be on a mission as she tackled everyday activity and her leisure with fervor. She liked a clean slate and was impatient when any of life's menial problems refused to be solved or even left loose ends. The bigger the problem, the more frustrated she became if the solution wasn't close at hand.

This was Sarah's third time to get in trouble in the last two months, and Barbara was at her wit's end. On top of that, it appeared to her that Bob gave no real support in her effort to discipline Sarah. She didn't like being the heavy but someone had to do it. And he seemed in no hurry to enter the fray this time either.

Bob made no effort to acknowledge that Barbara had turned her attention toward him. Without change of expression, he continued to draw intertwining circles on the pad. Sarah could see that this added to her mom's frustration.

"For God's sake, Robert!" Barbara blurted. "Don't you have anything to say? Your daughter is making us the laughing stock of Cibolo Falls, and all you can do is sit there and draw your stupid doodles!"

The tension built in the small room as Bob continued to ignore his wife. Sarah's discomfort increased. She wished her dad would say something—anything—before her mom moved up to her next level of frustration, which usually meant nothing but trouble for everyone.

Much to Sarah's relief, she saw her father flip the pencil on the desk. She knew that was an indication he was getting involved. Without a hint of acknowledgement toward his wife, he gazed at his daughter for a long uneasy moment with piercing light brown eyes, his jaw subtly working on chewing gum. Although cut short and receding, his hair was the same sandy-brown as Sarah's. He also had high prominent cheekbones, a bushy brow and a good tan. In spite of being in the pizza business, his body was trim and fit due to frequent time in the gym. In contrast to his wife, he seemed to be in complete control. Because Sarah knew he would act more rationally, she wanted him to be the one to confront her and was anxious for him to get involved.

"Well, it's obvious if most of the things the newspaper said were true, we would've known something was going on beforehand. So, do you want to tell us what the hell is going on—the real story?"

"Yessir," Sarah answered, relieved they had avoided her mom's potential meltdown—at least for the moment. "Where do you want me to start?"

Bob had both elbows propped on the desk with his hands folded together. "The beginning is good. Start wherever is necessary to tell the whole story."

Sarah pensively weighed the benefits of telling just enough to get her temporarily out of trouble. *I'd better tell the whole story now so I don't have to go through it again later. They aren't going to believe me, anyway. Geez, I think I would have been better off just running away from home.*

Sarah told the complete story the best she could, starting three weeks before when Spook first spoke to her. As she progressed she could see her parent's growing concern, particularly when told about everyone and everything being God. She charged on, determined to tell them everything—to get it out into the open as clearly as possible. When she had brought them up to the present, she paused for the questions she knew were to come.

"An interesting three weeks you've had, to say the least," Bob said. "Now, if you don't mind, let's get back to...so your mom and I can get this straight. Spook just takes over anytime it, he, wants too. What if you don't want him to talk to you? What then?"

"He said he would leave me alone if I didn't want his help. All I had to do was say so."

"And obviously you haven't told him that you don't want his help?"

He and Barbara noted a meek smile and a faint nod.

"Satisfy my curiosity," Barbara, asked as she resumed her pacing. "Have you asked him to help you get out of this mess that he got…that you're in? Where is he when you need him?"

"Yes, ma'am. He didn't answer, so I guess this is one of those experience times. I don't know."

"Uh-huh. Sounds like a real choice friend, uh, *guardian* angel you have," Bob remarked.

Barbara stopped her pacing and stood behind Bob, her hand resting on his shoulder. "All right. What's done is done. I'm sorry this happened, but you didn't use good judgment in your actions at school. You just can't go charging in and take over the assembly, and then shout slogans, particularly 'I am God.' I hope you learned something for the future. Always think things through. Most of the time it will keep you out of trouble. Understand?"

Bob could see a wave of relief pass over Sarah's face as she locked her eyes on her mom, nodding her head.

Wow. Maybe I'm going to get through this after all. If she's already in the advice stage, I couldn't be in too much trouble. I'm as good as out-of-here. If only they can think of a way to handle the newspaper article.

Sarah's thoughts were interrupted by her dad. "I can kind of see where you're coming from. I agree with you, to an extent, that God is everything and everywhere. However, there's a certain group, the majority to be exact, that believe that God is the Supreme Being, the Creator and Eternal Spirit of the Universe. He's the one in charge of our lives. He is to be worshiped and honored for what he is to mankind. I, and I think I speak for your mom, agree with that, although we aren't what could be judged as religious."

When Bob hesitated, Barbara added, "We don't feel the need to worship God in a church atmosphere, and perhaps we've fallen short in guiding you and encouraging you in a religious environment. But that doesn't mean that we don't believe in God and try to live our lives, shall I say, in a godly manner, treating our fellowman with love and respect."

Barbara saw Sarah nod her understanding, but knew she had a problem when she drew her brow together and curled the edge of her mouth. Barbara gestured for comment.

"Why can't I believe all that, but also believe that God is a part of me and everything else? Why can't I believe that we are created by God, and are a part of God? And why can't I believe that His spirit and our spirit is all the same spirit, so we are all God?"

Bob was about to answer, but Barbara tapped him on the shoulder with her finger, indicating she would do it.

"Sarah, although it is said that we are made in the image of God, it is accepted among the majority of the world's religions that we are, however, separate from God. They are very clear on this. So, what I'm trying to get across is, people out there just don't accept what you believe and most probably never will. Their beliefs are important to them, and, I might add, are right for them. So, if you throw something at them that is unacceptable to the very core of their being and teaching, you'd better expect them to fight tooth and toenail for their beliefs. And I'll tell you something else: this battle you aren't likely to win." Barbara offered her daughter a compassionate smile. "Do you understand what I'm saying?"

Sarah nodded. "Yes, ma'am. Spook said the same thing."

"He did?" Barbara's mouth gaped as she moved to the side of the desk between her husband and daughter.

"Yes. He said that not too many people will believe that God is a part of us, and that I need to let those that don't believe it to have their own truths. I should love and respect them anyway."

"This gets better by the minute. What, may I ask, are their own truths?"

Sarah smiled in hesitation. "I think it means beliefs."

An employee rapped on the door, calling for assistance. Bob left the office without comment. After he closed the door behind him, Barbara asked, "This 'angel' seems to have some interesting information. You say you've been keeping a journal; everything he says is written there?"

"I've kept a journal the best I could. He gave me so much stuff over the last two weeks...and some of it was confusing me in the beginning, so I didn't write too good, uh, too well. I didn't get all of it. He said that we'll go back over it later, when I begin to understand stuff more."

"You know, it's not normal for someone to hear voices inside her head, angel or otherwise. Doesn't that bother you at all?"

Bob returned with three Cokes, and could tell Sarah was thirsty when she discarded the straw and took a long gulp before setting it in front of her on the desk. She immediately picked it up again and had another long drink. She crunched on a small piece of ice and set the Coke back down. She answered with another piece of ice rolling around in her mouth, garbling some of the words:

"It did at first, but later on I decided that he wasn't going to hurt me. And anyway, I like what he says. It makes me feel good, like I'm a real necessary part of things." One last crunch and the ice was gone. "Spook told me that I'm as important as everyone else, not someone that God has forgotten. I really do believe he is my guardian angel."

"Most people would probably say you have a screw loose—perhaps a little crazy," Bob commented matter-of-factly, a hint of humor in his eyes.

"Yeah, I've thought about that. Some of the guys that heard about Spook didn't believe me at first."

"But they do now?"

"Yes, sir."

"Why did they change their minds?

"About two weeks ago, Spook made an image of me on the river at the edge, to prove to them that he was real."

Sarah saw her parents again exchange confused glances. Barbara asked, "I don't understand. He made an image of you. What—?"

"On the top, on the surface of the water. It's me with a large garbage sack. On the side of the sack there's some words."

"Words—what?"

"It says, 'Clean up your earth.' After the guys saw the image, they believe Spook is really real. They think it's cool, so now they want to do some of the stuff he suggested."

"Oh," Barbara nodded doubtfully. "And how many of your friends saw this image?"

"There were about twenty of us that day. When others heard about Spook, they went to the river to see the image. I don't know how many saw it before the assembly, but this morning there were about ninety at the meeting. All of them saw it."

"This is kind of hard to believe," Bob frowned. "Maybe they were just seeing their own reflection?"

"No, Dad. Nobody saw their own reflection. They all saw just me. In the image I'm smiling. I pick up a paper cup and put it in the sack."

"Is it still there?"

"Spook said that it will be there for a while, so others will believe me when I say he talks to me."

"Well, this I have to see," Bob said to Barbara. "Maybe we ought to take a little trip to the river." When he saw Sarah shake her head, he asked, "You have a problem with that?"

"Spook said that some people won't be able to see it."

"Oh, that's convenient," Barbara countered. She sat down and picked up her Coke. "And why would that be?" she asked as she took a sip.

"Because they don't believe in spirits. He said that you also have to be in tune with your spiritual side, like you have to have the right energy or vibration."

Bob nodded, "Well now, I guess you'll have to take your mom and me to see if we have the right 'vibration.'"

"I really want to, Dad. When do you wanna go?"

Bob ignored the question. "You know, once word gets around that only select people see the images, there is going to be a lot of disbelief. They'll think those that see it are having delusions or something. It'll be controversial, and you're going to be caught right in the big middle. You realize that, don't you?"

Sarah thought for a moment, and then answered hardly above a whisper: "I guess, but I don't—"

"Well, hell," he muttered. "Who knows how this is going to play out? Along with the newspaper already on your case, if this image stuff gets loose, which it probably will with so many having seen it, it could certainly get interesting."

"Well, I'm not believing it until I see it," Barbara stressed. "And if I don't see it, I just don't know what I will or won't believe. If there really is an image, it would make things easier if Spook would just make the image visible to everyone."

Bob and Sarah watched as Barbara wrestled with her feelings. "But, then again, if everyone could see it, some would call it a miracle and, you know what, I don't think I want my daughter in on a miracle."

Each sat in quiet contemplation, then Bob broke the silence, "Well, only time will tell. Now, where do we go from here?"

Sarah exaggerated a grimace. *Geez, here we go. Please make it easy. I won't cause any more trouble.* "Punishment, I guess."

Bob shook his head and emitted a throaty chuckle, then resigned, "I have the job of punishing God?"

The three of them laughed, relieving the tension that hung in the room. Sarah knew she had her parent's support for what lay ahead.

Bob continued: "Maybe your judgment wasn't too sharp, but I think your intentions were noble. I can't slight you for that. I do think you need to lay low for a few days and, hopefully, everyone will forget. Once things cool down, I don't see any reason why you can't go through with your plans to clean up the neighborhood, that is, if you have any help left. However, if you are going to continue with this, there is one thing I will require of you as your parent and, I might add, as one of those in charge of you."

"Yes, sir."

"Some of those groups that are out to change the world think they can break the law to accomplish their goals. Even the little laws, like trespassing on someone's private property. I don't know what your plans are, but if you demonstrate or anything like that, honor other people's rights," he smiled, "and truths. Just because they think differently than you, or don't agree with you, gives you no special rights, even if you are God." He took a swig of his Coke. "The way I see it, if what you say is true, even the scum of the earth is God, too. Am I correct?" He raised a brow while nodding at his daughter.

"And let's stop the 'I am God' stuff, until this blows over a little, okay?" Barbara added.

"Okay, Mom. I've learned my lesson." She saw that her dad had more to say, so she fixed him with a stare and waited.

"People can be downright ugly if they think differently than you, particularly if your views are threatening to theirs, or if they think you should embrace their beliefs instead of your own. If anyone says anything to you, just keep quiet, don't argue, and get away from them as quickly as possible. It will usually do no good to argue with them because, chances are, their beliefs are so deeply ingrained that they will never change, no matter what you do. So, just forget it—get away."

"Okay, Dad. I think I get it."

"Something else, Sarah," her mother spoke slowly as if she was still formulating what she had to say. "You may not agree with me, but I want to set up an examination with a doctor to see about the voices you hear. Sometimes people hear things when they have a mental or physical problem developing, so I just want to be sure. If everything checks out okay, I assure you, you will get our full support, and we'll also listen with an open mind to what your angel—if he is an angel—has to say. We won't necessarily agree with him, as you yourself shouldn't, but we will listen. Agreed?"

"If that's what you want?" *Do I have a choice? What else can I do?*

"That's what we want," her father answered. "And there's one more thing."

"What?"

"The journal. I want the doctor to see what your Spook has to say."

"Meaning, I'm going to one of those head doctors, huh?" Sarah answered, increasingly anxious about what she was getting into.

"A psychologist or psychiatrist," her mom nodded. "We have to be sure there is nothing abnormal physically or mentally. The journal will hopefully give the doctor some insight. It may help him in finding out where the voice comes from, if it's an angel or something other than yourself, or perhaps a hidden personality, or whatever. We can't just guess about this." Barbara nodded her compassion. "You're too precious for us to be guessing if you need some type of help."

Bob quipped, "Amen."

"I guess that's all, huh?"

"And by the way, Sarah," Barbara said. "I think you have suffered enough during the past few weeks. You're no longer grounded."

Barbara saw a wave of elation gross her daughter's face. "Thanks, Mom," Sarah gushed. "I don't have time to be grounded."

After checking the clock, they decided that they had enough time before peak dinner rush to take a quick trip to the river. Sarah tried to put on a happy face but was worried that her parents would not see the image and she would lose their support. *Spook, if you're there, you'd better do something.*

Later, when Bob and Barbara gazed over the edge into the water, they stared for a moment, then shook their heads in disbelief.

Barbara was the first to speak: "Well, Sarah. It looks like you've got all the makings of a miracle here. Good luck, 'cause you're certainly going to need it."

"Thanks Mom—Dad. I think I'm gonna need your support."

Sarah saw tears in her mom's eyes. "We both love you Sarah. You know that, don't you?"

Sarah didn't answer but her lips were pressed in a tight smile.

Journal Note

"You will never, ever be presented any issue or experience that you are not ready to handle."

CHAPTER 6

Sarah had drawn kitchen duty for the dinner shift, which was fine with her. Cooking pizzas was so much easier than serving them because many customers, she had learned, were inconsiderate, no matter how cheerful, efficient, and prompt the service.

Although the phone rang now and then, there had been very few of the call-in, take-out orders that usually kept the kitchen extra busy. As business was also slow in the dining room, she busied herself cleaning the large refrigerator that had needed it for quite some time, both inside and out.

The phone rang again and a moment later the kitchen door swung open; it was her dad. "Some gentleman on the phone wishes to speak to a Ms. Sarah McPhee," Bob announced with a grin. "He says it's of utmost urgency."

"Utmost urgency? I don't—?"

"Yeah, and tell Ralph that disguising his voice doesn't work. I'd know it anywhere."

Sarah giggled. "He doesn't want you to know it's him, because of the trouble."

"I figured as much. Well, tell him, next time I see him, there's going to be a royal blood-letting, because of the part he played."

"I can't do that. He'd leave town if he thought you were after him." She replaced two large pots in the refrigerator and dashed to the phone.

"Hi, Ralph. What's up?"

"How'd you know it was me?"

"Dad said so."

"Man, you can't get anything past that guy." He lowered his voice as if he were in the same room. "Hey, you don't sound so bad. What'd they say?"

"That I went about it all wrong, As long as I don't screw up again, I should be okay. I took them down to see the image. They really believe me about Spook now."

"Hey, that's beautiful. My parents want to see it. So does Juanita's. Donnie's parents are out of town, but he's going to take them when they come back on Sunday."

"So, you guys didn't get into trouble either?"

"Naw, I'm cool, and JB told her parents last night. When the paper came out this morning, they already knew the real story. But, they did blame JB for letting you get up on that stage and make a fool of yourself."

"Great," Sarah laughed, relieved that, so far, no one was in trouble.

"And that ain't all. Jody and Smiley's been checking up on the group to find out how their parents are taking it. We lost about twenty since this morning, either because their parents made them quit, they didn't agree with the God stuff, or some were afraid of getting into trouble. That's not too bad."

Sarah breathed relief. "Good, great. Now we can get back to work, if the newspaper will leave us alone."

"Jody says about fifty of the guys put in their time today, picking up litter on the streets and parks around town."

"Awesome!" Sarah exclaimed. "I wish I could have seen that."

"Thought you might like that. And let me tell you: Smiley and Derick Bradford made up some poster-board signs and demonstrated in front of O.P.A. Supermarket."

"What'd their signs say?"

"One read something like, 'Save waste. Bring back your grocery sack next trip to O.P.A.' Underneath, in small letters, he signed it, 'GARBAGE.' The other sign read, 'You can help save a tree. Bring your own tote sack next time you shop for groceries.' It was also signed the same way."

"I love it! I love it!" Sarah gushed. "The store manager didn't get mad or anything, did he?"

"They asked if it was okay. As soon as he saw the signs, he was cool. Hey, if customers brought their own grocery bags, O.P.A. would save a bundle on plastic and paper sacks. He's not stupid. And that's not all. That reporter guy who was at the assembly—"

"John Holland. The one who wrote the article."

"Yeah, him. He came by and took a picture of Derick holding up his poster."

"Did he say anything?"

"Hey, this dude's a piece of work—a real nerd. He wanted to know why Smiley and Derick were demonstrating. Smiley said, 'Hey, man, can't you read? The sign speaks for itself.' Then the reporter asked what GARBAGE meant.

"When Smiley told him it what it stood for, Holland said that he couldn't understand why he hadn't ever heard of it. Smiley told him that there was a whole lot of stuff going on in Cibolo Falls that the reporter didn't know about. He offered to fill him in, sometime, on all the stuff the reporter didn't know. That's when Holland got mad."

Sarah laughed, "That's great."

"Hey, there's more. Holland made a big deal of leaving Smiley out of the picture to punish him for his disrespectful attitude. Smiley said, 'I'll probably lose about two minutes of sleep because of being left out of the picture.' Then Holland really went psycho. He cussed Smiley out quietly so no one else could hear. Smiley flipped him the bird when he drove off."

"Smiley didn't tell Holland that I'm involved with GARBAGE, did he?" Sarah asked.

"Naw, because of the story in the paper this morning. Smiley says we shouldn't trust him, and I agree. He thought the reporter might change it all around and use it against us."

"Right," Sarah agreed. "If he can't tell the truth, we'd better avoid him."

"Yeah, we need to tell everybody that John Holland's off-limits. Right now, the less he knows about us, the better off we'll be."

"How about the shoppers? Did anyone say anything?"

"That's a no. Smiley and Derick said that people definitely noticed, but not much was said."

Sarah unconsciously twisted the phone cord around her finger. "Well, maybe we'll survive the assembly mistake after all."

"I don't think you should be too quick to say that. Some people out there don't understand, and I don't think they want to."

"What'd you mean?"

"Mom said that she overheard some people where she works. They were talking about a boycott of the Pizza Shack, to show you people that there is only one God. She said that they could probably do it, too. They're big churchgoers, and just a few phone calls could do it."

The sinking feeling returned to her stomach and she felt that same wall of regret that she had when she saw the newspaper. "You're kidding. Why would they do something like that? My parents didn't do anything. It was me."

"Some people suck, Sarah. That includes some who think they're Christians. Mom says that they aren't gonna let you say you're God, but that doesn't apply to them. They're happy to be your judge, jury, and executioner—in God's name, of course. And they'll probably enjoy teaching you a lesson, just because you don't think like they do."

"Shit!" she exhaled after taking it all in.

"Hey, deal me in."

"I think it's already started, Ralph. Things have been really slow around here this evening. I'll bet that—Hey, Ralph, I'd better go. Mom and Dad are going to be pissed big-time when they find out."

"Okay, call me later to let me know what happened."

"I'll try. Bye." Sarah hung up the phone and hurried back to the kitchen. Her father had taken over the cooking chores, and looked up when she came wearily through the swinging doors.

"Problem with Ralph?"

"He said that some people might boycott the Pizza Shack," she replied, hoping he wouldn't be hear or understand. Sarah was confused about the lack of response from her father as he methodically added topping to a pizza.

He turned and slid the pizza into the oven, wiped his hands on a towel, and nodded at Sarah. "Yeah, we've figured that out. And there's more—much more. We've been getting quite a few crank calls. Some have been downright nasty, considering they have to be coming from

God-fearing people."

Bob saw a wave of regret sweep across his daughter's face. Suddenly dizzy, she grabbed the only stool and sat down. "Oh, no, Dad. I'm sorry. I didn't mean for this to happen. It's all my fault."

Bob smiled at his daughter and took her arm for her to stand. The dizziness had subsided, but she still was a bit woozy.

"Hey, come on, now. Be strong," Bob said softly, taking her into his arms.

His warmth and obvious strength were always welcome, and she wondered why it was only during times that she was down or sad that he held her. His smell reminded her of when she was much younger. She would sneak into her parent's bed on cold mornings and escape imagined dangers of the world under sheets with the same smell.

She was thrust back into reality by her father's voice: "I don't understand how people can do such a thing, but they are. All we can do now is hold on and hope they see the truth—that you don't mean them or anyone else any harm. Perhaps this has been just another slow night. We have them on occasion. If this is a boycott, we'll survive. I guarantee that." A new worry line appeared between his thick brows.

Sarah spent a very restless night. Although daylight was a long time coming, it was welcome nontheless. She was up, showered, and dressed by six. As she descended the stairs she was aware of a weakness and tiredness in her legs that she had never felt before. She figured it was because of the continual stress and pressure she had been under for the last several days—and she wondered if it was going to let up anytime soon.

She noticed the kitchen light on and found her dad sitting at the table drinking coffee. He looked up and smiled. "Hey, gal, a bit early for you, isn't it?"

She was happy to see him although she didn't show it. "Can't sleep."

"Me neither."

"Well, damn," Sarah muttered under her breath. The misery of the night—and now the new day—haunted her. "I'm really sorry, Dad. I'm trying to do everything right, but it keeps...You know, sometimes I wish Spook would just leave me alone. Things were so much easier before he came."

Bob nodded his compassion. "Well, maybe, but if you remember, your glorious cousin led you astray before Spook showed. Maybe you're just going through a bad phase. You know, things go in circles. You go along, bumping into walls, then for no reason at all, you suddenly start sailing over them, carefree."

"Well, I don't like the stuff that's happening to me, but it's not as bad as what—the trouble I've caused you and Mom, and my friends. The more trouble I get into, the more I get everyone else in trouble. It's just not fair to everybody else. And it's all my fault."

"We'll be okay. All of us, and that includes your friends. We just have to keep plugging along." Bob noisily slurped his hot coffee, and watched as Sarah poured herself a cup. "Uh-oh, I've never seen you drink coffee before. Things must really be bad."

"I saw on TV that coffee kind of gives you a kick-in-the-pants, like a Coke does. Well, I don't think I can drink a Coke at six in the morning." She took a sip and grimaced. She put a spoonfull of sugar in the coffee, stirred it, and sipped it. No help, so she got a carton of milk out of the refrigerator and poured in a hefty amount. She tried it once more, then made a production of pouring it in the sink.

Bob laughed. "You thought we were having fun, drinking all that coffee, didn't you?"

"Ugh. That sucks—sorry Dad—that was terrible."

"So, what's the deal on Spook? Did he show last night?"

Sarah got a glass out of the cabinet and poured it half full of orange juice from the refrigerator. She sat down across from him at the table, and answered. "No, and I didn't try to call him, either. I don't think that there's anything he can say right now that'll help me...us get out of this mess."

"Well, the way I see it, if this guy is really your guardian angel, he's not going to do any physical stuff to help you. Apparently he can't. I assume he's just going to give you information that will help you live your life better." Bob studied Sarah's face and was alarmed at the gauntness and the dark circles under her eyes. She appeared to be much older than her fourteen years.

"Or worse," She countered. "Has the newspaper come yet?"

"I checked right before you came down. Should be here by now. Expecting good news, are ya?" he quipped, trying to cheer her.

"Not really. I'll be lucky if there is no news at all."

"Well, tell you what. Let's get the paper and go to Busby's for breakfast. Maybe we can celebrate no news."

"What about Mom?"

"She was sleeping like a baby when I got up. We'll leave her a note and she can catch up with us at work later."

They backed out of the driveway with the newspaper still in its plastic wrapper on the seat between them. When they arrived at the café, they ordered breakfast and spread the paper across the tiny table.

Apprehension surged in Sarah's veins as she eyed the headlines. She knew today would be no better than yesterday. There it was:

"Cult group grows to 100"

"Local clergy voice concern"

As her dad read silently, she watched the corner of his mouth twist up. Next his jaw flexed, and it was obvious he was not happy.

"Well, it appears that some of those at the meeting yesterday spilled the beans to their parents. The first paragraph pretty much sums up. Let's see, 'close to one hundred showed up…kids promised excitement for the summer'…yada-yada-yada."

Bob's finger passed over several paragraphs and stopped. "Here we go: 'In an effort to clarify the intent of the group, several local clergymen gave insight into why the kids speak of themselves as God, and what might motivate the group.'

"Let's see now. This is Gerald Morris of United Methodist: 'The child appears to be a victim of society. With the pressures of today on our youth, it is no wonder that a child would seek refuge of this nature.'" Bob shook his head and said, "A brilliant way to say nothing."

Sarah didn't comment but Bob could see the concern and uncertainty on her face.

"You want more?"

She nodded, "All of it."

"You sure?"

"Dad, just do it."

"Okay, the Reverend Mr. Donald Crosswhite, pastor, Northwood Community Church. 'The devil works in strange ways to capture the hearts of the weak. This is definitely the work of Satan, to lure our vulnerable youth into his service.'

"More?"

"All of it."

"All right, quickly now. This is Mr. David Saske, pastor of Riverview

Baptist Church: 'It appears that this is, once again, another unfortunate soul, misguided by those misinformed New Age types.'

"Dr. Mark Hightower, pastor of Hill Country Chapel of God: 'This is surely a guise by the devil to ensnare our youth. I shall begin a campaign, immediately, to protect our children from anyone claiming to be God. I will not rest until I have rid our town of anyone leading our precious young ones astray. Today, more than ever, church and family must work together to provide an environment to keep our children out of the grasp of those as deluded as these. We must gather together and act now, today, before it's too late, to cull those troublesome weeds from our midst.'" Bob exhaled noisily through his teeth. "This sounds like a real choice guy.

"There's more from him. Let's see, he went on 'to urge that the police restrain the leaders of this group from further corruption of our vulnerable youth.' I assume that means you."

The waitress brought their breakfast and set it in front of them. He pushed his aside to make room for the newspaper. Sarah picked up her fork but didn't attempt to use it as she waited for her dad to continue.

"Police Chief Donald Sheck, contacted late Friday, said, 'I have been receiving calls all day long from angry parents and members of the clergy, and there's not a whole lot I can do about their complaints. I have no plans, at the present, to even contact those involved at the park this morning. To my knowledge, there were no laws broken, and I certainly don't plan on making any of my own to rectify the situation. I was hired to maintain the law. There were no laws broken. It's as simple as that.' Good for you, Chief. The only rational one in the bunch.

"That's it for the lead article," Bob said as he turned to page two.

The waitress returned to fill Bob's coffee cup. "Something the matter with the eggs, hon? You haven't touched 'em."

"No, ma'am. I'm just a slow eater," Sarah answered. The petite waitress fluttered away. She stopped and straightened the salt and pepper shakers on one table, and the sugar on another. She reminded Sarah of a hummingbird, checking out all the flowers.

Bob skimmed over several related articles concerning cult activity, but didn't pass on the information to Sarah. She saw his eyes light up and knew good news was coming.

"What?"

Bob folded the second page over once again and creased it. He moved her plate over and slid the paper across to her, tapping a picture with his finger.

He detected a trace of a smile appear on his daughter's face—her first of the day. There was the picture that Ralph had described. Derick stood in front of O.P.A. Supermarket with his demonstration sign. Although there was no accompanying article, the caption said, "Despite the unfavorable publicity surrounding Cibolo Falls' teens recently, Derick Bradford, age 14, found time Thursday to campaign for a good cause. GARBAGE, printed on the bottom of his sign, identifies the new ecology group in town, Grassroots Alliance for Reviving and Building A Greater Earth."

By the time lunch was over, it was obvious that there was a boycott against the Pizza Shack. Normally Saturday was the busiest lunch of the week, but today was less than half what it had averaged on previous Saturdays. Two days of headlines and crank calls ragged Sarah out, so she begged off for the remainder of the afternoon. Depressed, she hoped a nap would help before meeting up with JB and Ralph for their GARBAGE activity at three-thirty.

When she arrived home, she dragged up the stairs to the peace and quiet of her bedroom. She lay down on the bed, closed her eyes and tried to calm herself. She heard the familiar echo-like voice of Spook from deep in her mind. With the metallic resonance of a bell, he announced:

"Good afternoon, little one. Remember, you will be confronted with many issues to deal with in the future. They will come in many forms and in the most unexpected ways. You should consider these issues, that you refer to as troubles, are only problems you have presented to yourself, to remind you of who and what you are. As I said before, you are nothing more or nothing less than an extension of God's soul or spirit in a physical body. He, as the Creator, knows all there is to know, but He has, in the very distant past, existed only in spiritual form. His just knowing wasn't enough. He wanted to experience what He knows, so He would be complete. His soul split, and you, as well as all things on the planet, were created to experience for Him physically, as well as experiencing for yourself. You and all creation, although you are on the phys-

ical level of existence, are spiritually connected on the soul level with each other and God. Therefore, you are all a part of each other and, more importantly, are a part of God. So, in essence, you are God."

When he was done, she focused her attention deep inside herself. Spook, she thought as she tried to close out all other mental activity, I understand I'm a part of God, and I try to accept that the issues I have are very important. As I work through them, I not only experience for myself, but for the whole universe and God. You say everything that happens to me is for this purpose, and when I experience these things, the universe becomes a better place.

You told me that the bigger the issue I have, the more I or we can experience and learn from it. But this isn't fair. What I did got me into trouble. I guess that's okay, because I can learn something. But the stuff I did made some big problems for Mom and Dad—my friends, too. It's not fair that they have trouble because of what I did. I want to change that, but I don't know how.

"I know this is hard for you to understand, but please know that your mom and dad, as well as your friends, are voluntarily playing this experience game with you, for the good of their selves and the universe. They may not realize the reason why they are involved, but it is very important that they are. Even those that you perceive as being against you are playing an equally important part to their selves, to you, and the universe. Again, they may not understand why they are playing this experience game as you do, but their part is as important as yours. And neither side is right or wrong."

I try to understand that, Sarah projected to Spook. But, still, it's real hard to experience stuff if everyone is against me. The newspapers are against me. The churches are against me, and people are saying I'm the devil's helper. Everybody is against me. I don't know what to do. I don't know how to fight this. What they are saying about me seems right if you look at it from their side. But what I meant to do isn't anything like they are saying. And I don't even know what to say to them if I have a chance to explain. It just looks to everyone like those people talking about me are right and I am wrong.

Sarah watched a spider hanging off the ceiling as she tried to clear her mind, hoping Spook would answer.

"We have spoken of this very thing in the past. You place too much emphasis on what others have to say, because they appear to have more

experience than you do. Some, like Dr. Hightower, command a large audience, because they are thought to be educated in godly matters. To many, Dr. Hightower's words are definitely true, while to many others, they are not and may be harmful.

"So, my main message for you, today, is that you should not necessarily value other people's acts or opinions over your own, no matter how right they appear. You cannot possibly be wrong if you truly and deeply feel you are right.

"Little one, I will now part with this final but important message. Write it down, because it will come in handy many times in the days to come. The message is: you will never, ever be presented any issue or experience that you are not ready to handle."

The message was completed and Sarah jumped up from bed and wrote down everything that Spook said in her journal. The last part of the message, she rewrote on a small slip of paper and placed it in her purse as a reminder, just in case.

She closed the journal and placed it in its special place on the bookshelf. As she crawled into bed she wondered what the doctor would think about what Spook had said. Oh, well, there's nothing I can do about it now. I've written the truth. I hope he doesn't think I'm a psycho like the rest of the world does. With Spook's voice still echoing in her ears, she fell asleep.

It seemed she had only been asleep a few minutes when the phone rang; it was JB. "Are you okay? I thought you were going to meet us at three-thirty."

Sarah glanced at the clock. It was after five. "I'm sorry. I was really out of it. I meant to sleep only an hour. Did you go ahead without me?"

"Yeah, *no problema*. Me and Ralph talked his brother, John, into helping with his pickup. We picked up three more of the guys on Riverside Drive, and went down to Lover's Lane. John says that there's a lot of activity going on down there at night."

"I'll bet. So, what'd you guys do?"

"It was *muy caliente*, about ninety degrees, this afternoon, like it turned summer since yesterday. Everybody was sweating. Anyway, the place was a mess. It was a dump. We loaded up an old sofa, some tires, a mattres, and a bunch of other trash, and hauled it off to the real dump."

"Well, darn. I'm sorry I missed it," Sarah complained. "But that's great. If we could get more older kids to help, we could use the wheels."

"No kidding. There're about four more loads out there, and John says he knows several other places that need cleaning up real bad. He'll help us, but he wants us to keep it quiet. His friends will laugh at him if they find out he's been hangin' with little kids."

"Hey, we'll keep it quiet. And with Derick's picture in the paper, maybe we'll get more support instead of all this cult stuff. How about the others? Did they go out today?"

"According to Jody, the same ones went out as yesterday, and because of Derick's picture, a few more of the ninety we had at the meeting came back. Everybody is working clean-up, right now. A bunch of them worked the old downtown area today. Jody said it really made a difference. You don't realize how dirty everything is until you clean it up."

"That's really cool. Maybe we won't lose so many after all," Sarah replied. "I need to get my shit in order, so I can help more."

"Yeah, Ralph said we need your dirty face to guide us. Whatever that means. And along with that, we'd better start thinking of some bigger projects to keep the guys from getting bored. I know fifteen or thirty minutes a day isn't overworking 'em, but they're going to need some variety, to keep 'em interested."

"I know," Sarah answered. "Before Tuesday's meeting, we should add to our job list and start doing stuff as a group, instead of everyone doing his own thing all the time. That way, maybe we can get the city to do something about recycling and stuff."

"That's gonna take some big-ass demonstrating, Sarah. Right now, we've gotta get everybody off your case, so you can get out on the street with us, without giving us all a bad rep."

"Thanks a lot, JB. I'm really in trouble when my own friends don't want to be seen with me."

"That's life," JB laughed. "Screw up once, you're gone."

"I'm glad I have such loyal friends. I don't know when I'll be able to show my face. Some people are really mad. And Dad is sure the Pizza Shack is being boycotted. Business is way down."

"Really? I didn't think they could ever get people to give up enough pizza to hurt your business. Could it turn into a big problem?"

"It already has. Mom says our budget can't stand for this to go on very long, or we'll have to shut down the place."

"Umm" was the only reply Sarah heard from her friend. She waited. JB's voice came back over the line. "I'll betcha Ralph can get the town to eat more pizza. I'll have to talk to him"

He paced back and forth across the carpeted floor. His anguish tormented him. His hands shook as he picked up a glass-framed portrait off the desk, glared at it for a moment, then slammed it back down.

He resumed his pacing and picked up his speed as he wrung his hands. Again he picked up the portrait and held it close to his chest. He began to sob:

"Father, she has returned and, to show my loyalty to you, I will do as you say. I will prove it to you. Please listen. Don't send me away. I would give my life to please you. You must know that."

He fell to his knees, his body shook as he sobbed, the torment of years of unmet need taking its toll. He clutched the portrait tighter to his chest and pleaded, "I beg of you, Father, accept me for what I am."

Journal Note

"When you experience something that you feel is undesirable or that you do not want, remember that you are not being singled out to have these so-called bad things happen to you. You are merely being given a chance to experience it all. When you have experienced it all, again, what you consider good and bad, then you can make a better choice of who you are and what you will want to become or be—which is love and God."

CHAPTER 7

Sunday morning's *Gazette* relegated news that concerned the youth of Cibolo Falls to page two, and that was an upbeat article on activities of the new ecological group, GARBAGE. Since many of the kids had banded together and cleaned up litter in the old downtown area on Saturday afternoon, it couldn't help but attract attention of the business owners in the area. One called the newspaper, which promptly sent out a reporter and photographer. When the reporter, John Holland, asked any pertinent questions about the organization, the kids were so evasive they wouldn't even give their names, thus giving the reporter little usable information. Nonetheless, the article and two pictures were positive, and generated additional curiosity and interest in this helpful group of teenagers.

Although the alleged cult group was missing as an item in the news section, it certainly heated up the "Letters to the Editor" section. In a short note before the letters, the editor apologized that space wouldn't allow printing all fifty-four of the letters and e-mails. Instead, in fairness he chose excerpts from several that most approximated the views of all the letters and e-mails:

"If Sarah McPhee chooses to worship herself as God, who is to be positive that she is not right. Although worshiping one's self is not new, it appears that it might possibly be a welcome change to the cold, corporate-type, self-serving religions of today." Joseph Janse

"All society is in agreement that there is no greater sin than calling yourself God. This blasphemous action is not only an intolerable threat to God's church; it is a threat to the individual, the family, the community, and all of society. We must act now, today, to put a stop to this erosion that will take our children away from us. Our procrastination today will take its toll tomorrow. How will we ever forgive ourselves if we let this heinous cancer spread among our youth, eating away at the very foundation and moral fiber of the future leaders of our country? Please join with me in removing this beast from our midst." Dr. Mark Hightower, Hill Country Chapel of God.

"Why is it that society always labels anything that doesn't fit in one of its well-defined pigeonholes nor follows its own biased narrow-minded path as a cult? *Webster's* defines cult: 'Great devotion to some person, idea, or thing, especially such devotion viewed as an intellectual fad.' Doesn't this define a certain church in this fair city, where the rich social-minded parishioners appear to be worshiping the pastor as much, or even more, than God? God save God, excuse me, Sarah McPhee!" Jeannie Bastrop

"How can we, in the name of God, let that self-worshiping cult contaminate our vulnerable children with their lies and propaganda? Who knows where this group is going to lead our children? Those who insist on practicing this activity should be asked to leave our loving community, immediately." B.R.T.

Sunday and Monday fared no better for the Pizza Shack, and Bob realized that if Sarah's situation wasn't resolved soon, the boycotters could very well achieve their aim of closing them down. He had run a special two-for-the-price-of-one special in the Sunday *Gazette,* but this only brought enough business to break even for the day.

As if this wasn't enough for the Pizza Shack to contend with, Sarah's alleged cult activity was the catalyst to unify the religious community of Cibolo Falls under one banner. For several years Dr. Mark Hightower, of Hill Country Chapel of God, had attempted to bring together not only the clergy of the different churches, but lay leaders as well. He felt that as a single organization the churches could better serve the spiritual needs and resolve any interdenominational problems that might affect the community as a whole. He, of course, hoped to become the leader and driving force behind the new organization.

On Monday evening the Cibolo Falls Council of Churches met for the first time. The lay representation of CFCC was limited to one for each three hundred members of their church, elected by their own congregation. By this method, because of its membership of over three thousand, Hill Country Chapel of God was allowed ten lay representatives, roughly one-third of the CFCC lay membership. This was instrumental in Dr. Hightower's being installed as president.

Dr. Hightower immediately implemented his objectives for the organization. Passed by a strong majority, the first order of business was to issue a proclamation that urged the Christian community to take all necessary measures to protect the youth of Cibolo Falls from unhealthy influences and activities. Although not mentioned by name in an article in the *Gazette* Tuesday morning, this action was clearly aimed at Sarah McPhee and the Pizza Shack.

On Tuesday morning Sarah had an appointment with Dr. James J. Gerick, the psychiatrist recommended to Barbara as the man who might have an answer to the reason for the voice that Sarah heard. The doctor had warned that tests would take much of the day, so Sarah missed the second meeting of GARBAGE.

The GARBAGE meeting place was changed from under the bridge at South Park to the pavilion at the fairgrounds. Ralph felt it best that the newspaper and, now, the Cibolo Falls Council of Churches not have any hint that GARBAGE and Sarah's "cult group" were the same organization. Ralph was relieved that Sarah couldn't make the meeting because, for his plan to work, she needed to distance herself from GARBAGE until it was carried out.

If Jody's figures were correct, the number of kids sitting on benches and tables in the large pavilion numbered ninety-two. Compared to the gloomy, sour note that had ended the previous week's meeting,

JB's enthusiasm was a sharp contrast as she bounded up on one of the tables in front of the group. Her dark skin and shiny black hair were magnified by a yellow T-shirt and matching shorts. Brown eyes sparkled as she stood high above her audience and looked them over.

"This is so tight, guys!" she exclaimed. "Last week it looked like we were *no mas*, but now, with all the good pub in the newspaper, our rep is great." The group clapped and congratulated each other. "But this is only a start. Although we have done a great job picking up litter and cleaning up the place, we gotta do other heavy stuff to really make a difference." She lifted a hand to keep their attention. "That doesn't mean that we quit the litter work. That'll always be a problem. Maybe someday people will figure out they shouldn't litter to start with. Until that happens, we'll just have to pick up after them. Okay?"

JB waited for the group to settle down, then continued. "I see we have some new guys with us today. Thanks for helping out. Before you leave today, please leave your e-mail address and your phone numbers with Jody. That way, if any emergencies come up we can find you. Now, I've got news. Smiley's mom has been helping Ralph, Smiley and me design a website. I guarantee, it'll be looking good. So, if you see Mrs. Schultz, thank her, 'cause we couldn't have done this without her. She's also dropping a few coins on this, so if this group ever gets *mucho dinero*, she gets first dibs." JB pointed at the owner of a hand sticking up. "Yeah, what's up?"

"When we gonna be online?"

Mrs. Schultz still has work to do, but she said we can be online within a few days. That way, people will be able to at least check us out. You know, see what we really are, instead of all the cult crap they're getting now. Later on, we'll be adding all the important ecological stuff and updating when we need, you know, worldwide eco-news, information about our own local meeting schedules, demonstrations," she grinned and spread her arms, "marching on City Hall. That sort of thing." We might even sell some of Smiley's special GARBAGE T-shirts and other stuff online to make some money, so we'll be a dot com instead of dot org.

"What's the name going to be?"

"This is really neat. It's going to be called *garbageangel.com*, for the name of our group and Spook." She looked over the group for additional questions or comment.

"Okay, on Sunday we're going to tell the whole world about Spook, but a lot of stuff has to happen, and happen right. And this is important: we need to keep everything about this meeting, about our group, and about Spook secret until Sunday.

"All right, enough of me. I'm going to turn the table," she grinned, "over to Ralph." She winked at Jody, did a quick pirouette, and hopped off the table.

Ralph replaced her on the table and with a quick toss of his head flipped the ever-present lock of hair out of his eyes. He straightened his glasses and reviewed his notes, then dropped the notebook on the table. "Hey, guys. I also wanna tell you, you're doing a kick-ass job. It's cool when the newspaper gets it right. So, now it's time to start bugging the city to do the stuff that we can't. What'd you think?"

His audience clapped, cheered, and laughed in response. They hushed when Ralph continued. "By the time school starts, we'll have everybody wanting to help, and there might be a few people in this town who'll wish we'd go away. It won't be easy getting people to start protecting the Earth instead of destroying it, but we'll convince them, one way or another. As Sarah said last week, our leaders, the government, and businesses really aren't gonna do anything but talk about it until we push them a little. So, it has to start with us, right here in Cibolo Falls, Texas."

"Right on, Ralph, my man," Smiley affirmed.

"Now, let's start our first big job. Next week, while you do your litter work, we want you to carry around a petition for people to sign. The petition will ask the Cibolo Falls City Council to contract with the garbage company to start collecting materials for recycling. Our garbage is buried on the same Earth as everyone else's and space is running out. Just like in the big cities, we have to recycle before it's too late."

Ralph watched Donnie rub his bald head with a beefy hand—something he always did when he had something important to say. "Big dawg. What's up?" Ralph asked.

"Hey, dude. You know the city council ain't gonna listen to us."

"Then we'll just have to sic you on 'em," Ralph countered. "Anyway, Jody and Smiley will give you guys a bunch of stuff today. One of the things you'll get is a petition. Hit up your family, all your neighbors and friends—get 'em all to sign it. After you've got all the names you can, bring it to our meeting in two weeks. Then we'll take it down to the next council meeting." Ralph smiled, raising and lowering his brow repeatedly. "We'll really have fun, if you know what I mean."

"Why aren't they already doing this?" Derick Bradford asked. "It doesn't seem like much trouble, and I saw on television the other night that a lot of towns are doing it."

"Probably 'cause we ain't kicked 'em in the ass yet," Ralph smirked. "Might need garbage up to their noses before they'd do it on their own. And they might be scared to bring it up because it'll cost more."

"How much, in case we're asked?" a girl called out from the back.

"If people ask, tell them that it'll probably add about a dollar-fifty per month to everybody's bill. If that's too much, what can you do? Sooner or later we'll definitely have garbage up to our noses."

"How many?" asked the girl.

"How many what?"

"How many signatures do you want?"

"Oh, about three thousand should do. The council has to listen to that." Ralph grinned at the doubtful looks he received. "Yeah, that's a lot, ain't it? Think you can do it?"

"No problem," Jody affirmed. "It's done, my man." Others nodded their agreement.

"Okay, the next thing we want to do is, write at least one letter or e-mail this week to a city council member, our state representative, or senator. Tell him, her, whomever, that you want them to do something about the garbage. As usual, my trusty dawgs—Jody and Smiley—have put all the names and addresses you'll need, plus a sample letter, in the stuff you're getting. But don't copy the letter just like it is; write your own. You know, show them how educated you are."

"Why the state?" came a question from the back from the little redhead.

"Because, if the state would pass a law on recycling, the cities and towns would have to go along with it." Ralph shook his head, raising a finger of caution. "But, that probably ain't going to happen. My dad says that the higher up you go in government, the less you're going to get done. But, we should try anyway."

JB watched as Ralph looked over the group. She thought it was cool the way he fussed with the lock of hair that forever fell over one eye. "As you know, Sarah is stressed to the max. The churches are boycotting the Pizza Shack 'cause they think she's some kind of weirdo. It looks like they might have to go out of business. Hey, I don't know about you guys, but I can't do without Mr. Mac's pizza. So, what'll we do?"

Ralph grinned when Smiley yelled out, "Eat more pizza!"

"Right. Listen up. Get your family to eat there at least once this week, so the Macs can hold on a little longer. We're working on a plan to help them out, and we need your help on Saturday morning and all day Sunday for extreme GARBAGE work. After Sunday, if our plan works and we get the town off of Sarah's case, maybe we can kick back and chill. Can you help us out?"

He smiled and shook his fist at the enthusiastic group. "Great. Jody and Smiley have a duty list for both days and what the jobs will be. Be sure to sign up. It's really important. Besides the petition, a sample letter, and addresses, they'll also give you a list of stuff you can do by yourself, if you ever get tired of litter work. Okay, any questions before we breakup?"

"Sarah," JB coaxed.

"Yeah, Sarah. For the rest of this week, don't tell anybody that Sarah is a member of this group. Also, we don't want the newspaper to find out that GARBAGE is the same as Sarah McPhee's "cult group"—you know, the one that met last week under the bridge. So, don't use the Earth Salute this week. These two things are really, really important for our plan to work this weekend."

Journal Note

"Because you are an extension of God's spirit in the physical body, honor, respect, and worship the God that is in you. Try to live life as simply as you can, in a truthful and wise manner."

CHAPTER 8

Bob and Barbara broke away on Wednesday afternoon to consult with Dr. Gerick about Sarah's test results. The news was both a disappointment and a relief. He had done a battery of expensive tests including an EEG, an MRI and the CT scan. He found no evidence of any physical problem such as temporal lobe epilepsy that could cause auditory hallucinations. Sarah also had taken a score of mental tests and the MMPI, ruling out all mental disorders including paranoia, schizophrenia, and multiple personalities. "I am most confident that Sarah is normal," the doctor informed them, "both mentally and physically."

This was good news, but Barbara still needed to know why Sarah heard the voice. When she pressed Dr. Gerick for more answers, he suggested a local research group that might be able to help. Barbara wasn't very enthusiastic about the referral, but if they could get any answers at all, it would be worth the time and money. Gerick said that he would forward the results of all the tests he had run and a copy of Sarah's journal to the director so that he might have time to study them before the McPhees arrived.

* * *

As Ralph had anticipated, most of the kids were bored with only picking up litter, so many opted for other jobs the rest of the week. Along with urging people to sign the petition, sending letters and e-mails in support of garbage recycling, some went to O.P.A. and other supermarkets in town. After they received the store managers' permission, they demonstrated with signs that carried a variety of messages that urged customers to do such things as buy products in bulk or family size containers to reduce overall packaging and garbage. Others urged shoppers to save their used glass bottles, metal containers, and newspapers, because the city would soon have a recycling program.

Taking Smiley and Derick's cue from the previous week, some signs urged shoppers to bring their own grocery tote bags, noting how one large family could save a tree in a year's time this way. Other signs urged mothers to buy cloth diapers instead of disposables, showing that disposables make up close to three percent of all garbage in the country. One sign showed the savings of using cloth diapers over disposable, even if using a commercial diaper service.

Armed with information from the local water company, some went door-to-door to urge families to take measures to reduce unnecessary water use, such as installing inexpensive aerators to all faucets inside their homes, thus saving about fifty percent inside water use. Others distributed energy savings pamphlets provided by the local electric cooperative that listed many energy and money saving techniques around the home.

Several of the more industrious kids, promising the owner good publicity in the future, begged some small trees off a local nursery. They planted them in a barren, seldom used area of a neighborhood park. The nursery owner, after he observed the fine job they had done, offered them several more trees if they would plant them in a park near his home. The kids agreed when the nurseryman volunteered to deliver the trees directly to the park.

It became apparent to many of the people of Cibolo Falls that this group was making a difference and deserved thanks, if not support.

The sign in front of the old three-story home, remodeled into an impressive office building read:

Central Texas Parapsychology Institute

A Foundation for Research on the Nature of Man

Upon reaching the top of the steps Bob and Barbara stepped onto a large wooden porch. To the left of the entrance was a staff directory. At the top of the list was the gentleman they had come to see: J.P. Pauley, Ph.D., Executive Director of Research.

They entered the front door into a foyer. Straight ahead was a staircase with a hallway to the side. To the left, paneled glass doors opened on each side of a large doorway leading to what was once the living room—now the reception and waiting room. They were motioned to enter by a sprightly receptionist at an antique desk surrounded by all the trappings of the usual business office. The woman greeted the McPhees and handed both a pamphlet about the center, just as they were joined by Dr. Pauley.

After introductions he escorted them down the carpeted hall next to the staircase to a charming office that had once been a parlor or library. The McPhees each took a seat in a leather chair in front of a large desk, cluttered with stacks of files and journals.

Barbara was fascinated by the short, bald middle-aged man taking his seat across the desk. He wore small, round, wire-rimmed reading glasses balanced delicately on the end of a long, pointed nose. A well-trimmed salt-and-pepper mustache and beard adorned his elongated face. Barbara thought he looked a lot like pictures of Dr. Sigmund Freud she had seen, and wondered if Dr. Pauley intended this look.

After the usual small talk, Bob and Barbara waited while the doctor stroked his beard and read through Sarah's file. With a nod that made him appear to be agreeing with himself, he laid the open file down and rested his elbows on the desk. With hands folded in front of him, he peered over his glasses:

"Let me give you an overview of our objectives. First off, our foundation is funded by private grants and donations. We were founded twenty-six years ago to study paranormal activity. This takes in a whole range of subjects from extrasensory perception, clairvoyance, psychokinesis, and telepathy to other bizarre occurrences like crop circles.

"Bottom line, we do scientific investigation of phenomena that contradict the generally accepted laws of science. In other words, we're interested in experiences for which there seem to be no explanation based on scientific principle."

He paused and grinned. "I guess you could say that there are those who think we are weird. And, to an extent, that's true. To study the weird, you have to be somewhat weird."

Barbara tapped the pamphlet on the arm of the chair and spoke hesitantly, "Well, we definitely have a problem that falls under weird, as you saw when you read over Dr. Gerick's notes. We don't understand what's going on, and frankly we're more than a little concerned."

"Of course, I understand. Dr. Gerick is thorough, so I trust his judgment and his findings. Having said that, I believe that I can give you some insight in what's going on with..." he looked down at the file, "Sarah."

He scanned the file. "I would like to say before I give you my opinion that I believe what is happening to Sarah, although a concern to you, is fascinating from the standpoint of the work that we do here. It is remarkable and exciting.

"I believe it's essential to both of you, as well as to Sarah, that you understand all that you can about Sarah's situation. Unfortunately, although many cases of these voices are documented, nothing concrete is really known, because most of the cases vary in some way. I think it is very important that you have an open mind because, if you don't, it severely limits the possibilities, confining you to our own conscious little world."

Bob and Barbara stared blankly at the doctor. "Your puzzled looks are expected." He picked up the copy of Sarah's journal from the corner of the desk. Leafing through it, he paused, "Do you believe in God, Mrs. McPhee?"

"I haven't been to church in years, or lit any candles lately, if that's what you mean. And after the way we've been treated by the church community this past week, it'll probably be a cold day in hell before I return."

"Understandable. But the question is, do you *believe* in God?"

"Sorry. Yes, I do believe in God."

"Has Sarah ever had any religious training or education?"

"None in particular."

"And before the last two or three months, had she ever spoken of God in any way?"

Barbara glanced at Bob and they both shook their heads.

"How about her friends? Are any religious or, as far as you know, have any, shall I say, shown an overbearing interest in God?"

"There's none that we could put in that category." Bob replied.

"I assume you've read this material?" he asked as he put his hand on the journal.

"Yes," they answered in unison.

Dr. Pauley looked back to the journal page and began to read: *"You are here on Earth for one reason. It is because you are of the creative force. You must learn, teach, and express the Godness of you."* He furrowed his forehead. "That's pretty strong stuff for a fourteen-year-old without any religious background, wouldn't you say?"

"That isn't Sarah talking. We've gone through all the reading material in the house," said Barbara. "Unless she has hidden it for some reason, she didn't get it from a book. As you've probably noticed, there are some words misspelled in the journal. If she was copying from another source, I believe she would have at least copied correctly."

"I agree." Dr. Pauley looked back to the journal: *"Because you are an extension of God's spirit in the physical body, honor, respect, and worship the God that is in you. Try to live life as simply as you can, in a truthful and wise manner."* He looked up from the journal. "Is that the Sarah you raised?"

"Those statements didn't come from her," Bob answered. "There is an outside source giving her this information, without a doubt. If it's an angel or whatever, I have no idea. I do believe her, however, when she says she hears a voice."

Barbara warily eyed Dr. Pauley leaf through a few more pages of the journal, doubting that this visit was going to answer any of her questions. "An education in itself," the doctor said as he read a few lines. "Listen to this: *Whenever you eat a plant, the plant acknowledges and agrees that it will become a part of you, giving its spirit a new destiny.* That's very interesting, wouldn't you say?"

Bob waited for Barbara to answer. When she didn't, he said, "That's leading into the part about us all being a part of the whole, and what happens to one affects us all, whether it be plant, animal, the air we breathe, or the water we drink. I think she based that salute—the one you may have seen in the newspaper—on this. It's supposed to remind them that they are all God or part of the whole, and to act like it."

"Yes, and this next entry expands on it," the doctor followed. "Get this: *Remember, we are all connected on the spiritual level. One of the greatest things you will ever experience is that feeling of unity and harmony with everything in the universe. And, little one, attaining that feeling should be your goal in every thought and action.* That's pretty deep, wouldn't you say?"

"Connected on the spiritual level?" Barbara frowned.

In order to explain his thoughts on Sarah, Dr. Pauley needed to know precisely the McPhee's beliefs. "Do you believe that?"

Barbara considered the question for a moment. "That's a tough one. But I guess it's no tougher than asking me if I believe in God. You know, we've all been taught to believe only what we can touch, see, smell, hear or—"

"Take to the bank," Bob interjected, bringing chuckles from Barbara and the doctor.

"Yes, and I'm believing that even more this week," Barbara countered as she patted Bob on the knee. "Anyway, if something isn't right here in my own conscious, physical space, I have a hard time accepting it. The same goes for believing in God."

"Meaning you don't believe that we are connected spiritually if the plants and rocks and trees can't interact with us on the sensual level?" Dr. Pauley quizzed.

"Now, wait a minute. I didn't say I didn't believe it. I said I have a hard time believing it."

Dr. Pauley studied Barbara, a hint of tongue pushed against his cheek. "You do believe, then, that just because something isn't perceivable to your senses doesn't mean it doesn't exist?" He stopped to consider what he just said. "Did that come out right?"

"Yeah, I get your drift." Bob and Dr. Pauley watched Barbara arch her neck and study the ceiling. She looked back at the doctor and continued: "Yes, I do believe that something can be real, even though I don't sense it."

"Uh-huh. Now let me make sure I understand you. What you are agreeing to is, there are possibly other realities on the spiritual level that you aren't consciously aware of. And just because they don't show up on you sense screen doesn't mean they don't exist."

Barbara and Bob laughed nervously. "Did I say that?" she asked. "Okay, okay. I believe that there are other spiritual realities that I'm unaware of in my own little physical world. I don't know what they are, but they're there I'm sure, I think."

Dr. Pauley fixed Bob with a stare and waited for his opinion.

"Yeah, I'll buy it. It's within the realm of possibility; there are things happening on the spiritual level we aren't aware of." Bob nodded tentatively. "It certainly would be a lot easier, however, if we could at least get an occasional glimpse of these other realities, spiritual or otherwise."

The doctor held up Sarah's journal. "Perhaps you are."

Neither Bob nor Barbara commented as they considered what Dr. Pauley had just said. The doctor leafed through a few pages of the journal and stopped on a page stuck with an orange marker.

"All things on Earth and throughout the universe are God, many manifesting on different levels, but all interconnecting on the spiritual level. That is how it is with you and me." Dr. Pauley looked over his glasses at Barbara, then Bob. "Any comment?"

Bob watched Barbara. He could tell that she chose her words carefully. "I assume that means the voice exists on another level—whatever that level is—and is communicating with Sarah on the spiritual level?"

"Uh-huh. Perhaps the voice really is her guardian angel. Have you noticed how many movies have come out lately with the central theme built around guardian angels? There are also several weekly shows on television that have an angel as the central character. And just recently, there have been a couple of special programs of supposedly true incidents of angels rescuing people in trouble or danger. I guess, what I'm trying to say is, more and more people are accepting that angels not only exist, but they will interrelate with us, given the opportunity."

"I guess I kind of feel that, yeah, angels and even miracles do exist, but not for me." Barbara paused and fanned herself with the pamphlet. "It always happens to someone else. It's just something you read about in the newspaper or see on a newscast."

Dr. Pauley spread his hands, "Why not? Why can't it happen to you? Why not your own personal bona fide, card-carrying guardian angel or why not your own personal miracle of the day? Why, if we believe in miracles and angels, can't we experience them on a personal basis?"

"I believe in lightning too. But it hasn't struck me...well, not yet anyway," Bob countered. "Maybe we're not the lucky...or, should I say, the unlucky ones who get visited, struck or whatever?"

"Yes, do we really want either one?" the doctor asked with a grin. He pondered for a moment and lightly tapped his fingers on Sarah's journal. "You know, there's another aspect closely related to this voice that we could examine. It is considered by some to be about the same, if not exactly the same, as having a guardian angel communicating with us. Consider this: the voice that Sarah is hearing could be a spiritual communication from another of the many dimensions of herself. Sarah, as well as every individual, could have a whole group of what we might call multidimensional beings or entities involved with her on a higher or spiritual level. It's called the God-self or higher self of the individual. It not only includes other past and future incarnations of the individual, but other experience levels as well, such as spirit guides or guardian angels."

Barbara got up from her chair and inspected some photographs on the wall as Bob and Pauley watched. She turned back toward the doctor. "Higher self, multidimensional beings, other incarnations—how many people believe this?"

"Well, let's see. For starters, 78 million adults in the United States believe in reincarnation, and as for people hearing voices, that has been going on for over two thousand years that we know of. I wouldn't be surprised if the voices that the prophets of the Bible heard were from the same source as Sarah's—an angel or another dimension of themselves. I think it's pretty much accepted that those with psychic ability have a similar connection, if not the same one Sarah has.

"It appears that on a higher spiritual level, there is access to the Akashic records, Heaven's so-called computer, giving information not only on the past, but possibilities for the future as well. Psychics, through their spiritual connection, whether it be to their higher selves, angels, or whatever, seem to have an open window or channel to the Akashic records. I suspect that Sarah through her so-called angel has the same connection."

"It sounds to me like you're saying Sarah could be psychic?" Barbara frowned as she sat back down. She wondered just how much of this she should believe or even wanted to hear.

"We all have a certain amount of psychic ability. Why shouldn't some have more than others? In fact we're currently testing three people from here in the hill country who are experiencing voices, angelic or otherwise. One, close by in the little town of Comfort, actually speaks the voice and has divulged some very interesting information. My staff all strongly feel the voices are indeed those of a guardian angel or some other spiritual part of the person involved.

"In our research we find over and over, whatever or whoever these entities are, they stress love and respect for one another and have other practical information for us, if we will only listen. Mrs. McPhee, it appears to me that Sarah has the same connection. I certainly would classify it as psychic."

"Or psychotic," Barbara grinned in resignation. The doctor cocked a curious brow, but smiled. She continued, "I just don't know if I, now or ever, will feel comfortable about some angel or multidimensional whatever taking over my child, and putting her up to leading the town's youth on some harebrained scheme to save the Earth."

Until now Bob had been content to merely take in the dialog between Barbara and the doctor. "What if this entity decides to go a step further, and the kids all end up in jail for breaking the law? I don't think a judge is going to accept an angel or voice from another dimension as an excuse. In fact, that would probably be his laugh of the day."

"Perhaps you could let her open up to you on what's going on in their little group," Dr. Pauley countered. "That way you can keep an eye on her 'angel.' Maybe you could even join them or, at least, help them out. I believe that it would also be advisable to accept the voice for what it is. After all, if it is an angel, her higher self or both, it appears to me that this spiritual connection brings her a little closer to God. Isn't that kind of what she's saying? 'I am God.'"

"Keep an eye on her is right. This voice has already gotten us into a heap of trouble, at least financially. No matter how close she is to God, her 'I am God' statement is going to sink us for sure, if the church has anything to do with it. And I don't know if it's a good idea for her to continue with that, no matter what her, or our, beliefs are."

The doctor leaned back in his chair as he considered what Bob had said. He responded slowly, as if weighing each word individually: "You know, in our research of those with a heightened psychic ability, all seem to have a higher or stronger affinity for God. They all stress this, and we all agree that, by working with these people, we've become a little more, shall I say, closer to God.

"By the same token, most all of these highly developed psychics become soured or turned off by today's organized religion. It appears the psychics' unfavorable attitude stems from the doctrine of most religions, both modern and ancient, that dictate a complete separation of man and God. A true psychic knows he's not separate. They may not go as far as Sarah's 'I am God' statement, but all definitely recognize the spiritual connection."

The doctor observed Bob lean forward as he listened. Barbara shifted uncomfortably in her chair, again tapping the pamphlet on the chair arm. He waited for comment from either.

"Maybe Sarah and the kids have the right idea. It seems to me, if we all acted a little more Godlike, this would be a heck of a lot better world. And maybe the church doesn't have all the answers. The whole world seems to be headed for some sort of spiritual revolution, but I wonder just what part the church is playing, or even if it wants to play a part. Many people, perhaps you folks as well, have given up on the church, because they feel it is no longer providing the answer to their inner spiritual needs. They don't want to go back to the church, but they want something to help them feel secure, and they want to feel like they are being watched over and taken care of. I guess they're all searching for deep meaning or a real reason for their very existence.

"The church is supposed to be doing that, but I wonder. It's kind of a paradox in a way. People are searching for God but no longer have confidence in the church to guide them in their quest. So, what do they do? They turn to fundamentalist Christianity, some New Age guru or—why not?—a convenient angel."

The doctor stood up and strolled absently around the room. He stopped at the bookshelf and selected the Bible. He thumbed through it for a moment, then closed it abruptly and pointed it at the McPhees. "However, when all is said and done, I wonder what's going to happen. On judgment day, if there, indeed, is a judgment day, those who follow certain belief systems may all end up with egg on their faces."

"You have a good point," Bob interjected. "Maybe the whole system, from Christianity to Buddhism, and the New Age movement, is going to be in for one big *Gotcha* when time comes to cash in our chips or chits."

"Exactly," Dr. Pauley countered. "Who really knows? I certainly would like to hear what Sarah's angel has to say about this. Maybe he can give us some insight on who to follow and where we are headed if we do."

He placed the Bible back on the shelf and returned to his chair. "Questions abound." He made a fist and rapped his knuckles on the desk once for each question: "Should we follow anyone or anything? Is there no God? Should we spend our lives bouncing aimlessly off walls with no direction or guidance? Is that the price we have to pay for the privilege of being here?" He rapped the last time: "And should we even listen to Sarah's angel, or any other angel? Most of these questions you'll have to answer for yourself. As I will and everyone else will."

Dr. Pauley waited for additional questions. He watched as Bob and Barbara exchanged quizzical glances, but didn't comment. "Well now, folks. You've come to me for an opinion, whether you want to believe it or not. Having seen perhaps three dozen cases similar to Sarah's, I feel she has a gift of a large amount of psychic ability. And it is showing up through her connection with whatever you want to call the voice. If the voice says he is her guardian angel, then why not? Perhaps you don't welcome this happening to your daughter, but it is, indeed, happening. I would strongly suggest, at this point, that you support her and the voice. I certainly wouldn't ignore or repress this gift."

By this point, the McPhees had already separately decided the voice Sarah heard was real. And since there didn't appear to be any other choice, they would cautiously accept it and carry on, supporting her in every way possible.

When it was apparent to Bob that Dr. Pauley had no more to say, Bob said, "Doctor, there is something I think you might be interested in, because it is definitely paranormal activity. Last Friday, Sarah took Barbara and me to the river. She showed us an image of her on the water's surface. It was definitely an image—not a reflection, because when both of us looked, there was no reflection of either of us. It was an image of Sarah, holding a garbage sack and picking up litter."

Pauley stared at Bob, then Barbara in complete surprise. "You sure?"

"I would say that perhaps three-hundred or more have seen it by now—mostly Sarah's group but also many of their parents and friends. I'm surprised the newspaper hasn't gotten wind of it."

The doctor nodded for a long moment. "This is exciting. I must see it. Can you show me where?"

"I'll have Ralph, one of the leaders of the group, contact you. He'd love to take you."

"Great. I would like to study it before the masses get the message, before this becomes a carnival."

Barbara nodded, "That's what we're afraid of."

"Your fears are not unfounded, I assure you. People have a thirst for the unknown, particularly when it comes to spiritual matters. Yes, please have Ralph call me as soon as possible. It would be nice if we could have an explanation or at the very least an educated guess before the press gets hold of it."

He passed the journal copy across the desk to Barbara. "Now, I have a proposition for you folks. For over a year now, we've been unable to accept any new subjects for research because we haven't had the necessary staff. As a result of a grant we've just received, in September we are bringing in one of the country's best researchers in paranormal activity. This will open several slots for subjects. As I have final say on whom we accept, I would highly recommend Sarah—that is, if you agree. There would be no cost to you and since you are close by, this would save us the expense of room and board."

"What exactly do you do?" Barbara asked.

"First off, the subject is thoroughly tested, as Sarah was tested by Dr. Gerick. If there are no physical or mental abnormalities, we begin an extensive program of testing to find out all we can about the subject's gift, and we also concentrate on improving or magnifying the gift. We usually work with a subject about six months, but sometimes longer."

After the McPhees questioned the doctor for a few more minutes, they told him that they would seriously consider his offer, thanked him, and left. They left confident that Spook was indeed a gift to Sarah and wasn't to be feared.

The phone rang at four o'clock at the Pizza Shack, and Bob stuck his head through the kitchen door. "JB's on the phone."

Sarah followed her dad out to the cashier's desk and picked up the phone. "Hi."

"How did it go? Did you pass?"

"Did I pass what?"

"The guy that the shrink recommended. What did he tell your mom and dad?"

"I don't know. They haven't locked me in the closet or anything, so I guess everything is okay."

"Great! No news is great!" JB exclaimed. "Now we can put our plan into effect tonight."

"What plan. I don't know of—?"

"That's because we haven't told you," JB interrupted.

"Oh," Sarah hesitated. "Do you want me to do anything?"

"That's a big no. And Ralph doesn't even want you to know what's going on. But you're going to love it, and it's going to be a big surprise. Trust me."

"Now, wait a minute, JB," Sarah said defensively, hurt that she was on the outside of planning for the group and that the plans they made were being kept secret from her. "You guys aren't going to get us in any more trouble are you? After the terrible business we've had the last few days, my mom and dad will kill me for sure if anything else happens."

"No problem, sweetie. This plan is perfect and, if we make it happen, everything will be cool by early next week. What's your schedule the rest of the day?"

"Come on, girl. Now, really, why won't you tell me what's going on? I'm the one that started all this, and you won't even include me in the plans."

"How do you…? Yeah, I know: *colloquial mantener la calma*. That's it."

"JB, stop that. I don't know what you're saying. Just tell me why?"

"I said, just be cool. Everything is going to be all right. You'll see."

Sarah was silent for a moment, then said in resignation, "I have to work until seven, then softball at eight."

"Good, that should keep you busy. We've called an emergency meeting of everybody available for five-thirty at the pavilion, and it would be best if you aren't there, just in case we're discovered by the wrong people."

"You're sure there's not going to be any more trouble?"

"Sustantivo promesa femenino. Even if it doesn't work exactly like we planned, it can't make things any worse. However, Ralph just knows

that it will get the newspaper and everybody off your case. The church, who knows, but we can live with that, right?"

"I guess so," Sarah answered. *I wonder if I should allow them to do whatever they're planning. If it causes Mom and Dad more trouble, that would be the end of it. They'd never let me out of their sight again. And they'd make Spook go away.*

"Sarah. Sarah, are you there?" JB's urgent voice came over the phone.

"Yeah. Sorry, JB. I guess I tuned out or something. I'm just so stressed that something else is going to go wrong. I really can't take much more of this, not knowing what's going to happen next. Or what's going to happen to the Pizza Shack. I'm really scared, JB. Promise you aren't going to make more trouble for Mom and Dad."

"Sweetie, I'm cool. Trust me. Nothing but good is going to come out of it. It could be fantastic. Don't worry about it. Okay?"

"All right, if you say so," Sarah answered with a sigh.

"Has business been bad today?"

"About half of what we usually do at lunchtime. Who knows about tonight? We'll find out."

"Well, Ralph says his little scheme will definitely solve the boycott problem," JB said cheerfully. "He says that people will be eating pizza at Pizza Shack who have never eaten pizza before."

"I hope you're right," Sarah replied. "Should I tell Mom and Dad?"

"No way. Ralph said that he would give your dad the details tomorrow afternoon after everything's ready."

"And you're not telling me about what's going on, right?"

"Nope. All you have to do is hang in there and get some rest. You're going to need it. We'll do the rest." JB waited to see if Sarah had anything else to say. "Gotta go, sweetie. I'm late for the big meeting."

"G*racias*. I sure hope Ralph's plan, whatever it is, works."

"It will. It will. See ya, girl."

Journal Note

"In your experience in the physical body, there are no accidents, little one. Everything that happens to you, even what you might consider insignificant, has an important reason. And on a spiritual level, you had a part in choosing for it to happen."

CHAPTER 9

When she arrived home after Friday night's softball game, Sarah fled to her bedroom. Although physically and emotionally fatigued, she didn't sleep well because of the guilt she felt over the trouble she had gotten her family into. If the Pizza Shack had to close from lack of business, it would clearly be her fault. And the problems would not let up. In fact, they multiplied in spite of what she did or didn't do. It was as if every problem took on a life of its own. And now it was possible that JB and Ralph were about to cause more trouble with their new scheme without even telling her what was going on or even asking her to help in thc planning. She felt that she had no control over anything. If Ralph's plan backfired, how would she ever explain it to her mom and dad?

Early Saturday morning she gave up trying to sleep. She rolled over and opened the blinds to let in the morning light. She couldn't believe it was still dark until she noticed the clock. Gee, it's only five-fifteen. Will this night ever get over with? Yeah, right. Will this week, this month, this year, this life ever get over with? And why am I complaining about the night, anyway? At least in bed I'm safe from the newspaper, the church, the boycotters, the—

Sarah's thoughts were interrupted by that familiar whiteness that clouded her mind before Spook made an appearance. There was a faint hum, then the metallic resonant voice came from deep in her head:

"You should not be so hard on yourself, little one. You are doing exactly what you chose to be doing—as is everyone else. The issues you are experiencing now are very valuable to you. And I must remind you, these experiences are neither good nor bad; they are just that—experiences."

"But I can't handle anymore," Sarah blurted out.

"I know your concern. Remember, I am a part of you, and I am here to guide you and encourage you to carry on when things seem a bit troublesome or confusing to you. Now, what I am about to tell you is very important. You must remember these words in the days to come:

"Little one, in your experiences, you will never, ever take on or be given more than you can handle, emotionally or physically. Remember, the more you experience, the better decisions you will make now and in the future, for yourself and for others. And because of this, you will make the Earth a better place."

Tears welled up in Sarah's eyes as she waited for more from Spook. When nothing came, she thought to herself: yes, Spook is right. I must try to always remember what I am and who I am. Then I won't be afraid anymore. I won't worry so much and things will always work out in a way that is best for me.

"As they shall, little one. Much in the coming days depends on you, JB, Ralph, your parents and other friends. Always remember, their desire is to assist you the best they can, and they love you very much. And likewise they depend on you, all of them, to love and help them, likewise. The love, the give and take between you, is certainly a model for the Earth. Always remember that."

"I will, I promise," Sarah stated. "Thank you, Spook. I'm glad you came and are with me this morning."

"My pleasure. My love to you."

"Are you sure he's going to be there, this morning? If he's not, it'll blow this whole operation apart." Ralph called over to JB as they rode their bikes toward Town Square, a small park across the street from Hill Country Chapel of God.

"He'll be there. I called again this morning. His secretary said he never leaves before noon on Saturday! He always works on his sermon on Saturday."

"You sure?"

"Look, *stupido grande*. I said I'd get him there, just like you asked." Juanita retorted. She pedaled harder, leaving Ralph behind. She called over her shoulder, "You just do your part, okay?"

"All right, already! Hey, hold up!" he called out, his voice squeaking nervously. "Did you call that dorky reporter?"

"Yeah, Ralph. I've done everything you told me to do. I told him that if he wanted to find out who the leader of GARBAGE was, he'd better be at the park at ten-fifteen, because that's what time Dr. Hightower was going to meet with the leader."

"Great! Then it's all set. I hope this is a success. If it ain't, Mr. Mac will kill me for sure."

JB didn't reply as she watched Hill Country Chapel of God come into view. A monument to not only God but to its pastor as well, the new church buildings and parking lot occupied the whole block east of the park. Painted in white and trimmed in brown, the main chapel's twin steeples cast a majestic shadow over the park.

Waiting in these shadows, as if under the protective umbrella of God, were seventy-two of the group. Ralph parked his bike, reached into his bag, pulled out his small tape recorder, and placed it inside his shirt. Buttoning back up, he modeled for Juanita. Receiving her silent nod that the recorder was not visible, they joined the waiting group.

Ralph took off his glasses and with one finger flipped the lock of hair out of his eye. He replaced the glasses and spoke, his voice agitated: "Hey, guys. Glad you could make it. Ready to go to work?" He waited for a few scattered replies, then continued: "Now, remember, although we want to get this whole area sparkling within the next hour, our main job is to put on a good show for the good Reverend Dr. Mark Hightower"—he gestured toward the church—"when he comes over. You guys are playing a very important part, and there can't be any mistakes. Don't say anything to the Rev or our reporter friend unless it's necessary, and don't use the Earth Salute. That would be a sure give-away.

"Now listen up. This is important. If either of those guys ask where our leader is, just refer them to JB or me, or tell them she hasn't showed up yet. We'll handle it from there."

Ralph looked over the group and exaggerated a devilish grin as he rubbed his hands together in anticipation. "Any questions before we set our little trap?

When there were only a few scattered whispers, he nodded, "Good! We're ready! Okay, everybody stay with the job you were assigned yesterday. After you finish that, help out some of the others or go down some of the streets leading from the park and work litter. Those of you that are painting the park benches and seesaws, be sure to leave a wet paint sign on each, so we don't get into trouble. If you're assigned to work the church parking lot for litter, wait until the Rev shows himself. That should get his attention, right quick. Okay, guys, put on a good show, for Sarah's sake."

A murmur of excitement swept through the group as they scattered to take on their jobs. As if on cue, John Holland and a photographer drove up in the reporter's late model, blue Chevy and parked next to the curb.

"Okay, JB, this sucker's mine. I'll stall him while you make the call." He turned when JB didn't answer. She had drifted off with Jody on one of her flirting missions. "JB, come on. We ain't got time for your love making! Do your job, okay?"

"Right." She whispered something to Jody and scampered off to her bike to retrieve her cell phone from her pack.

Ralph paused to pick up a cigarette butt as he worked his way toward the newsman's Chevy. John Holland and the photographer get out of the car and surveyed the working youth. Ralph sized up the short, overweight reporter. He disliked and distrusted the man on sight. Holland attempted to hide his heavy midsection by keeping his belt extra tight and wearing clothes that were too small, only magnifying the problem. His thick black-rimmed glasses on a puffy face brought attention to his dark seedy eyes. He attempted to cover his partial baldness by combing his light brown hair over from one side, which only drew more attention to his lack of hair.

Holland spied Ralph. "Hey, kid!" he barked. "Where's your leader? I need to talk to him."

Ralph picked up another cigarette butt as he ignored the reporter.

Yeah, sure. I'll bet you do.

"Hey, you, kid!" Holland called out, much louder than necessary, making no effort to hide his irritation. "Your leader. Where is he?"

"Not here."

"Well, when's he going to get here? Do you expect him anytime soon?"

Ralph enjoyed the game. A shrug was his only response.

"What the hell's the matter with you people?" Holland blurted in frustration.

Ralph observed a twitch develop at the corner of the reporter's mouth. Staring in fascination, he was jolted back to reality by the reporter:

"I can't get anyone to tell me jack shit." When Ralph didn't comment, the reporter and the photographer went over and sat on the hood of the Chevy. Holland mumbled something to the photographer that Ralph couldn't understand.

What's going on here? JB wondered as she dailed the number for the third time. When there was no ring she panicked. Then she noticed that the phone's battery was low. *Oh, no, that's all we need. Well, Ralph is going to just love this.* She replaced the phone in her pack and headed for Ralph. Without saying a word, she slipped the phone off his belt. After an instant of confusion, he muttered something under his breath that JB didn't hear.

"Don't worry about it," she retorted. She dialed the number as she walked away.

"Hill Country Chapel of God," came the answer.

"Yes, ma'am," JB said in her most adult voice. "I'm with the *Cibolo Falls Gazette*. Tomorrow we are running a follow-up piece on the youth cults of Cibolo Falls, and I would like to see if Dr. Hightower might have any additional comments he would like to make?"

"Why of course," the secretary responded. "If you hold momentarily, I'll—?"

"Yes, ma'am. I'll be happy to."

A strong confident voice came on the line: "Good morning. This is Mark Hightower. How may I help you?"

"Oh...uh...yes, Rev...uh...Doctor," JB sputtered. "I...this is Mary Sessions. I'm Mr. Holland's assistant with the news...the *Gazette*. I'm calling to see if perhaps you had some additional statement to make on the youth cult movement. Mr. Holland tried to call you earlier, but couldn't seem to...so, as he is going to be out at Town Square all morning, to get a statement and pictures of the leader of GARBAGE, he thought he might miss—"

"Town Square?" the minister interrupted.

"Yes, to get pictures," JB affirmed, musing to herself about the little wheels that must be turning in Hightower's head at the prospect of some easy publicity.

"Oh, I see," he responded enthusiastically. "Well, that's just right here, I mean, across the street. Why don't I just walk over and see if I can find Mr. Holland? That way I'm sure I can save his—"

"Oh, would you, sir?" JB interjected. "I'm sure he would—That's a great idea! Then perhaps he could take some—" The line went dead. JB laughed as she switched off Ralph's phone and stuck it in her pack. "Not in any hurry, are you, Rev?"

When Ralph saw JB laugh, he spread his hands for explanation. She winked and held up a thumb. He grinned and raised a fist of success.

"Right on," Ralph whispered to himself as the side door of the church swung open and out stepped Dr. Hightower. "Tight," he said as JB joined him. "Not bad, not bad," he added as he stuck a finger in her ribs. "Now, for the kill. You ready for this?"

"Intentar algo," she smiled uneasily, knowing they could still foul the plan up.

"Huh?"

"Go for it, Ralph."

When John Holland saw the minister, he and the photographer jumped into action. Ralph and JB fell in step a short distance behind them as they approached Hightower. Ralph reached inside his shirt and turned on the tape recorder and spoke softly, "Saturday, June 5th, twelve minutes after ten A.M., Town Square. The Reverend Mark Hightower and reporter John Holland. GARBAGE represented by JB Martinez and Ralph Coggins."

A tall, well-tanned bachelor in his late fifties, the Reverend Doctor Mark Hightower's long silver gray hair bounced as he bounded across the street. His captivating light blue eyes quickly sized up the four people approaching. He buttoned the top button of his tailored gray suit, and turned on the charismatic smile familiar to the people of

Cibolo Falls. He extended his hand well before he reached John Holland and boomed in his best pulpit voice, "Mr. Holland, it certainly is good to see you again!" He nodded at the photographer, JB, and Ralph.

The twitch at the edge of the reporter's mouth increased in relation to his agitation. *Of course it is. It was only yesterday.* He deeply resented the publicity Hightower attracted, a large amount due to the articles Holland himself was forced to write as part of his job. He felt Hightower was a phony and had, over the years, developed a deep mistrust for him.

"Good morning, Dr. Hightower," he forced, limply shaking the minister's hand. "Sir, if you don't mind, we certainly would like to get a picture of you with the leader of this GARBAGE group, and perhaps a comment for our Sunday edition."

"Why certainly. It would be my pleasure. Your office called and said that you might...Who is the—?" The minister looked at Ralph and JB.

JB answered with a shrug, "She can't be here. She can't get off work."

"Aw, that's too bad. And who might you be?" the minister asked, a bit condescending.

"I'm JB," she replied as she gestured toward her friend. "And this is Ralph."

The minister shook each one's hand, a bit too firmly JB thought. "My pleasure, I'm sure," the minister said.

"And my pleasure," Ralph mocked. *You asshole. It's going to be my pleasure, I'm sure, to see you go down in flames. I could use your help.*

Hightower turned his attention back to the reporter. "Well, it's too bad that the leader of these GARBAGE kids couldn't...I was looking forward to this meeting." He exaggerated a frown of disappointment.

Yeah, so what else is new? Frustrated by not being able to meet the leader, thus losing his story, Holland forced a smile for the minister. "Perhaps all isn't lost. As you see, Dr. Hightower, the kids are doing a pretty good job of cleaning up the park." He gestured toward those in the church parking lot. "They're even cleaning the church property. I wonder if you might have any comment on the—hold it right there, so we might get your picture." He motioned for the photographer, who jumped into action.

Not one to shun any photo op, Hightower adjusted his tie. He spoke, all the while smiling for the camera: "I certainly do have something to say. The youth of this town have been taking a lot of flak because of the cult movement that has taken hold. Sometimes in our effort to stamp out the work of the devil, we neglect giving proper recognition to the kids of our community who are out here doing good—doing a service to their community."

Ralph watched the minister pause dramatically as Holland played right along, nodding his readiness as he held his pencil over the pad. These guys are total stuffers, thought Ralph. He glanced sidelong at JB. She covertly rolled her eyes.

"In particular, I would like to praise the leader of this GARBAGE group," Hightower said.

Yes, yes, Ralph's heart leaped. You go, Rev. Just what we want.

The minister looked toward JB. "It's a young lady?" he asked.

JB nodded and smiled, "Fourteen years old."

Dr. Hightower studied JB for a moment, nodding slowly with pressed lips. "Fourteen years old," he said, turning back toward Holland. "It's apparent that the leader of this group is a fine upstanding young woman and a treasure of the community. While working at another job, she still finds time to organize her friends to come out and help clean up the town. I admire her leadership and unselfishness, and I'm looking forward to meeting...What did you say her name was?" He looked at Ralph and JB for assistance.

Oh, shit, thought Ralph as a sudden wave of panic hit. He glanced at JB, hoping she wouldn't respond. She had a blank expression as she looked out over the park; no way was she getting involved in this problem.

Ralph considered making a name up but realized it would show up in tomorrow's paper. That would destroy their plan. He was aware of Holland and Hightower waiting his answer. He began to panic. *Hurry. Say something, anything. Too much time is passing. Do it, now.*

"Well, you know," he replied awkwardly, "she's kinda...she gets real embarrassed when...she just doesn't want anyone to, you know, make a fuss over—"

"A treasure, indeed," the minister interjected, much to Ralph's relief. "Now, Mr. Holland, that's a story for you. The young lady is a true child of God. Put that in your story about these...these GARBAGE kids. It's so refreshing. She doesn't even want anyone to know her name. I must meet her, and soon," he commanded as he turned back toward JB and Ralph.

JB suppressed her elation as she nodded at the powerful man in front of her. "You will, sir. I promise." *And you aren't going to like it one bit.*

He fell for it, thought Ralph, having a hard time holding back his excitement at the first part of his plan working—imperfectly, but working. He reached inside his shirt and turned off the recorder.

As the minister posed for some pictures with the kids at work, JB stifled a laugh. "Sarah gets embarrassed when someone makes a fuss over her?"

"Hey, it worked, didn't it?" Ralph whispered back. "I thought we were going down the shitter. I didn't know what I was going to say."

After the photos, the minister patted both Ralph and JB on their heads, thanking them for their time, shook hands with Holland and the photographer, and excused himself. As Holland watched Dr. Hightower retreat to his church, Ralph noticed the twitch reappear at the corner of the reporter's mouth.

"You shouldn't grimace so much when the preacher touches you," Holland castigated, turning his attention to Ralph. "He really cares for you. I can tell."

"Get lost," Ralph followed with a grin. "The man knows perfection when he sees it."

"Yeah, right. We can see that you are perfection without equal," Holland retorted.

Ralph's grin vanished as he narrowed his eyes and glared at the reporter. He shot back, "You just wait. Very soon, now, you're gonna see what perfection is." *Like tomorrow. Then you'll see who's perfect. You're such an asshole. You'll be begging me for help.*

The reporter chortled but didn't answer. He turned and opened the trunk of the Chevy for the photographer to store his equipment, then they got in the car.

"And good-bye to you, too!" Ralph yelled out to the reporter as the car sped off.

The kids gathered round and exploded into celebration as Ralph and JB gave them the news of their success in phase one of the plan. They were dismissed after Ralph reviewed plans for the second phase of action to occur the next day, Sunday. JB and Ralph sat down on the grass to take care of two more chores before their day was complete.

JB retrieved Ralph's phone from her pack, called Smiley's mom, and told her everything was right on schedule for tomorrow, so Mrs. Schultz could call her contact in San Antonio.

Ralph then called the Pizza Shack.

"Pizza Shack."

"Uh, Mr. Mac."

"Yeah, Ralph. What's up with you? You want to talk to Sarah?"

"No, sir. You, if you have time?"

"I'll tell you what, Ralph. Business has been so bad lately, I've probably got about an hour to spare. What can I do for you this morning?"

"About tomorrow."

"About tomorrow?"

"Yes, sir."

"Well, what about it, Ralph?"

"You're going to have a lot of business, tomorrow," Ralph blurted out. "More than you've ever had before. Maybe a week's worth of business in one day. Do you have enough food?" There was silence on the other end as Ralph formulated his answer to the question he knew was coming.

"Okay, Ralph, I'll bite. What're you up to?"

"We're going to have a promotion. All the kids in GARBAGE are going to get their parents and friends to come in for pizza tomorrow to pay you back for the business you've lost because of the newspaper."

Bob's voice came back over the line: "So, that's about a hundred pizzas, Ralph. That's good. We can handle it, and we'll be ready. Thanks. We need the business or we're going broke, right quick. I really don't want to go job hunting, but it's getting close."

"No, Mr. Mac, twice that many!" Ralph's voice broke into treble. "Maybe three hundred or more! And hire some—have all your workers come in until closing. Hey, I know. We'll have some of the group help you. They can clean tables and wash dishes, sweep up or something."

"Whoa, Ralph, just cool it now," Bob said in concern. "I can get enough makings for three hundred pizzas, but there's no way you can—"

"They'll be that many, Mr. Mac. I promise. So, be ready. Okay? Then you won't have to get a job."

"Okay. I'll arrange for all the help to work all day, just for you. But,

I'll have to pay all those people, and if I don't have enough business to keep them busy, I'm personally going to come after you. You understand that, Ralph?"

"Loud and clear, Mr. Mac." Ralph answered despite having sudden doubts about being able to deliver.

"Anything else, Ralph, as if I really want to know?"

"Yes, sir," Ralph's voice cracked. "I wonder if we could borrow some water tomorrow?"

Already steamed about the lack of business during Saturday lunch, Bob glared at John Holland, who appeared in the open doorway of his cubbyhole of an office. Bob stood up but ignored the offered handshake. "Something I can do for you, Holland?" he asked gruffly. The reporter backed into the hall and held up his steno pad in defense.

"Yes sir, Mr. McPhee," the reporter answered. "If I could, I'd like to speak to Sarah."

Bob forced a grin but didn't answer as he glared at the uncomfortable reporter. He saw a chunky weasel of a man that nervously tugged at his open collar. Holland glanced to see if his escape root was clear.

"Sarah?" Holland repeated. "But, then, perhaps I could come another time, if, you know, she can't—"

"What the hell is with you, Holland?" Bob steamed. "It hasn't been important that you talk to her the last week and a half, but hardly a day has passed without your printing something nasty about her! I can't imagine why it's so important that you talk to her now! Just make up something else to write! All that shit you've been writing is nothing but garbage, anyway. You don't need her for that. So, what do you really want?"

Holland took another step back and again checked out his exit. He broke into a sweat in spite of the cool office. "Well, because we...I want to get both, I mean her side of the story."

"Both sides! Her side!" Bob exploded in astonishment, louder than he intended, startling the reporter even more. "After all the damage is done, and the sensationalism has served your purpose, you suddenly decide that being a good journalist is important! Is that it?"

"Well, I'm just trying to do the best job I can," came the meek reply. "I assure you, I have only written what I perceived to be the story—"

"Perceived?" Bob cut him short. "Tell me I didn't hear you right. Perceived? You've only written what you *perceived* to be the story? The way I see it, it is your job to report the news as it unfolds, backed up by accurate information on all parties involved! Over a week ago, you observed an event, got only one side of the story—not even the most important side—then wrote several biased articles supporting your fabrication, because you knew it would sell a lot of newspapers and make you look good! And you know that's a crock of shit, particularly when you're screwing up a lot of lives in the process!"

Bob turned and picked up the Thursday edition of the *Gazette* off the desk, rolled it up, and pointed it at the reporter. He spoke softly as he stood in the doorway: "This, my friend, is not investigative reporting. At best, it's biased editorialized bullshit." He took two steps into the hallway and tapped the shoulder of the reporter with the newspaper. Holland backed against the wall, his face a mask of alarm.

Bob took another step closer to block any additional retreat the reporter might consider. "Now, after the damage is done, you expect to come walking in here, all high and mighty, and get our cooperation?"

Bob twisted the newspaper as he shook his head. He reached over and unfastened two more buttons of Holland's moist shirt, and the reporter pressed closer against the wall, his eyes filled with fear. Rivulets of sweat ran down his neck. Bob peeled open the shirt and stuffed the newspaper inside, down to the reporter's pot belly. After methodically buttoning the top of the reporter's shirt, he patted the bulge, stepped back into the doorway, and glared. "No thanks. We don't need anymore of your lies. We've had plenty, I assure you."

Given room, Holland ducked away from Bob to gain a better angle on the exit door. With his escape near, he regained some confidence. He shook his fist at Bob. "You can't do that! That's assault!"

Bob responded calmly, "Yeah, right. Look, you pip-squeak. If I wanted to assault you, they would have to scrape you off the floor with a putty knife when I got through. If you don't like the way you've been treated, I suggest you call the law. Better yet, why don't you get a high-powered lawyer and sue me? But if you have ideas about doing either one, I think you'd better think long and hard about it, because you'll have to justify in courtroom every bit of that crap about Sarah being the leader of a cult group."

Bob studied the nervous man in front of him. "Why don't you get the hell out of here, before I really do assault you?"

Holland stood frozen, his lip twitching violently as he considered his plan of action. He opened his mouth to speak but then clamped his lips together. He backed down the short hall and out the exit door.

After the door swung shut, Bob stared at it. With a quick shake of the head, he returned to his office and slammed the door behind him.

Journal Note

"You have no obligation to take on this task or any other. You do have an opportunity to take on a task that will benefit you and the rest of the universe. If you do not choose to take this or any other opportunity, do not fret. It is simply a missed opportunity—nothing else. You will be no less for not taking it."

CHAPTER 10

Jody and Smiley waited outside the loading dock at the *Cibolo Falls Gazette* long before dawn on Sunday. As soon as the workers brought out the first bundles of the Sunday edition, they purchased one, jumped on their bikes, and pedaled to Westside Budget Printers.

JB, Ralph, Donnie, and his father, Jerry Rimkus, the owner of the print shop, received the newspaper with anticipation. Ralph scanned the front page, and then turned to the second as the others looked over his shoulder.

"Bad ass!" he exclaimed, bringing a like reaction from the other four. The headline over a two-column article about GARBAGE was more than they had hoped for:

"Dr. Hightower praises youth leader"

In addition to quoting Dr. Hightower calling the leader of the group a treasure to the city, the article went on to say that the minister praised the group's activities, such as creating ecological awareness and doing their part to clean up the City of Cibolo Falls. The article had a small picture of Dr. Hightower helping two of the kids pick up litter.

"Looks like this is just what you need," Jerry stated as he sat down at the computer. He folded the page before him and pointed to the headline. "Why not lead off with that?"

Everyone in agreement, he proceeded to move the headlines over what he had written earlier. He then moved down several spaces on the screen, changed a sentence, and added a quote out of the news article. He looked up for reaction. The kids nodded their approval. After a few minutes, Jerry had completed his changes and reviewed the completed version along with the kids. He made a few minor changes and everyone agreed that they should go with it.

The laser printer quickly spit out five copies and Jerry handed one to each of the group for review. "Make sure that's what you want, because you can't afford any changes after they are printed up."

The Reverend Dr. Mark Hightower:

"Sarah McPhee a true child of God"

Saturday morning, in a complete reversal of his earlier position, the Reverend Dr. Mark Hightower called the leader of Grass-roots Alliance for Reviving and Building a Greater Earth "a true child of God" for her leadership and unselfishness. Dr. Hightower also emphasized that the leader was a "city treasure." The leader of the organization, better known as GARBAGE, is fourteen-year-old Sarah McPhee.

GARBAGE is a newly formed Cibolo Falls youth group. According to Ms. McPhee, the chief aim of the group is to recognize Earth's ecological problems, and act on a local level toward solving those problems.

She has been criticized for her belief that everything on Earth is a part of God and, therefore, is God. In honoring these beliefs, the group hopes to raise public awareness to the need for cleaning up Earth and restricting the use of its natural resources before it is too late.

The *Cibolo Falls Gazette*, mostly through the efforts of reporter John Holland, has accused Sarah of being the leader of a youth cult group. Also highly outspoken against Sarah's alleged cult activities has been Dr. Mark Hightower, pastor of Hill Country Chapel of God and President of the Cibolo Falls Council of Churches.

These accusations are not true and Dr. Hightower has since called Sarah a child of God. We urge you to read of Dr. Hightower's complete change of position on page two of today's (Sunday) edition of the *Gazette*.

As a result of the accusations against Sarah, various religious groups of Cibolo Falls have launched a boycott against the McPhee's family-owned and operated pizza restaurant. Because of this unfair and wrongful action, the Pizza Shack, a favorite among youth of Cibolo Falls, may be forced out of business soon.

The approximately one hundred youth involved and many of their parents urge you to counteract the efforts of this boycott. Today, GARBAGE invites you to attend and enjoy PIZZA SUNDAY IN CIBOLO FALLS, at the Pizza Shack. With your purchase of a "Pizza Grande" (Family Size Pizza), you will receive a free car wash, compliments of GARBAGE, right on the parking lot of Pizza Shack, while you and your family enjoy your meal in the dining room.

With the attached coupon, help us break this unjust boycott. Coupon good this Sunday only at Pizza Shack, located at the corner of Broadview and Phillips Streets in Cibolo Falls. Prompt car wash service on orders to go.

Thank you,

Youth of GARBAGE

"Hey, that's tight, Mr. Rimkus," Ralph declared. "Let's do it."

"Okay, guys," Jerry nodded. "About how many you want?"

Well, here we go, thought Ralph. I hope Mr. Rimkus is the great dude that Donnie says he is. He looked for assistance from JB.

"Well, we took up a collection and came up with about thirty-six dollars," she offered as she raised her perfectly arched dark brows and hoped for assistance from Mr. Rimkus.

"That certainly won't buy much printing, but, it's a good cause. I'll tell you what: I'll spring for the remainder. But, there's a catch. If your organization ever gets big and rich, I expect to be your printer at fair market prices. Deal?"

"Deal," the kids answered in unison.

"All right, then. How about three thousand for starters? We can always print more later if necessary."

"Awesome!" Ralph exclaimed. "How long will it take?"

"Once they start coming, it'll be pretty quick. In about an hour we'll have enough to get your people out on the street. Is that soon enough?"

"Perfecto," JB exclaimed. "We'll have about forty of our group here by eight o'clock."

Between eight and ten o'clock, thirty-eight kids fanned out over the city, distributing the freshly printed leaflets to anyone that would take one. They worked traffic lights, grocery store parking lots, residences, and businesses. They even left leaflets on the windshields in church parking lots during services, and some of the more daring kids even passed them out to parishioners as they left services. The campaign was in full swing to right the wrong done by the newspaper and churches of Cibolo Falls.

At ten o'clock, half of those distributing leaflets left to join the first shift at the Pizza Shack for car wash and duty inside.

"You're going to what?" Bob laughed. He, Barbara and Sarah stood by Ralph at the window of Pizza Shack and watched a group of kids arrive with hoses, buckets, and other equipment on their handlebars. "Bud, when you say you're going to drum up business, you mean it."

Ralph winked at Sarah as he handed a leaflet to each of them and then watched for reaction.

"Well, now I see. You were the one behind that article in the paper this morning; I kind of figured you had a hand in it," Bob declared when he finished reading. "How in the world did you pull that off?"

"It was easy. Let me put it this way: the Rev has met his match. He stepped right into our trap. It was totally cool."

"Did he actually say Sarah was a child of God?" Barbara asked, her brow gathered in concern.

"Well, kinda," Ralph sputtered. "He said that the leader of GARBAGE is a child of God. She's our accepted leader, so what can he say? Ya shoulda been there to see a real master in action."

"I wish I'd been there," Sarah pouted. "I always miss out on the fun."

"Poor thing. Never gets to have any fun." Bob teased his daughter. He turned back toward Ralph and cautioned, "You realize, he's probably going to be a bit peeved at you and everyone else involved. He'll maintain that he said no such thing, that the reporter got it all wrong—that he was misquoted or something."

"He can say what he wants. Ralph, boy genius, is too smart for him. I got the whole thing on tape. I dare him—I double-dog-dare him—to deny he said it. And Donnie is going to tape the Rev's sermon, this morning, just in case he sticks his other foot in his mouth."

Barbara accidentally dropped a shaker she was filling; salt scattered across the top of the table. She raked it into a pile with the side of her hand. "I can't believe you guys are going to this much trouble. I'm impressed. And the leaflets—they must have cost you quite a few bucks."

"Mr. Rimkus says our credit is good."

Sarah watched her father stroke his chin in thought. She knew this was always followed with something good. She was not disappointed.

"Well, since you guys are going to bat for us, I'll tell you what: if we have all the business you say we're going to have today, your group can have a hefty fifty percent of this week's profits over what we usually clear in a week. That should give you enough for the printing plus some left over for your next project."

"Hey, that's great, Mr. Mac," Ralph gushed. "We've been wondering how we could raise some bucks. Smiley and Jody have spent a lot of their own money on supplies for the handouts, and Smiley's mom is going to have our website online early next week. She said she would help us out, but she's doing enough with all the time she's putting in."

"Hey, you guys getting a website? That's great," said Barbara. "Sarah, how come you haven't told us?"

Sarah grimaced. "Well, I didn't think you were in the mood for this stuff, when we already gave you so much trouble."

"Now, look here, Sarah," her mom scolded as she shook her finger. "We're supporting you the best we can, and we want to know the bad and the good. Understand?" She broke into a grin.

"Yeah, Mom, you're right. From now on, I'll tell you everything. Even the boring stuff."

Barbara smiled at her daughter. "Good, I'm glad we understand each other. Now, I've just had a sinking feeling. Just how many of these leaflets did you pass out this morning? I don't know if we can handle—"

"Don't know, about twenty-five hundred, maybe three thousand. Hey, I have enough people. How many do you want?"

"Geez," Bob laughed. "I can see it already. This is going to be a day to remember. How about, let's see...about ten at a time, two-hour shifts. I think that should be enough. Can you handle that?"

"You got it," Ralph affirmed. He took charge and thoroughly enjoyed it. "And if any of 'em give you grief, or aren't doing their job, just let me know. We'll send you in a fresh one. If you decide any are good enough to hire full-time, go right ahead. GARBAGE don't charge no employee finder's fee."

"I certainly am glad you're on our side, Ralph," Bob replied. "If we survive the day, we'll be indebted to you and your friends. I don't think I need to tell you, things are approaching the crisis stage around here." He grinned and winked at his wife. "I was even considering sending my wife out to find a job."

Ralph smiled when Sarah flipped the lock of hair out of his eye with a finger. "It was all for Sarah. We look out for our friends."

"Thanks, Ralph. I was wondering last night if you were going to get me in trouble again. I guess I was wrong."

"Come on, Ralph getting you in trouble? No way, just no way," he protested as he projected a hurt look. "Okay, your highness, get back in the kitchen and get that oven cranked up. Today is pizza day in Cibolo Falls."

Ralph started for the door, but stopped short. He turned back. "Hey, Sarah. It'd be a good idea of you stay looking good today. You know, like keep your hair brushed, clean apron, that sort of thing."

Sarah locked her squinted eyes on Ralph. She hated it when he threw out hints but wouldn't tell the whole story. "Ralph! You're doing it again. Will you tell me what's going on?"

"Me lady!" Ralph bowed with a flourish. "You wanted a better rep, so we're going for it while we have the attention." He smiled wickedly, turned, and headed out the door. "Ten common laborers coming up!" they heard him call back as the door closed.

By ten-thirty, when the Pizza Shack opened for business, there were already four cars waiting. Smiley, the head of the car wash detail, had divided his people into six groups of four, enabling, he hoped, each group to wash one car every ten minutes. By eleven o'clock, they had already washed eighteen and had another waiting when each was completed.

Likewise, on the inside of the restaurant, Sarah, her two regular helpers, and four GARBAGE kids kept the oven full at all times, easily staying ahead of the orders. Although the dining room wasn't filled to capacity, Bob expected by one o'clock to have customers waiting for a table. He gave his new help instructions on taking pizza orders, serving, busing, general cleanup, and dish-washing because he wouldn't have time once business picked up.

Ralph set up a schedule so that each worker would rotate to another job every two hours, to avoid boredom during the long day. The favorite job, because of less work involved, was that of demonstration and leaflet distribution. There were always twenty kids out carrying handmade signs dealing with not only the Pizza Shack boycott, but Sarah's "I am God" statement and GARBAGE ecological issues. They were divided for duty in the parking lot and on the three major traffic intersections near the restaurant.

Donnie had reported in at twelve-thirty that his mission was a success at Dr. Hightower's early sermon. He turned over the original tape and four copies he had made afterward. Ralph borrowed Bob's office to listen to the tape, and upon hearing Dr. Hightower making the same glowing comments about GARBAGE and its leader to his congregation, he made packets of the tapes. Into each of four envelopes he placed a single copy of the tape he had made the day before at the park and one of Donnie's sermon copies. He put them aside for later use and returned to his supervision of the work at hand.

By two o'clock, Pizza Sunday had turned into all that Ralph had hoped, and he figured, even with a probable letup between three and six, they could possibly wash close to three hundred cars. He felt apprehensive, however, because the expected visitors had not shown. The *Gazette* would surely send its people, since his flyer mentioned the controversy that had been page one or two material the previous ten days. At two-thirty he limited himself to outside supervision, just in case any of the possible visitors showed.

Close to three o'clock John Holland and his sidekick cruised by the Pizza Shack in his familiar blue Chevy. Coming to a halt along the front curb, they got out and surveyed the activity on the busy parking lot. Ralph waited for the right moment to approach them. As Holland looked on, the photographer took pictures of a couple of demonstrators with signs that said: *EATING AT PIZZA SHACK IS A VOTE FOR EARTH*, and *SURE GOD EATS AT PIZZA SHACK—DON'T WE ALL?*

The reporter projected a hostile stare when he saw Ralph approaching. He knew he would have to do something about the boy who set him up the day before. He couldn't let it happen again. "You're a little smart-ass, aren't you, Ralph?" he asked as he reached up and smoothed the hair over his bald spot.

Ralph projected an air of self-confidence that he knew would irritate Holland but was unsuccessful in trying to repress his amusement at outsmarting him. "Just trying to do my job. I don't like it, but, you know, Mr. Holland, someone has to do it. Sometimes you just have to use a little brain power to get the real truth out."

Holland knew he had screwed up by embellishing his original story about Sarah, essentially reporting a falsehood. It had already caused him some professional as well as personal problems. Now it was important, more than ever, to interview Sarah and write an article to rectify the problems he'd caused, so he could, at the very least, save his reputation and maybe even his job. If he couldn't get to Sarah through her father, perhaps Ralph could help him, if he worked it right.

"Right, Ralph," the reporter responded. "Everyone stumbles onto success once in a while. Now, you've had your day. Congratulations are in order, but now you need to get on with your measly life. You know, you could help out in this situation if you wanted to."

"Ha," Ralph retorted. "Meaning you want—no—you *need* something from me, to help get you out of the mess you're in, right?" The reporter starred back blankly. "Hello," Ralph said, as he waved his hand in front of the reporter's face. "Hello. You in there? Mr. Holland, you can wake up now."

"Yeah. Sure," Holland responded. "I do need...perhaps you could get me an interview with the...with Sarah. I tried to talk to her yesterday, but her father said she was too busy. You know, she couldn't take time from her job, and I had too much to do, so I couldn't, you know, hang around."

Ralph fixed Holland with an intense stare. "Uh-huh. I feel your pain," he said with all the seriousness he could muster. "Well, I dunno. I guess...maybe something—Now, wait a minute. What's in it for me? What's in it for GARBAGE?"

Holland glared down at Ralph. "Look, you little twirp. If you had leveled with me yesterday, all of this crap wouldn't be happening. I don't guess you've ever tried dealing truthfully with people?"

Ralph, hands planted on his hips, leaned toward the reporter and exclaimed, "Hey, asshole! Don't you, don't *you* talk to me about truth! All that shit you've been printing about Sarah isn't anything close to the truth, and you know it! Sarah ain't no cult leader and you've known it all along! Now the truth is biting you in the ass and you think you can come here and get the real story. Then everything's cool. John Holland is The Man again."

Ralph felt elated about his little outburst in front of his friends, but he had to make a quick decision. If Smiley's mother was able to come through for them, after this afternoon they wouldn't need the reporter, not on his terms anyway. If she wasn't able to do as she promised, they would definitely need Holland and a positive news story. He needed to stall for more time, so he backed off.

"That's a no. Mr. McPhee won't let you talk to Sarah," Ralph added evenly to the reporter. "He mentioned earlier that he couldn't wait to—" He stopped as if trying to remember what Bob had said. "Oh, well, I can't—" He gestured flippantly, "I can't remember exactly. I just don't think it would be a very good idea for you, or even me, whom he thinks the world of, to ask him right now." Ralph's face lit up for the reporter's benefit, as if he had an idea. "Hey, you know what? Like later, another reporter is gonna interview Sarah. Maybe you can kind of, you know, listen in. That way you can get your story, without having to deal with Mr. Mac."

What the hell's going on here? Is someone taking over my turf? I can't let this happen. "Wait a minute. Another reporter? Who? I'm the only—"

"From San Antonio," Ralph interjected, delighted to see the reporter squirm. "They've shown some interest since you...I mean, since Cibolo Falls has been so divided, you know, since Sarah was dissed and called a cult leader, and then your friend Dr. Hightower decided to hurl a little barf. I guess they want the real story, Mr. Holland."

The reporter's confusion was evident. However uncomfortable the alternatives, he was being forced to decide on a plan of action. Should he leave and perhaps miss the story or stay and face the humiliation of playing second-fiddle to a reporter from the big city?

Ralph waited for a reply from Holland. *If the San Antonio reporter shows, then I've got you, shit-head.* He gestured for a response.

Holland answered as he looked around the parking lot as if Ralph or anything he had said didn't bother him: "Look, Ralph. First off, Hightower isn't now, or has he ever been, my friend. Don't you forget that." He ignored Ralph's grin. "Second, did you write that leaflet that your group put out this morning?"

"Some of it. Pretty tight, huh?"

"You know that Dr. Hightower is going to be a little upset. He's going to deny saying any of that. He has to answer to all those people who follow him around, and he can't lose face over a bunch of loud-mouth kids."

"So," Ralph answered with an indifferent shrug, "defend yourself. You're the reporter. You wrote it because he said it. If he says that he didn't say it, it's your word against his. No one should know better than you that the *truth* always wins out."

"Ha," Holland scoffed, "who are they going to believe? A reporter who works for a podunk newspaper or someone everyone thinks is God's anointed one?"

Ralph slowly shook his head in mock disappointment. "Aw, man. I thought you were number one in this town. That's the way you act, anyway. Stand up against the man. Make a big deal out of it, just like you made a big deal out of Sarah being a cult leader." He gestured at the kids washing cars. "There's a lot of us kids...uh...cult members in this town who'll linkup with you if you take the Rev on. All you have to do is write some good articles about us. What can you lose?"

"Yeah, right," Holland answered with a wry grin. "Like the support of some dumbass kids will really help me."

Ralph turned to attend to his other duties but took one last stab, "Don't underestimate Sarah's *dumbass* friends. We just might have more power in this town than you think."

Stone faced, Holland watched Ralph walk away. A few minutes later, Ralph sneaked a look and found the reporter and his photographer sitting on the hood of the blue Chevy. Just as Ralph had hoped, they stayed to see if the reporter from San Antonio showed. They didn't have long to wait.

At ten past three, a large white van with a video transmission dish on the top rounded the corner, stopped for a moment, then entered the lot of the Pizza Shack. On the side in large blue letters was the logo of KGEX TV 8, The Eye of San Antonio, Texas. A svelt reporter and her frumpy cameraman got out of the van and looked around the busy parking lot.

Ralph silently thanked Mrs. Schultz for her connections. He looked for JB and found her striking a sexy pose in the carwash detail. She nodded her understanding of his signal and walked toward the restaurant. Ralph approached the news crew, smug in the knowledge that Holland was an unwilling spectator of the arrival of the television crew.

Ralph looked over the tall slender woman, smartly dressed in a gray pin-striped suit. "Man, this is one hot lady," he mumbled to himself, awed by her short curly blond hair and brown eyes adorned by gold-framed glasses, and a radiant tanned complexion.

The reporter had an air of confidence about her as she spied Ralph approaching. She smiled. "Hi, there. I'm Joyce Brown from KGEX, in San Antonio. I wonder if you could tell me where I can find…"—she consulted a pad—"Ralph?"

"I'm your man," Ralph said as he extended his hand.

"Ralph. It's nice to meet you," she greeted and shook his hand. "I'm told you might help me find Sarah McPhee. We would like to get an interview with her for our evening newscast."

Wow, I wish I was about ten years older. This is my kind of woman. I wonder if she can hear my heart pounding? "Yes, ma'am," he answered heartily, trying to be as businesslike as he knew how. "I'm her representative and best, you know, friend," he grinned. *I wonder if I'm in love.* "You want me to bring her out for your interview?"

"Yes, Ralph. I do, and we're in somewhat of a hurry. You know, time scheduling for the *Six O'Clock News,* and maybe again at ten. That is, if it works out. You know how it is." She nodded at Ralph. "Time is very important."

Now, this is more like it. "I gotcha, Ms. Brown. Have her here in a minute," he called over his shoulder, breaking into a run. He glanced over to see John Holland mingle with the adults and kids gathered nearby to watch. *Eat your heart out, you jerk.*

Ralph burst through the restaurant door to find many of the workers and diners gathered at the windows, curious of the activity around the TV van. He picked out Sarah, stopped and gathered his composure. He announced formally: "Ms. McPhee, Channel Eight wants you." His smile broad, he clapped his hands together. "This is it, Sarah. You wanted fair reporting, you get fair reporting."

Sarah and Barbara looked at Ralph in surprised confusion, their mouths agape. "They're here to talk to Sarah?" Bob asked.

"You got it. Now come on," Ralph urged Sarah. "If you're good enough, they want you on the *Six O'Clock News* in San Antonio."

Sarah stared at Ralph in stunned silence. "I don't…They…? I can't talk—" She looked to her dad for help.

Bob smiled at his daughter. "It's your show. If that's what you want, go for it. However, what you say could get you in more trouble. If you say any of that 'I am God' stuff, you'd better be prepared to pay the consequences, because people may continue to turn on you. Can you face up to that?"

Sarah's face mirrored bewilderment as she looked to at Ralph. *What can I do? This is just too much all at once. I can't handle being on TV or even being interviewed. What if I mess up? What if I say something I don't mean to say and we get in more trouble?*

Spook, are you there? Yes, that's it. Spook said that I would never choose or be given any task that I wasn't ready to handle. That I would only have to deal with issues that I am capable of handling. But the group is depending on me. I just can't let them down. Not when we're so close to getting the publicity we need to succeed.

"Come on, Sarah," Ralph prodded.

Sarah closed her eyes in deep concentration. She opened them and blew out a long noisy breath. "All right, Ralph. You're right. This is our big chance. Let's do it." She beamed in confidence at her mom and dad. "Okay?"

"It's up to you," Barbara affirmed. "Just be yourself and you'll do fine. We'll support you. We can't help you, but we'll be there for you."

"Thanks, Mom...Dad," she whispered as she hugged both. She untied the string to take off the red-checkered apron.

"No, leave it on," Ralph urged. "Ya gotta have a little humility—you know, woman just out of the kitchen. If God can pick up litter, God can work in the kitchen, right?"

Sarah retied the string and turned toward Barbara. "Do I look okay, Mom?"

"You look fine. Now, go wow 'em and be cool, no matter what. Don't let them get to you, okay?"

"Right, Mom," Sarah answered with a wide smile.

"Come on!" Ralph urged as he pulled Sarah by one arm toward the door. "They won't wait all day."

As they walked out into the sunshine, JB fell into step with them. "How'd it go?" Ralph asked.

"Well, I made the call to his residence. Some lady answered, probably the housekeeper. He wasn't there, so I asked for his cell number. She wouldn't give it to me, so I left the message. Maybe he'll get it; maybe he won't."

"Good. I'm sure they'll reach him,"

"What're you talking about?" Sarah asked as they approached the crowd that surrounded the TV reporter.

"Don't worry about it. Just do your job and we'll take care of the rest," Ralph smiled confidently, taking Sarah by the hand. "Okay, guy," he whispered as the group parted to let Sarah, JB, and Ralph through, "go for it. You may never get a chance like this again."

"Ms. Brown, this is Sarah McPhee," Ralph said as they approached the reporter. "Sarah, this is Joyce Brown."

Sarah released Ralph's hand and extended hers to the reporter. "Hi, Ms. Brown. I'm glad you're here. I'm surprised because Ralph didn't tell me you might come."

"Hello, Sarah. I'm glad to talk to you," Joyce nodded as she shook Sarah's hand. She looked over Sarah somewhat surprised. *So, this is the girl that's causing all the trouble. She certainly looks harmless enough. This should be interesting.* "We've been made aware of some of the problems you've had, and I would like to hear your side. Would you mind answering a few questions in front of the camera, so that we might use it on this evening's newscast?"

The cameraman gestured that he was ready, and Joyce Brown began to ask Sarah about the controversy that surrounded her since the school assembly. As the interview progressed, Sarah and the reporter worked well together and Sarah relaxed. She answered the reporter's questions with confidence in manner and delivery, and her brown eyes beamed with enthusiasm. Bob and Barbara watched close by, surprised at the maturity their daughter showed in the interview, despite the controversial areas it covered. They knew that Joyce Brown was impressed because she backtracked over several issues, getting the minute details of the goals Sarah had set for GARBAGE and the reasons behind her statements about everyone and everything being God.

John Holland tried to hide his note-taking from those around him as he took it all in. Much to his discomfort, Joyce Brown delved into the *Gazette's* articles on Sarah's involvement in cult activity. Sarah fielded the questions with light humor and ease. She took full blame for her part in creating the controversy but refused to blame either the newspaper or the religious community for their part.

When the interview concluded, Joyce Brown appeared pleased. She gained permission from Bob and Barbara to tape a segment on Sarah's work with GARBAGE later for a weekly news series she hosted on ecological issues.

Later, just as Joyce completed a wrap-up in front of some strategically placed demonstrators with signs, a black Cadillac drove up next to the curb and stopped. With no lack of flair, Dr. Mark Hightower got out of the car and surveyed the activity on the parking lot, aware of the attention his arrival garnered. Still dressed in his Sunday morning best, it was as if he knew he'd be on stage. He paused and crossed his arms over his chest before he shook his head, then proceeded toward the woman near the camera.

"Who?" Joyce asked Ralph.

"That's the man," Ralph answered. "The one and only Dr. Mark Hightower. This will make your newscast complete." Ralph couldn't resist adding, "But watch out. Sarah ain't in the same league as this guy. A few minutes with him and you'll know, without a doubt, who the real God in Cibolo Falls is."

"Thanks, I'll keep that in mind."

Ralph backed away as Joyce circled with a finger for the cameraman to keep filming. He nodded and took a strategic position to catch the full profile of the self-assured man who approached through the crowd of parents and kids. Sarah joined Ralph; she wanted no part of the confrontation that was imminent.

Joyce watched the minister come ever closer, his chest thrust forward as he smoothed back his wavy silver-gray hair. "Mark Hightower," he declared without a hint of his usual cordial smile as he extended his hand to Joyce. "I'm minister to the people of Cibolo Falls, through Hill Country Chapel of God."

She shook his hand and forced her most confident smile. "Joyce Brown. Channel 8, San Antonio."

"I see. And I suppose you're here to give unnecessary publicity to these..." he paused and swept his hand across the kids and parents gathered around, "blasphemous misguided children."

Surprised by such a blatant statement, Joyce's jaw dropped. She composed herself. She would not be intimidated by this man, no matter who he was or who he pretended to be. She glared back at him and spread her feet to hold her ground. She pointed a finger at Hightower and said, "Sir, for your information, it is not now, nor has it ever been my intention to give anyone publicity about anything. My main job is to gather the news, in any way I can, then present it to the public in the fairest way I can. That is all. This is a news story and I fully expect to cover it fairly and truthfully—"

The minister interrupted, "Well, now, I understand what—"

"Pardon me. I haven't finished," the reporter glowered. "I want to hear all the facts and opinions, pro and con, concerning Sarah McPhee and her group. Your position has been reported in the local newspaper, but I am most happy to hear all you have to say on the issue of cult activity and Sarah McPhee as well." She forced a smile. "I believe I've made myself clear. Do you wish to make a statement, or would you be content to just answer my questions?"

"Well, Ms..."

"Brown, Mr. *Watertower*."

"*Touché*. I can see that you are one to be reckoned with. It was foolish of me to forget your name."

"Dr. Hightower," Joyce replied as she tried to stay calm. "I'm on a strict timetable. If you have something to say, I suggest you get on with it. If not..." She turned away from the minister and prepared to leave.

"Ma'am, wait, you have my most humble of apologies. It wasn't my intention to be rude. It's just that I have been under a bit of pressure lately. When that happens, I become short, disrespectful—God forgive me—even mean. Again, forgive me. Ask your questions, please. You have my full attention and cooperation."

Joyce turned and faced the minister. "Fine. Dr. Hightower, for some time now, you and the Cibolo Falls Council of Churches have lead a boycott against the restaurant behind me. This happened after the daughter of the owner said some things you disagree with. Do you care to comment or state your group's position on this matter?"

"I certainly do. These kids, lead by Sarah McPhee—" He stopped short and scanned the crowd for her, although the newspaper picture of her at the school assembly was all he had to go on.

JB, who had joined Ralph and Sarah, nudged Sarah and whispered, "He's looking for you, sweetie. Wanna volunteer?" Smiling hesitantly, Sarah shook her head.

Hightower turned his attention back to the reporter. "This town is rife with devil worshiping activities by our youth. And these kids think they can seduce the people into believing that they are doing some kind of good, despite my attempts to expose their activities. Sarah McPhee is not a healthy influence on our children, and I will not rest until I stop this blasphemous activity, acting under the guise of cleaning up the earth."

"But, sir," Joyce countered, "has it been proven that these kids are involved in any type of devil worship? All this was based on the observations of one reporter for the Cibolo Falls newspaper. Is that correct?"

"And the assistant principal and other faculty members of the school as well," the minister ignored the first question. "And my own observations."

"Now let me be sure I understand you, Dr. Hightower." She gathered her brow and looked the minister in the eye. "You're saying that, by your own observations, these kids, mainly Sarah McPhee, are involved in devil worship, yet didn't you say yesterday to a reporter from your local newspaper that the leader of this ecology group is—and I quote—a child of God, and a treasure to the City of Cibolo Falls?"

"No, ma'am, I did not!" the minister retorted vehemently. He shook his head and clenched a fist as his face turned crimson. "I said no such thing! I was misquoted by that incompetent reporter!" He turned and pointed at John Holland. "Ask him! Ask him if I said anything close to calling the leader of this group a child of God! He knows he can't stand behind the article published this morning!"

Holland, unwilling to take on the confident charismatic man who accused him, remained silent and tried not to show any emotion. He rested his hand on the side of his mouth, well aware the twitch could betray him. He could feel his stomach twist in knots as he seethed at not only Hightower, but at Sarah and Ralph as well.

Ralph enjoyed the spectacle that played out in front of him. *Keep digging, brother Hightower. We'll bury you in your own bullshit.* He turned, cupped his hands around his mouth, and whispered to Smiley, who stood behind him: "On Mr. Mac's desk there are four big white envelopes. Get two of them and bring them to me."

"Gotcha, boss."

Hightower glared at John Holland, then turned back to Joyce Brown: "You see! The man won't even come forward and defend his article. He knows he has wronged me and, in the process, has helped this bunch of misguided kids with his irresponsible reporting."

Joyce held the microphone closer.

Dr. Hightower reached into his coat pocket and pulled out a copy of the flyer the kids distributed. He dramatically unfolded it and held it up to the camera. "All lies. These kids have slandered God, the church, and me by spreading these leaflets all over town. I have not called the leader of this group, or Sarah McPhee, or anyone else for that matter, a child of God. Not now or ever. I have been blatantly misquoted, and I intend to take every legal means at my disposal to right the wrong that has been done by the reporter of the *Gazette*, and all other parties responsible of smearing my good and respected reputation in this fair city."

Hightower displayed a confident, triumphant smile at Joyce Brown as he methodically refolded the flyer and stuck it back inside his coat pocket. *Well, that will teach them. That should take care of all of them in one swoop. The threat of a lawsuit works every time.* He smiled smugly. "The people of Cibolo Falls know me well. They respect my judgment and trust my actions in all spiritual matters. They, of course, will continue to support me in my time of being wrongfully attacked by those representing the forces of Satan."

Although Joyce had nothing more to ask of the minister, she thought she had better wait a moment more.

"I believe I've said all that's necessary at this time. We all should have more important things to do on the Sabbath than hanging around a pizza cafe and supporting the forces of evil." He paused again and waited for question or comment from the reporter as he flashed a wide smile at the camera.

She smiled at Hightower: "Thank you, sir, for your time."

The minister nodded at Joyce Brown, brandished a smile of moral victory at John Holland, turned, and walked briskly to his Cadillac. Just as he opened the door, a voice boomed out from the middle of the crowd:

"Hey, Rev, does this mean you don't want your free car wash?"

Hightower jerked his head around to see who the culprit was—laughter and cheers filled the parking lot—glared angrily at the crowd, then jumped in the car, slammed the door, and sped away. The crowd applauded his exit.

Those nearby gathered around and congratulated the guilty party on his outburst, each trying to get their turn at rubbing his bald head. Donnie Rimkus basked in his little moment in the limelight.

Well, that certainly was a bad-ass interview. Now, let's see how you can hold up against the words of one of Cibolo Falls' finest citizens—yourself. Ralph approached Joyce Brown and handed her one of the packets. "I think you'll find these interesting."

Joyce eyed Ralph warily as she opened it and discovered two tapes. "What—? You didn't?" she laughed, loud enough that others turned to see what the commotion was. "Let me guess: Hightower, right?"

"Yes ma'am," Ralph answered with a confident smile. "Yesterday, in an interview with the reporter from the *Gazette*, and this morning in the pulpit of his church."

She studied Ralph. "You're very thorough, aren't you."

Ralph moved a step closer to the reporter so he could get a last whiff of her perfume. "Just covering my behind, ma'am."

"I'll bet. Well, if you're intent on collecting evidence," she quipped, "next time get video. That way I can use it on my newscast."

Ralph twisted his lips in regret. "Now, why didn't I think of that?"

"Watch the *Six O'Clock News*, tonight. Sarah will be on it. Then again at ten."

"All right! Thanks!" exclaimed Ralph. He turned and gave thumbs-up to JB, Sarah, Bob, and Barbara. "We'll be seeing you again, right?" he asked as he turned back.

"Yeah, Ralph. If not to see Sarah, then to see you. I think you young people are on the right track with GARBAGE, and I have this feeling that Dr. Hightower isn't going to leave you alone anytime soon, do you?"

"Probably not." He stuck out his hand. "Thanks for coming. We needed you." *I guess since she thinks I'm young people, I don't have a chance with her.*

"Ralph, you are a breath of fresh air," Joyce laughed. "I'll look forward to working with you again."

Ralph turned away from the reporter, although he fantasized staying close to her forever. He searched the thinning crowd for John Holland. He spied the *Gazette* reporter and his helper about to pull away from the curb. *Oh, shit. Don't let him get away.*

"Mr. Holland! Mr. Holland!" he yelled. When the reporter stopped his car, Ralph ran over and dropped the other packet of tapes through the open window into his lap. "I think you need this. Don't say I never did anything for you." He turned away before the reporter had a chance to respond.

At six o'clock, Bob switched on the big dining room TV at the Pizza Shack. Despite being filled to capacity, the dining room got quiet a few minutes into the newscast when the anchor introduced Joyce Brown. She stood in front of the Pizza Shack, and behind her were three kids with demonstration signs. One sign read WE LOVE PIZZA SHACK! And another, SHE GOD, ME GOD, WE ALL GOD! The third read, GOD LOVES PIZZA—WE ALL DO! The three demonstrators each held up their free hand in the familiar Earth Salute.

"I'm coming to you from seventy miles west of San Antonio, in Cibolo Falls. For the last eleven days, this town has been embroiled in controversy, all because of a fourteen-year-old by the name of Sarah McPhee. Because of a voice she claims to hear, she has taken on the task of doing her part to clean up the Earth, with the help of about one hundred of her friends."

All kitchen and food-service activity came to a halt as everyone watched, spellbound. In Joyce Brown's dialogue with Sarah, they briefly covered the arrival of Spook, the purpose and plans of the group, the reasons for the 'I am God' statement, the devil worshipping allegations, and the boycott.

The picture switched back to the studio with Jerry Monsoto, the anchor seated at his desk, and Joyce Brown at his side:

"That was an interesting interview. Sarah McPhee seems to be a very charismatic child," he said to the reporter.

"Yes, she is. Sometimes we overuse the term 'self-assured,' but, considering her age, she is just that—at least, on the surface. I might add a sideline on this Cibolo Falls problem: Dr. Hightower, the minister I mentioned, is extremely upset. He says the kids tricked him into saying that the leader of GARBAGE is a child of God, as was reported in the local newspaper. I interviewed him this afternoon and he denied saying anything of the sort. He threatened to sue all those involved for slander. However, the kids are in possession of audio tapes of the minister saying just that—that the leader is a child of God."

"That's interesting," Monsoto nodded. "Will you be doing a follow-up on this story?"

"We'll be watching the situation closely, and I hope to have a segment on Sarah's group on my *Ecology Today* program."

"Well, we wish Sarah and her friends luck in cleaning up the Earth." Monsoto turned back toward the camera. "I want to say to our viewers, Joyce Brown's story ran a little longer than our usual news segment because we felt it that needed to be told in its entirety." Another pause and Monsoto changed his tone of voice: "In other news, today..."

The packed restaurant exploded in applause and cheers, because everyone knew they had scored an important victory in Cibolo Falls. Not only had they apparently succeeded in their efforts to break the boycott, they had also cleared the way for the group to do their work with support of most of the townspeople and news media.

The rest of the evening went smoothly, and by closing time the kids had washed 273 cars. The restaurant had also sold a like number of Pizza Grandes. The final tally resulted in a profit of $332 for GARBAGE.

Journal Note

"If it is in your mind, if it is an idea you have, then first talk about it to anyone who will listen. Then, just do it—make a physical effort to make it happen. If you truly believe it and act on it, you can create it."

CHAPTER 11

Monday business had been better than usual at the Pizza Shack, so Bob pronounced the boycott broken. After closing cleanup was complete, Sarah convinced her mother and father to stop at the local coffee shop for a snack before going home. As soon as they entered the small café, two of Sarah's friends greeted her with the Earth Salute. This drew attention from other customers, several of whom smiled and acknowledged Sarah.

"Well, look who's a celebrity," Bob teased when they got settled in their booth. "Even the adults. One time on TV and the whole town knows you."

Sarah blushed and had a sheepish grin. "Yeah, I noticed. What's going on? Other than you two, Jessie and Sheryl are the only people I know in here, but everyone is smiling and nodding as if we've been friends forever."

Barbara's eyes crinkled in amusement. "That goes with the territory, Sarah. If you want publicity, often a little notoriety goes with it. People like to know someone that everybody else is familiar with. Particularly if they are—you know—a movie star or, as in your case," she winked at Bob, "a TV star."

Sarah studied her mom. *Was she joking?* She decided she was serious. "You mean, like I'm a star just because I've been on the evening news?" She ran a hand through her hair. "I don't want people staring at me everywhere I go. I guess there's no way we can get publicity without me having to be on TV, is there?"

"You get publicity wherever you can get it," Bob advised. "When you don't have to pay for it, it's even better. TV news is free."

Amused at her daughter's dilemma, Barbara smiled and said, "And either you do it or you don't. You take what publicity you can get and possibly become well known, or you forget the publicity and become a regular person like everyone else. You more than likely can't have it both ways."

Sarah girded herself with resolve. "Well, GARBAGE needs the publicity, so I'd better take it while I can, while the news people still want to talk to me. Maybe once we get the town behind us, it won't be so important. But until then..." Her voice trailed as she looked up to find the waitress smiling down at her. "A piece of apple pie, warmed up, with ice cream on top, and a

Coke, please," she grinned. "Vanilla."

Bob and Barbara ordered, and the waitress scampered off. She returned shortly with their order. They watched as she meticulously set pie á la mode in front of each, and two coffees and one Coke. She stepped back, admired her presentation, and buzzed off. "Being a celebrity has its advantages," Bob chortled. "Of all the times we've been in this place, that's the first time anyone has returned with our order in the same hour we placed it."

Barbara rolled her eyes at her husband and continued, "So, what's in store next for the group?"

"Our main goal is education. We want to show everyone what they can do to clean up, not only our own city, but also the whole world. It isn't enough to just clean up Cibolo Falls, so we've got to find a way to tell everyone, all over the world, to get involved. That's why we need the newspaper and television."

"Tall order for a kid from a town that very few outside of Texas know about," Bob replied. "Does your angel have any ideas stashed away?"

"I asked him that," Sarah answered. Her parents watched as she carefully pushed the ice cream off the pie with her spoon so it wouldn't melt so fast. She took a small bite of the ice cream and licked her upper lip with her tongue. "He said for me to just do what I can here in Cibolo Falls and not worry about it. He promised that leaders will show up at just the right time to help, but until then I should just keep working at it. So, if I have to become a star to do this..." She raised her nose and added dramatically, holding a limp hand in front of her, "Then I'll certainly do so."

Her parents laughed, both proud that she had accepted the price she would have to pay if she wanted the group to succeed. "So, what else are you guys up to?" Bob asked.

"This week we're going to start what Ralph calls, 'Educating Cibolo Falls.' At tomorrow's meeting, we're going to get everyone to paint up an Earth-minder. This is JB's idea. Each week we'll decide on a different slogan, and each of us will make small signs and put them in our yards, in vacant lots around town, or maybe in windows of businesses that will let us. Each sign, of course, will be different, but all will have the same slogan. On a certain day each week, we'll replace the sign with a new one with a different slogan. After a while, if the people keep reading the same slogan over and over, hopefully they'll decide that what we say makes sense and will do their part to help out."

"Great idea, Sarah," Bob congratulated. He deftly filled his fork with equal portions of the pie and ice cream. It quickly disappeared down his throat. "If you have about a hundred signs all over the city, people can't help but read them."

Sarah could see that her dad was apprehensive and waited for him to continue: "I might caution you, however. You must remind your people to keep an eye on their signs. If it rains or the wind blows it down, there are certain individuals around town that might decide that your group is doing more littering than anyone else. Once talk like that gets started, it's hard to stop it. Remember, the image you project is very important. It has to be impeccable."

Barbara took a sip of her coffee, then grimaced. "Ugh...bitter. People will always be quick to criticize you for not doing the very things you're advocating. You have to be real careful." She added a packet of sugar and slowly stirred the coffee. Pointing the spoon at her daughter, she continued, "Also, people may say things like, 'If you're so interested in cleaning up the earth, what about the car you drive?

It puts out emissions that cause all kinds of problems, but you still drive it. It seems to me, you're only doing the things that are convenient for you.'"

"I agree. Spook says this will always be a problem. People will have different ideas about what needs to be done and what is important. He said that the only answer is, as long as we're really trying hard to make a difference, and don't wan...ton—I don't know the word..."

"I think he is saying, 'wantonly,'" Barbara prompted. "It means unrestrained, unjustified, or perhaps, indiscriminate. You shouldn't go about indiscriminately destroying the countryside, animals, a tree, our resources, or whatever. You always need a very good reason for doing so."

"Yeah, that's what I thought. You shouldn't destroy or use stuff unless it's necessary, so we won't run out of…stuff—resources."

Bob drained his coffee cup and set it back in the saucer. "Okay, that takes care of wantonly destroying the stuff. What else?"

"Well, let's see. We're each going to start writing at least one letter or e-mail each week to one of our government representatives, either on the state or national level, asking them to help pass laws that might help Earth. We're going to try to keep up with what's going on, so we might get them to vote the right way on environmental bills. Smiley says he saw on the news that Congress is working on a bill, right now, that concerns the environment. The bill is not very good for the environment, but it's supposed to pass anyway. So, we're going to write letters to get it changed, before it's too late."

Bob winked at Barbara. "These kids just might pull some strings in Washington, even though they can't vote. That would be a change, for sure."

Sarah realized he was making fun of her, so she defended herself: "It won't hurt to try. If enough of us...you'll see. Anyway, pretty soon we're going to do a lot as a group. We're already getting signatures on petitions that we're going to take to the Cibolo Falls City Council in a couple of weeks. We're going to ask them to pass an ordinance for recycling garbage."

"Well, don't get your hopes up." Barbara toyed with her pie. "You may be completely ignored. Those people don't do anything because of kindness or because it needs to be done. One of the lessons you'll learn about politicians is that their first goal is to keep their jobs, meaning getting reelected. The second lesson is, they will only react when they are pressured, which means doing whatever is necessary to keep their jobs—the same as the first goal."

Bob picked up where Barbara left off. "To get politicians' support, you must show that you have enough people behind you to vote them out of office. Anytime you can show this kind of power, suddenly the politician will agree with anything you say, right or wrong."

"Well, that's exactly what we intend to do—force them to do it," Sarah resolved. "If they don't listen and do something, next time we'll get the right signatures, and force an election. Joe Cantu's father is a lawyer, and he said he would help us do it legally."

Barbara was impressed at their plans. She wondered if they would be able to keep up the enthusiasm when things didn't go quite as expected. "Well, this I can't wait to see, and I'll be the first to sign the petition." She winked her approval. "What else?"

"Later on in the week, we're planning to demonstrate in front of the shopping centers to raise awareness on some issues, particularly littering."

"You're kind of doing that already, aren't you, with your Earth-minder signs?"

"It's the creation thing."

"The creation what?"

"Spook says that for us to create what we want, just thinking of it and talking about it isn't powerful enough. We have to act on it. You know, do something physical to get the energy flowing. The more physical effort we put into something, the more chance we have of creating it. So, even though the Earth-minder signs take a small amount of physical action and are important, it's even better if we're out there giving it one hundred percent physically, getting the message across. He says it's all about energy."

Bob was silently amused as he watched Barbara, tongue in cheek, slowly nod at Sarah. "Uh-huh. It's all about energy? You've got to get the energy flowing?"

"Yes, ma'am. God's energy is creative energy. And to get this creative energy working at its best, we need to get involved physically. This will eventually result in people becoming more conscious...uh...conscientious about the issue, littering or whatever. Spook says we will be creating an attitude."

"Spook's 'tude," Bob jested.

"I like that. That's cool," Sarah retorted. "We'll be creating Spook's 'tude."

"You know, sweetheart," Barbara said carefully, "don't think you're going to change the world in a day. People are set in their ways and, even if they agree to change, it's going to take time. But, I will say this: as long as you keep trudging along, changes will come, and these changes will, over a period of time, add up. You just have to keep pushing."

"Absolutely," Bob affirmed as he flagged down the waitress for their check. "Don't expect everybody to do exactly what you want. Many people in this country don't think we have environmental problems and won't give a rat's behind about what you're saying. That won't change until they have an incentive to change, like a crisis or something. So, I don't know what to tell you. With the environment, a crisis may be too late, if it's not already."

Sarah held back her reply until the waitress left the check. "That's exactly what Spook said. And that's why we need more newspaper and television coverage, to tell the people what needs to be done. We aren't going to give up."

"For someone that didn't want people to notice you after being on TV, you certainly do hunger for being in the public eye," Bob remarked as he scanned the check and left a tip.

As they slid out of the booth to leave, Sarah replied, "That's the only way people are going to learn, Dad. We have to keep telling them over and over, until they accept that we really have something important to say." A sigh of resignation escaped her. "Even if I have to be on television."

Across town, the man stood at a street side phone kiosk. He nervously squeezed the portrait against his ribs with his left arm as he clutched the phone receiver in his left hand. He dropped two quarters in the slot and dialed the number for the fourth time.

"Damn it!" he shrieked when the answering machine again picked up. He beat the receiver against the phone box and slammed it back in the cradle. He lost two more quarters.

He set the portrait on the small shelf next to the phone. "I'm trying, Father!" he shouted, his voice belligerent. "Can't you see that? I'll do as you ask! I always do as you ask! I'll send her back to hell where she belongs! No, Father, that's not true! I'm not Beelzebub! Please, Father, don't say that!"

The man grabbed the portrait and took the few steps to his car. Jerking the door open, he flung the portrait on the front floor. He glared at the portrait, then slammed the car door and returned to the phone kiosk.

His hand shook as he retrieved his last two quarters from his pocket, dropped them in the slot, and redialed…

The phone rang as Bob opened the front door. He stepped back as Sarah ran to answer it. "I wonder who could be calling at this hour?" He checked his watch; it was eleven-twenty.

"Hello?" Sarah answered. "Yes, I'm Sarah McPhee….I don't—"

Bob and Barbara saw Sarah's jaw drop and her face pale as she listened to the caller. Sarah turned toward her parents, a prickly chill going up the back of her neck. Her eyes reflected her fear as she trembled. "No….I'm not who—stop it! No, please….No!…That's not true! I don't—"

Although not able to hear what the caller said, it was obvious to Bob that he could not let this continue. He took the phone from Sarah just as she began to cry. He listened, but heard nothing. "Who is this?" he demanded, only to have the person hang up. Bob stared at the phone as if it was going to answer and then hung it up.

Sarah shook with despair as she cried in her mother's arms. Bob watched, his jaw clenched in anger.

After Sarah had calmed down, she reconstructed the conversation the best she could and Bob wrote it down. He had to stop and wait several times as reliving it brought back Sarah's tears. They finished and she assured her parents they she was okay before going up to bed.

Once behind her bedroom door, she closed it and threw herself down on the bed and cried. She tried to muffle the sounds in her pillow so her parents wouldn't hear. She didn't want to burden them any more.

It was not a surprise that the familiar hazy whiteness began to cloud her mind. A faint hum cleared the whiteness and introduced the metallic voice of Spook:

"My best to you, little one."

Great, this is all I need, thought Sarah as she buried her head in her pillow. She answered, "Your best always gets me in trouble. And it's all because you're suggesting I do something that turns out wrong every time. Now someone wants to send me to hell. I don't know why, but he does, and it's all because of you. I don't know if I want to do any of the stuff you say anymore. I just want to be left alone for the rest of the summer. I want to be like everyone else. I don't want to save the environment—not even Cibolo Falls' environment, and I don't want to have an angel that talks to me, if what he says always turns out wrong and leads to trouble."

"Granted, granted. You are correct. Perhaps you have taken on a bit more than you can handle, if you feel it is so. It was not and is not my intention to lead you down a path where you do not clearly want to go—or are unable to go. My intention is only to guide you, if that is your wish. Of course, if you do not wish for my assistance, I will stand by, as I said I would. If in future times, you need my assistance—"

"No, please don't—" Sarah voice softened as she sobbed, "I don't want you to go. Not now, please. I want you to help me, to help us. It's just that I...You said that I would never take on more than I can handle, but I don't...I can't handle this anymore. I don't want to go to hell or die, or get hurt. I just want things to be all right and be easy for a while."

"There is more, little one. Speak it out."

She delayed her answer, overcome by her tears. "It's this love thing. I just can't do it. You told me that I should always try to love everyone and everything. But how I can love or respect someone who is trying to hurt me? That's not fair."

"It is certainly not meant that you stand by while someone else attempts to harm you. You should, by all means, take measures to protect yourself. You would also be strained to love such a person whose path here on Earth differs so much from yours. However, since he is also a part of God, you would be wise to honor and respect his decision to live how he sees fit, providing, of course, he doe not harm you or others and does not require that you live as he does. After all, he has his issues to live out, as you do, and you should respect that. Remember, you are related on the spiritual level, and on the spiritual level, nothing is either good or bad. It just is."

Sarah got out of bed and fumbled around her dressing table for a tissue. After she wiped her eyes and blew her nose, she tossed the tissue and sat on the edge of the bed. She rested her elbows on her knees, and supported her bowed head with hands covering her eyes.

"Little one, let me review the lesson on love. It is, of course, a matter of experience. Love depends on all the emotions, because you cannot totally love until you know or experience all the other emotions that are the opposite of love. The ones you are experiencing now are hate, fear, and anger. You feel this person hates you, and you hate him in return. You also fear that he is going to harm you, so you have become angry with him and, of course, me. Now, perhaps you are feeling that these emotions are bad, but they are not. They are only the opposite of love.

"Love is not fear, nor hate, nor anger. It is not jealousy or many other emotions that you might again consider bad. But, you need to experience all these emotions, so that you will truly know what love is not. That way, when you choose love over those opposite emotions, your choice is based on the real thing—what you have actually experienced.

"Of course, all this is a part of being God. Loving and being God—it is all the same. And to be better at loving and Goding, you need to experience it. All of it. That is going on with you today. Don't you see?"

He's right, thought Sarah, knowing that Spook was probably reading her thoughts. But I'm just tired of all the trouble I have to go through. Maybe I should give it one more try and just be careful that I don't get hurt. And I've got to quit being so scared of people. I also have to quit worrying about whether I'm making progress or not. I should just do what I can, and if it doesn't get done, whatever.

She leaned back and supported herself with her arms stretched out behind her on the bed. She looked at the dark ceiling with an odd pattern of streaks made by the street light that entered through the closed blinds. "Okay, Spook, I'll keep on working, if you keep on helping us," she said softly. She waited for a reply, but none came. "Spook, are you there?"

"Good choice, little one. Remember, you are special. I will leave you now. Much power and love to you."

"Thank you, Spook. I love you too."

Within minutes Sarah had drifted off to sleep. Despite what she had been through, she slept quite soundly that night.

The following morning, although still upset over the phone call, Sarah insisted that she be allowed to attend the GARBAGE meeting at the bridge. There were well over 190 in attendance, several of them older kids. Ralph's older brother, John, helped by the newscast, had convinced some of his buddies to come along, providing three pickup trucks.

With the money from their work at Pizza Shack, the group would be able to pay off Westside Budget Printers, order other needed pamphlets, leaflets and supplies, and pay the expenses of starting the website. According to Smiley's mom, they would be online by the next morning. Also coming out of this meeting was the first week's Earth-minder slogan: WHO PAYS THE TAB WHEN THE CITY PICKS UP YOUR LITTER?

Sarah reminded the group that the petitions on garbage recycling needed to be turned in by next Tuesday and suggested that everyone send at least one letter or e-mail to a local, state, or national government representative, then adjourned the meeting.

Police Chief Donald Sheck leaned back in his chair and listened as Bob, seated across the desk, recounted an ever-too-familiar story. "Is this the first call like this you've received?"

"For the past two weeks, since Sarah's assembly fiasco, we've been receiving a lot of what you could probably call crank calls but none this threatening. At least Sarah hasn't mentioned any others."

"You're sure she was actually threatened? Because, if you are, this is a different ball game from just a crank call."

"Yeah, well, according to Sarah, the exact phrase the caller used was—I've got it written down here." Bob removed a small paper from his shirt pocket and unfolded it. "Okay, here is what he said: 'You are next to the devil in power and, as God's emissary, I have been called to return you to your place in hell.'" Bob looked up and shrugged his shoulders. "I guess we can split hairs here, but it certainly sounds like a threat to me."

"Yep. Sounds like it. Did he call her by name?"

"No, he called her something else. She said it sounded like Billy Bob...but not actually. Earlier she had said Billy Bub, so it has to be something relatively close to those two. I can't even guess..."

Chief Sheck opened a file folder lying on the desk in front of him and leafed through a few sheets. Selecting one, he ran his finger down the sheet, then looked up: "Beelzebub?"

Bob considered for a moment, then shook his head. "Could be. She was pretty emotional at the time. It took us a while to get the whole conversation on paper, but that's pretty close. Beelzebub? Who...?"

Bob watched the chief nibble at his mustache, knowing that the chief already had experience with the caller.

Well, here we go again, thought Sheck. He was itching to get something concrete on this guy, if for no other reason than to just get him out of his hair. He seemed harmless enough, but Sheck had no idea who else this man was harassing. "Just another crazy."

"I'm sorry. I didn't catch that," Bob frowned.

"Oh, sorry. I was just mumbling. It seems we've had several complaints about this Beelzebub character in the past. I'm relatively sure he's a little wacko. But dangerous, I just don't know. All the reports are similar to Sarah's, and all except one have been about phone calls that warn the victims to either change their ways or they would be sent back to hell, Lucifer, or the devil. To date, however, no fire or brimstone. They seem to be hollow threats."

"And the other one?"

"It was in letter form, written in care of us, in fact," the chief answered as he looked through the folder. He removed one and placed it on top of the others. "Do you remember that nurse, three years ago, who murdered that kid under her care, saying it was God's will?"

"Uh-huh. Who doesn't?"

"Well, obviously, this guy couldn't reach her on the phone, so he sent her this typed letter with no return address, threatening to send her back to hell. That's how we finally got the correct name—Beelzebub. Until then, we only had names like Sarah came up with."

"Any idea who this Beelzebub is?" Bob asked, his brow drawn.

"There was a lot of speculation around here until one of our dispatchers, a college kid, ran across it in John Milton's *Paradise Lost.* Since then, we've also found various references in the scriptures, spelled in different ways."

"I don't suppose you've come up with any reason why he calls his victims Beelzebub?" Bob asked. "What significance could that have?"

Sheck searched through the folder and pulled out another sheet. He read over it without looking up: "It seems that this Beelzebub was one of the angels that fell out of grace with God, along with the devil. When God decided to throw Lucifer out, for good measure, he threw all the rebellious rascals out. They were all sent to hell. According to Milton, Beelzebub was the devil's right-hand man, or number two devil. So, this is what we think: when this caller decides someone is rubbing him the wrong way, he claims the person is the devil's assistant, hence, Beelzebub, and threatens to send them back to hell."

"Sounds like a religious fanatic, if you ask me," Bob countered.

"Possibly one that is a little tetched in the head." He cocked his bushy brow for Bob's benefit and grinned. "Got anyone in mind who could have made that call to Sarah?"

"Umph..." Bob answered, dourly. "You read the papers. You tell me."

"The way he's been ranting and raving, it certainly sounds as such, don't it? My first impulse is to drag old Hightower down here and see what makes him tick, but we can't do a hell of a lot without some positive proof. Threatening a life is serious, but my hands are tied until someone can come up with a handle on this guy...if he is indeed the guy. Without reasonable evidence, he could, and would, hang me out to dry and still get off scot-free. He's a powerful figure in this town—if not the most powerful."

A shadow of irritation crossed Sheck's face. "I'll tell you what, Bob. There ain't no way I'm even going to ask this guy a few questions without enough evidence to keep my head out of the noose. If he is the caller, he won't tell me, so I've accomplished absolutely nothing. On top of that, I'd be fired in a minute if he spouted off to just one council member. They already think that I'm just a little too independent. That's all they'd need to give me my walking papers."

"But the guy has threatened my daughter with her life. I realize it might be an empty threat, but what if he's serious? What if he decides to carry out his threat? I can't just lock her up until things settle down. And how would I know, anyway, when he's decided she's not worth the effort, and goes on to other 'godly' things?"

"Bob, right now, as far as I can prove, he has done nothing other than speak out against what he sees as actions contrary to what his church believes. I don't like this predicament, but I can't act until I get some meaningful concrete evidence. This guy has rights and, I assure you, he is well aware of what his rights are. Until he does something criminal, I can't do a thing."

Bob knew the man in front of him was right. He had confidence that the chief would help if there was any way he could. For a moment they both sat in uneasy silence.

Sheck was feeling both frustrated and helpless that he couldn't at least offer some reassurance. Several times in his career he had cases where he knew who was responsible but was unable to do anything because of the lack of concrete evidence. He saw the need for laws that protected the suspect, but sometimes these safeguards actually made it dangerous for the victim. This was another of those times.

Sheck broke the silence: "If it's any consolation, I want this scum as much as you. If you come up with anything—anything at all—give me a call. If it'll hold water, we'll go after him. I don't know how far we can take him, but if he is the one making the threats, we'll take him for a merry ride. Do you have Caller ID?"

"No, I don't."

"Then I suggest that you get Caller ID on your office and home phone, immediately. This may be the only way we can track this guy down. If he has any smarts at all, he won't be using his own phone. But you never know."

"Yeah, Barbara suggested last week that we get it, just so we could identify some of the cranks, but I nixed it, thinking the whole thing was going to blow over. Not much you can do about a crank caller anyway, except maybe return the call. Then you become just like them."

"You're probably right. An eye for an eye usually just breeds more problems. But, then again, who knows? Sometimes you have to fight fire with fire.

"Now back to the...For a while, I suggest that you not let Sarah go out at night, unless she is with either you or your wife. In the daylight hours, tell her to always have several of her friends with her, even to the point of their walking her right up to the door. If she doesn't have a cell phone, get her one, and tell her to always have it with her and turned on. Okay?"

"She has a cell phone and we'll get Caller ID." Bob rolled his head and massaged the tense muscles in his neck. "You know, we've been sitting back, hoping this thing with Hightower and the churches would blow over, but it hasn't. We've even considered getting a lawyer to convince him to back off. What he is doing is tantamount to slander...and against a child at that. Just because he believes a certain way gives him no right to set out to destroy another individual who thinks a little differently about things. He's nothing more than a thug, in my opinion."

"He would be appalled. Imagine someone getting a lawyer to threaten the big preacher. I'd certainly like to see his face when that comes down. Maybe a lawyer nipping at his heels is just what he needs. It seems he's way too big for his britches."

"Well, we would have already hired an attorney if it wasn't so expensive. I just can't afford to spend that kind of money just to rattle his cage, but it definitely will come to that, if he doesn't back off."

At the Tuesday night meeting of the Cibolo Falls Council of Churches, the Reverend Mark Hightower received his second setback in three days. Much to his surprise, over sixty percent of those present passed a proclamation that urged him to cease publicly denouncing Sarah McPhee as a cult leader and instrument of the devil. The main reason for this action against Hightower was the Joyce Brown news telecast. The majority of the members felt that his actions in days preceding the telecast were biased, unfounded, and unfair.

Hightower, insulted, stalked out of the meeting. Following adjournment, many of the religious leaders present privately discussed the likelihood that the CFCC would cease to exist because of the unfavorable publicity.

Rumors circulated about town on Wednesday afternoon that the board members of Hill Country Chapel of God also had a lengthy session with Dr. Hightower in a specially called meeting that morning. It was not known what was said or decided, but rumor had it the minister was angry afterward. He refused to even communicate with his staff. When called by reporter John Holland looking for information of what transpired at the meeting, the members refused comment. Dr. Hightower was unreachable for the rest of the day.

His publisher apparently reprimanded John Holland for his original features that labeled Sarah McPhee as a devil worshiper. In a small back page column of Thursday's *Gazette,* he retracted several things he had said about Sarah, blaming them on unreliable witnesses. He apologized for any problems he might have caused.

Journal Note

"You should always trust the universe. An experience will be of great value to the overall education of your soul, as well as the other souls involved. Your primary reason for living on Earth today is to experience everything, so that you might be more perfect. You are also here to teach and express God's unconditional love. Love, honor, respect, and worship all that God is—all that you are."

CHAPTER 12

The man had called asking for Sarah three times during the evening rush period, and Bob became agitated. Caller ID had listed the originating number, and it had been the same on all three calls. He had been tempted to call Chief Sheck but hesitated because he wasn't sure the man was the Beelzebub caller. He considered putting Sarah on the line to find out for sure, but he couldn't possibly put her through that again. Somehow he had to find a way to get the man to reveal himself.

"No, you cannot speak to Sarah until you identify yourself and tell me the purpose of your call," Bob said through gritted teeth.

Bob's abruptness didn't appear to affect the caller, who persisted in a muffled male voice: "Sir, my business in not with you, so I have no need to share my identity. Now, if you will, it's very important that you put her on the phone."

Although it was familiar, Bob couldn't place the voice. The accent didn't sound like Texas, unless maybe east Texas. It had a touch of a twang, but not like this part of the state. Perhaps the muffle distorted it to the point he was hearing something that wasn't there. *I've got to get this guy to show himself. I might not get this chance again.*

"Hey, asshole," Bob barked into the phone, "I don't think you quite understand me. Let me tell you again, real slow: no one is talking to Sarah until I know exactly who he is and what his business is. Do you understand that, or do I need to spell it out?" He waited for response. When none came, he added, "Okay, fine. I have a business to run here, so I don't have time to play your idiotic games. I certainly would appreciate it if you wouldn't bother us with your bullshit. Okay?" Bob started to hang up when the caller spoke:

"I am Immanuel, the son of God."

Surprised, Bob managed a laugh of disbelief for the caller's benefit. "Of course you are, and I'm the Queen of Sheba." This was the same man that had threatened Sarah, he was sure, but for Chief Sheck to act, he needed true identity.

"Okay, I'll buy it. So, you're Immanuel. I suppose that makes you the Emissary of God who called Sarah last Monday night. Am I correct?"

There was awkward silence. "Yes, I am the chosen Emissary of the Almighty, and I pledge that I will carry out his desires."

"Yeah, right. I can't imagine what your god—if you really want to call him that—desires. This must really be an important job, for him to pick such an asshole as you. Why don't you enlighten me?"

"I have come to collect the fallen one, Beelzebub, to return her to her mentor," came the impatient answer. "And you are obstructing God's intent. You may also have to answer to his wrath for your actions."

Bob laughed in an attempt to goad the caller. The sound of uneven heavy breathing came over the line. He knew he had to make the caller angry enough to get added to his hit list. It was the only way he saw to draw him out.

"Hey, Jack," Bob shot back. "I don't even believe in God, at least not the god you're nosing around with. That makes you absolutely nothing in my book. And as far as I'm concerned, any god that would choose you as an emissary is not much of a god to start with. Why don't both you and your god just go to hell? Then we'll be done with you. Do I make myself clear, or do you want to hear more?"

"How dare you rebel against the wishes of God Almighty!" the man blurted out. "Beelzebub must be returned to Lucifer because of her blasphemy! Now you may also have to join in her descent into hell!"

Bob answered calmly as his anger would allow: "You know, that's interesting. But, why blasphemy? I don't understand."

"She professes to be God, and in his name I must punish her."

"Let me see if I understand you correctly. It's all right for you to call yourself Immanuel, the Son of God, but it's not all right for Sarah to call herself God. Is that what you're saying? I want to be sure I have this right."

"How dare you, sinner!" came the sharp retort. "Now, you must pay for doubting the will of God and doubting my existence as the Son of God! You are now to join Sarah. Both of you will now suffer the wrath of the Almighty!"

"I can't wait. And I suppose you're the one, in all your holiness, that's going to do the punishing?"

"Sinner," the caller shouted. "You have burdened God with your malediction! The time is nigh for you to pay for your sins!"

Bob knew he needed to stay calm. Getting into a yelling match would not help. He had to make the caller think he wasn't being taken seriously. "Uh-huh," Bob forced a calm reply. "And when are you, the glorious Son of God, going to do this punishing? I don't think you can do it. I really don't think you have the power. In fact, I think you're a fake. And you know what? I think you are the one who should be going to hell."

"In God's name, I will come for you! You are about to suffer the confines of hell!" Immanuel retorted.

"When?" Bob asked. "When do you want to do this, so I can pack my bags?" There was no answer. "Well? God is going to be disappointed big-time, if you don't get the job done. What's he going to say if you put this off?"

"Right now! In the name of God, I'm going to send you to the devil, right now. Do you hear me?"

"Good, now you're talking. God would want it this way. And the sooner the better. I don't want to keep the devil waiting. Your place or mine?"

"What...what do you mean?"

"What's your problem? What kind of Son of God are you anyway?"

Bob chastised him. "You've got a job to do, and I am going to make it easy for you. Now, where do you want to meet?"

"Well...I—"

"Geez, it sounds like you are a little chicken shit to me," Bob badgered. "I'm all set to go to hell, and it looks like you're trying to back out. What's your problem, fella? Being the Son of God a little too much responsibility for you? God certainly is going to be dis—"

"Yes, yes! It's time for your journey into Lucifer's den. Meet me...meet me at...at—"

"The Miller Pavilion at the fairgrounds, in thirty minutes," Bob coaxed. "That would be ten o'clock."

"Yes, ten o'clock," came the sharp reply. "And you'll be returned to the devil where you belong, as Beelzebub will also be delivered in days to come."

Bob's heart sped up when he realized what he had gotten himself into. He hung up the phone. *I need a plan. I have to arrive at the pavilion first. Why didn't I allow myself more time? And what if Sheck isn't on duty? This could be more than I can handle.*

He dialed the police department. "Hello. Is Chief Sheck in?...Oh, when do you expect him?...He is. Well, can you contact him?...Okay, call him and tell him Bob McPhee called. Tell him I'm going to meet the Beelzebub caller....Yes, that's B E E L Z E B U B....Yes, tell him that I'm going to meet him at the Miller Pavilion on the fairgrounds at ten o'clock....Yes, tonight, in about twenty minutes....Okay, but hurry. I'm leaving now....Yes, ma'am....I'll just have to see him there. I can't wait. If I miss this guy, we may never get this chance again....Okay, and take down this number: 990-8491. Tell Sheck that's the number the call came from, and I'll have my cell phone with me. He has the number....Yes, good-bye."

Bob hung up the phone and pulled off his apron. "Barbara!" he called out through the open office door. She appeared in the doorway, shocked to see her husband checking the bullets in his 38-revolver pistol.

"Bob, what are you doing with that? What's happening?"

"I've lured our friendly caller out into the open,"

"Here?" Her eyes reflected her fear.

He stuck the gun in his back pocket and shook his head. "No, the fairgrounds."

"Oh, no you don't! You're not going anywhere!" Barbara countered as she grabbed Bob by the arm. "You call the chief and let him handle it! There's no sense in you getting hurt! He's experienced at this, and that's what he's paid to do!"

"He's out of pocket right now. I can't let this opportunity pass. If we don't get this guy, he may harm Sarah. I would rather deal with him face-to-face."

"No. Absolutely not! You're not leaving here!" she shrieked. "You don't know what you're doing!"

"What's going on?" An alarmed Sarah stood in the doorway. "Is something the matter?"

Barbara released Bob's arm and attempted to calm down. She tried to push back her fear, but it didn't work. She couldn't bring herself to answer her daughter. "No, Bob, no," she pleaded. "This is crazy and I won't let you go out there."

"Tell me," Sarah cried, her stomach churning in fear and frustration. She stared at the pistol in her dad's pocket.

Barbara answered with all the calmness she could muster, "Your father just talked to the man who threatened you. He wants to meet and—" She turned toward Bob and asked, "Just what are you going to do?"

Sarah covered her mouth with her hand as she looked first at her mom, then at her dad. She tried to reply but nothing came out. Feeling queasy, she found the stool and sat down under her parents' watchful eyes.

"I don't know what I'm going to do. I guess I'll just play it by ear. I do know he wants to send me to the devil. I don't have any idea how he hopes to do it. And that's the bad part. I don't know what or who I'll be up against."

Barbara studied her husband with piercing eyes. "No, just forget it! You're not going out there! Not only do you not know who—or what—you're dealing with, you have to do it in the dark. You wouldn't have a chance. The man is crazy, and I won't allow you to walk into a trap. There's no telling what he might do."

"Barbara, it's either him and me on more or less equal terms, or him against me or our daughter when we don't expect it. I'm going. There's no other way," he answered with a hint of fear in his voice that even he heard.

Barbara thought it was a crazy idea, and couldn't accept that there wasn't some other way to handle this situation. She saw tears well up in Sarah's eyes, and she walked behind the stool to put her arms around her daughter. "Please be careful."

Sarah began to sob. "It's my fault, again, isn't it? I don't want you to go. I'll be okay. I won't even go out anymore. So why don't you stay here?"

Bob forced a comforting smile. "No, it's not your fault. The world is full of crazies, and we have to deal with them when they get in our way. That's what I'm going to do. Then, maybe we can be rid of this guy, once and for all. I'll be careful, and I'll be all right." He squeezed her shoulder, met Barbara's eyes for an instant, and left.

Bob drove twenty miles an hour over the speed limit to beat the gunman to the fairgrounds, and to gain the help of any patrolman who stopped him for speeding. He pulled into the parking lot of Miller Pavilion, disheartened that Chief Sheck was not there. The area sat in complete darkness except for a security light at one end of the open-sided structure. He drove to the dark end of the building and parked the car. The dash lights glimmered off the pistol lying on the seat. Bob reluctantly picked it up, got out of the car, and quietly closed the door. He stood still for a moment and listened while his eyes adjusted to the dark.

He began to tremble and no matter how hard he tried, he just couldn't stop. He had doubts about being able to go through with what lay ahead. He hadn't fired the gun in three or four years. The way he was shaking, he probably couldn't hit something ten feet away. Did he even want to shoot somebody, no matter who he was or what he'd done? He had to pull himself together. This was the only way. Bob could either face the man now on Bob's own terms or later on Immanuel's.

Unable to hear or see anything suspect, Bob made his way into the dark pavilion. He wondered if his heavy breathing or the sound of his steps were going to give him away. His sweated profusely—his shirt was soaked, droplets rolled down his temple, and the gun became slippery in his palm. Coupled with the way his hands were shaking, he doubted that he could even hold the 38 tight enough to pull the trigger.

He forced his rubbery legs to carry him around and between the rows of tables toward the lighted end of the pavilion. At any moment he could be confronted by his nemesis. His legs cooperated more with each step, so now he could at least concentrate on the job at hand. In spite of the warm temperature, the light breeze that blew through the pavilion made his sweaty skin feel cold.

As he neared the lighted end of the pavilion, Bob collided with a wooden bench. The sound was answered with a soft thud. It sounded as if it came from about fifty yards away from the pavilion in the darkness near the cattle-judging barn. Unable to see past the light of the pavilion, Bob crouched down behind one of the tables just as a shot rang out. He ducked as the wood of the table splintered just inches from his head. *Shit, this isn't what I had in mind.* He fell to the floor as a tingle rushed through his body. His slippery pistol in one hand, he grabbed a leg of the long table with the other and jerked it on its side in one swift move. He slid it around to act as a barrier between him and the direction he believed the shot had come from.

On his knees, Bob peered around the table to locate his attacker. He fired his pistol in the direction of the barn—the noise rang in his ears.

Another shot answered from the dark; it plowed into the table. Bob ducked back in fear the table would not provide enough protection.

"Use two tables."

He fell back into a sitting position and pressed up as close to the table as he could get. "What the hell was that?"

"Use two tables. Make a V with the tables to protect you from three sides."

"Shit, now I'm hearing voices," Bob muttered to himself. "Is that you, Spook?"

"Yes, this is Spook. Now, use two tables. It will afford you more protection. Quickly now."

"If you want to help, how about saving me from the idiot that's shooting at me?"

"I am sorry, I have no ability to make major physical changes, so I am limited to advice."

"You can make images on the water. That's seemed pretty physical to me."

"The image was very difficult. It took the help of many of my associates. Now, this is no time to argue. The table."

"Whatever you say." Bob laid the gun on the concrete and returned to his knees. He reached out, grabbed the leg of the next table, pulled it close in one motion, and turned it over as he had the first. He slid both tables together in a V. "How's that?"

He got no reply from Spook and he wondered if he had imagined Spook talking to him. "What about the light, Spook? He still has the advantage." He still received no reply.

After several minutes of silence, Bob hazarded a peek around the table. He listened to make sure Immanuel wasn't changing position. A new tactic was necessary:

"Hey, Immanuel, you clown!" he shouted out, his voice quavering in fright. "Some Son of God, you are! I would think you to be more creative in your methods of delivering the wrath of God—like lightning or some minor miracle or something! Instead, you hide in the dark and shoot at me with a cheap gun! God is sure going to be disappointed in you! Why don't you just show yourself like a real Son of God would? After all, you are protected by God, aren't you? What about it, Immanuel?"

Two more shots rang out from the dark, one struck the table and the other disappeared into the night. Bob fell back into a sitting position and listened to make sure the gunman wasn't changing his location. Confident that he wasn't, he tried to figure out how to get the advantage on his attacker. He wasn't making any progress penned behind his barricade.

Several minutes later, the lights of an auto appeared at the far end of the parking lot. A vehicle came slowly toward the pavilion. When it came close enough for Bob to recognize it as Sheck's squad car, he motioned that he was under siege and toward the direction the fire was coming. The car stopped, and Bob's cell phone rang.

Bob fumbled for the phone in his back pocket and answered, "You're just in time."

"Looks like you've gotten yourself into a little predicament," Sheck responded. "Where is he? What's going on?"

"I think he's over by the cow barn. He's shot at me four or five times."

"Are you okay?"

"So far. It's been kind of a one-sided war. I can't see diddly."

"Well, I'm coming to join you. Maybe we can get a bead on where this guy is holed up." Just as Sheck opened the door and stepped out, a shot shattered the window on the driver's side. The chief ducked back into the car. He worked his way over to the passenger side away from the line of fire, opened the door, got out and crouched behind the right front fender. His voice came back over the phone. "Shit. That ole boy's a pretty good shot from that distance. He must have a cannon."

"You ain't telling me nothing," Bob answered nervously. "What next?"

"Hang on. Let me check on my back-up." Sheck worked his way back to the door, reached in for the radio mike, and asked about the status of his two officers. He apprised them of the situation, instructed one to come into the fair grounds through the back entrance to block the escape of the attacker, and the other to join Sheck. He replaced the mike, removed his 12-gauge shotgun from its bracket, and pumped it once, casting an ominous threat into the dark, still night.

He worked his way back to the front fender, and Bob heard his voice come over the phone. "Can you make it over here?"

"Afraid not. I'm a sitting duck in this light."

Sheck took quick aim with the shotgun and shot out the security light, the explosion creating an echo reverberating off the buildings of the fair grounds, followed by the tinkling of glass falling on the cement floor of the pavilion.

"How about now?"

In the same pitch dark as his attacker, Bob felt a measure of safety. He crawled between and around the tables and chairs, eventually joining Chief Sheck. "Glad you could make it," Bob stated as he leaned back against the front tire in a sitting position.

"You sure you're okay?" the chief asked, looking over Bob the best he could in the dark.

"Just scared shitless. I've never had anyone shoot at me before. For a minute there I thought I was a goner."

"Umm," Sheck replied as he looked over the hood. "Where is he? I didn't see where the shot came from."

Bob crouched, looked over the hood and pointed toward the cattle-judging barn. "About that direction. I think it was right behind the south corner, the best I could tell. You think we can flush him out?"

"We should have help here any minute. We'd better wait until they arrive, so we'll have his get-away blocked. I'd hate for him to slip through, particularly when we have him right where we want him, with no one hurt. We may not get this chance again."

"Yeah. You're right. Sorry to interrupt your movie."

"Thanks," Sheck chuckled. "It was one of those kid's movies. I thought it was never going to get over with. You gave me a good excuse to leave."

"Yeah, to get shot at. I'll tell you what. I'll watch a thousand kiddy movies to save having to go through this again. I'm glad I don't have your job. I would have quit after the first time someone shot at me."

A squad car, emergency light flashing, screeched on the pavement as it slowed to enter the parking lot. A moment later it pulled to a stop next to them. The officer got out and crouched next to Bob and Sheck.

"What do you have?" the officer asked.

"Guy with a gun, next to the barn," Sheck replied as he pointed toward the corner. "Turn your spot on that area and see if we can locate him. But be careful. He's already shot out my window, so he's pretty good, even at that distance."

The officer scurried back to his unit for the portable spotlight. When he returned, he crouched behind the fender and pointed the light toward the barn. Scanning up and down the barn, and around the nearby trees and shrubbery failed to turn up a sign of anyone.

"Well, damn. Where are you?" Sheck said under his breath. He opened the door and reached in for the radio mike. "Unit Five, this is Unit One. What's your twenty?"

"Unit Five, here. I'm at the west entrance. No action here. What am I looking for?"

"We are searching for what we believe is a lone gunman, possibly mentally deranged. He may be on foot or in a vehicle. Apprehend anyone who is suspect. Do you read?"

"Loud and clear, One."

"Unit Five, work your way toward the cattle barn on foot. Be aware that we will be working toward you. There are three of us—one in civies."

"Read you, One. I'll be working my way toward the cattle barn on foot, searching for one or more gunmen. Will be on the lookout for two officers and one civilian on foot."

Sheck turned to the officer. "Bring your light, and let's work our way around the barn. You go to the right and we'll meet you on the other side."

With a spotlight in one hand and his revolver in the other, the officer sprinted off toward the south end of the cattle barn. Although there would be a measure of danger, Sheck felt Bob would be safer if he tagged along than he would be if left behind alone. With Bob close behind, the chief made his way toward the north end of the barn. After several minutes of fruitless searching, they met up with the officer from squad Unit Five. The gunman had either driven away before the west entrance was blocked off or escaped on foot over the fence.

"Well, shit," Sheck said in frustration. "We had that sucker right where we wanted and let him slip away."

Bob felt a chill. "Oh, no, Sarah and Barbara are alone at the Pizza Shack. What if he decides to go ahead and—"

Chief shook his head. "At least I did that right. When I got your message, I sent an officer over there. I told him to stay until he heard from me."

"Good," Bob said, then grimaced. "Geez, you know, it just now dawned on me, that guy could have lured me out here and had a free shot at both of them. I guess I wasn't thinking too clearly."

"Yeah, I guess we've all made some mistakes tonight. I should've never let that clown get away. Well, at least we're all in one piece."

As they walked back to their cars, the chief told Bob that the phone number his Caller ID picked up was a payphone in the downtown area, so they were back to square one in their pursuit of the Beelzebub caller—now the Beelzebub gunman. They would definitely have to be take him more seriously.

The lone squad car parked beside the park road near the bridge was a chilling reminder to Sarah and the other kids of her constant danger. If there had been any doubt of the seriousness of the problem, it had dissipated with her father's confrontation with the gun-wielding man the night before.

Police Chief Sheck had put out the order for an officer to be close by anytime there was a scheduled GARBAGE activity. And when a reporter from the *Gazette* picked up the trouble at the fairgrounds on his scanner, Sheck told him it had been a false alarm. He figured that if the gunman did indeed have a mental problem, any kind of publicity might trigger further acts.

Ralph saw to it that the kids were given every detail about the shooting—at least, the details that he knew. He also felt it was important to rally around Sarah, not only in support but in protection. Bob had called early Tuesday morning before the meeting to ensure Sarah always had several friends with her.

There were already about 230 kids present at the meeting under the high South Park bridge, about half in the shade of the bridge and the other half soaking up the morning sun. JB delayed calling the group to order a few minutes longer as others arrived. She and Ralph took the opportunity to try settling Sarah down.

They could see that last night's trauma with the gunman had really gotten to Sarah. Her face, absent the usual smile, was drawn and gaunt, partly because she had slept very little the night before, but more so due to the constant stress of the past few weeks. She looked totally freaked out. Ever since they had picked her up on their bikes, she had said very little other than the usual greetings. They were determined to draw her out, to get her to talk about it.

"Hey, Sarah, did Spook have anything to say last night after your dad got home?" Ralph quizzed. "Any words of wisdom to help you get through this?"

Sarah, still sitting on her bike, reached into her pack and pulled out her journal. She flipped through a few pages and handed it to Ralph. "See for yourself," she said flatly.

Ralph silently read a few lines as JB looked over his shoulder. Puzzled, he shot a sidelong glance at Sarah, then read out loud:

"*Within every experience, little one, there is a lesson to be learned. And it is apparent this time you as well as your parents have chosen an extreme experience for the dramatic lesson involved. No matter how this continuing experience expresses itself, you must remember to love, honor, respect, and worship all that God is—all that you are.*

"There is one who feels he must avenge a wrong done his God, but however misguided or misinformed, he still deserves the respect of being an extension of God. As you have, he has chosen this experience. In days to come, you are urged to remember this."

Ralph looked up from the journal and exaggerated a grimace. "'No matter how the coming experience expresses itself—' Man, that takes in a lot of territory. It's totally scary, if you ask me. What does he want you to do, nothing, while you wait for this extreme lesson? Doesn't he give you any advice for protection at all?"

Without expression, Sarah pointed down the page. Ralph continued to read:

"Be cautious and take measures to protect yourself. However, you should also trust the universe in these matters. When all is added up, this experience will be of great value to the overall education of your soul, as well as the other souls involved. You would be encouraged to concentrate on surrounding yourself, as well as the other players in this experience, with God's loving, healing light. Your vibration of creative thought will manifest this light energy as a protection to you and all others involved. It is a matter of creation."

Ralph slapped the journal shut, his face wearing a look of anguish. "This is total bullshit. He's got to be kidding. He wants you to protect the very guy that's trying to kill you and your dad? Maybe Spook is really your dark angel, and he's leading you, and all of us, to destruction? I don't know if I even trust him or his advice anymore. Maybe it's good for you, but it ain't for me."

Sarah merely flipped a hand in resignation.

JB pinched Sarah on the arm. "It ain't easy being God, is it, sweetie?"

Sarah laughed nervously along with JB and Ralph, then JB took her usual place before the kids to open the meeting. After they had completed the Earth Salute and the group quieted down, JB thanked them for coming, then turned the meeting over to Ralph.

Ralph announced that though the website wasn't totally complete, they were now online at *garbageangel.com* and suggested that everyone check out the site and also have all their friends do so. He also urged everyone to get a GARBAGE T-shirt that could be purchased at a local T-shirt shop. He held up one of the shirts and praised Smiley for his artwork on the logo, and had him stand to have his success acknowledged by the group. Ralph then reviewed the previous week's activities and invited those that had interesting experiences during their GARBAGE work to share their stories.

As the meeting progressed, JB touched Sarah on the arm and gestured toward the road where an old red Jeep CJ had come to a stop. The occupants of the Jeep, three older boys, appeared to be amused.

"What do you think they want?" Sarah asked.

"Who knows? The one driving lives right down the street from me. He's supposed to be some big football hero or something—a senior next year, I think."

"Not bad-looking, huh?" Sarah quipped, forgetting the Beelzebub gunman. "Too bad we're not about two years older."

"Hey, you're better looking now than most of those juniors and seniors. Go for it. I've talked to him a time or two. That makes us old friends. Let me introduce you."

"Yeah, a time or two, like you stood behind him in line at McDonald's or something," Sarah replied, not really believing anything JB said about boys.

"Who cares? You want to meet him or not?"

"Well, we could use his Jeep for some of our cleanup jobs. I'll bet it'll hold a lot of garbage."

"Sweetie, hello. Anybody there?" JB chided as she lightly rapped her knuckles on Sarah's head. "What about you and him? Forget the Jeep. You want to be single the rest of your life?"

"Yeah, I guess you're right," Sarah answered wryly. "Especially, since, any day now, I'm going to be sent to the devil. I'd better get some major love while I can. At least, kissed." She grinned, "Just kidding, of course—I think. Well, let's do it."

She grabbed JB by the hand and pulled her toward the Jeep. "Now, you do know him, don't you?"

"Well...you know, kinda."

"Great. Thanks a lot. I'll remember this."

When they reached the Jeep, Sarah waited for JB to say something. JB said nothing as she winked at the boy on the passenger side. Sarah kicked her lightly on the foot. "Hi, guys," Sarah said. "I'm Sarah, and this is JB, my friend."

The driver held eye contact with Sarah. "Steve Forest. That's Sonny Johnson in the back." Gesturing toward the boy on the passenger side, he added, "This is Pinky Willman."

After a round of polite hellos, Steve again fixed his eyes on Sarah. "What's up? What are you guys doing over there?"

Sarah hesitated and JB jumped in: "We've organized a group to help clean up the Earth. You guys want to help us out? We sure could use your help." *We could use your gorgeous bodies, too. Especially you, Pinky Willman. You're hot. I'll pick up litter with you any day.*

"No, I don't think so," Steve answered indifferently. "We've got better things to do. Anyway, the government takes care of all that.

They'll see that the Earth is," he smiled at Sarah, "kept clean. You're just wasting your time."

Sarah didn't bother to answer as she glared at Steve. *What a jerk. Good- looking, but still a jerk. You're so stuck on yourself that nothing else matters. Well, I've got news for you, big man football star. We also don't need you or your friends.*

When neither JB nor Sarah responded, the uneasy silence unnerved Steve. "And, even if we did help, we'd be the only ones doing anything. So, who cares? Your little group couldn't possibly clean up C. F., much less the whole world. Why don't you just give it up?"

Sarah continued to glare with narrowed eyes at the boy in front of her. *We don't need you or your Jeep. If you were my boyfriend, I'd definitely tell you a thing or two.* She made an impatient gesture and turned toward her friend. "Come on, JB, we've got work to do." She grabbed her by the arm and pulled her away from the Jeep. JB followed reluctantly as she glanced back for a good-bye wave. She pointed at Pinky and waved again.

"What's the matter with you? What'd you do that for?" JB complained as she stopped Sarah before they returned to the group. "How can we make any friends if you're so rude?"

"Come on. We don't need them as friends and you know it. They are just jocks and they don't care about anything except themselves. They have no right to act that way."

"Now, wait a minute," JB objected, her lips puckered in annoyance. "I'm on your side, remember? I just wanted to meet some good-looking guys. I don't care if they don't want to save the world with us. Anyway, if they don't care what shape the Earth is in, and don't wanna help, it's our job to teach them. I thought that's why we formed this group—for education."

Sarah stuck her temple with a finger. "Duh, how stupid can I get? We're sent someone to educate and I blow it. Sorry.

"Wrong, *guerida.* You just don't have a clue, do you? Education? Come on. Look at the whole Earth-shaking, far-reaching picture here. We were sent some good-looking guys to meet, and you blew it. This has nothing to do with saving the Earth. It has to do with finding a real live boyfriend. I want to hook-up with somebody—anybody. I want to get down and make out, girl. And when some hottie shows up, I don't want to run away. *Compriende, mi hija*?"

They looked back at the sound of the Jeep pulling away. "Well, darn," Sarah resigned. "I guess it would be cool to get our minds off all this stuff once in a while. Okay, I promise, next time, I won't screw it up. If there ever is a next time." JB laughed and put her arm around Sarah as they walked back to the group.

"...and that's why we might take a new direction, this Thursday, with our demonstrations," Ralph informed the group. "We've been asked to help another local group by doing some demonstrating at Cibolo County Court House. This chance just came up this morning, and I think you'll like it. Okay, Gerald Cochran's dad wants our help, so I'll turn the meeting over to him, so he can tell you what's going on."

"Hey, dudes and dudettes," Gerald greeted as he looked over the group with a ton more self-assurance than the majority of those in front of him. His rugged and chiseled, acne-pocked face was framed by a square jaw. His large boxer's flattened nose further commanded attention. A muscular body was magnified by ragged cut-offs, a time-worn sleeveless T-shirt, and jogging shoes that should have long ago been discarded. The group immediately shut their busy mouths and got set for anything he had to say. He had the appearance of someone you didn't want to reckon with. He knew this and had no problem using it for his own comic pleasure.

"Can't wait to get you guys in high school," he said gruffly, intimidating a large part of the group. He glared over those in front of him, who wondered just how to take him. His sudden smile brought a few snickers from those that knew him, followed by laughter from the whole group. "Hey, just kidding. But, I still can't wait to get you in high school.

"Okay, I only got a few minutes, so I'll make it short," he said, referring to his notes. "My dad is the organizer of a group called CFWAC, which means Cibolo Falls Water Action Committee. The main purpose of the group is to watch over the C. F. area leaders who control growth and water use. In case you might want to know what they are, you have, Cibolo County Commissioners Court, C. F. City Council, Upper Guadalupe River Authority and Headwaters Underground Water Conservation District." He looked up and grinned. "Boy, that last one was a mouth full.

"CFWAC has more than 3,500 signatures on petitions to stop golf courses from getting built in the area until they figure out if we have enough water for them, say, ten years from now. Hey, if we don't have enough water to drink, then we don't want to use it to water the golf courses. Simple as that.

"You guys probably remember that the city had water restrictions last summer, and that's what my dad's group is complaining about. Before you let anyone build new golf courses that use a lot of water, the group wants the government to take enough time to figure how much water we will need in the future during dry spells. It's called a water master plan.

"I told my dad that we were demonstrating Thursday over littering, and he asked if we would help them out—in water conservation." Gerald panned over the group and smiled. "You guys with me so far? Okay, here's the deal, if you guys want to help. Thursday at two o'clock at the Courthouse, the Cibolo County Commissioners are meeting to discuss whether they're going to support the new golf course.

"That's when my dad and other members of CFWAC will deliver the petitions. Right now, the commissioners appear to be divided on what they want to do, but my dad says that if we demonstrate during the meeting, and we get our usual publicity from the newspaper, it will help bring more pressure from the people of Cibolo Falls. Then, maybe the commissioners will hold off on backing any new golf courses until we have a water master plan. So, if we want to, he suggests that we demonstrate outside the courthouse from about one-thirty to three-thirty. I really think it's a good idea. Like Ralph and Sarah have been telling you, this is what GARBAGE is supposed to be doing—protecting our resources."

Gerald looked toward Ralph and pointed a finger at him, indicating he was finished. He received good-natured ribbing from his buddies as he retreated to the rear of the group.

Ralph took his place in front of the group. "Cool, Gerald. Okay, is everyone okay with changing our demo to the Courthouse for water management?" He looked over the group. "Anyone have a problem with it?"

JB grinned. "Yeah, my dad loves golf. I'll probably get killed if I demonstrate to quit building golf courses." Several of the others nodded their agreement because they had the same problem.

"So, what are you going to do?"

"Demonstrate, of course," JB laughed. "I guess I'll have to wear a Halloween mask."

"Now, about the demo signs," Ralph announced. "We'll send you some suggestions by e-mail later tonight. Those without e-mail give me a call later. Now, Smiley's turn."

"Okay, everybody! Earth-minder time." Smiley announced. "Our first slogan this week was a real hit. We had about two hundred signs and posters plastered all over the place and everybody saw them. That's want we want, right?"

"Right!" the group answered in unison.

"Gotta tell ya, we need ideas for slogans. Send'em in. If it's good, you'll get your week. Okay, now get this, the slogan for this week is WHAT HAVE YOU DONE FOR EARTH TODAY? NOT AS MUCH AS EARTH HAS DONE FOR YOU." He looked over the group, smile in place. "Short and simple, but it says a lot. It was suggested by Joe Lopez." He gestured toward Joe, "Way to go, Jose!"

Smiley said to keep the signs professional looking and cautioned the group to keep an eye on their signs so that they didn't litter. He then turned the meeting back to Ralph.

"Okay, two more things, and we're outta here. I took that Dr. Pauley guy from the Parapsychology Institute to see Sarah's image. He thought it was really awesome and said they're going to do some research on it, which is good for us, I guess. Anyway, all you guys need to take your parents and friends to see it. Once word gets around, it'll be good pub for us. Gotta remember, though, some people won't be able to see it, for whatever reason.

"Last deal. About 5,000 signatures have been turned in on garbage recycling. That's great, guys. Meeting adjourned. See you at the one-thirty on Thursday at the Courthouse."

After the majority of the kids went their separate ways, JB, Ralph, Smiley, and Sarah rode their bikes into town to Cibolo Falls City Hall. They checked with the clerk to make sure GARBAGE was still on the council meeting agenda for Thursday of the next week. The clerk checked the schedule and affirmed that Sarah McPhee of GARBAGE would be allowed five minutes of council time at about three-fifteen.

The three kids then escorted Sarah to the Pizza Shack for her eleven-thirty kitchen shift. They were greeted by Bob with news that Joyce Brown had called earlier about taping a segment Thursday for her Friday *Ecology Today* segment. She was to arrive about one o'clock in the afternoon.

The phone rang several times and Sarah, putting a pizza in the oven, waited impatiently for her father to answer. She was expecting a call from JB, but her father instructed her not to answer the telephone because of the chance it might be the gunman. The phone kept ringing. Sarah wiped her hands on her apron and peeked out the kitchen door. Her mother, busy with a customer, nodded for her to answer. "Pizza Shack. Sarah speaking," she greeted cheerfully.

"Hey, sweetie," JB gushed across the line. Let me tell you what happened today." JB rambled for about five minutes, then said she would try to come by later if she could get her mom to spring for a pizza.

As soon as Sarah hung up the phone rang again.

"Hello."

"Well, well, I finally have you, Beelzebu*b*," came the familiar muffled voice over the phone.

A chill ran up the back of Sarah's neck and she regretted having answered. Her first thought was to hang up. *Do it now. Don't even talk to this man.* But something held her back. It was as if she needed to hear what he had to say. She wanted to hear more about his confrontation with her father at the fairgrounds. She had to know why he wanted to harm her. Somehow, deep inside, she felt that it was all a misunderstanding and the man would stop if she could only explain that she had never meant to hurt him.

"What do you want? Why don't you quit calling me? And leave my dad alone. He hasn't done anything to you. Me neither."

"Oh, no. I can't do that," came the muffled reply. "You see, I made a promise to Father to return you to the devil, because of your blasphemous behavior. You do understand that, don't you? I have been given this honor, and I shall carry out my duty. I failed last night in eliminating your protector, but no, I shall not fail again. The power of God Almighty is with me, and you will not escape your just punishment."

Tears filled Sarah's eyes as fear and helplessness engulfed her. A wave of nausea and dizziness forced her to sit down on a stool behind the cashier's counter. She could think of nothing to say but felt she couldn't hang up. She wanted to end this nightmare, now, once and for all. A morass of jumbled thought, intense anger, and paralyzing fear made her oddly wish that he was standing in front of her, so she could lash out at him—physically destroy him. She couldn't take anymore; she had to fight back.

A sense of protection spread through her. Love and compassion pushed away her fear and anger. Then confusion took over. How could she feel love for this man? How could she possibly feel compassion for the man who threatened to kill her and her father? Why do I feel this way, Spook? She projected. How can I feel love for someone that wants to destroy me? Help me understand, Spook. Please.

Sarah didn't see her dad come through the front door holding a broom and dustpan. He stopped when he saw his daughter with the phone cradled in both hands, leaning with her head against the wall. Although her eyes were closed, tears trailed down her cheeks. It took but an instant for him to understand.

"I...I am God, and I love you. You are also God. I know that, and no matter what you do to me, I will still love you. You must understand that."

Bob, astonished at what Sarah said, touched her on the shoulder, took the phone, and put it to his ear.

"No! That cannot be! You're the emissary of the devil! You can't love me! I'm Immanuel, the Son of God! You are the devil! I don't want your love! Don't love me!"

"Hey, creep!" Bob exclaimed. The line went dead. Bob replaced the receiver and reached out for his daughter's hand. He assisted her in standing and took her into his arms. She felt so small and fragile as she buried her head into his chest. "You did right. That man needs your love. He needs all the love he can get. That may not even be enough."

Journal Note

"If you feel uncomfortable in whatever you are doing, whatever you're experiencing in life, change it—create a different life. Do whatever makes you feel good inside. If you have indecision, go with what sparkles, what is open and alive. Never go with what looks dull. Then you cannot be wrong. This is what love and God are all about."

CHAPTER 13

The timing of the demonstration at Cibolo County Courthouse was perfect. Joyce Brown and her *Ecology Today* cameraman arrived just after the group got started. KGEX TV's video, along with John Holland's photographer captured the group of 210 as they silently carried their signs and flashed the Earth Salute. When Joyce was satisfied that she had ample footage of the demonstration, Sarah, Ralph, and JB accompanied her in the news van on a tour around town to get video of the Earth-minder signs. Close behind followed the ever-present Cibolo Falls squad car.

The tour guides then dropped their little bomb on Ms. Brown—a visit to Sarah's image on the water. After their initial shock, the reporter and her cameraman spent over an hour taking video footage of the image and interviewing Sarah at the water's edge. They also got pictures of the stream of locals who had come to see for themselves what everyone was talking about.

The reporter knew full well the ramifications of the image and what it could mean not only to Sarah and GARBAGE but also to her news program and possibly her own career as well. After their return to the demonstration, she held another short interview with Sarah on the Courthouse steps and then left for San Antonio. She was anxious to get back and start editing because the show was due to air the following night.

With only a short time left in their planned demonstration time, Sarah borrowed a sign that simply read, WATER OR GOLF—WHICH WILL IT BE? She and Ralph fell in step with JB and the other demonstrators slowly making their trek around the Courthouse. After a few minutes, they saw Steve Forest's familiar Jeep CJ pull into a parking space in front of the Courthouse. Two boys got out and sat on the hood. JB was quick to notice that Pinky Willman was with Steve. She nudged Sarah, who smiled her acknowledgment.

"Wow!" Sarah exclaimed. "I don't know what's the matter with me! My heart is beating too fast, and I feel more nervous than I do when Ms. Brown interviews me."

"Hey, sweetie," JB giggled. "You must be in love."

"But he's such a jerk, and what chance would I have with him anyway? All those high school girls are probably all over him. And after the way I treated him the other day, he probably won't even speak to me."

"Think again, *querida*," JB countered. "Look, he sees us. He just pointed us out to Pinky. Sweetie, I think you're going to get another chance."

As they approached the Jeep, Sarah nudged JB, "I'll try not to act like a fifth grader this time."

"Good plan, but ignore them. Make them come to us."

"Ignore them? What if they don't do anything?

"They will, I promise. Go, girl."

"Hey, how's it going?" Steve said as the girls passed in front of the Jeep.

"Hi, Pinky, Steve," JB answered smiling. Sarah waggled her fingers.

Both boys stepped down from the Jeep and joined the girls. JB and Pinky slowed to let Sarah and Steve go ahead. "Hey, Sarah," Steve stammered. "I don't know if I like you best as a TV star or as God."

Sarah smiled and continued to walk. "So you like me, huh. That's news to me."

Steve fidgeted for an answer as he tagged awkwardly along with her. She glanced over at him and liked what she saw. His height and muscular build, the dark eyes and angular jaw, and even the slightly crooked nose were really cool. Add on the bronze skin and dark brown, windblown hair and he turned into a real hottie. She wasn't too thrilled about the tattered cut-offs or the ragged-out black running shoes without socks, but she was sure, given time, she could polish him up nicely.

"Well, you know, you're okay. It's kind of like, you know, I've never known anybody that's a celebrity. Tuesday I didn't even know who I was talking to."

"I'm the same person today as I was then."

Steve kept in step with Sarah as he kicked a small stone along in front of him. After a few agonizing minutes, he broke the silence. "I suppose, since you're God and all, I guess you're going to strike me down or send me to hell if I don't agree with you and still play golf?"

Sarah, amused at not only his statement but his awkwardness as well, could tell he was frustrated because of her distant attitude. As they passed the squad car parked on the shoulder, she rapped her knuckles on the fender and waved at the occupant.

"Hi, Officer Riley. Good to see you." She greeted him openly.

Unsettled, Steve blurted out, "And if I waste water and throw my litter all over town, I suppose you're going to send me to hell for that, too?"

"No, not at all, Steve. As far as I'm concerned, your can do whatever you want. I may not agree with you, but I'm not your judge. If you wanna trash out the Earth, it affects us all, and that bothers me. We're part of the whole Earth, you know, and it's like your actions, good and bad, have an effect on me, you and everybody else. Get it? Whatever you do, I can only love you and allow you to live in what you believe to be the right way."

Steve stopped in mid step, raised a doubtful brow and grinned as he hurried to catch up with Sarah. "Say what? You love me? Hey, wait, already. I didn't think...I mean—"

"Never mind, Steve. You don't understand."

He walked along beside her scratching his head, his lips pressed tight and his jaw set in concentration. He gave her a wary sidelong look. "What do you mean? I don't understand. One minute, you...then you tell me that you love me, but then you…what's with you, anyway? You sure do have a lot of crazy...you know, beliefs. Do you learn that in church or what?"

"No, I don't go to church. Most churches around here don't even agree with how I think or what I know. But, I do have a special way of finding this stuff out. Maybe someday I'll tell you...if we become friends."

Steve knew she was weird, however cool and sexy. It concerned him that she didn't treat him like the other girls did, that she didn't like him, and that she was turned off by him. She did tell him she loved him, but the way she said it, it was like she was talking to her mother or sister. In the two times that they had talked, she made him feel so unsure, but he still felt good being around her. The whole thing was crazy. He wanted to reach over and touch her to see if she was really real, suspecting, however, that she would probably kill him if he did.

Steve turned around to look for support from Pinky, but he and JB had stopped almost where they had started. They sat on the curb and talked. Steve looked back for Sarah as she walked away from him. He sighed in frustration and quickly caught up with her. As he fell into step beside her, she was aware of his return but didn't respond.

"Okay, okay, you win," he resigned. "I guess I believe what you say. I promise to support water conservation, and help to get the city all cleaned up, and do my best not to litter. I'm a changed man. Now, are you happy?"

"Wrong, Steve. You're not doing it for me. You're doing it because it needs to be done, not just today, but everyday. If you don't want to commit to that, why bother? It seems to me you should want to do it anyway, whether you're my friend or not."

"Come on, girl, you don't give up, do you?" Steve protested. "Give me a break. Nobody—not even you—can go through life doing exactly what's right for Earth. That would be impossible and you know it."

Sarah sensed it was best not to push him. She needed to become his friend, then help him understand.

She smiled and grabbed his arm. "Hey, I do something wrong everyday, but I keep trying, and I try to keep learning what needs to be done. If everybody did the same, we could really change the whole Earth. Maybe that will never happen, but I'm going to try."

When he didn't respond, she stopped and boldly pulled on his arm, turning him toward her. "You know what, Steve? I'm sorry. I had no right to say those things to you, because I don't know you." Letting go of his arm, she touched him on the cheek, letting her fingers linger there for a moment. "I like you. I really, really like you." Sarah turned away to resume her walk. *I can't believe I said that.* A faster step and a few deep breaths seemed to settle down her rapid heart rate. She was just about to get her head together when he caught up.

They walked along without speaking. After a few uneasy minutes, he reached over and took her demonstration sign. "So, how do you carry this thing?"

She slipped her arm inside his, and felt an odd shift in her chest, releasing a tension she wasn't even aware was there. A strange energy passed between them that she had never experienced with anyone before, and she felt it taking her breath away. She had never hooked-up with a boy before, and it made her feel really good. She wanted to hold onto this special moment of exhilaration forever if possible.

They continued to walk until they had made the full circle of the Courthouse. As they approached JB and Pinky, JB was the first to see Sarah on one of Steve's arms and the sign in the other. She touched Pinky on the shoulder and pointed: "Damn…would you look at that."

Because Thursday was a slow news day, the Friday edition of the *Cibolo Falls Daily Gazette's* headlines read: "GARBAGE takes to streets." The sub headline: "Sarah's group joins with CFWAC to halt new golf course."

In addition to two pictures of several of the demonstrators, John Holland had written a positive article on the various government entities concerned with water and their actions thus far on the new golf course request.

In another article, Holland discredited the rumor about the so-called phenomena at South Park. He reported that he and his photographer had investigated for themselves and neither could see an image of Sarah McPhee on the surface of the Guadalupe River. "It is all a hoax," he declared.

If the *Gazette's* follow-up story on the demonstration wasn't enough to convince the people of Cibolo Falls that GARBAGE had become a driving force in the ecological arena, Joyce Brown of KGEX in San Antonio was. In her Friday news magazine program she appeared on the street in front of the Courthouse. Kids occasionally crossed behind her toting demonstration signs. With her usual air of confidence, Joyce spoke:

"This week, in our search for local crusaders who make a difference in the ongoing battle to save and maintain a strong and healthy environment, we have traveled to Cibolo Falls, Texas, an hour's drive northwest of San Antonio. Behind me you can see a group of kids demonstrating in front of the Cibolo County Courthouse. Their main goal, says the leader of these kids, is to do their part to clean up the Earth, and educate the public about conserving resources. Today, they have teamed up with Cibolo Falls Water Action Committee, a local water conservation group, to protest the proposed building of a new golf course in Cibolo Falls. They claim the large amount of water needed to maintain the course could threaten the water supply.

"The kids' group is called Grass-roots Alliance for Reviving and Building a Greater Earth, or GARBAGE. What makes these kids so interesting is their 14-year-old organizer and accepted leader, who maintains she converses with a guardian angel. Because of information she has received from this angel, she believes she is God. In fact, she says, we are all God and she urges us to act like it to help our planet.

"You may remember on our newscast last week, I spoke of this teen God, Sarah McPhee. At that time, the Cibolo Falls Council of Churches, led by Dr. Mark Hightower, the charismatic minister of Hill Country Chapel of God, boycotted The Pizza Shack, Sarah's family-owned and operated restaurant. It was their intent to force Sarah to discontinue what Reverend Hightower termed as 'her blasphemous ways.' Undaunted by the religious community's opposition, the kids fought back, not only forcing the church to back off, but winning over the support of the majority of this town of 20,000 in the process.

"Spurred on by this success and the favorable publicity, the kids have stepped up their campaign to not only clean up Cibolo Falls and the state, but have taken their movement Earth-wide.

"We caught up with this whirlwind of a teenager today, as she and over two hundred of her cohorts demonstrated in front of the Cibolo County Courthouse to gain the attention of the County Commissioners. The commissioners have a say in whether a planned new golf course will be given the go-ahead."

Joyce Brown turned and gestured for Sarah to join her.

"Here I have Sarah McPhee. Sarah, you appear to have taken on a big job here. Do you really expect to stop the building of a new golf course in Cibolo Falls?"

"I don't know. We're only asking the commissioners to wait to approve it till studies are done and rules set up. Everybody knows that golf courses use a lot of water. That might not seem so important now, but it could be in fifteen years. We've already had water rationing in late summer, so we feel that future water needs should be figured out before any new courses are built. Maybe the Water Action Committee can make a difference with their petitions, but I don't think the commissioners care what us kids have to say."

"So, why are you here, if you don't think the commissioners will pay any attention to you?"

Sarah began to relax and enjoy the interview. "Somebody has to tell the people of Cibolo Falls what's going on, so it may as well be us. Then maybe they'll put pressure on the commissioners."

Sarah flashed a confident smile and looked up at Joyce: "Programs like yours are the biggest help, because you can reach more people than we can. We appreciate the opportunity to be on it. People can also check us out on our website at *garbageangel.com.*"

"And we appreciate your taking time from your busy schedule to talk to us. Now, what else is your group doing to achieve your goals?"

"Our main goal is education. If we can persuade the people to help out, it will be much easier. Everyday, each one of us spends fifteen minutes on some project to help out Earth. Some write letters, some pick up litter, and some go door-to-door passing out conservation literature. Each week we select a slogan, then we make signs and place them around town."

"And what was this week's slogan?" Joyce asked.

Several of the more creative signs danced across the screen. Sarah beamed, "WHAT HAVE YOU DONE FOR EARTH TODAY? NOT AS MUCH AS EARTH HAS DONE FOR YOU."

The camera returned to Sarah and Joyce. "I was told you have a big project coming up, Sarah. Would you tell the *Ecology Today* audience what you have planned?"

Sarah felt at ease in front of the intrusive camera as the interview continued. Her confidence had elevated to the point that whatever question was asked, she had an answer and, because she and Joyce thought so much alike, she could even anticipate what Joyce was going to ask. Sarah's self-assurance showed in every word and gesture. She gained control of the whole scene. "Yes, next week we'll ask the Cibolo Falls City Council to start garbage recycling in Cibolo Falls. We already have 5,000 signatures supporting us."

"That's about one-fourth of Cibolo Falls' population. Do you expect the council to listen to your pleas?"

"Well, since we don't vote, we don't have that kind of power, but because of the newspaper and your program, we hope some people will hear our message and vote for us."

"Sarah," Joyce Brown said in a more serious tone. "By now, everyone knows that you have said that you are God, and that you got this information from your guardian angel, a voice you hear in your head. Would you comment on that, and how it applies to the work you are doing with GARBAGE."

"Oh, no, please. I don't want anyone to think that I'm the only...not just me." Sarah held out her left hand, palm up, as if holding a globe. She tapped a finger around the imaginary globe as she spoke: "The whole Earth, it is God. We are all God. Even the rocks and trees and birds and animals. We are all a physical extension of God." She continued to tap the globe. "The whole Earth is made up of trillions and trillions of sparks of God. You and I, and everyone else is one of those sparks." She pitched the imaginary globe up, her face glowing in awe. "All God," she smiled.

Joyce followed Sarah's demonstration with fascination. *This kid is either totally nuts, a con artist, or a developing genius. Whatever, this is a fantastic program..*

Sarah held both hands out in front in a pleading gesture: "If just one of the sparks is lost, the whole of Earth, meaning you, me and everyone else, loses something. We all suffer. If people would only understand, there is a higher harmony going on between all the parts of Earth, and when there is even the smallest disruption in that harmony, when even a little spark of God is lost, we all lose. We must not, in any situation, harm any other spark of God."

"Uh, yes, I see." the reporter nodded, "And this…your guardian angel gave you this information?"

"Yes, ma'am. He speaks to me nearly everyday."

"Let's go to the river, Sarah."

The program broke away for a commercial and returned as Sarah and the reporter stood on the bank of the Guadalupe River. "Sarah, something very exciting has happened. Will you tell us about it?"

"Yes ma'am. A few weeks ago, we had trouble getting other kids to join our group, because they didn't believe that Spook really talked to me. Spook told me that he'd do something to convince them."

"Spook? Who is Spook?"

"Oh, I'm sorry. Spook is what I call my guardian angel. Anyway, they didn't believe me, so Spook made an image of me on the top…on the surface of the water. When the kids looked on the water they didn't see their own reflection—they saw me. I'm picking up some trash and putting it in a garbage sack. The words on the side of the sack say, 'Clean up your Earth.'"

"After they saw your image, then the kids believed you?

"Yes, ma'am, and my parents, too. That was good, because I don't think they believed me very much before."

"Do you think that I might be able to see the image, Sarah?"

"That would be great. I'll bet the people watching television can see it, too," Sarah gushed. "It's really cool."

"Sarah, before we have a look at the image, we're going to have to take another commercial break. I just want to thank you for being on *Ecology Today*. I want to wish you and your group good luck and hope you achieve all your goals, for Earth's sake."

Sarah smiled and shook Joyce's hand. "Thank you for having us. You make our job easier."

After the commercial, the program continued with Joyce Brown in the KGEX studio:

"Welcome back. Before I saw what you are about to see, I was a little skeptical of Sarah and her story of the angel. I'm sure, after you see the following video footage, you will agree that Sarah McPhee is no hoax—she is not performing any magic. This is real. And Sarah does have a guardian angel or some other paranormal entity speaking to her.

"I must tell you, Sarah mentioned before we looked at the image, yesterday, that there are those that don't see it. We have found the same to be true with the video. Nearly everyone in our studio has viewed it. There were two that saw nothing on the water's surface but the reflection of my assistant and his video camera. Now, the image of Sarah on the surface of the Guadalupe River in South Park, Cibolo

Falls, Texas."

After the video was shown, Joyce Brown made no further comment on the tape, letting it speak for itself. She smiled with confidence. "Sarah McPhee. Remember the name. I'm sure you haven't heard the last of her. This is Joyce Brown with just another of the many stories of humankind's struggle to live on Earth in a way that's compatible with nature. See you next time on *Ecology Today.*"

If not the most popular citizen of Cibolo Falls, Sarah became the most sought after. The *San Antonio Express News*, San Antonio's only daily newspaper, expressed interest in publishing a public interest piece on Sarah to appear the coming week. The reporter dropped in unannounced at the Pizza Shack on Saturday morning, so Bob called Sarah on her cell phone, interrupting a big meeting at Ralph's. She, Ralph, and JB biked to the Pizza Shack, where the reporter interviewed them for two hours in the office. They ended the session by taking the reporter to the river. They had to wait in line for a few minutes before the reporter got to see the image for himself.

At noon, Sarah and her parents received another surprise when a producer from Cable News Network called to see if he could come by. He wanted to do a segment on Sarah and GARBAGE for their weekly *Earth Scope* program on CNN, a thirty-minute segment much like Joyce Brown's *Ecology Today*, only broadcast worldwide. The producer, on vacation in San Antonio, had seen Sarah on Joyce's program and drove to Cibolo Falls to see the image for himself on Saturday morning. He arranged to tape all day Thursday, so they could film Sarah as she addressed the Cibolo Falls City Council.

With all the excitement generated by the *San Antonio Express News* interview and the CNN call, Sarah provided very little kitchen help Saturday afternoon. Bob accepted the fact that, on this day, she had absolutely no value as a pizza cook and called in another employee to take over for her.

The new cook had just arrived when Steve Forest dropped in for a visit, and Sarah introduced him to her parents.

"So, you're the famous linebacker that has so much promise this year," Bob jibed as he wiped his hand on a towel before shaking Steve's. Barbara smiled and shook Steve's hand. She cocked a knowing brow and decided her daughter had picked a live one. *How did she do it?*

"Yeah, that's what they're hoping," Steve stammered. "I'm just one guy, though, and we have a lot of holes to fill." Rescuing him from her parents, Sarah grabbed him by the arm and led him off to a booth.

"One Pizza Supreme, coming up," Bob called after them. He turned to Barbara and whispered, "She could've done worse. Kinda big, isn't he?"

"Sexy enough," she grinned. "Better hold me back or I might move in on her. What's the linebacker stuff?"

Bob laughed, "I'm sure you could. You're still the siren you always were. I don't think Sarah would go for that, though. Linebacker is a defensive position on the football team. When Sarah told us about Steve the other night, I asked Donnie Rimkus about him. Well, Donnie hates football players, but don't kid yourself; he keeps up with the team and knows all about who plays what. He says that Steve is better than good, whatever that means."

Barbara smiled as she turned away. "I think I'll just stick with the sexy part."

"Hands off, lady," Bob laughed, popping her behind with the towel.

Barbara delivered the pizza and two large Cokes, and returned to the stool behind the resister for surveillance. Barbara watched Sarah talk endlessly as Steve scarfed down the pizza, slice by cheesy slice.

Bob retreated to the kitchen, but Barbara continued to watch as Steve started his fourth slice. She wondered just what her daughter was so animated about. *She's probably driving him crazy with her save-the-world stuff. She's got to stop the serious talk and drool over him once in a while—at least I would.* Her own girlish thoughts continued through the incessant ringing of the telephone.

"Get the phone, Mom," Sarah called out. "Are you gonna get it or what?" She slid out of her seat just as Barbara jumped up and rushed over to answer.

"Sometimes she's completely out of it," Sarah said as she slid back into her seat. "I think all this stuff going on is getting to her. There's all kind of shit coming down that we can't control." Sarah took a large draw on her Coke, and Steve nodded his understanding.

Engrossed in Steve's battle with the pizza, Sarah became fascinated with a smudge of tomato sauce on his chin. She dreamed of licking it off his face and then replacing it, only to lick it off again. It suddenly became a tomato sauce fantasy, so much so she felt her face flush in embarrassment. If Steve noticed, he didn't comment. He devoured the last slice.

Back to reality, Sarah glanced over at her mom who was still on the phone. Bob stood nearby. Ever mindful of the reaction of whoever answered the phone, she excused herself and joined them. Steve, aware of Sarah's mood change, watched the three of them as he gulped the last swallow of Coke and wiped his mouth with a napkin. New to the group, he was not yet privy to the problems of the Beelzebub caller. Their reaction, however, told him the phone call was very important.

It appeared to Sarah that her mom enjoyed her confrontation with Immanuel. "No, she is not, and even if she was, you definitely couldn't talk to her....Oh, yes. I know exactly who you are. You're the idiot that took shots at my husband in the dark....Yes, you got that right....Of course, and as far as I'm concerned, you can crawl right back in the hole you came out....Yeah, you're also a joke...."

Bob couldn't help but be amused at Barbara's handling of the caller. He tried to imagine what was being said on the other end of the line.

"Oh, is that so….Yes, I certainly did. You say you are a man of God, yet you act like the scum of the earth....No, I'm not afraid of you or your god....By all means, be my guest." Barbara shook her head at Bob and circled a finger around her ear. "Add me to your list....Hot dog. I sure will. See *you* in hell would be more like the truth....You'll need more help than God, mister....That's right, and the first thing he's going to ask you is, 'What about all those people you terrorized in my name?' Just what are you going to say to him, then?...Oh, really?...You sound pretty chicken-shit to me, you worm....What's the matter? Don't you want to talk to me anymore?...Ha, and good riddance."

Barbara slammed down the receiver and turned toward Bob and Sarah. She flashed a thin smile of triumph. "That'll teach him to mess with me," she said as a matter of fact and left to attend her duties. Sarah and her dad scurried after her, intent on getting the other side of the phone conversation.

They cornered her in the kitchen, but she put them off, saying it was just more of the same old story that Bob and Sarah had both heard. She didn't seem upset, so Bob and Sarah left her alone. Sarah returned to Steve's booth and slid in. Largely because of the cool way her mother handled the conversation, Sarah felt at ease despite the continuing harassment.

Steve studied her, aware that something was wrong. When no explanation came, he asked, "Hey, you wanna tell me about it? What's up?"

After a moment of awkward silence Sarah told him the whole story, from the original phone call, including Spook's part, through the Beelzebub call the day after Bob's confrontation at the fair grounds.

Silent throughout the long story, Steve stared at Sarah, overwhelmed by it all. "Man, how do you do it? I'd be afraid to show my face outside."

She took a long drag on the Coke straw. "I can't just go home and hide. Mom and Dad already won't let me go to my softball games or anywhere else at night. But, the whole thing is really a problem, particularly since CNN is coming. This is our big chance to reach the whole country. Maybe even the whole world. I'm really, really scared, Steve, but I'm not going to let him make me stop, just when we're getting the good publicity we need. No matter how much trouble this guy is or how dangerous he is, he's just going to have to wait."

"Shit," said Steve under his breath. "I wouldn't be able to sleep at night."

"Some nights I don't."

Steve picked up the larger crumbs on the empty pizza platter and tossed them into his mouth.

Unable to stand his silence any longer, Sarah touched him on the hand. "What are you thinking, Steve?"

"Nothing, really. I just came over here today to...Hey, look. It's not important. Let's talk about something else."

"No, I don't want to. Why'd you come over?" When she still didn't get an answer, she removed the straw from her Coke, methodically licked it off, and slid out of the booth. She put one knee on his bench, leaned over, and stuck the straw against his neck and held it there. "Steve Forest, why did you come here today? I want to know, right now, or you'll regret it the rest of your life. Your picture will be in the paper tomorrow with a straw sticking out of your neck. The headline will say, 'Sarah McPhee strikes again.'"

Steve laughed and pushed her away, embarrassed. The four other customers in the restaurant were highly amused at the spectacle. "Okay, already. I came over here to ask you to go see a movie tonight. But, I guess, with a gunman out there looking for you, that's a no, huh?"

"Really?" Sarah blurted out, but collected herself as she slid back into the booth. "You mean it? You want to take me to the movies?" she asked as calmly as her excitement would allow. "I've never—"

"Yeah, I want to take you to the movies," he interjected, gesturing wildly with his hands. "Is that such a big deal?"

"No—Yes, it is. I've—" She stopped short and frowned. "I don't know if...I'd better check with Mom to see maybe she might—" Sarah slid out of the booth and trotted off to find her mother.

"Geez," Steve mumbled. *This is crazy. I might get us both shot. Maybe we should wait awhile until this idiot is caught. I should've never brought it up.*

A few minutes later, Sarah returned with her father in tow. She grinned and winked at Steve as she slid back into the booth. Bob towered over the booth. Steve had been in situations with girlfriends' fathers before but never quite like this. He doubted that there was any way he and Sarah could go out.

"You're aware of what the situation is with Sarah?"

"Yes, sir," Steve nodded. "We won't go anywhere else, except maybe to the Dairy Queen for a Coke or something afterwards. And I'll make sure we're always with a bunch of friends."

"And back here by eleven?"

"You've got it," Steve answered, confident that permission was close at hand.

"You've got a top for that monster you drive?"

"Aw...Dad. That takes the fun out of it," Sarah protested, using her Daddy's-little-girl-asking-for-a-big-favor pout.

Bob turned to leave. "Take it or leave it."

"You've got the top. Back here by eleven," Steve quickly replied, getting a face-splitting smile from Sarah.

Steve left shortly to "wash the mud off the Jeep"—a major job as he had not cleaned it in months. Sarah called JB, who was ecstatic to hear the news that Sarah had been able to wrangle a date out of Steve so quickly. "*Esto es un milagro*!" she exclaimed. "Well, at least a little miracle, anyway."

JB followed, "*Querida,* just hold up. We need a plan. The first time you guys met, the impression you gave was *cátastrofe femenino.* You can't have any more screw-ups, particularly on your first date. It may mess up the rest of your life. It has to be perfect—"

"Will you hurry up, JB," Sarah interrupted. "I only have three hours and I don't have anything to wear. What am I going to do? Maybe I should go buy something."

"Sweetie, trust me, you've got everything you need. Let me see...Okay, I've got it. This is what you're going to wear. You don't want to be too dressy..."

Sarah looked like a flower sprouting out of the sofa as she sat cross-legged in her white low-slung bells with a mini-web belt and yellow jelly sandals, impatiently waiting on Steve. It took her and JB a while to pick out her clothes, and she hoped Steve would be impressed, particularly with the yellow tee and its red embroidered outline of a cat on the front. The tee allowed an acceptable portion of her belly to show at the bottom and its V neck, a sensuous resting place for a small heart dangling from a thin gold chain. Her matching small drop earrings were chosen to not to detract from her face, which was highlighted by a small amount of makeup and eye shadow. The overall effect emphasized Sarah's delicate beauty which somehow enhanced her strength and confidence. The whole look made her feel incredibly sexy, something she had never felt before.

When she heard the sound of the Jeep pulling into the driveway, she immediately ran out, something JB had told her not to do. She opened the door and gracefully slid into the front seat of the sparkling clean Jeep and smiled a self-assured hello to the surprised Steve.

"Let's go. I'm ready," she laughed.

Steve hesitated a smile, but before he could comment, Sarah laid her hand on his shoulder and beamed: "Hey, you clean up pretty well. Like the shirt." *And the tight jeans and the way you smell, and the confused smile about me coming on so strong. JB would kill me if she knew.*

"Thanks," he stammered. "Check out the ride. Pretty tight, huh? Took me about two hours to clean it up. It even runs faster, I think."

As he backed out of the drive, she was acutely aware of his sidelong glance checking her out. *Man, this is one hot lady. She is even more sexy now than she was this afternoon, and coming on strong. This is weird. If I can just figure out what's going on in her head maybe we can really hook-up.*

They arrived at the local theater right before the start of the movie and avoided Steve's friends, including Pinky, to sit alone in the back of the theatre. If JB asked Sarah later what the movie had been about, Sarah would be clueless. Her focus had been on cuddling up under Steve's arm and resting her head on his shoulder, beginning to experience all the boy-girl stuff that she had heard the older girls talking about. The elation of touching and being touched, the building desire for more, the laughter, smells, anticipation, apprehension—it was almost more than she could stand. And she liked it.

After the movie, Steve talked briefly with Pinky and they all agreed to meet at the Dairy Queen for a snack before heading home. It was dark when Steve and Sarah left the theatre, arm-in-arm. Although the parking lot was lighted, it still held dark areas that could possibly spell trouble, and both had a feeling that it could be dangerous. They were suspicious of everything and everyone around them as they stepped up their pace, looking for the Jeep.

"Look over there," Steve cautioned as he pointed across the street from the parking lot. They could make out the silhouette of a lone man sitting in the front seat of a car parked at the curb. "We'd better get out of here," he declared as he took her hand.

"Should we run? If we do, he might see that we've seen him and—"

"Let's go for it. Once he sees us, we may not have a chance to get away, unless we get a head start."

The Jeep was only four rows away. They ran between two cars and down between the rows, then between two more cars before reaching the Jeep. They both jumped in at the same time. After fumbling with his keys, Steve started up, and raced down the parking lot, nearly running over a couple of people in the process. They could hear the pair cussing them as they entered the street and fled away from the parked car.

"Let's forget the Dairy Queen," Sarah said breathlessly. "Let's go to the Pizza Shack."

"Good thinking." Steve looked over at Sarah and broke into an uneasy grin. "That was fun."

"Speak for yourself," Sarah answered as she slumped down in the seat.

As they neared the Pizza Shack, Steve checked the rearview mirror one more time, and patted Sarah's hand. Things were going to be okay.

Bob saw the fear on Sarah's face as she came through the door.

"Have a problem?" he asked calmly.

They explained what happened.

"What kind of car was it?" Bob asked.

"Looked kind of like a Chevrolet, maybe four or five years old," Steve answered. "It was too dark to tell for sure."

"It wasn't a Cadillac?"

"No, sir. Not a Caddie."

After Sarah and Steve had a small pizza and Cokes, she decided she didn't want to be at home alone, so they agreed that she would stay at the Pizza Shack until closing and ride home with her parents. As she walked out to the Jeep with Steve, she couldn't deny the spark of excitement and anticipation of getting her first kiss. *What do I do? How do I hold my mouth? Will my nose get in the way of his, or do I tilt my head to one side? Who decides? Do I wait for him to make the first move or do we do it together?*

When they reached the Jeep, he leaned against the fender and took her in his arms. She pressed against him, burying her head against his chest and losing herself in his fantastic smell. She wondered if he could feel her heart beating—she certainly felt his. The strange inner excitement, the energy between them was building to the point it was taking her breath away. *Does he feel that? He's got to. When is he going to kiss me?* Unable to hold back for another second, she tilted her head back and their lips met.

Journal Note

"You must not worry or fret over your progress in cleaning up the Earth. As long as you diligently go about your business, good changes will come. Even your small group, if you are dedicated to the task, can change the world. But you must push, push, push. Then your energy will multiply tenfold, then one hundredfold, then infinitely. Remember this, because it is so."

CHAPTER 14

Ralph made sure that the *Cibolo Falls Daily Gazette* had the news about CNN's Thursday visit. It got front page coverage and a picture of Sarah in Monday's edition. Coupled with Joyce Brown's television segment on Friday, it boosted the interest of local youth in GARBAGE. Tuesday morning's meeting found over four hundred kids attending. Due to the influence of senior class president Gerald Cochran, about fifty of those were to be high school juniors and seniors next school year. Alongside the sea of bicycles under the bridge, these older teens added six pickups, nine cars, and Steve's Jeep.

The meeting was largely spent in preparing the kids for what to expect during the CNN visit. As the C. F. City Council meeting would be the focal point, Ralph urged everyone to not only attend, but also dress appropriately and act in a courteous, businesslike manner. He stressed again, for publicity and educational purposes, CNN could perhaps provide the momentum needed to convince millions of people to change their attitudes and take responsibility for the sad state of the environment.

After the meeting, the kids took a reprieve from the ninety-eight degree heat to plunge into the river. The ever-present policeman at all GARBAGE events, Officer Riley, pulled closer to the river under the shade of a tree. He sat on the hood of the car, kept an eye on Sarah, and wished that he, too, could escape the heat by joining the party.

After a short swim, several of the kids, including JB, Gerald, Ralph, Smiley, and Donnie, joined Sarah and Steve as they spread their towels under a cypress tree along a grassy area of the bank. Pinky, never one to let an occasion pass without refreshment, brought a small cooler of soft drinks from the Jeep. After everyone settled down, Ralph flipped over several sheets on his clipboard that listed possible shots for the CNN people to consider taping. He took suggestions for additions and changes, taking care to show respect to what Steve and Gerald had to say. He knew that it was the natural tendency for them to resent his being in charge, being three years younger. However, if there was any resentment on the older kids' part, it wasn't visible.

"Yeah, I'm trying to get an appointment at the *Gazette* for eleven o'clock on Thursday morning," Ralph responded to a question from Gerald. "I called John Holland to see who to talk to, but he wasn't any help. I don't know what his problem is. He gets pissed every time we make some news."

JB nodded her agreement. "Yeah, I noticed that. He's a grade A nerd."

"I think asshole is a better description," Ralph added.

"You'd think he'd be happy since he's usually the one that writes our news for the *Gazette*."

"Who is John Holland?" Steve asked as he scratched his temple.

"He wrote the first article. You know, the one calling Sarah a cult leader," Ralph answered. "Since then, he's been on and off our case, depending on his mood of the day."

"Yeah, I think *el jefe* at the newspaper went ape-shit," JB clarified. "He made Holland apologize for screwing up the story. I think that's what really pissed Holland off. He thought he was a big crime scene investigative reporter uncovering a devil worship sect. I'm sure he hoped we were a bunch of psychos sacrificing chickens and drinking their blood. When Ralph tricked him and the Rev, he was really dissed."

I don't think he likes the Rev at all," Ralph added. "Even before our world famous sting, he wasn't real anxious to interview Hightower. Seems to me like Holland wants to make the news, not report it."

"Yeah," JB laughed. "But Sarah and Hightower keep getting in his way." She hoisted her Pepsi and after a long gulp added "ahhh" at the end.

Donnie Rimkus jibed as he rubbed the top of his bald head. "Watch out, Britney Spears. JB wants your Pepsi spot."

"And Hightower keeps getting in my way," Sarah said softly. She adjusted her sitting position, to lean against Steve's knee. "My dad thinks that Hightower is the one making the Beelzebub calls. I guess I'll be getting one pretty soon, because of the article that's supposed to be published this morning in the *San Antonio Express*, and with CNN coming. The more publicity the group gets, the madder he gets."

"You haven't heard from the Beelzebub guy since your mom talked to him on Saturday?" Smiley asked.

"No, nothing."

"I went to the library yesterday, to see what I could find out about Beelzebub. John Milton wrote some pretty cool stuff."

"Yeah, Ralphy" JB replied, dragging his name out. "Only you could find Milton co-ool."

The others laughed and Ralph shrugged it off. "Laugh not, ye stupid ones." He thumbed through a green library book. He found the page and said, "Listen, this is tight. *Paradise Lost*. Okay?"

"Sure, Ralph, hurl a little barf on us," JB heckled to the continued amusement of the others.

"This is where God throws the devil out of heaven, because the devil was a troublemaker and wanted to take over the whole operation." Ralph ran his finger down the page. "Yeah, here we are. Listen to this:

For those rebellious, here their Prison ordain'd
In utter darkness, and their portion set
As far remov'd from God and light of Heav'n

"Ugh," Donnie groaned. JB exaggerated a yawn as she covered her mouth. Smiley rolled his eyes. "I think I'm going to be sick," added Pinky.

"Come on, guys. Listen up. This is important.
As from the Center thrice to th' utmost Pole.

O how unlike the place from whence they fell!
There the companions of his fall, o'rewhelm'd
With Floods and Whirlwinds of tempestuous fire,
He soon discerns, and weltring by his side
One next to himself in power, and next in crime,
Long after known in Palestine, and nam'd
Beelzebub…

Ralph looked up from the book for reaction from his audience. He received blank stares, then laughter.

"Go ahead and laugh. But you gotta know, whoever is making those calls is one mixed up dude," Ralph said, snapping the book shut. "Just thought you might want to know about Beelzebub, Sarah. That's pretty heavy stuff."

"I'm aware of what the caller thinks of me, Ralph. But thanks for going to the trouble, even though I wonder if I even want to hear that stuff." She closed her eyes and Steve patted her lightly on the head, bringing a hint of a smile.

Later that Tuesday afternoon, Bob answered the expected phone call. "If Beelzebub addresses the City Council on Thursday, I have been instructed to carry out my mission at that time."

Before Bob could reply, the caller hung up. Bob checked the Caller ID to find the same number as before—a pay phone in the downtown area. He called Police Chief Sheck. The chief suggested that Bob not allow Sarah to speak before the council, but he said he would have several officers on the scene if she decided to go forward with her presentation.

Sarah insisted that she be allowed to appear and her parents agreed reluctantly, considering the importance of her cause and the promise from Chief Sheck that she would be well protected. Sheck also called CNN's producer on Wednesday afternoon and filled him in on the death threat. The producer said he wanted to go ahead if Sarah agreed.

The Cable News Network crew noted the squad car that followed at a distance as they pulled up to the curb at the *Cibolo Falls Daily Gazette* on Thursday morning. They were also followed by a van that carried the director of *Earth Scope*, host Robert Bruce, Sarah, JB, and Ralph. They were shown to the office of the publisher of the Gazette,

Harlon Shiner, who relished the opportunity for his newspaper to be mentioned on CNN. He ushered in the kids, followed closely by the CNN crew. The cameraman filmed as Shiner introduced himself and motioned for the kids to be seated. After a few minutes of small talk, the CNN crew excused themselves and left.

A short time later, the kids emerged from Shiner's office with an agreement for a trial run of a new feature to be published on the editorial page. Written by the kids and named GARBAGE NOTES, the weekly column would deal with different environmental problems from a teenager's point of view.

When the publisher appointed reporter John Holland to work with the group and edit the column, Holland became incensed first at the group, then at the publisher. A week ago he asked the publisher if he might write a similar column but had been turned down cold.

After a short lunch break, the CNN crew taped GARBAGE activities that included several youths as they loaded two pickups with refuse that had been dumped on a lonely riverside road, and some other kids in different parts of town as they picked up litter. They followed with footage of a reenactment of the demonstration at the Cibolo County Courthouse over the golf course issue.

When the director felt they had enough filler for the *Earth Scope* segment, the caravan made its way to the river to see the image. They were not disappointed. The host, Robert Bruce, then interviewed Sarah by the river. They finished just in time for the City Council meeting.

When they arrived at Cibolo Falls City Hall, it was just as Sarah, JB, and Ralph had hoped. The crowd of kids and other spectators had already overflowed the chambers into the hall, down the steps, and onto the sidewalk. The CNN director had Sarah wait outside until they were able to get the cameras set up inside the chamber. The cameraman took some quick shots of the crowd, then the crew made their way inside the building to set up their equipment.

Sarah, JB, and Ralph followed in the wake of the crew into the building, bolstered along the way by enthusiastic encouragement from the kids. As Sarah appeared in the doorway of the chamber, everyone turned, and many of the kids broke out in applause and flashed the Earth Salute. Embarrassed by the display, Sarah blushed and forced a smile. Followed by Ralph and JB, she made her way up to the seats near the front saved by Steve, Pinky and Smiley.

The CNN camera followed them until they were seated, then panned the first ever standing-room-only Cibolo Falls City Council meeting. Stationed around the chamber were Police Chief Sheck and four of his uniformed officers. Sheck was positioned close to Sarah's parents, within a few feet of the Reverend Doctor Mark Hightower, who sat in the second row across the chamber from Sarah and her group.

"You're a real celebrity," Steve, who sat on her right, whispered to Sarah.

"Yeah, it's weird," Sarah answered as she laid her hand on Steve's knee. "I didn't know it was going to be like this. I want the people to get excited about the Earth, not about me."

"Well, you've got their attention, whether you like it or not. Are you ready?"

"I don't know if I can speak in front of all these people. It's kind of scary," Sarah whispered as she looked around the chamber. To her surprise, she saw Hightower sitting on the far side, near her mom and dad. She could tell he was upset as he glared around the chamber. As their eyes met, his anger and resentment sent a wave of fear through her. She looked away only to meet the eyes of John Holland, who stood by the far wall. The twitch worked overtime. It appeared to Sarah that he was disturbed over the brief visual exchange between her and the pastor. It crossed her mind that the reporter was somehow aware of the problems she and her family had been having with the Beelzebub caller.

Sarah leaned to her left toward Smiley, "What's the Rev doing here?"

"Not only 'what's he doing here?'" Smiley replied loud enough so that Ralph, on his other side, could hear. "What's he doing on the speaker's list? He wasn't on it Monday, but he is now, and that ain't exactly two week's notice. I just talked to John Holland. He was bitching about Hightower talking his way onto the list—as if it's any of his business. He said that Hightower is up to his usual publicity-grabbing tricks."

Ralph removed a sheet of paper from his clipboard. "What's the speaking order?"

"They've just revised it because of the crowd. They moved Sarah up to first, hoping that we'll clear out afterwards. The Rev is second."

"Good," Ralph grinned mischievously. He tore the sheet of paper into eight pieces and jotted down a message on one. He handed the message and half of the remaining pieces of paper to Smiley. "Copy what I've written on each piece, then give them to our members in different areas of the chamber and even out in the hallway. Tell them to pass them on, until everyone sees it."

After Smiley read the message, he nodded, showed it to Sarah, then copied it. She smiled in agreement and repeated the message in Steve's ear. Smiley took those that Ralph had copied, added them to his own and left to pass them out to the group. He had just returned to his seat when the City Council and Mayor Rayford Johnson filed in and took their seats.

The mayor shuffled papers in front of him as he basked in the presence of the crowd. Since never more than a few dozen attended usual City Council meetings, this huge gathering made his heart step up a beat. He relished this opportunity to appear before a possible national audience, even if in support of a hometown hero.

The assembly saw the mayor light up with excitement as he scanned the assembly and break into an open smile upon meeting Sarah's eyes. His face and partially bald head flushed with perspiration, he welcomed those in attendance and extolled far too long the finer points of Cibolo Falls. The CNN cameraman, out of courtesy, filmed away. Following his opening remarks, he cleared his throat.

"Before we begin the open forum portion of our meeting, I would like to deviate from our normal routine so that I might comment on the activities of our first speaker and the group she represents. Following a rather controversial beginning, *Grassroots Alliance for Reviving and Building A Greater Earth*, a local group of teenagers led by our speaker, fourteen-year-old Sarah McPhee, has become a driving force in Cibolo Falls on issues concerning the environment."

The chamber erupted in applause and the mayor dutifully waited it out, pretending that it was for him. When it died down, he continued:

"In just five short weeks, the group, now numbering over four hundred, has made a difference not only in the physical appearance of our city, but in our attitudes toward the Earth we live on."

"Right on," came a muffled utterance that brought on a few chuckles and scattered clapping. "Right you are. Its activities have already made some favorable changes in city jobs, and have saved the city some valuable tax dollars. Due to the group's clean-up efforts, we have been able to transfer two of the three employees hired for this purpose into other departments to fill badly needed positions without hiring additional workers.

"I have, within the last week, received favorable calls from others citing the work of these youth. Of course, we are all aware of the work they have been doing in opposing the new golf course until a comprehensive water plan has been put into effect. Mr. Chester Gaines of the Cibolo Falls Water Board also informs me that last year he ordered 2,000 water conservation kits to be distributed free of charge to C. F. residences. Each kit could save a possible 22,000 gallons of water in a year's time. Mr. Gaines told me that despite his advertising the availability of these kits, few residents had requested them. Since the GARBAGE group went door-to-door two weeks ago explaining the kit, his phone has not stopped ringing with requests. He has had to order an additional 2,000 to meet this unexpected demand."

Mayor Johnson looked over the large audience in front of him. "I don't believe I have to tell you, my friends, this is service to the community. In a time when our water is becoming more precious by the year, it is time we learn how to conserve. Along with your C. F. Water Board, these kids are in the forefront, helping to educate us. I, as mayor, appreciate that; you should too."

The mayor beamed as the audience burst into applause. The kids carried on until he held up his hand to bring the noise to a halt. "The enthusiasm that the kids have shown for their chosen task has been contagious because more and more people in our great city are joining in, becoming aware of our environmental problems. These teens hope their movement will spread state and nationwide. The value of the service they have and will give us is immeasurable, and we owe them a debt of gratitude."

The mayor gestured toward Sarah. "Ladies and gentlemen of Cibolo Falls, I would like to present the leader of GARBAGE, a first-class citizen of our city and our first forum speaker this afternoon: Sarah McPhee."

Unlike the usual speaker at City Council meetings, Sarah was greeted with a standing ovation and loud boisterous cheering by her peers. She remained in her seat as she experienced a combination of embarrassment and awe at the reception. Steve urged her up and gave her an easy push to get her moving.

When she reached the lectern the applause halted. She turned toward the chamber audience and raised her hand in the Earth Salute. The kids, still on their feet, repeated the gesture as the CNN camera panned over them. Sarah dropped her hand and turned toward the council as the others sat down.

She adjusted the microphone as she looked over her notes. A bundle of nervous anticipation, she acknowledged the mayor and the individual council members. To keep her hands from shaking she gripped the side of the lectern, then launched into a five-minute speech that urged the council to initiate a garbage recycling program.

After she finished and the applause died down, the mayor turned on the microphone in front of him. "Well, Ms. McPhee, I see that you have done your homework. You are to be commended on the research you have done in preparation for your presentation here today. I assure you, your request for a garbage recycling program will be discussed in the coming weeks, and we'll make every effort to see if your recommendations warrant passing an ordinance."

As Sarah returned to her seat, the mayor glanced down at the schedule in front of him. "Now, I believe we have the Reverend Doctor Mark Hightower of Hill Country Chapel of God, who has asked for time to discuss a...uh—" He looked toward the clerk. She shrugged. "Well, now, we have Dr. Hightower," the mayor announced simply as he gestured for the pastor to come forward.

Without his usual charismatic smile, Dr. Hightower approached the lectern and raised the microphone. He folded his arms across his chest and stared at the council members. The spectators watched as tension filled the chamber. The council members stole quick glances at the mayor and waited for either Hightower to speak or the mayor to respond to his silence. Other than a light cough from the audience, the silence dragged on. The CNN crew filmed the odd spectacle, just in case something newsworthy became of it.

The mayor cleared his throat. "Dr. Hightower, I believe that you're allotted only five minutes to state your purpose or make your…presentation."

"Five minutes? Five minutes, you say?" Hightower shouted, startling several of the council members. "You will allow me all the time I want!" he exclaimed as he slammed his fist down on the lectern. "How dare you? You are elected to a position of trust in this city—a

God-fearing city. How can you stoop so low as to honor this blasphemous child, who...who claims to hear angels and professes to be God Almighty? I tell you here today, I'll do everything in my power to—"

Hightower stopped his tirade because of a noise behind him. He turned to see all the youth began to file out of the chamber—some smiled, several flashed the Earth Salute and others waved good-bye to him. Sarah, Steve, Ralph, and the small group that had sat around them made no gesture nor showed any emotion as they followed the others toward the back door. They ignored the pastor.

"Stop! Stop, I said!" Hightower yelled out to the kids. "How dare you walk out when I'm speaking! Come back and take your seats! I demand you—!" He looked toward the police chief and commanded: "Chief Sheck, stop them! You can't let them walk out on me!"

Sheck shrugged as the last few kids approached the chamber door. Reporter John Holland held the microphone of his recorder out toward Hightower. CNN filmed on.

The minister pointed a finger at the chief. "I'll have your job, Sheck! I promise!" he shouted. He shifted his point to John Holland. "And you, you little...you cut off that recorder before I do it for you!" The reporter shook his head and cupped his hand around his ear as if he didn't hear what the pastor said.

Hightower, obviously shaken, balled his fists. His eyes darted around the chamber, then back to the council members. "And you"—he pointed at the mayor—"you planned this! And I won't forget it, I assure you!"

The minister glared at each council member, his fists still clenched, jaw muscles rippling in anger and his face flushed with perspiration. He wheeled around and stomped out of the chamber. A police officer preceded him out the door and another followed.

As the doors of the chamber closed and the small audience and council buzzed over what had transpired, Bob stepped up behind Chief Sheck. "The man is dangerous, and he's going to hurt someone before this is over. Can't we do something about him?"

"I agree," Sheck replied. "But he ain't broken any laws yet, at least not that I know of. My hands are tied until he does."

John Holland passed on his way out. "Are we having fun yet?"

Bob and the chief watched the reporter until he passed through the doors and out of sight. "I'm beginning to think that this town has more than its share of weirdoes." Sheck looked back to find the council preparing to continue their work. "I guess we'd better get out of here. I don't want to hang around and listen to these guys."

Sheck, two other officers, and Bob and Barbara followed the CNN crew outside to find the kids in celebration of their day's activities. The Reverend Doctor Mark Hightower was nowhere in sight.

Incensed at the spectacle before the CNN cameras at the City Council meeting, Mayor Rayford Johnson reacted swiftly. Despite Mark Hightower's respected position in the community, the mayor faxed a letter to the board of Hill Country Chapel of God. In harsh words he protested the unnecessary and offensive behavior of the pastor at the council meeting, which would disparage the city before a national, possibly worldwide audience.

There was no immediate response to the mayor's letter to the board. However it was rumored later in the week that Mark Hightower appeared before the board on Wednesday morning. Like the board meeting two weeks before, the congregation was not privy to the purpose or the minutes of the meeting. Rumor had it that Hightower threatened to resign his position of pastor of the church if the board didn't approve of the manner in which he carried out his duties. Feeling the church would not be able to carry on financially if it lost its charismatic leader, the board reportedly backed down after issuing Hightower a private reprimand.

"Yes, we've had eight calls since the council meeting," Bob answered the chief who sat across from him in a booth at the Pizza Shack.

Sheck licked some cheese off his fingers as he gazed around the dining room filled with the noon rush of pizza lovers. "Did Sarah talk to him?"

"No, and he didn't ask to talk to her or anyone else in particular. He just expressed his regret at not being able to carry out his mission as planned. He promised to do so as soon as the appropriate time presented itself."

"Did you say anything in return?"

"He always hangs up before I can comment. Same for Barbara."

"They come from the same phone?"

"Yeah."

Sheck was silent for a moment. "I'm getting more worried about Sarah's safety. Maybe you'd better not let her out of your sight, unless she's going to a specific group activity where we have an officer on hand. I don't think this guy will make a move unless there are no witnesses."

Bob studied Sheck. "Why don't you just move in on the guy? We know he's the one."

"Some high-powered lawyer would have him sprung in an hour. I've got nothing to hold him on except some insane remarks at the council meeting and in the newspaper."

"Well, we've got to do something. It's driving Barbara and me crazy, and who knows what it's doing to Sarah. She's clammed up about it."

"Well, I've got an officer working full-time on his background—where he's from, family history, previous jobs, the works. Maybe something will turn up. This afternoon, I'll see if the judge will give the okay for a wiretap on the phone. Also, we'll see about attaching a video minicam to the pole above the phone. If we can get some good tape of this guy along with his conversation, we'll nail him to the wall."

"Sounds like a good plan. I hope it works. Again, I appreciate your help. I know this whole show is a pain in the ass."

Journal Note

"Harmony is God's spirit in action. Disharmony results from the obstruction or withdrawal of God's spirit. To achieve harmony in a difficult situation, love is necessary."

CHAPTER 15

Immanuel sped down Interstate 10; his hands tightly gripped the steering wheel. Tears traced down his cheeks as he stared ahead, oblivious to the traffic he weaved past. "No, Father. Please don't send me away. I'm trying to do what you want. You must know that."

He pounded the steering wheel with his fists. The car veered off the pavement and sprayed gravel on the shoulder as it slid sideways onto the grassy roadside. Although tears blurred his vision, he made no attempt to brake and the car shot back onto the pavement. It narrowly missed a minivan that swerved just in time to avoid a collision. He sped on.

"You must give me another chance, Father," he sobbed. "Please, Father, it's just not fair. I will send *Beelzebub* back where she belongs. I promise."

Ralph decided Sarah needed support and invited himself and several others to the Pizza Shack to watch CNN on Thursday evening. Over seventy kids showed, near the capacity of the small restaurant. Bob had rented four additional televisions and had the cable company hook them up in different corners.

The kids staked out their tables and booths, and kept Barbara, Bob, and two helpers busy with an endless supply of pizza and drinks.

"Hey, dudes, listen up," Donnie boomed to gain attention from several tables close by. He waved the Thursday edition of the *Gazette*. "JB wrote this badass column for GARBAGE Notes. It's called *Just One Little Can*. It follows an aluminum can from the can-making factory to when it gets tossed in a ditch and we pick it up. She compares the cost of a can being recycled to another new can made from raw material. Saves a lot of bucks and aluminum, too. It's cool, so you gotta read it."

Sarah felt like she was going to burst. Would the show turn out as she expected? Would she come across well or look like a doofus? She busied herself by helping her parents wait tables. Aware of her nervousness, her dad winked his understanding. Barbara teased him, saying it was as if he were the one on stage and not his daughter. She was having the same feelings. She kept busy filling the crushed pepper shakers and napkin holders at each table, although very few were low.

When a commercial signaled the end of the newscast preceding *Earth Scope*, Sarah sat down in the booth next to Steve. JB, Pinky and Ralph were squeezed onto the bench across the table. She held onto both of Steve's hands as the seconds ticked closer.

At eight-thirty the *Earth Scope* logo appeared on the screen and the restaurant became quiet. Opening music introduced the host, Robert Bruce, who appeared standing on the bank of the Guadalupe River. The wind blowing across the river tousled his hair as he peered into the camera. The midday sun cast multiple small shadows over the chiseled ridges of his face.

Ralph pointed out the reporter's red plaid shirt, blue jeans, and hiking boots. "I betcha he don't dress like that in Atlanta," he remarked, hoping to ease the tension in the room.

"As seen time and time again on this *Earth Scope* series, the quest to clean up our environment and protect Earth's resources is seldom easy. The environmentalist has to battle and overcome uncompromising government standards and laws, age-old mores and customs.

"He encounters uncaring bureaucrats, selfish businesses or companies, insouciant politicians, narrow-minded special interest groups, pompous individuals, and, of course, greed. Overcoming these obstacles can be overwhelming and sometimes dangerous. But, time and time again, the most unexpected environmental warriors rise above the muck.

"I'm coming to you from the banks of the lazy Guadalupe River in the hill country of central Texas. In Cibolo Falls, a city of some 20,000, such a battle has been raging for six weeks now. It's a developing story about a group of youth struggling to do their part to save the environment. They are winning despite efforts to have them disbanded and, recently, threats on the life of the group's controversial leader."

The host explained the purpose of the group, its membership, and how it came to be formed, as video footage showed the group demonstrating at the Court House. He noted the Earth-minders as a sign paraded across the screen with the slogan, YOUR SURVIVAL DEPENDS ON A HEALTHY BODY AND A HEALTHY EARTH. STOP POLLUTING BOTH—BEFORE IT'S TOO LATE. The kids watching at the Pizza Shack laughed when the *Gazette* visit yielded some humorous shots of the publisher, Harlon Shiner, as he preened in the limelight.

The scene cut back to Robert Bruce at the river. In the background Sarah knelt down at the water's edge with her back to camera. She reached into the water and pulled out a stone.

"This morning at the *Cibolo Falls Daily Gazette,* we examined the many articles and letters written about the leader of our young environmentalists. She has, without a doubt, polarized this town. Folks around here are either for her or against her—her beliefs, that is. From an outsider's perspective, the town is rocked by paranoia. Some actually believe that fourteen-year-old Sarah McPhee is a threat to 2000 years of religion."

Robert Bruce turned toward the river and gestured toward Sarah: "Let's meet this young self-appointed mini-savior of the Earth, Sarah McPhee." He walked down to meet his guest. "Sarah," he called as he approached.

She turned her head toward him and stood. She smiled as she wiped her wet hand first on her jeans, then across the GARBAGE logo on her T-shirt. She extended it to Bruce.

He gestured across the glassy water. "It's such a beautiful river, Sarah."

Sarah beamed as she followed his gaze. "Yes, it is. My friends and I hang out here a lot during the summer. It's sort of a meeting place.

There's always something going on."

Bruce and Sarah began to stroll together down the riverbank. "Sarah, I'm told that you got the idea to start GARBAGE from a voice that you hear in your head. Do you have any idea where the voice comes from or what it is?"

Sarah threw the stone side-armed and it skipped several times over the mirror-like surface of the water. "The voice tells me it is my guardian angel. He wants to be called Spook," she replied as she watched the ripples on the water's surface. She ran her hand through her hair and let it fall back into place.

Viewers worldwide watched as Sarah told her story to the host. As she became more at ease and confident with Bruce, she became more animated. She accepted blame for the assembly problem and humorously told of the fear she had when Spook first made his appearance. Right before a commercial break, Sarah talked about the Earth Salute, future plans for the group, and the need for viewers all over the world to take on individual and group projects to help clean up Earth, save its resources, and make it a better place.

After the break, the host covered what Sarah and the group had been through in their ongoing battle with the church community. The video, all the while, showed pictures of some of the newspaper headlines and also captured footage of some of the local churches including Hill Country Chapel of God. Sarah was straightforward as she explained how the churches turned against her because of her "I am God" statement. She told of the frustration this caused her family, the fear brought on by the death threats she received, and the attempt on her father's life.

The video returned to Sarah and Bruce at the river. "That's frightening, Sarah. How do you handle it, knowing that someone has threatened your life? How can you keep going?"

Sarah got choked up. "There's work for us to do, and I can't spend my life hiding from someone I don't know. It really scares me a lot, though. I wish he would quit bothering me. I'm not doing anything to hurt him."

Bruce nodded. "I'd be scared too, Sarah. Do you think the threats are coming from a religious person?"

"That wouldn't be fair for me to say because I'm not sure. I really don't know."

"Sarah, in the beginning you had trouble convincing your friends that the voice you hear, Spook, was real. As a result, they weren't too eager to follow you in your quest. What happened to convince them?"

"There's an image of me on the water down there." She pointed a short way down the bank where a group of people were gathered at the water's edge. "When they saw it, they knew I was telling the truth."

"Well, let's go have a look, shall we." As they walked toward the group, Bruce continued: "I want to tell our viewers that we consulted with Dr. J. P. Pauley, a Ph.D. with Central Texas Parapsychology Institute, a local research group. He and several of his colleagues who investigate paranormal activity have studied the image and have no answer for why it's here or how it's composed. They have stopped short of calling it a miracle, but they are baffled by it. They also have no explanation as to why a small percentage of people cannot see the image, even on video tape."

As if on cue, the group parted for Sarah and Bruce. The video showed the image of Sarah on the water with her garbage sack.

"Tell us about this, Sarah."

"Spook did it."

"That's simple enough, Sarah, but still confusing."

Sarah seized the opportunity to slip in her own commercial. "If anyone wants to know more about the image and GARBAGE, they can check out our website at *garbageangel.com*. The website has an article written by Dr. Pauley about Spook and the image. We also keep a daily journal on the site about what we're doing, and the site also has links to other websites that deal with the environment."

"That's great, Sarah."

Sarah smiled as Bruce checked his watch. "Well, it looks like it's time for the City Council meeting. We don't want to be late. Shall we go?"

The program cut away to the long mid-program commercials, and the kids erupted in cheering and applause. Sarah, pleased about the program, said very little all through the commercial break as she accepted congratulations for her performance. The program resumed at City Hall. The first footage, narrated by Robert Bruce, was of Sarah, Ralph, and JB entering the council chamber to applause. The scene switched to excerpts of Mayor Johnson's introduction of Sarah, snips of the enthusiastic assembly of spectators and Sarah's Earth Salute.

The kids at Pizza Shack were glued to the TV sets as the video showed Sarah opening her notes and speaking directly to Mayor Johnson. When the camera again panned over the audience, a smattering of whispering spread through the restaurant as everyone tried to find themselves in the shot.

A close-up of Sarah appeared on the screen. "Because I don't have time to go into detail about the savings gained through recycling, the members of GARBAGE have attempted to provide each of you this—"

She was interrupted as the mayor and council members laughed. The mayor commented: "I assure you, Sarah, the council and I are aware of the reason why you're here. Each of us has received over three hundred e-mails, snail mail, and telephone calls on this issue."

Sarah laughed along with the spectators. "It's nice to know that each member of the group is taking responsibility to make sure his councilman and woman is well informed. The members of GARBAGE and I hope each one of you will take the time to read over the material that we have sent.

"Now, let me tell you about garbage recycling." Sarah counted on her fingers as she briefly gave the council the major reasons that recycling was a necessity for Cibolo Falls. She was relieved that she got through her list without leaving anything out.

"As I'm running out of time, I want to leave you with a final thought. We, as individuals, want to take responsibility for our environment and what happens to that environment. Our taking time to recycle will be of no benefit if we have no way to channel it in the right direction. We need your help. Please consider this recommendation for a program of garbage recycling in Cibolo Falls. Now, a member or GARBAGE will present you with a petition with over 5,000 signatures supporting you in this action. Thank you."

As Sarah left the podium to applause, the video showed Ralph dropping the petitions on the desk in front of Mayor Johnson.

The scene changed, showing Robert Bruce on the steps of City Hall:

"Following Sarah McPhee's presentation to the City Council, Dr. Mark Hightower, pastor of the three-thousand-member Hill Country Chapel of God, took a moment at the lectern to have his views heard, upset with the City Council for allowing Sarah to speak before them."

The video returned to the earlier taped chamber meeting with Hightower standing before the council members as he slammed his fist down on the lectern. After a short segment of his outrage against the mayor, the council, Chief Sheck and reporter John Holland, the video switched back to the steps with Robert Bruce. Sarah had joined him.

"Sarah, it seems that your group was quick to walk out on Dr. Hightower. Was that planned beforehand?"

"Does it matter?" Sarah rebutted. "He had no right to talk like that. We haven't done anything to him."

"Does his tirade against you for stating that you are God change your mind at all—make you think that you might be wrong and this man is right?"

"No," Sarah answered, her posture and jaw set in determination. "That's just more of the same stuff. He's been bashing us all along. And anyway, what he's saying is not near as important as the job we're trying to do. We are just helping clean up our little part of Earth. What difference does it make what we call ourselves?"

The picture left Sarah and zoomed in on Bruce. He looked directly at his audience. "Every group battling to save the environment runs into its own particular problems along the way. Some seem insurmountable, some aggravating, but most are solvable with persistence. Sarah McPhee and her group, Grassroots Alliance for Reviving and Building A Greater Earth, are not without theirs. Whether you agree with Sarah's beliefs, one thing is for sure: she is a driving force in an effort to make this a better planet for us to live on. I'm Robert Bruce from Cibolo Falls, Texas, bringing you another story of Earth's survival. This has been *Earth Scope*. Please join us again next week."

As the credits rolled down the screen, a wide-angle background picture showed Bruce and Sarah on the steps of Cibolo Falls City Hall. She held up her hand in the Earth Salute.

Before the credits had finished, the kids at the Pizza Shack erupted in celebration. Most had no idea that the program was going to so detailed and were delighted they had been such a big part of it. Sarah was also pleased, not only in her own performance, but in the footage of both JB and Ralph at several intervals. They had spent considerable time working behind the scenes, and received very little recognition. She knew that this was important to Ralph and had asked that he be the one to present the petitions to the mayor, hoping *Earth Scope* would not edit out that part.

When the majority of the kids left for home, JB, Ralph, Pinky, and Steve stayed behind to help clean up the mess made in celebration. The job was just about complete when Bob and Barbara joined them in the kitchen.

"Well, the program didn't set too well with our friendly caller," Bob announced as he waved an order ticket.

"Oh, no," Sarah moaned. "Why doesn't he just leave us alone? Every time something good happens, he spoils it." She threw down the towel she was using and sat on a nearby stool, her arms folded across her chest.

Steve came up behind Sarah and laid a hand on her shoulder, at a loss for what he should say. Apparently his touch helped as a trace of a smile crossed her lips. "Well, what did he say this time?"

"You okay?" her mom asked, not wishing Bob to burden her with more if she wasn't ready.

"Yes, I need to hear it. If I don't, I'll wonder all night long what he said. I want to hear it now. What did he say?"

"It was short and kind of confusing. He was reciting a poem or something. I got the distinct impression that he was reading it. I wrote it down the best I could but didn't get the last line or two." He held up the order ticket showing his writing around the margin. "Here's what he had to say:

"For those rebellious, here their prison ordained in utter darkness, and their portion set as far removed from God and light of Heaven, as from the center'—I think I missed a word there, but then he said, 'to the utmost pole,' or something to that effect. Then there was one or two more lines, but he lost me by then." Bob slapped the back of his other hand with the order ticket. "It doesn't matter. It didn't make sense, anyway."

"Hey, I know what that is!" Ralph blurted out in treble. "It's the same—! Hold it a minute!" He rushed out the swinging doors of the kitchen only to return as he leafed through his notebook. He jabbed at the sheet with his finger. "Just as I thought. Listen to this. This is a continuation of what Mr. Mac just said:

As from the center thrice to the utmost Pole.
O how unlike the place from whence they fell,

With floods and Whirlwinds of tempestuous fire.

Ralph looked to Bob. "That's it, Ralph. That's the last line he said. Where did you get that?" he asked as he took the notebook from Ralph and looked at the sheet.

"Milton, it's Milton," JB answered for Ralph. "That's the same verse Ralph read us at the park."

"Yeah, *Paradise Lost*," Steve affirmed as he stood behind Sarah, still resting his hand on her shoulder.

"See, I'm no doofus after all," Ralph pompously interjected. "Who has the last laugh now?"

They all laughed and patted him on the back, humoring him until he couldn't stand it any longer. "All right, already. Enough, enough. I know you think I'm the greatest, but don't damage the goods. Unhand me, please." He backed away from his friends as laughter and a somewhat lighter mood returned to the kitchen.

"Did the caller say anything else?" Barbara quizzed her husband. This drew everyone's attention back to the subject at hand.

Bob handed the notebook back to Ralph and looked toward his daughter. "His exact quote was, 'Your Beelzebub will soon meet the same fate as the one in my verse.'"

In defiant response, Sarah threw her head back and boldly planted her hands on her hips. "Just leave me alone, Immanuel, you creep. I don't want you bothering me anymore."

Friday's *Gazette* led with large headlines: "World watches Sarah." The sub-head line of the lead article read: "Local environmentalist puts C. F. on world map."

Several companion articles appeared on the front page. One, written by a new reporter, Jeff Broom, gave the background and events that surrounded the unreported attempt on Bob McPhee's life. Although most residents were well aware of the feud between the McPhee family and the religious community, very few already knew about Bob's incident because Police Chief Sheck had not reported it to the press until Sarah spoke about it on the CNN program. Beelzebub was not mentioned in the article.

Another article, written by John Holland, was an in-depth chronicle of events that involved the actions of Dr. Mark Hightower in his religious war with Sarah McPhee, culminating in his unfavorable appearance at the City Council meeting. The reporter conveniently left out the part he had played in starting the feud. The article was critical of Dr. Hightower and, oddly, was not particularly positive about Sarah and her group either. This left the group confused as to where they stood with Holland, particularly since he was the editor of their weekly column.

Journal Note

"Be cautious if you must. But above all, little one, you must not live in fear. When you have fear in any situation, you lose the power of love. When you lose your loveness, you lose your Godness."

CHAPTER 16

South Park, already expected to be at capacity due to the Fourth of July weekend, could not possibly accommodate the mass of curiosity seekers that flooded to see what the Friday edition of the *San Antonio Express/News* dubbed the "Miracle of the Guadalupe." During the park's nine-to-nine hours Sheck had to provide two officers for each of two shifts to control traffic. The City Parks and Recreation Department also added two rangers on each shift. They estimated about seven hundred-fifty viewed Sarah's image on Saturday, followed by over eleven hundred on Sunday, July Fourth. Due to the CNN program, visitors began to arrive from all over the United States. Calling it a stroke of incredible tourist good luck, a group of forty-two Japanese visiting San Antonio chartered a bus so they could get a glimpse of the image before returning home.

Midmorning on Monday, Barbara answered the Pizza Shack telephone, expecting it to be Immanuel. The call for Sarah was from the organizers of the first World Environmental Symposium, scheduled for the last week of July in New York City. Although Sarah was out on a GARBAGE project, Barbara accepted an invitation for Sarah to speak at the event. An hour later, Steve dropped Sarah off for her kitchen shift. Her parents were waiting when she came through the door:

"Hi, Mom, Dad," she greeted, then was stopped short by their smiles. "Okay, so what's the deal? What happened?"

"New York wants you." Barbara answered.

"Huh? What do you mean?" Sarah asked as she looked from her mom to her dad. "New York, what...?" She pitched her backpack behind the counter.

"The World Environmental Symposium, three weeks from now. They want you to speak."

Barbara saw a mask of confusion cross her daughter's face. She waited for the question she knew would follow. "I don't...what's a synponium?"

"Symposium, Sarah. It's kind of like a conference or convention—a big meeting. A lot of people get together and discuss things. At this symposium they'll be discussing how to improve or protect the environment."

"Wow! Really?" A big smile crossed Sarah's face only to disappear when she realized exactly what her mom had said. "Dad, is she joking?"

"It's like she said, New York wants you," Bob affirmed.

Apprehension swept over Sarah. "Me? They want me to speak at...at a meeting on the environment. Are you sure?"

"They called about an hour ago. It appears you're a hot item after *Earth Scope*. They're looking for someone to stimulate youth interest, and they feel sure that you're what they're looking for. You'll be speaking to about five thousand scientists, government officials, and environmentalists from all over the world."

"Geez...five thousand. No, come on..." Sarah whistled through her teeth as she sank down into the closest booth. As doubts began to build up, she cleared her throat and muttered, "I don't know if...I can't. There's no way I can speak to...I'd be scared to death." She grimaced. "That's impossible, Mom. No way. I can't do it."

Her parents understood how she felt. This would be a lot to ask even of a seasoned speaker, and she had no experience other than the City Council speech and a few minutes being interviewed before television cameras.

Bob took care not to show his own doubts. "Sure you can. This is exactly what you've been working for. You said you wanted to reach the world. You did it Thursday night, and now you have the chance to do it again. Now, go for it; get the job done."

"How long?"

"How long, what?"

"How long do I have to talk?"

Bob chortled, "Your friendly angel would ask, how long do you *get* to talk? Be positive."

"Okay, how long do I *get* to talk?" Sarah asked, her stomach knotting in a cold lump.

Barbara interjected as if it were no big deal, "The man said they were still working it out, but they felt like it would be close to an hour."

Sarah's false smile disappeared as her mouth fell open and her eyes widened. "Shit! Uh, sorry, Mom. No way. I can't speak for an hour. I don't have that much to say."

"Yes way." It was Bob. "You have plenty to say," he added, although he silently agreed that to speak for an hour would be a stretch. "You wowed them at City Hall."

"Yeah, right. Sure I did," Sarah dismissed. She slid out of the booth and began to pace. "I talked for about five minutes...and I was scared to death. I'll wet my pants for sure, in front of five thousand people," she mused as panic set in.

"There were many more than five thousand watching you on CNN, I assure you," Barbara encouraged as she thumbed through a stack of yesterday's checks, "and you handled that like a pro. That's why these people want you. They see the light that shines from you, and they want that light to shine on them. This won't be any different than talking to Joyce Brown or—what's his name?—Robert, on CNN. You just have to get prepared, then go for it." She wondered how anyone could pull this off. "You have plenty to talk about. It's just a matter of organizing it. We'll get Ralph over here and, together, we'll write you a speech that'll knock 'em dead. Every night you can practice it on us or the customers."

"There's too much other stuff to do before school starts and...and we've got to make plans to keep the group busy during the school year. I just don't have time to work on a speech."

"And what do you think Spook would say about this?" Barbara quizzed with a smile.

Sarah fixed her mom with a curious stare. She retrieved her pack from behind the counter and took out her journal, flipped through several pages, and stopped. "Okay, first we have 'an issue that can make me a better person—better God.'"

Her finger ran down the page. "Second, 'it'll benefit the universe.' Third, 'I don't have to do anything. I can walk away if I want to.'" *Is that supposed to make me feel guilty?* "Fourth, 'there will be other experiences if I don't choose this one.'

"Then, 'there's no punishment if I don't,' and next, 'what do I want?' That makes it simple enough," she quipped. She closed the journal and replaced it in the pack.

Sarah walked to the kitchen, pushed open the doors, stopped, and turned. "I guess I have to bake pizzas before I write any speeches, huh?"

Bob and Barbara nodded their heads in unison. "I shoulda known," Sarah mumbled as she left the doors swinging behind her.

"You have any idea what we're getting into?" Barbara asked as she stared at the closed doors.

Bob massaged the tension in the back of his neck. "Sounds like loads of fun to me."

"Honey, I don't know how much more of this I can take. I've been worried sick about her every time she gets out of our sight. Now, this added pressure. And that's just me. I can't imagine the fear she must feel. She's got to be afraid of everyone she doesn't know."

"And even some she does know," Bob added. "But I understand how you feel. When she and Steve went to the movies, I had this urge to follow them, just so I could protect her if anything happened."

"Then why did you allow her to go?"

"The kid needed a diversion from all the pressure and threats. But when they saw that guy in the parked car, it just caused more stress."

The phone rang. Bob picked up his order pad and pencil for the usual call-in order. He answered and, satisfied that it was neither an order nor the Beelzebub caller, summoned Sarah to the phone. He returned to his preparations for the noon rush.

After talking for several minutes, Sarah hung up the phone and motioned for her parents to join her.

"That was the producer of *Earth Scope*. The program brought on a lot of interest all over the world, so they want to do a short follow-up on this Thursday's program. He wanted to know if anything unusual had happened here that they might include."

"Hey, good things are happening all around!" Bob exclaimed. He expressed more excitement than he actually felt. *I can see the merry-go-round picking up speed.*

Barbara's concern about her daughter's ability to cope built as she wiped the countertop with a paper towel. "Did you tell him about the symposium?"

"Yes, ma'am. He said they would mention that. He also said that people all over the world are excited about the image, and wanted to know if more people were coming to see it since the program. He laughed when I told him about the Japanese."

The phone rang again. Bob reached behind the cashier's counter and picked up the receiver: "Pizza Shack....Oh, hi, Ms. Brown. It's good to hear from you again....You did....Well, I'm sure she'll—Yes, but you'll probably have to take a number....Yes, several....I'll let her tell you. She's right here....Sure....Okay, hold on."

Bob handed the phone to Sarah. "You sure are popular today. Joyce Brown." Sarah took the phone, and her parents exchanged a wary glance, each wondering if this madness should be stopped before it got completely out of hand. And would they dare stop it if they could?

"Hi, Ms. Brown," Sarah breezed into the phone. Barbara saw her daughter's face brighten as she listened. "Really?...I would love to, but—if I can. In two weeks I have to—I mean—I *get* to go to New York....Yes ma'am. To speak to the World Environmental Symposium....I don't know yet.Mom said five thousand....Yes, that would be even better. Then, you—Yes. That would be best for us, too....Yes, afterwards....Great!...Thanks....Okay, bye-bye."

Sarah hung up the phone. "ABC," she informed them as she headed back to the kitchen. "After I get back from New York."

"And when did this happen?" Sheck quizzed as he leaned up against the front fender of his squad car, his arms crossed over his chest.

"That would be twenty years ago," John Stroud, the department's lone detective answered. "He had another church in Waco after that. He was pretty popular there, because they didn't want him to leave to come here."

"But he actually got fired from Rutledge?"

"Yeah, they ran him off. He apparently got a little too big for his britches. I'm told by an old-timer that he was more interested in what the people could do for him than what he was doing for them. The shit hit the fan when he 'asked' some long-time parishioners to leave the church because they didn't agree with his philosophy. The congregation revolted in support of those he threw out."

The chief looked out across the front lawn of the department and wished he was on his ranch, sweating in the sun. "Sounds like the Hightower that we know and love. Anything else?"

"Naw. Other than that, he's pretty clean. Been divorced. Never remarried. It's rumored that he has a few women fans here in C. F., but nothing unusual there as far as I can find out. On the local level, Jeri Lynn checked out the Hill Country Chapel of God's website and came up with some interesting stuff. Apparently Hightower isn't a real bad dude—at least to the people of Waco. He was voted Humanitarian of the Year by the Waco Chamber of Commerce before he left to come here. He used his ministry to help several poor families get back on their feet after a tornado completely wiped them out. The mayor of Waco also issued a special proclamation in his honor declaring Pastor Mark Hightower Day. This was for his help in organizing the local community to raise over a million dollars to help a local orphanage that had fallen on hard times."

Sheck cocked a brow. "Mark Hightower Day?"

"Yeah, and that's not all. He's written several books"—the detective checked his notes—"*My Father's Father*, which was a bestseller about fifteen years ago. According to the website, it still sells pretty well." Stroud again checked his notes. More recently he wrote *The Crusader's Last Stand*, and *The Battle for the Christian Mind*. They're marketed through the site but it didn't indicate how well they're selling."

Sheck curled his lips as he thought about what Stroud had said. "Well, keep on him. We need anything we can get on this guy. What about the phone?"

The detective pulled off his coat as the late morning temperature began to rise. "The tap and minicam are in place, but we've bombed out so far. Immanuel has called twice since I talked to you on Saturday but used a phone on the corner of Welch and Court. We got some pretty good fingerprints off the receiver that I hope will match up with

Hightower's."

"How you gonna get his?"

"He eats breakfast every Wednesday at Julie's Kitchen. I'm going to just happen to be there and see if I can talk Mae Bess out of his water glass after he leaves. Then we'll see if we have a match."

Chief Sheck stepped away from the car, stretched, then hitched up his pants. "Damn, that's day after tomorrow. Well, give me a holler as soon as you find out anything. I have this crazy feeling that something is about to happen—and I'm not going to like it."

Sarah decided to view all the news she received as a positive step for both her and GARBAGE. All the publicity gave her confidence she could overcome the obstacles her inexperience presented. She couldn't wait to start work on her speech and to practice it on anyone who would listen. It would be a success because she would create and deliver a speech that everyone would appreciate, adults and kids alike. Ideas flooded in—pictures of the group for a slide show, information on how to form a group, personal video shots, and some clips from the CNN program to show the kids in action. Smiley's mom volunteered to set it all up on Powerpoint and loaned Sarah her laptop for presentation on the symposium's big screen. This was Sarah's big chance to tell the world about GARBAGE, and she would not allow herself to fail. She just couldn't.

An uneasy feeling lingered deep in the back of her mind as she prepared for bed. Immanuel always intruded into each of her little successes, and the more she succeeded, the angrier he became. Why would this time be any different? She couldn't help but feel him lying in wait, ready to spoil her plans.

But what could he do? she pondered. If he's going to harm me, wouldn't he have already done it? And how can his words hurt me? They can't unless I let them. Still I can't shake this creepy feeling. Does this urging I have to be careful mean something or am I just being a wimp? What was it Spook said about fear? I'll have to look it up in the journal tomorrow. Right now, I'm just too tired.

She ignored the whole mess, took off her clothes, and tossed them in the hamper. She thought about the rented video movie that she and Steve had watched, and reflected on how great it had been to cuddle up on the sofa and just forget it all for awhile. She opened the top drawer of the dresser and removed her favorite yellow shorts and the GARBAGE T-shirt for the next day. After she removed her makeup and took a quick shower, she slipped into bed. As she turned out her bedside lamp, the clock read eleven-thirty. *How did it get to be so late? Tomorrow's going to be a busy day.*

She closed her eyes and tried to remove any thoughts, to clear the way for any messages that Spook might have. He responded quicker than usual:

"You are correct, little one. Rest is most important at this time. Rest is necessary to keep up your strength in the days to come.

"There will be times when you feel, shall I say, out of sorts, because of a confrontation with someone. During these times, it is as well you remember, all that happens to you is for a well-planned purpose. You must remember this. Take each and every experience, even if you feel it is what you call a negative experience and use it to your advantage. Let me say that again: use it to your advantage."

"Are you warning me that something bad is going to happen to me?" Sarah asked in the dark.

"Any experience is bad if you label it as such. There is potential for growth in every experience, if you desire it."

"Meaning you aren't going to tell me if I have a bad experience ahead of me, right?"

"Let me repeat myself, little one: good experiences and, as you say, bad experiences, are both the same. They are opportunities to teach, to learn, to indeed simply experience...or live. That is life. You must have trust in yourself, and trust the God that is you. Only then can you face life's dilemmas unafraid and confident."

"Are you done, Spook?" she asked testily. When nothing came, she turned on the small lamp beside her bed and wrote in her journal, the best she could, what Spook had said. Turning off the lamp, she laid back. "Thanks, Spook...I think," she mused sleepily.

"You are entirely welcome...I think," came the reply.

"I don't understand," Ralph complained. "Spook talked to your dad. Why won't he talk to me. I betcha I've called to him ten times now, and he never answers."

"Come on, Ralph. Just give it up," Sarah replied, sitting back-to-back with Steve on the cool cement floor of the pavilion. "He isn't gonna to talk to you. That was a special time with Dad. He was being shot at. Maybe if you get shot at, he'll talk to you."

"I bet he would if you'd ask," Ralph pressed.

Sarah tuned out Ralph just as Smiley's voice rang out:

"IT'S ELEVEN FIFTY-NINE—TIME IS RUNNING OUT FOR EARTH. That's the Earth-minder for the week," he announced to the group of about six hundred gathered at the fairground on Tuesday morning. They had changed their meeting location to Miller Pavilion because the large crowds coming to see the image at the river would be a distraction.

JB made a dramatic effort to exaggerate her own smile, making fun of his ever-present grin. He winked his recognition of her joke and tried to produce a frown for her benefit. The surrounding laughter proved his lack of success, so he gave up and relaxed into an easy smile as he sat down on top of a picnic table.

The big event of the week was simultaneous demonstrations at all the supermarkets in Cibolo Falls to get customers to conserve plastic and paper grocery sacks by bringing their own reusable totes for shopping. Kids would also carry signs and give out leaflets that urged customers to call their council members in support of the garbage recycling proposal.

"Listen up, everybody," JB called out. "Hear me all right?" She pointed toward the very back. "*Bueno.* We may be demonstrating over what may appear to be no big deal to most people out there, but it is a big deal if everyone, all over the world would do it. So, let's don't screw it up this afternoon. Remember which of the seven grocery stores is your demonstration site. And be there on time. Dress nice and don't act crazy. This is serious. We don't want any unnecessary criticism. Everyone knows we've had our share." She winked at Sarah.

"And make your signs neat. Point out the issue, but please, no sarcasm or cuss words. We need to be professional about this, guys." When a few good-natured boos, hisses, and general complaints from the older kids interrupted, JB merely stuck out her tongue at them. "Questions?"

"Yes, ma'am…I mean, yes," a boy about twelve asked, "can we demonstrate the full three hours or just during our scheduled hour?"

JB smiled at the kid. "Just make sure your hour is covered. If you want to demonstrate all afternoon, go for it, but don't forget it's supposed to be close to one hundred degrees. We don't want you to die from heat stroke," she joked.

The kid, wide-eyed, nodded seriously, bringing laughter from the older kids. Several patted him on the back for asking such a good question. He also took them seriously as he beamed his pleasure.

"One big happy family," JB continued to the amusement of the group. "Okay, settle down. Any more questions?" She looked over the group and pointed at Donnie. "Quickly, big guy."

"Any TV today?"

"Ralph's foxy lady, Joyce Brown from KGEX in San Antonio, might be here. She's going to help ABC do a segment on us when Sarah gets back from New York. She said they needed some fresh pictures of us demonstrating. I called her this morning, but she didn't know if she could make it today or not. Donnie, go ahead and buff your head anyway just in case." She grinned as the laughter subsided. "Anybody else want a smartass answer? Okay, then, meeting adjourned. See you this afternoon."

The pavilion emptied except for a few who sat on top of the picnic tables and drank Pinky's sodas. "Well, six hundred of us should send a strong message," Steve said. He had his arm draped around Sarah's shoulder, but she felt a tension between them—like something bothered him. She dismissed the feeling and snuggled closer against him.

"Yeah, we could have a fair-sized riot," Ralph chimed in.

"Speaking of delivering a message, Ralphy," JB followed, drawing his name out to irritate him. "Have you delivered your column to John Holland? Deadline is two o'clock."

"Not quite through yet."

JB was quick to show her displeasure with Ralph. She slowly shook her head and clicked her tongue. "Better get through, mucho-quicko. Super-nerd John Holland, is just itching to tell—what's-his-name?—the publisher, that we aren't holding up our end of the deal, so he can write the column himself. Then, Sarah," she winked at Sarah, "be hurling a little barf at you, Ralphy boy. *Comprehende*?"

"I know, I know," Ralph snapped. "Don't come unglued. I'll have it there by three."

"Ralph! Two o'clock!" JB pressed. "Not three! I'm telling you, he'll cause trouble for us if you screw it up!"

"Just shut up, JB! Don't worry about it, okay?" Ralph's frustration kicked up a notch. "You just take care of your job...if you can handle that, and I'll take care of mine! If I need your help—dream on—I've got your number!"

JB stared at Ralph as the others waited for what was coming next. She shifted gears on him, her voice now soft and velvety, "Okay, Ralph. You're right. I should stay out of your business." She walked over to Ralph and, before he could defend himself, kissed him on the check.

"Ugggh!" Ralph cried out, his voice cracked to a higher pitch. He jumped away as he rubbed the kiss off with his hand, to the laughter of the others. "Would you just quit? Just leave me alone, you...you sex pervert!"

"May I speak to Mr. Holland, please." Ralph used his most businesslike voice over the phone to the receptionist of the *Cibolo Falls Daily Gazette.*

"Yes sir. Who may I say is calling?"

"Coggins, ma'am. Ralph Coggins."

"Please hold, Mr. Coggins. I'll put you through."

Ralph tapped his fingers to the piped music that came over the phone line. The music stopped as the phone was picked up on the other end.

"Yeah, *Mr.* Coggins," Holland answered, his voice heavy with sarcasm. "Now, what can I possibly do for you, Ralph?"

"Mr. Holland. I'm so glad I caught you." Ralph ignored Holland's usual foul mood. "I'm going to be a few minutes late with this week's article. I'll drop it by about three o'clock, okay?"

"Few minutes, my ass, Ralph!" Holland retorted. "That's one hour late! Just don't bother! I had to rewrite the first one, anyway!" After a moment, Holland continued in a much more amiable tone: "I may as well write this one from scratch. It would be a hell of a lot easier, and better, I might add, because I can use my own material."

Ralph was not surprised at Holland's attitude but was caught off guard by his outburst, then the complete turnaround. Ralph waited for what would come next. He didn't have long to wait:

"I really don't care for this arrangement," Holland's voice came back over the line softer and more cordial. "I do all the work and, as usual, you guys get all the publicity and credit."

Ralph came back, again in his most businesslike tone: "Mr. Holland, sir, we're trying real hard to do our part, and I promise you, we'll get better. If you don't want to work with us and, you know, kind of help us out, maybe you should ask Mr. Shiner to replace you with someone who really enjoys his work. We don't want you to have a stroke or something." Ralph held the phone away from his ear, expecting another outburst.

He wasn't disappointed. "Look, you little twerp!" Holland shouted in reply. "You just get the damn article here on time from now on! I'll keep on carrying you guys to make sure the town stays in love with you, but you won't get any special treatment—not from me! You and that uppity little bitch, Sarah, would be nothing without me! I made you and I can break you! Understand?"

Shit. This guy doesn't give up, Ralph thought as he twisted the phone cord around his finger. He really thinks he's God's gift. Well, Sarah's gonna go psycho when she finds out, but I ain't taking this shit anymore.

"Hey, dude," he retorted angrily, his voice rising an octave. "What the hell is your problem? You ain't got no cause to talk to me or anybody else that way! And if you want to talk 'twerp,' maybe you should take a good look at yourself! No, sorry, that's wrong! I think 'asshole' might better describe you! And you know why? Because, that's what you are! In fact, you're a royal asshole!

"Now, I suggest you get off my case, or I'll pay a nice little visit to Shiner's office!" Ralph tried to calm down a bit. "You know what, asshole? I've had this feeling for quite some time that you're on Shiner's shit list, and I'm sure he'd really love to hear you called Sarah a bitch."

Ralph prepared himself for the tirade that was sure to follow. He could nearly feel the anger from Holland flowing through the phone line. For a moment he heard nothing but Holland's ragged breathing.

"Have the article on my desk by three, Ralph," came the smooth reply.

"Uh, yeah, sure," Ralph answered. *What's with this guy? He's either putting on a great act or he's crazy, one or the other.* "You'll have the article by three. You need anything else?"

"Yeah, what's your group up to today?" Holland asked without a hint of animosity.

"We sent you a note. We'll be demonstrating at the seven grocery stores in town from three to six."

"Oh, yeah, sure. I see. I have it here. I just misplaced it somewhere, I guess. Uh, what I really wanted to know is, where's Sarah going to be?"

"Super City. Why?"

"For pictures. Yeah, we want to get some new pictures of her in action. You know how it is. The people out there are hungry for more Sarah." Before Ralph could reply, Holland asked, "The column by three, right?"

"Yeah, sure. By three," Ralph promised. "I'll bring it by personally."

"Well, it certainly has been nice talking to you, Mr. Coggins. See you at three."

This guy is out of his mind, Ralph thought as he said good-bye and hung up the phone. "Ralph," he muttered to himself. "You're headed straight for the shitter because you'll never get that article finished by three and you know it."

The first order of business at the Tuesday City Council meeting was the rapidly growing South Park visitor problem. They decided to erect a temporary fence surrounding the image area with a gate for both exit and entry. Next, they agreed that the city could not afford to keep two park rangers and two police officers on duty for twelve hours a day if the image continued to be an attraction for an extended time. Their solution was to start charging each visitor one dollar at the entrance to the image site to pay for the rangers and police officers.

At precisely three o'clock, the man dialed the phone. "Is he in?...Okay, thanks....Hey, it's good to see that you're working today....Yes, good....Well, I've decided that now is the time, if you're sure you want to do this....Yeah, really....Sarah McPhee is demonstrating right now at Super City....Everything. Just be there and we'll get it over with....Yeah, it's going to be one big surprise....Yeah, come immediately." He grinned in satisfaction as he hung up the phone.

Journal Note

"Please remember in days to come, there is much value in all of your experiences. This will hold especially true in those events that you interpret as being sorrowful or troubling. This I can not stress too much, little one."

CHAPTER 17

Ralph didn't have time to wait for the elevator so he ran up the stairs as fast as his skinny legs would carry him. He panted at the second floor reception desk as he glanced up at the clock. It was five minutes past three o'clock. *Well, shit. I hope Holland won't let five minutes bother him. But, you never know about that guy.*

He tried to gain the attention of the woman behind the front desk engrossed in a computer screen. "Uh, ma'am. I need to see Mr. John Holland. Do you think maybe I could—?"

"Just missed him." She didn't bother to look up as she barked at the computer, "Come on. What's the matter with you?" She shook her head in agitation, stroked a few keys, and said something under her breath when the graph on the screen changed.

"One of these days I'm going to pitch this machine. It's nothing but trouble. What do you want him for?" She looked up and broke into a smile. "Well, hello there. You're one of those GARBAGE kids, aren't you?"

"Yes, ma'am. I'm Ralph. Look, I was supposed to leave this article for him at three o'clock, but I kinda got caught up in...Anyway, could I maybe leave it on his desk so it'll be here when he gets back?" he said breathlessly. "He'll be real mad if I don't. Do you know where he went? Maybe he's still here in the building or something?"

"Hey, slow down. One question at a time, hon. Yes, you can leave it on his desk. Yes, I know where he went. And no, he's not in the building."

Ralph's glasses had fogged up after his run up the stairs. "Where?"

"He said something about a demonstration at Super City. I assume it's something you GARBAGE kids got going. Say, you want to clean your glasses?" she asked as she handed Ralph a tissue.

Taking the tissue, he removed his glasses and wiped them off. "No, I mean, where is his desk, so I can leave the article?"

"Oh, why didn't you say so?" She gestured down the hall. "Last door on the right. Just go right in. He always leaves it open."

Ralph nodded and smiled as he handed back the tissue. He replaced his glasses, said his thanks, and turned to leave. He turned back and asked as if an afterthought: "By the way, was he...you know...mad or angry when he left? When I talked to him earlier, he wasn't too happy with me."

"Join the club. You aren't the only one he's yelled at today. That guy is going to crack up one of these days if he doesn't settle down. He certainly wasn't happy when he left here. I told him, I said, 'Hey, you can't treat me like I'm your wife. I have to put up with that at home, and I'm not about to take it from you. They don't pay me enough to take your grief.' All I did was ask him where he was going and he bit my head off. But I gotta know. It's my job."

Ralph nodded and shrugged his what-can-you-do at the receptionist as he backed away, holding up the article. "Well, thanks for your help."

"Anytime, sweetie."

Ralph looked back down the hallway as he approached Holland's office and found the receptionist still absorbed in the computer screen. He entered the small cubicle, switched on the light and dropped the article on the desk. He wrote an apology across the cover sheet for missing the reporter. As he turned to leave, a light green book on the edge of the desk caught his eye, but nothing registered. He switched off the light, closed the door, and headed back up the hallway.

"The book, Ralph."

"Huh?" Ralph looked behind him, back down the hall to see who had said something. "Hearing things," he mumbled.

"The book, Ralph. Check the book."

"Shit!" Ralph exclaimed, then looked up the hall to see if the receptionist heard. The computer still had her complete attention. "This can't be. Is…is that you, Spook?"

"Yes, that is what I am called."

"Well, damn. It's about time. I've been trying to get you to talk to me for a month now. It seems like I—"

"Ralph, there is no time for talk at this time."

"Okay, sorry. What's up?"

"Get the book."

"The book? What—"

"The reporter's book, in his office. Examine it."

"Oh, yeah…why?" Ralph waited for a reply. "Spook, why?"

Giving up, Ralph ran the few steps back to Holland's office, turned on the light and closed the door behind him. He picked up the book, turned it over and found written across the jacket, just like the one he had checked out of the library, the simple title, *The Works of John Milton*.

Well, that's interesting. Holland's reading Milton. He flipped the book open to where it was marked by a folded sheet of paper. Highlighted in fluorescent green, a passage leaped out at him:

For those rebellious, here their Prison ordain'd
In utter darkness, and their portion set

Being all too familiar with the verse, he didn't need to read what followed. He opened the sheet used as a marker and stared at the page in confusion. "Why would he...unless—Oh, shit!" he exclaimed. "Holland and Hightower are in this together."

Ralph slapped the book closed and removed his cell phone from his belt. He dialed and impatiently drummed his finger on the desk as the phone rang. "Come on, answer the phone. Hurry, dammit."

"Pizza Shack," came the answer after the fifth ring. It was Bob.

"Mr. Mac, this is Ralph. I'm at the *Gazette*."

"Sure, Ralph. What's up with you?"

"John Holland's the caller…along with…and Hightower, too," he blurted out.

Bob's curiosity peaked. "How do you know this, Ralph? What happened?"

"I'm here in Holland's office. He has a book of Milton's work, just like the one I checked out at the library. It proves it. He's the caller."

"Now, hold on. I really don't think that makes him the caller, do you? I'm sure a lot of people out there could be interested in Milton. That doesn't make them all the caller."

"No, no, you don't understand," Ralph pleaded as he tapped the book on the desk. "The same part of *Paradise Lost* is highlighted that the caller quoted to you on Thursday night. And get this: Sarah's name, along with Hightower and some others, is on a sheet of paper used as a marker. Sarah was last listed on Thursday night at nine-thirty. That's when he called after the *Earth Scope* program. And he called the Rev just a few minutes ago. They've got to be in this together."

"Does Sarah's name show up after Thursday night?"

"Yes, on Saturday, Sunday, and Monday."

That's great. Ralph's right. We've finally got that sucker. "Does Sarah's name show up at any time before?"

"Yes, sir."

"Okay, what is the first date that her name shows up?"

Ralph skimmed up the list. "Monday, June the seventh. It's got your home phone number."

He is the one. Now, what to do? "Ralph, is Holland there?"

"The receptionist said he went to the demonstration. She said he was very pissed."

"Does he know which store Sarah is going to be at?"

"No, I don't think—oh, shit!—yes, he does! He asked me earlier and—oh, no!—I told him!"

"Don't worry about it, Ralph. It's done and you had no way of knowing. Now, listen: how far away is Super City for you?"

"About ten blocks, I think."

"You're on your bike, right?"

"Yes, sir."

"Okay, get over to Super City as fast as you can. Go straight to the policeman on duty there. Tell him what you told me. I'll call the police station, so they can call him on the radio. He should already know by the time you get there, but you never know. One of us will surely get through in time to stop—whatever—I'll call Sarah on her cell phone and tell her to get the hell out of there."

"Gotcha, Mr. Mac."

"Now hurry, and be careful. Okay?"

"On my way," Ralph said as he ended the call, stuck the phone in his belt, and tucked the book under his arm for evidence. He ran down the hall past the receptionist's desk, pushed the stair door open, and flew down the stairs three steps at a time.

"Hey, what's the big hurry?" he heard the receptionist yell before the door swung closed. Seconds later he was in the street. He stuffed the book in his bike pack and pedaled off.

Bob called Sarah as Barbara waited, wringing her hands. "For God's sake, Sarah, what good is it to have a cell phone if you don't answer it?" he exclaimed as her recorded voice message came on. He didn't leave a message. "You have any idea what JB's cell number is?" he asked as he dialed the police department.

Barbara thumbed through her address book; her hands shook in fear.

"Nothing." She dropped the book down on the desk and tears flooded her eyes.

Bob didn't reply as he waited for the police department to answer. He nervously rubbed the back of his neck.

Barbara took the phone from Bob. "Get over to Super City as fast as you can. I'll talk to the police. And call me as soon as you get there."

Sarah heard her phone ring, but in the middle of her busy interview with Joyce on the sidewalk in front of Super City, she chose to ignore the call. JB was close by but not close enough to hear the ring.

After Sarah's announcement that she would be attend the World Environmental Symposium in New York City, Joyce Brown decided to film a short interview to be used on newscasts right before Sarah's departure in two weeks. Just as she and Sarah were about to wrap up the interview, John Holland arrived.

He cruised past the blue and white patrol car, parked across from the demonstration, and cut the engine. He got out, sat on the hood of his car, and watched the twenty-eight kids in the first shift solemnly march back and forth just off Super City property, each carrying a sign.

Joyce Brown finished the interview and instructed her cameraman to get some footage of the kids' demonstration for use with the later ABC program. When Sarah rejoined the marchers, she noticed John Holland across the street. She waved and smiled. When he didn't acknowledge she exaggerated her gesture, only to be ignored. Sarah could see him mop his red face with a handkerchief, and thought it odd that he wore a sport coat in the ninety-nine degree heat. *Wow, that guy is really weird.*

"It looks like Holland is his usual self." Sarah pointed the reporter out to Steve, JB, and Pinky, who walked nearby.

"Betcha Ralph didn't show up with the article on time and now Holland wants his revenge." JB added. She moved up next to Sarah and nudged her with an elbow. "Hey, sexy. Why don't you ask him what his problem is?"

"That's a no. I can tell when I'm not wanted. And anyway, if I wait five minutes, he'll probably forget why he's being such a horse's ass. Then he'll fall all over himself, trying to be nice to us."

"He can't stand it because we're out here attracting attention while all he can do is watch and write about it," Steve said. The others nodded their agreement.

"That's it!" Pinky jested. "Let's offer him a sign, so he can make news for a change. Then, maybe he'll be happy."

"Just shut up and keep walking," Sarah commanded her friend, playfully hitting him on the head with her sign. "Look at the way he's watching us; he knows we're talking about him."

Officer Riley felt he was slowly being baked alive as he sat a short way down the street in Unit Seven. He got out of the patrol car earlier but the sunshine and lack of breeze made him even hotter, so he scrambled back inside. Disgusted, he opened the thermos of lemonade he always carried, knowing full well it was already empty, drained the last few drops into the plastic cup, and dismally shook his head.

"Well, that's a crock..." he mumbled to himself. *Why can't these kids pick a shady spot to do their demonstrating? Who cares about saving trees, anyway? Man, I can't take this anymore. I've got to get something cold to drink before I melt.* He picked up the radio mike and keyed the switch: "Dispatch. This is Unit Seven. Over."

"Go ahead, Seven."

"I'm down at the Super City demo. Everything is quiet. I'm going to take a short run across the street to Quick-Stop for a soft drink and restroom break. I'll be on the portable radio. You Copy?"

"Ten-Four, Seven."

Riley replaced the radio mike and got out of the patrol car. As he stretched his legs he glanced down the street at the demonstrators. Aware that he had gained John Holland's attention, he acknowledged the reporter with a nod and crossed the street. When he entered the store he realized he had left his portable radio on the car seat and dispatch couldn't reach him. Rather than go back for it, he dashed to the restroom to take care of business as quickly as possible.

Steve touched Sarah on the arm and gestured as Hightower's black Cadillac approached. It rolled to a stop on the same side of the street, down from the demonstrators and across the street from the reporter. The engine and air conditioner continued to run.

"Oh, shit," Sarah muttered. She tensed up, her eyes brimming in concern. She bit at her lower lip as she turned to Steve for help.

"Just hang loose and we'll get out of here," Steve assured her as he looked down the street for Officer Riley. *Where is that guy when we need him?* He tried to look unruffled as he took Sarah by the elbow. "Okay, let's be cool now. The cop has disappeared, so stay close to me and we'll head for Super City. We'll have to walk past the Rev. Look the other way and act like you don't see him. Now don't panic." He gestured for JB and Pinky to close in around them.

Sarah's legs trembled so much that she felt they wouldn't hold up long enough to get to Super City. She wanted to run but her legs would not cooperate. *This can't be happening. He's right in front of me and I can't even run to get away.* Sarah held onto Steve's arm and ordered her feet to move.

Joyce Brown recognized the Cadillac and gestured to her cameraman to be on the alert for anything newsworthy. The cameraman caught her signal and they both circled around behind the kids to get a better angle.

Across the street, John Holland slid off the hood of his car to the ground and leaned against the front fender. His face twitched as he stared at the Cadillac. His hand shook as he wiped his neck and face again with the wilted handkerchief.

Ralph had covered all but two blocks of his trip from the *Gazette* to Super City. To save time he had crossed parking lots and took shortcuts in alleys behind businesses. He pushed his ten-speed with all the muscle his puny legs would allow. His lungs gasped hot air through a dry throat, his heart pounded in discontent as it heaved against his small chest, and his legs ached. He could see the blue and white police car in the distance, along with Hightower's Cadillac and the small group of demonstrators. "Come on, Ralph," he urged. "Just a little farther."

"Unit Seven. Unit Seven, this is dispatch. Do you read? Unit Seven, please come in. Unit Seven. Respond, please. Officer Riley, respond..."

Hightower appreciated the Cadillac's air conditioner, especially since as he could see the kids were suffering in the heat. He was about to cut off the engine and join them when he heard a voice:

"Hightower. I am Spook."

"Well, are you, now?" the minister said in amusement. "Sarah McPhee's Spook, I presume. Well, as you must know, I've said publically that you really don't exist. You're proving me wrong. I'm honored to have an audience with you."

Hightower. Hear me. There is danger immediately ahead. Be alert."

"Well, that's nice to know, my invisible friend. How do you know this?"

"You must be aware. Danger awaits you. I must leave you now. Go quickly—with caution."

When it was apparent the conversation was over, Hightower sat very still, marveling at being talked to by an angel. He turned off the ignition, opened the door, and stepped onto the pavement. Feeling the rush of afternoon heat, he took off his coat and tie, and laid them across the front seat. He surveyed the area as he closed the car door.

He spotted Sarah among the group of demonstrators, then John Holland across the street. Aware of the interest he provided the reporter, Hightower smiled in recognition, then made his way toward Joyce Brown, a short distance behind Sarah.

Sarah realized Hightower was going to block their way to Super City. She grasped Steve's arm tighter and dropped her sign. Her legs deserted her as she felt her knees about to buckle. She had no control and danger approached. *There's no way I can get away. He's going to hurt me and I can't do anything to protect myself. Spook, I need help. Help me, Spook.*

Pinky, on Sarah's opposite side, pushed JB in hopes that she would run away while she could. She held fast, determined that she could help if trouble developed. She moved in closer to Pinky to give him the silent message that she was going nowhere. She heard him whisper, "Idiot," under his breath.

"Be cool, Sarah," Steve assured. "He won't do anything with me and Pinky here." He was relieved to see Donnie Rimkus join them, his bald head glistening in the sun.

"My legs...my legs don't...Help me get out of here, Steve! He's going to hurt me. I know he is. Please, help me get away!"

"No. Just hold on to me," Steve urged. "Keep walking. He can't hurt you. If he makes a move, we'll get him first. Just stay by me." He glanced at Pinky and Donnie to see the same fear and doubt that he himself felt. He had the urge to run and drag Sarah with him.

The other kids, aware of the drama, drew back from their five friends, inadvertently leaving a clear path for Hightower. Pinky again shoved JB, urging her to join the others. She pushed his hand away and stood her ground.

With Hightower just a few feet away. Steve removed Sarah's hand from his arm. He and Donnie stepped forward to warn the pastor to come no closer.

"*Mark Hightower! Look out behind you! Danger! Turn now! Behind you!*" Spook exclaimed.

Hightower turned and caught the reflection of the sun off a shiny object in a man's outstretched hand. He saw the man point a pistol at Sarah. With all the strength and quickness he could muster, he lunged forward. He collided with Sarah and pushed her back just as the pistol fired; the bullet struck Sarah in the upper chest. The minister landed on top of Sarah. As they hit the ground, Sarah's muffled scream carried eerily across the parking lot. JB, Steve, Donnie, and Pinky were horrified as they looked down at the minister sprawled across Sarah. Kids dropped to the ground or scattered in different directions; they screamed and cried in terror as they ran.

"No!" Ralph screamed as he realized he was too late. He bore down on the figure of a man standing over someone on the ground. His glasses had fogged over and fallen down on his nose, but through a blur he could see the man taking aim at two figures on the ground. JB, Steve, Donnie, and Pinky were frozen, transfixed by the sight before them.

"Stop it, you bastard!" Ralph screeched to distract the gunman as he raced toward him. He knew what he had to do. He crashed into the man as the gun fired with an explosion that echoed through Ralph's head as if it had come from a cannon. He grabbed the man around the neck as he and the gunner tumbled to the ground, the bicycle on top of them, front wheel spinning wildly. The gun skidded out of reach.

"You shot Sarah, you dirty sonofabitch!" he screamed. With all the strength he could muster, he held onto the assailant's head and neck, determined to squeeze every ounce of life out of him for killing his friend.

Ralph felt several sets of hands grab at him and his captive. Thinking they were other assailants, he struggled with two people. He stopped fighting them off when, in a blur, he realized it was Donnie and Pinky trying to assist him. Ralph released his hold on the gunman after they assured him they had the man under control. When he got to his feet he could see the hazy outline of both the gun and his glasses on the ground nearby. He picked up his glasses and put them on, kicked the gun away as he had seen many times in the movies, and turned back to find the assailant, still pinned down by Donnie and Pinky, was John Holland.

Ralph stood over the dazed reporter with clenched fists "You bastard!" Ralph screamed. He kicked Holland in the knee, eliciting a childish scream from the reporter. "I should rip your heart out! I will if Sarah dies!" Smiley appeared without his usual smile, grabbed Ralph by the arm, and led him away. Smiley whispered softly to calm Ralph down.

Officer Riley heard the second shot as he was came out of Quick-Stop. "Oh, crap! I blew it!" He threw his soft drink and snack down, and sprinted toward the action. He got to the scene just as Chief Sheck arrived in his squad car.

They took Holland from Donnie and Pinky, cuffed him, and led him to Sheck's squad car. "My picture!" the reporter screamed. "I have to have my Father—to tell my Father! Please give me my picture!"

Sheck jerked the back door open and pushed Holland in. The reporter's head banged against the door frame—another cry of anguish. "All you're going to get is a jail cell, hotshot. Now shut your mouth while you're able." He slammed the door and headed for the injured. Riley stayed with the prisoner and called for medical assistance.

The emergency lights that flashed on Sheck's car told Bob there was trouble. He could only hope that Sarah was not involved, but he sensed the worst. He screeched to a halt beside the squad car, leaped out, and ran to Sarah's side. He dropped to his knees next to her. Those already assisting Sarah and Hightower tried to make them as comfortable as possible.

Steve, on his knees at Sarah's side, looked up at Bob and sobbed. "I'm sorry Mr. Mac. I should've saved her. It happened so fast."

Bob, aghast at the sight of his daughter lying crumpled on the street, could only squeeze Steve's shoulder and nod his understanding. Bob's face drained of color, dizziness and nausea overwhelmed him. He braced himself with one hand on the pavement to keep his balance and grasped Sarah's arm with the other.

He tried to calm himself as he forced a smile of reassurance for his daughter. Although not unconscious, she was obviously in shock because she didn't react in any way to his being at her side. Her white GARBAGE T-shirt was soaked with blood that extended from the left shoulder down into the chest and abdomen, and blood splattered in dark contrast over her yellow shorts. Her breathing was labored with periodic heaves and gasps for oxygen. Her color was ashen and her arm felt cold and clammy in Bob's hand.

Bob closed his eyes as he attempted to quell the continuing dizziness and nausea. While holding onto Sarah's arm, he covered his eyes with his other hand and softly cussed himself for encouraging Sarah's fantasies and allowing her to listen to Spook. Overwhelmed and helpless, he looked to Chief Sheck, who kneeled on Sarah's opposite side, for the least hint of hope. Sheck reached across and squeezed Bob's wrist.

"Help is on the way," he said.

Bob noticed that Sheck's eyes had teared over, and it occurred to him how many people would be affected by Sarah's plight, whether she survived or not. There were so many out there who didn't even know Sarah, but were taken by her and the positive energy that seemed to surround her. It occurred to him that she was indeed connected to everyone.

Despite a wound in Hightower's upper left leg that caused him a great amount of pain, he spoke coherently. His trousers around the wound were soaked with oozing blood and his white dress shirt was covered with blood in the chest area—presumably Sarah's. Joyce Brown, JB, and Pinky had to restrain him when he tried to get up and help Sarah. He put his own pain and injuries aside as he agonized over her plight and blamed himself repeatedly for being a split second too late to save her from her attacker.

The surrounding area became a bevy of activity as the kids that had been demonstrating gathered around. Many cried for their friend who, as far as they knew, had been murdered. Traffic came to a standstill, and people rushed from Super City and other businesses to see what happened. John Holland, under Officer Riley's close watch, sat in the back of the patrol car staring straight ahead. He was oblivious to the tragedy that he had so carefully planned and carried out, and didn't seem to notice the KGEX cameraman filming him through the front window.

The crowd parted for two ambulances from nearby Breckenridge Hospital that made their way through the stalled traffic. In a matter of minutes medical technicians whisked up the two injured and were off to the hospital with Bob following close behind in his Toyota, driven by one of the older kids. He speed dialed number one on his cell phone to make the dreaded call to Barbara at the Pizza Shack:

"Sarah's been shot, Babe," he blurted out when she answered. There was no way to soften the news.

"God, no!" she exclaimed as she dropped the telephone. Her knees buckled and she slumped to the floor.

"Dammit," Bob said under his breath. *Stupid. I should have gone over there and told her in person, he berated himself. There's no one there to—*

"Is she…? What happened?" Barbara's voice quivered over the line. "Will she…?"

"I don't know. She got hit in the chest. It's bad. Real bad."

"It's all my fault. I should have never…damn. Damn, damn, damn," Barbara cried as her head rested against the wall. "Where is she? I'm coming."

"Breckenridge. We're on the way, right now. Have Jason lock up.

Tell him, once the last customer leaves, clean up and go home. You'd better not try to drive. Have one of the staff bring you."

Pinky pitched Ralph's bike into the back of Steve's Jeep, and he drove JB, Ralph, and Steve, who was also too shaken to drive, off toward the hospital.

Most of the crowd of onlookers dispersed except for the kids who had witnessed the shooting, their relief shift of new kids arriving and kids who hurried over from other stores when they heard the news. They watched as Sheck's crew documented the crime scene with pictures and measurements. Several who witnessed the shooting gave their names and addresses to an officer for later interviews.

They sat on the nearby curb or milled around in small groups in a state of disbelief. They had been aware of the potential danger to Sarah, but it had all been a sort of game to them. Very few had given a second thought to Sarah being in any real danger, much less an attempt by someone to take her life. Parents arrived to comfort and assist their children in dealing with emotions caused by the tragedy.

Joyce Brown and her cameraman delicately recorded the open flow of emotions between the kids and their parents. Their plan was to get a closing shot at the hospital before sending the news over their satellite hookup for the *Six O'Clock News.* They packed up the video equipment and were about to drive off when Chief Sheck stepped in front of the van.

He came around to the passenger window and looked in. "You understand, Ms. Brown, I want that tape as evidence of the crime."

"Yes, sir. I'll see that you get an exact unabridged copy first thing in the morning, when I return for a follow-up at the hospital."

"Thanks. And I'll need a statement from the both of you, since you witnessed the crime."

"Fine. We'll allow enough time so that we can help out any way we can. I feel like I have a vested interest in this tragedy. I've been here almost since the beginning. This kid has somehow grabbed me and won't let me go."

Sheck didn't reply.

"It's really feels weird when some youngster can take over and you can't help but follow her to see what's going to happen next. But until now I've enjoyed it. I just hope it's not over."

Sheck studied Joyce as she looked over his shoulder at nothing in particular, a far-away look masking her face. He sensed that she was deeply hurt by this tragedy—more than she realized. His eyes moist, he replied, "Yes, I guess we all feel like we're a part of Sarah and her problem—or should I say, problems. There seems to be one after another." He removed his hat and ran his hand through his curly hair. "Whether this town realizes it or not, we needed someone like her, and to lose her would be a great loss."

Joyce patted his hand that rested on the window frame. "She'll make it. I just know it."

"I hope so. You people going to be around for a while?"

"We're going to the hospital for some footage, then we'll head back, depending on what happens. You need something?"

"No. Just curious." Sheck backed away from the van and waved good-bye.

Joyce leaned out the window. "You've already taken Holland in?"

"Yeah."

"Can we come by for a quick interview later?"

"Now, Ms. Brown, I think you know what the answer to that question is."

She smiled for the first time. "Doesn't hurt to try." She motioned to the cameraman, who slowly pulled away.

Sarah faded in and out of consciousness. She knew that she had been hurt and was also aware that she was in an ambulance with an attendant close by. An unbearable pain cut into her upper left chest and increased with every turn or bounce the ambulance made. She willed the pain to end to no avail. *Maybe the hurting will stop when I get where I'm going? Where am I going? The hospital? Will the pain end when I get there? How far is the hospital? Spook, are you there?*

In and out of consciousness, Sarah's mind rambled. *Where was I? What was going on when I got hurt? Am I really hurt? Why do I feel so cold? Don't they know I'm cold? Dry. My mouth is so dry.* She tried to wet her lips with her tongue; it seemed stuck to the top of her mouth. She shook her head as she tried to speak, to beg an end to this long trip. Again she felt herself slip away, falling through space, twisting and turning into a beautiful, bright, peaceful white sea of clouds where there was no pain.

Spook? Where are you, Spook? I need you, Spook. Her thoughts formed beautiful word-pictures that swirled about in colorful, sparkling waves of energy. *Spook, please. Talk to me, Spook.*

"These are important lessons, little one," came the hollow resonant voice of Spook, a certainly welcome friend. *"Face the unknown with confidence and trust. Because of this experience, you will realize, without a doubt, that you are the physical manifestation of God. You are the true spirit of God. You are God's message of love to the world, because you are, indeed, God's love. You are no more and no less than God. Believe that, and live as such, little one. Remember, release the fear and face what's ahead with confidence and trust."*

Sarah regained consciousness as she was being wheeled down the long corridor of the hospital. Her eyes opened to a blurred passing parade of ceiling panels and fluorescent lights. Her ears picked up a jumble of voices, machines, and hurried footsteps scurrying around her. A child cried in the distance.

"Hi, honey. You just lie still and you're going to be just fine," came a voice from an Afro-framed dark face suddenly peering down at her. Below confident eyes, a blue surgical mask puffed in and out at the mouth with each word spoken. The voice offered encouragement: "Don't you worry, now. Hang in there, 'cause you're gonna get fixed up real soon."

The voice had a calming effect, and Sarah attempted to smile, only to fade away into the now familiar and welcome colorful wave of pure energy.

Journal Note

"I encourage you to remember, little one, whatever happens to you, even if you feel that it is unfair or, as you say, 'bad for you,' to always look at it as if it is just another incident. However, this incident will affect the whole universe. Even the smallest of happenings affects the universe in some way. This is an important message for you to remember, because it is so."

CHAPTER 18

By six o'clock the number of kids that held vigil in front of the hospital numbered close to five hundred. Many of the demonstration signs had been changed to read, *SARAH*, and *HANG IN THERE, SARAH.* Others read, *THE WORLD IS WITH YOU, SARAH*, and *WE LOVE YOU, SARAH.* Joyce Brown and her cameraman, stationed a short distance from the group, recorded the solemn congregation of kids.

As soon as two teams of doctors arrived, surgery was started. They assessed the problems with the patients, then sent out word that both would need several hours of surgery. Due to the location of Hightower's wound, the doctor's felt he was not in a life-threatening situation. For Sarah, however, because the wound was in close proximity to her heart and its large arteries, the doctors were cautious at giving any premature hope. They would only know after surgical exploration.

The hospital had been quick to restrict the surgery waiting room to only immediate family members or close associates of the injured.

Bob authorized Ralph, JB, Steve, and Pinky to join Barbara and him as not only Sarah's closest friends, but as representatives of the kids outside. Dr. Hightower had no immediate family close by, but several members of the board of Hill Country Chapel of God and two assistant ministers waited for word of his condition.

Ralph jumped up and adjusted the volume on the waiting room television. *The Six O'clock News* had just started. Joyce Brown appeared on the screen standing in front of the lawn sign of Breckenridge Hospital. She conversed with KGEX anchor Jerry Monsoto at the studio news desk:

"Yes, Jerry. A shocking and tragic sequence of events has taken place in the ongoing story of young environmentalist Sarah McPhee, of Cibolo Falls. Sarah, while demonstrating over ecological issues, Sarah was gunned down by a reporter for the *Cibolo Falls Daily Gazette*, John Holland. A local minister was also shot. They both are at this very minute undergoing surgery.

"Jerry, we are going to show about sixty seconds of the actual tape that Jessie Santiago, our KGEX cameraman, caught of the shooting. We were filming for an upcoming ABC spot when it happened. It would be appropriate for parents viewing this newscast to exercise discretion in allowing young children to view it."

Barbara tightly held Bob's hand as they prepared to watch.

The tape showed Hightower approach Sarah, then the reporter appeared on the screen as he came from behind and to the left of the minister. Holland raised his gun and shot just as Hightower collided with Sarah. As JB, Steve, Donnie, and Pinky stood nearby, the reporter aimed at the minister and Sarah lying on the pavement, and fired again just as Ralph ran into him with his bicycle. After Donnie and Pinky took control of the gunman, Ralph screamed and kicked the assailant before he assisted Smiley, Steve, Joyce, and JB gently roll the minister off of Sarah.

Monsanto commented, "I see on the tape that you were an active participant."

"Yes, Jerry. I've become fascinated with Sarah and her group since we had a segment on her in our *Ecology Today* series. Immediately after the shooting, I'm afraid I forgot that I was on the scene as a reporter, not as a contributor in making the news. When I saw the minister sprawled out on the pavement lying on top of Sarah, I just had to help both of them any way I could.

"As many of our viewers will remember, Sarah has been in a continuing battle with some local churches, which began with a newspaper article written several weeks ago by the reporter who shot her. The article falsely accused her of being a cult leader. We reported on this feud during this newscast a month ago. And, last Thursday evening, CNN's *Earth Scope* series also featured this disagreement, which had escalated from telephone threats and a boycott of Sarah's family-owned pizza restaurant to an attempted shooting of Sarah's father.

"As strange as it may seem, the heroic acts of the minister, Dr. Mark Hightower of Hill Country Chapel of God, her nemesis in past weeks, may have saved Sarah's life. As you saw, he risked his own safety in an effort to foil the gunman's attempt to take Sarah's life. He pushed Sarah aside just as the gunman took aim and shot, hitting Sarah in the upper chest. The shooter then turned the gun on Dr. Hightower."

Joyce paused with a hint of a smile. "The boy on the bicycle who attempted to stop the gunman from getting off the second shot was a friend of Sarah's, Ralph Coggins. We originally thought this second shot was also intended for Sarah, however, as you heard on the tape, the gunman said, 'This is for you. One less preacher's lies to listen to.' It appears that the gunman somehow lured Dr. Hightower to the scene so that he might kill both him and Sarah McPhee at the same time."

Except for Barbara, the waiting room turned oddly quiet as the newscast ended. She was hysterical. She paced back and forth as she blamed herself and her husband for allowing things to go so far. She also ranted about Police Chief Sheck not doing his job. Bob and JB attempted to calm her but knew that comfort would only come when and if Sarah pulled through all right. It took a long time for her to settle down. She sat silently for a while, then got up and crossed over to the group from the Hill Country Chapel of God.

She wiped her eyes and attempted to gain control of her emotions. "I can't tell Dr. Hightower, right now, so I will tell you," she said to the group of men. "Your pastor did a very unselfish thing this afternoon. He sacrificed his own well-being in an attempt to protect my daughter from danger. I'm sure he knew that he would be defenseless if the gunman turned on him. I...I—" Barbara began to sob uncontrollably and it was obvious that she could not continue. The five men from the church were at a loss as to what to say or how to comfort Barbara, whom none had met before this evening.

Bob rose from his waiting room chair and took her into his arms. His eyes glassed over as he forced a smile for the uncomfortable men. "I'm afraid we haven't had much good to say about Dr. Hightower lately. If God was watching today, He is pleased. We will both personally give Dr. Hightower our heart-felt appreciation when he's recovered. In the meantime, if you will deliver our thanks, we would appreciate it."

The men smiled their understanding and gratitude as Bob and Barbara turned to rejoin the kids.

By eight-fifteen surgery was complete on the minister. His doctors reported that the bullet had damaged a small tributary of the femoral artery, which accounted for the copious amount of bleeding after the shooting. They were confident that their patch job would heal without complication and he would be back on his feet as soon as the muscle damage would allow. After the doctors' report, those who had waited on word about Hightower's condition departed, leaving the waiting room to the four kids, Bob and Barbara McPhee.

There had been no word on Sarah's surgery . The waiting room became quiet except for the soft drone of the television in the background. The kids huddled together in their little pack, but very little was said. Ralph watched Bob and Barbara in hopes that he would see some glimmer in their behavior that indicated Sarah was going to be all right. Bob never sat down. He paced the room, then roamed the hallway. Barbara was up and down. She never sat in the same chair twice, fortified herself with coffee, and kept a wary eye on both the clock and the door. They all wondered as time wore on if the delay was a good or bad sign. Fragile hope was high but confidence low.

Police Chief Sheck dropped by about nine o'clock, but considering Sarah's unknown condition opted to merely set up times the following morning to get the kids' statements on the shooting. He added that, since Joyce Brown's newscast at six o'clock, his office had been flooded with calls from different media and news services for information on the shooting. He said the hospital receptionist mentioned that she had also received numerous calls about Sarah's condition.

The kids could see that Barbara was peeved with Sheck. They watched as she followed him out into the hall with Bob trailing. They gathered at the door and peeked through the window to see what was about to happen.

"Chief, you blew it. This should have never happened," Barbara steamed, her jaw clenched and eyes narrowed. "You should have taken in Holland weeks ago. Now, because of your incompetence, we're going to lose Sarah."

Bob looked on, bewildered. He certainly understood Barbara's frustration and anger with Sarah's plight, but he felt the chief had done his best. He had hesitated in arresting Hightower and was right. Although belligerent at times, John Holland was never a suspect. Perhaps he should have been, but even Bob hadn't dreamed Holland was dangerous.

Sheck hesitated in his reply, torn by conflicting emotions. This wasn't the time to defend his action—or nonaction. He knew the McPhees needed to strike out at something or someone for their apparent loss of Sarah. To a lesser degree, he felt the same. But he didn't want to be the object of their anger. He certainly agreed that he should have done something about Holland had he suspected. However, like Hightower, he would have had no evidence to hold him on.

As Sheck spoke his voice wavered, "Barbara, I realize there is nothing I can say to make you feel better. I understand your feelings about what's happened. I would give anything to go back, knowing what I know now. But I can't."

Barbara folded her arms across her chest and glared at the chief.

"I'll tell you what: at your earliest convenience, y'all come by the office and we'll go over the investigation—what we found out about Hightower and what we didn't find out about Holland. Until then, I can only say I'm sorry."

Getting no comment from either, he said good-bye.

As soon as the chief left, two doctors dressed in surgical scrubs approached from down the hallway. "Mr. McPhee, Mrs. McPhee?" one asked. Despite apparent fatigue, his eyes flashed with strength and confidence. "I'm Dr. Fagan, and this," he gestured toward the other, "is Dr. Westhead." Westhead didn't comment, but his easy smile indicated success.

Bob and Barbara shook hands with the doctors, already relieved that it appeared the news wasn't bad.

Dr. Fagan opened the door of the waiting room to allow the other three to enter and join the kids. "Well, it was a little tedious, but Sarah is strong and held up well. She'll be in considerable pain for a few days, but she should pull through just fine."

Both doctors smiled at the somewhat controlled eruption of jubilation from the kids. "We apologize for keeping you in suspense for so long, but sometimes in surgery of this nature, there are a lot of minute problems that have to be taken care of for the surgery to be a success."

"Will there be any permanent problems we'll have to deal with?" Bob asked with concern.

"None that we are now aware of. On occasion there can be complications in cases such as this. But we don't anticipate any. Let me fill you in a little on...You see, the bullet hit in the upper left chest, just below the collar bone." With his finger he touched Steve in the chest to show the area.

"It damaged quite a bit of muscle tissue but in time that shouldn't be a problem. The bullet also shattered the outer angle of the first rib and became lodged in the subclavian artery, the main blood supply to the left arm. That is the reason for our taking so long. It was close to the median nerve, and we had to be extra careful to not injure the nerve during removal of the bullet and bone fragments. If the bullet had struck the nerve, she would've had some long-term problems with her left arm."

Again he demonstrated on Steve's chest as he drew the finger down toward the middle. "She was very fortunate with that, as well as not receiving the bullet a few inches down and toward the center. In that case, I'm afraid she wouldn't have made it. I've seen more of these gunshot wounds to the chest than I would like, and I assure you, she is lucky to come out of this as well as she did. She'll be left with only a small scar as a medal for her ordeal."

When Fagan didn't continue, Barbara wiped away her tears with a tissue and smiled, "We're thankful for that and also appreciate your help."

"Glad we could be of service," Fagan replied and then gestured toward his colleague. "Dr. Westhead will be keeping an eye on Sarah until she recovers. I'm just a phone call away, however, should he need assistance. There is nothing that he can't handle, but two heads are always better than one."

"We're very grateful, I assure you," Bob said.

After some discussion about the shooting, Dr. Westhead said that the nurse would notify the McPhees shortly when they could visit Sarah in intensive care, where she would stay the night. Although she would still be under the affects of the anesthetic, her parents would be a welcome sight as she regained full consciousness. She wouldn't be able to talk as she had a breathing tube, but they hoped to remove it by tomorrow afternoon. After Westhead assured the McPhees he would return first thing in the morning, he and Dr. Fagan excused themselves and left the waiting room.

As Bob and Barbara hugged in relief, Ralph motioned to Bob that the kids were going to give the good news to the others holding vigil outside.

When they approached the glass front doors of the hospital, Ralph, JB, Steve, and Pinky were surprised to find the kids all sitting on the massive hospital lawn in the dark, each silently holding a burning candle for Sarah. They swung the doors open, came through, and stopped at the top of the steps. A ripple of contained excitement spread throughout the group.

Ralph held up his hands to quieten the murmur, then shouted, his voice exaggerating its usual squeak: "She's okay!"

To a crescendo of applause and cheering from the kids, Ralph held up his open hand and then closed it into a fist. The kids answered his Earth Salute. A few joined Ralph on the steps and took pictures of the group flashing the Earth Salute with one hand and holding up the candle with the other.

As the celebration began to wind down, and several of the kids gathered around Ralph, JB, Steve, and Pinky for the particulars of Sarah's condition, Smiley balanced his candle on the edge of the large rock fountain in the middle of the hospital lawn. Taking his cue, another followed, then another and another until there were over five hundred candles lighting up the fountain. They backed away and some took pictures to show Sarah.

Joyce Brown and Jessie Santiago stood off in the darkness and recorded the end of the celebration. They were unaware that news outlets and media services all over the world had already requested their earlier tape of the shooting.

Considering what she had been through, Sarah slept very well in intensive care. She opened her eyes to find Barbara standing beside the bed.

Pale, groggy, and confused, she acknowledged her mom and looked around her strange surroundings. She remembered nothing about the night before, even after the anesthetic had worn off. Her mouth was dry, her tongue swollen, and partially stuck to the floor of her mouth. She forced a painful swallow, hampered by the breathing tube stuck down her throat. She looked quizzically at her mom for explanation and assurance. She was unable to speak.

Barbara touched her on the shoulder. "You can't talk because you have a tube to help you breathe. They will take it out later."

Sarah frowned, hoping her mom would understand.

"You got hurt, yesterday, at the demonstration. You're in the hospital."

Sarah stared at her mom as she forced herself to go back mentally to the day before, to remember what happened. She recalled the demonstration, then Hightower showing up and the fear she felt. She recalled the minister coming toward her and lunging out at her. She remembered both of them falling back with him on top of her, smothering her against the hard, hot pavement of the parking lot. And she remembered the intense pain. But what happened then? Again she frowned for explanation.

"You got shot, Sarah, in the chest."

Sarah tried to clear her throat, but found it difficult with the tube. She stared at her mom in disbelief. The reality of what had happened began to sink in. Lifting her right hand, she touched the tube coming out of her nose, then felt across her upper chest. The bulge of bandages affirmed what her mom had said. She felt over toward her left shoulder, then down into her middle-left chest area. She tried to lift her left arm. She flinched in pain and gave up—she had indeed been shot. She took a deep painful breath and released it in resignation, the cool air rasped in her throat.

Her thoughts were interrupted by the sound of someone coming through the door. She looked over to see a rotund and bald middle-aged man, dressed in an expensive suit and white physician's jacket, but without a tie. She glanced back to see her mom react with a smile.

"Well, now, how is the patient this morning?" Dr. Westhead asked as he tweaked Sarah on a toe that stuck up under the sheet. He had a self-assured, easy manner about him; however, he appeared tired, probably, Barbara thought, from too many long hours of practicing his craft.

"Good morning, doctor," Barbara greeted. "Sarah, this is Dr. Westhead. He is one of the doctors who operated on you last night."

"We've met," Westhead said. He took Sarah's right hand and shook it before she could lift it.

Sarah feebly reached up and touched the breathing tube coming from her nose. She gestured with her hand for him to take it away.

The doctor acknowledged with a smile. "We'll see." He pulled a small light out of his jacket pocket and looked into Sarah's eyes, then listened to her lungs with his stethoscope. Lifting her right shoulder, he slid the scope under her shoulder blade despite the discomfort it caused. "Well, you seem to be breathing pretty well. I guess we can remove it." He turned toward Barbara: "If you'll step out a moment, we'll have this tube out in a jiffy. Then Sarah can move to a regular room."

Barbara left as Dr. Westhead pushed the buzzer for a nurse's assistance. Thirty minutes later, a nurse helped Sarah get settled into her own private room, when her mom reappeared. Sarah talked hoarsely to the doctor:

"When I…move…ugh, hurts…my arm. Am I going to be…okay?"

"You bet. Well, you're going to have a lot of pain for a while. If it gets too much, tell the nurse and she'll give you something."

"When…go home?"

"Maybe in a week or so. We'll see how you do. By the time school starts, you'll be just like a new person," Dr. Westhead assured, only to see Sarah's expression of disappointment. Confused, he tilted his head. "That wasn't meant to be bad news. You have a problem?" He again checked her breathing with the stethoscope.

Sarah looked at her mom in dejection as she attempted to clear her throat. The nurse gave her a sip of water through a straw. Sarah pulled the glass back with her right hand for another sip, then answered: "I can't."

"Okay, I'll bite. What earth-shaking event is this recuperation interfering with?" Before either Barbara or Sarah could answer, he continued, "Wait a minute. I heard on TV, this morning. Let's see, you're supposed to go to New York, in three weeks, I think, for a—oh, yeah. You have to go to the...something about the environment?"

"Worl—" Sarah coughed. She reached up with her right hand and held her throat, grimacing in pain.

"The World Environmental Symposium," Barbara supplied as she watched her daughter to see if she was okay.

Sarah pouted for the doctor's benefit.

"I see...well, that's highly unlikely. Three weeks is a little too soon to be globe-trotting, but we'll see." He abruptly changed the subject: "Now, if you—?"

"What…ughhh…on TV?" Sarah interrupted the doctor, much to Barbara's chagrin.

"Pardon me?" he asked with a grin. "You're supposed to be recuperating from major surgery. Who cares about what's on TV?"

"Much…better," Sarah tried to adjust herself to a more comfortable position. She flinched in pain, but tried to cover it up. "I'm ready…go home, now…okay?" she fibbed.

"Yeah, sure you are." The doctor pointed a finger at his patient. "You have been through something very traumatic—something that usually keeps people in bed for weeks, if not months. So, don't get any ideas about going anywhere, young lady. Not until I, big macho doctor, decide. Do you understand, or do you want me to tie you to the bed?"

Sarah closed her eyes, too tired to argue with the doctor. *This argument is not over, doctor. It'll just have to wait.*

Doctor Westhead glanced at Barbara without expression. "I can see, right now, that we really will have to tie her to the bed before this is over."

"What…on TV?" Sarah asked hardly above a whisper, her eyes still closed.

"*Good Morning America* is the one I saw. The nurses tell me that *Today* and *This Morning* also had segments about your adventure. I'm told that CNN had a short segment and a gruesome tape of your ordeal a little after eight this morning. That means they'll probably have it on all day long."

Before Sarah fell asleep she mumbled something under her breath that neither the doctor nor her mom understood.

"All right, then. You get some rest, and I'll check back with you later on today. Okay?"

There was no answer from Sarah, so Dr. Westhead spoke to Barbara: "I think it best that we limit visitors today. If this turns into a parade, she'll never heal. She needs a lot of uninterrupted rest."

Barbara agreed and said good-bye to the doctor. As she pulled the sheet up around Sarah's shoulders, she realized that she, too, felt fatigued. She sat down in the chair and soon dozed off.

Bob returned around ten o'clock from the Pizza Shack. He touched Barbara on the arm to wake her. "How is she?" he whispered.

Startled, Barbara opened her eyes and checked her watch. She was surprised that she had slept for an hour, despite the nurses' continual interruptions. "Hi," she greeted. "She's doing okay, I think. The doctor seems satisfied. Sarah convinced him to take out the tube so she could talk."

"What did she think of the shooting?"

"We really haven't discussed it. The doctor came in just as we started talking about it."

"Tell me," Sarah said hoarsely when she woke up to the sound of their voices.

Bob lightly tapped his daughter on the nose with a finger. "Hey, lady. How you feel?"

"Better."

"What do you remember about yesterday?"

Awkwardly she cleared her throat. "Dr. Hightower. He hit me and made…he made me fall. He fell—he fell on—he shot me?"

"Dr. Hightower didn't shoot you, Sarah. It was John Holland. He shot you," Barbara informed her daughter, watching for her reaction.

"No. Not Mr. Holland. Why?" Sarah hoarsely forced as tears leaked from the corners of her eyes. "He was…friend."

Barbara didn't answer because she had the same impression of the reporter. She hoped that Chief Sheck would be able to shed some light on that question. "I don't know, dear. Perhaps he lost control or something. He definitely has a problem. He planned it, because he wanted you and Dr. Hightower close together, so he could shoot you both at the same time."

Sarah's jaw dropped, and she covered her mouth with her right hand as she stared at her mom. "He...Dr. Hightower didn't...?"

"He pushed you, to save you when he saw Holland pointing the gun at you. He was a second too late, because the gun went off right when he pushed you away. Then Holland aimed at him, but Ralph ran into him with his bicycle. The gun went off, anyway, and Dr. Hightower was shot in the leg, but he'll be okay."

Sarah was silent as she tried to remember more of what happened. She gave up. "Ralph…saved the Rev?"

Barbara watched her daughter struggle with her discomfort, and then answered, "Yes. And you too. He's a real hero. He was coming to warn the police about Holland, but he was too late. When he saw you get shot, he ran into Holland to keep him from shooting again."

"How did he know…uggh…Holland was going to—?"

"He was dropping off his article at Holland's office. He found a book that listed the names and times that Holland had made the threatening phone calls. Ralph called your dad, then rode down to Super City as fast as he could."

"Holland is…Immanuel?" Sarah quizzed in surprise, but didn't wait for an answer. "All the time…we thought that the Rev…but it was…I don't…why he—?" She closed her eyes and searched for a reason why the reporter would betray her and the gang.

Bob decided it was time to change the subject. He opened up the *San Antonio Express-News* morning paper for Sarah to see. The front-page headline read, "Young Cibolo Falls environmentalist shot." Barbara took the paper and skimmed the article, then folded it and placed it on the table beside Sarah.

"Well, if people didn't know who you were yesterday, they do today. What did the *Gazette* have to say?" she asked Bob.

With a flare, Bob unfolded the newspaper and held up the front page for Barbara and Sarah to see. There was nothing about the shooting on the front page. He grinned and turned to the second page. The headline on a corner column read: "Dr. Mark Hightower and Sarah McPhee shot on C. F. street."

Barbara stifled a laugh. "Second page, huh? The biggest story this town has had all year long, and since their employee is the culprit, they try to hide it on the second page."

"Yeah. Everybody in town knows, anyway. They would have been better off printing it in the largest headlines available, right on the front page. The way they've tried to hide it will just make them a laughingstock." He refolded the paper and placed it on top of the other.

He noticed that Sarah's eyes were closed. "Sarah," he said. There was no answer. "I called Sheck and he said, if it's all right with us, he could see us at his office around two o'clock, to fill us in on what he's been able to find out."

"Good. I need to apologize for last night," Barbara said.

"Well, in the meantime, why don't you go home and get some sleep? I'll hang here in case Sarah needs anything."

"What about the store? Won't they be shorthanded without either of us?"

"Ralph called first thing this morning and offered all the help we need. I called the regulars and asked them to work extra, so we would have some experience on hand to guide the GARBAGE kids through the rough spots. So I guess we'll be free for a couple of days. Maybe by then Sarah can pretty much make it on her own."

Barbara looked down at her sleeping daughter. Bob could see a trace of a smile cross Barbara's lips. "I think I will go home for a while and collapse. You sure you'll be okay?"

"Sure. The nurse at the front desk said Dr. Westhead has forbidden any visitors today, so that should hold down unnecessary traffic. I'll call Ralph in a little while and tell him to pass the word. I also told the receptionist to hold phone calls until further notice."

"Good," Barbara smiled. "Well, I'm out of here to get some shut-eye. Call about twelve if Sarah needs for me to bring anything. I'll try to get back here by twelve-thirty, so we'll have time to get a bite to eat before we see Sheck."

Spook interrupted Sarah's sleep: "*Quite an experience, little one. The world is watching you because of this incident. It has been an event that will affect the whole universe. You will now have many people who want to join you—who want to help in your quest.*"

Sarah thought for a moment before her mental reply: I don't know if I want to be hurt again like this. I don't care if it does affect the whole universe. I hurt, really bad, and I want to go home.

"That is understandable. And, I assure you, others are, indeed, feeling your pain along with you. As I said, the whole universe is affected. Others are sharing your experience."

Spook, why didn't you help me? I called for you. I needed for you to help me.

"I am limited in what I can do to help you physically. I can sway the events somewhat by encouraging you and others to help. But, the final event is what you have already chosen as an experience. If I change

it, you will merely create another situation to have the experience. Again, I can persuade others to help you make it a more perfect experience. As I did.

You persuaded others to make the experience better? Who?

"Those close to you."

That's no answer at all, Spook. Who helped, and how did you ask…uh…tell them?

"In due time. Let me say again, you have had a perfect experience, for you, the universe and all of God. I am honored to be a part of you."

Go away, Spook. I need to think.

"Much love to you, little one."

Yeah, right.

Journal Note

"Yes, you are indeed special, little one, but no more special than anyone else in this time or any other time. Each is equally special. Each is provided with an equal spark of God. Each is God."

CHAPTER 19

Bob and Barbara sat across from Chief Sheck at his desk. Sheck watched Barbara as she struggled for the right words. He knew by her embarrassment that she was no longer angry with him. "Donald, I'm terribly sorry for the outburst last night. I needed to lash out for what happened to Sarah, and you were…well, since I couldn't get my hands on John Holland…But there was really no excuse. Especially since you had no reason to suspect him."

"Can't say that I blame you," the chief followed as he straightened a stack of files on the corner of his desk. "If it'd been my daughter they brought into the hospital, I can't imagine what I would've done. And the police chief would have been as good a target as any.

"Have you people seen any of the television news programs today? Sarah and Cibolo Falls are hot items all over the country."

"Yeah," Bob answered. "She said she wanted people to hear what she had to say. I suspect she's going to get her chance. It's a shame it had to come this way, but..."

Barbara watched Sheck nibble at his mustache. He spoke: "It appears that, in her case, she was precisely in the right and wrong place at precisely the right and wrong time. She got what she was after but took a bullet to do it. It's very peculiar how things work out sometimes. It's as if she's on a strange journey—like it's all planned out."

"Everything she's done lately has attracted attention. Both Bob and I are having a hard time keeping up with all that's happening."

"I bet. If it's all right with y'all, I'd just as soon she left me out of the next chapter. I certainly missed the boat with this one. It just goes to show you; everybody's a suspect until the case is solved."

Barbara picked up a statuette of an old Texas lawman off the shelf next to her and examined it. "Holland was a little cranky at times, particularly with Ralph Coggins, but to go to that extreme, it makes you wonder. Sarah really felt he was her friend." She held out the figurine toward Sheck. "You?"

"Great Grandfather. Alpine, Texas. I'm told—pardon my French, ma'am—he was a badass."

"Pretty rugged-looking."

"Yeah, he'd been in six or seven gunfights, and no telling how many barroom brawls, so they say. He died at forty-two—kicked in the head by a mule."

"You have any mules on your spread, sheriff?" Barbara mused, bringing laughter from the chief.

Bob followed the conversation with interest but wanted to move on. "If you'd told me in our earlier talk that Holland was a suspect, I would've laughed. We had one little run-in with each other, but he acted like a royal wimp. I guess he had us all fooled. Thinking back to that night at the fairgrounds, we both thought that it was Hightower stalking around in the dark, taking pot-shots at us."

"Yeah, I thought about that this morning. That night I should've sent an officer to Hightower's home, just in case we missed him, but I thought we had him dead-to-rights. If I'd sent someone over there, and he was at home at the time, we would've had to find us another suspect. This case could've had a different outcome if we had gotten onto Holland sooner."

Sheck got up and opened the blinds, letting a flood of light into his drab office. "Have you thought of what might've happened if Ralph hadn't discovered what Holland was up to? If Holland had free reign, he would've gotten four or five shoots off. Ralph was the real hero yesterday. All ninety-five pounds of him."

"We'll have to do something special for him," Bob agreed. "He saved her life and is as much responsible for the success of GARBAGE as Sarah, but he gets very few kudos for his work."

"A celebration is definitely in order, just as soon as Sarah is able," Barbara added.

"Be sure to invite me." Sheck pointed a pencil at Barbara for emphasis. "That kid not only saved two lives, he probably saved my job, not to mention preventing a lot of misery for us all, especially you folks."

The chief picked up a file folder off the desk and laid it on the window sill. After he scanned the contents, he continued: "This could've been tragic, but I'm sure you'll now find this interesting. I stopped by the hospital, this morning, to get a statement from Dr. Hightower. He told me that he's been receiving harassing calls, the whole Beelzebub bit, for over three years. Every time his name appeared in the newspaper or he got any type of publicity, that night or the following day he could count on getting a call from Immanuel threatening to send him to hell."

Bob frowned. "Wait a minute. How come he never reported it? That certainly would've helped."

"No kidding. He thought the calls were harmless. In fact, he asked the caller to meet with him on several different occasions to work out their differences. He thought he could help the guy get back on track, but the caller resisted until, of course, yesterday. He called Hightower about three o'clock and said that he would meet with him at the demonstration. Hightower asked him what their meeting had to do with the demonstration. The answer was, 'Everything. It's going to be a big surprise.'

"When Hightower got to the demonstration, he spied Joyce Brown standing a short distance behind Sarah, so he decided to go chat with her while he waited for Immanuel. As he neared Sarah, that's when Holland went into action."

Bob looked puzzled. "Wait a minute; Holland had Sarah and Hightower together at the council meeting. Why didn't he act then?"

"Also at the parking lot of the restaurant during pizza Sunday," Barbara interjected.

Sheck looked out the window into the sunshine. "We discussed that here at the station. We assume that he didn't feel he could get them both, because they were separated by several feet with a lot of people in between. As soon as he got the first shot off, the ensuing panic would have made it impossible to get in a second."

He closed the file, left the window and returned to his desk. He dropped his body recklessly into the well-worn chair. "So, he arranged to get Hightower to come to the demonstration, hoping to get them close enough together to do the deed. If he couldn't pull it off, he would just wait for another chance."

"Does Hightower know that he was suspected of making the calls to us?"

"I don't know, and I'm not about to ask or tell him. That information will die with me unless someone else lets the cat out." Sheck raised a lone brow and cleared his throat.

"I think your, or should I say, *our* secret is safe with us," Bob said flatly. "After all, I was positive he was the caller."

"I'm glad we agree on that little detail," Sheck replied. "I must say, Hightower wishes he'd taken the caller a little more seriously. Maybe he could've prevented the shooting altogether."

"I guess it's easy for all of us to look back and ask, What if?" Barbara remarked. "But that part's over and fortunately everyone survived. What about Holland? What's in store for him?"

"He went before the judge this morning. Looks like we have a real nutcase on our hands. His attorney, the district attorney, and the judge have already agreed to psychiatric testing before going any further. Everything will be on hold until we hear what the doctors have to say. The judge has asked for a preliminary report early next week."

"That should be interesting reading."

"Well, whatever they decide, they'd better not put him out on the street," Barbara retorted forcefully.

"They're not going to do that. Not anytime soon, anyway. I won't be privy to the report, but the DA will give me the scuttlebutt when it comes in. I'll pass on what I hear to you. For what y'all have been through, at least you deserve that."

After talking for a few minutes about the heavy publicity surrounding the case, Bob and Barbara, anxious to get back to Sarah, thanked Chief Sheck, and said good-bye. Once back at the hospital, they stopped by the receptionist, picked up a stack of messages for Sarah, and told her to begin putting phone calls through to their daughter.

When they stepped into the room, they found it had morphed into a jungle. Flowers, plants and get-well balloons crowded the room and gave off an aroma Barbara could smell in the hallway. Sarah had the bed cranked up, lying in a semi-sitting position as the nurse intently took her blood pressure. Barbara was pleased that Sarah had gained much more of her natural color in the last two hours and appeared much more comfortable and alert. She had a thermometer dangling from her mouth.

Barbara swept her hand toward all the flowers. "Well, you seem to have a few fans out there somewhere."

Sarah mumbled something. The nurse removed the thermometer, recorded the temperature, and asked Sarah if she needed anything while she was there. She left when Sarah shook her head.

"Yeah…don't think…have room for more. I told 'em, if more come, bring me…card and give flowers…other patients."

"Well, that was nice of you. I'm sure there are patients in this hospital who never receive flowers." Barbara said while she felt her daughter's forehead for a fever like mothers always do. "Well, you're looking better. How are you feeling?"

"Legs and…right arm don't…hurt."

"So everything else does?" Bob laughed.

"Hurts when…I turn…head. I coughed…killed me."

"There were a lot of muscles involved in your injury, and I'm sure they assist in coughing." Bob tried to appease her. "The doc said your left arm might be bummed out for a while."

"Better hurry," Sarah said gruffly. She tried to relieve this by clearing her throat. Unsuccessful, she continued: "Got places to go."

"Now, don't you count on going to New York," Barbara said. "You heard what Dr. Westhead said."

"What?" Sarah asked with an innocent gesture and an intentionally overplayed frown of confusion.

"You know good and well what he said. You're not going anywhere until he says you're able. And I intend to see that his rules are followed. You understand?"

"Well..." Sarah answered smugly as a twinge of pain shot through her chest. "I'll tell him that—" Sarah was interrupted by the telephone. Puzzled, she looked to her father. He had said no calls would be put through.

"We thought that since we're here, you could take a few, but it's going off when we leave." Bob picked up the receiver. "Room 341. Sarah McPhee's answering service speaking. May I be of service?"

Sarah giggled, sending a quick pain through her chest. She put her right hand over the wound and grimaced as tears welled up in her eyes.

"Yes, she's doing quite well," Bob said to the caller. "Who did you say you are?...Oh, yes. Of course....Sure....I'm sure she would want to, but I don't know if the doctors will allow her to so soon....Okay, I'll be glad to....Okay, hold just a second."

Bob cupped his hand over the mouthpiece of the phone and raised his brow. "CNN wants to send Robert Bruce for an interview in the morning, for *Earth Scope* tomorrow night."

Sarah glanced at her mom for permission. The reaction she received wasn't favorable, but Sarah nodded to her father. Bob looked to Barbara for any objection to Sarah's decision.

"I don't think it's a good idea. You've been shot in the chest, for God's sake. You nearly died. Now, you want to be interviewed two days later. You're in no condition—"

Sarah croaked her interruption, "Aw, Mom. I'll be...okay. Please."

"What about Doctor Westhead? You know he's not going to like it."

Sarah's eyes narrowed as she contemplated her mom's concern. "It's...he won't...care."

"Yeah, right," Barbara answered as she shook her head in dismay. "This I've got to see." She turned and looked out the window. "Okay, you've got my vote, but you have to handle the doctor. I'm not going to fight this battle for you."

"No problem," Sarah retorted in a throaty yet flippant rasp. She winked at her dad to give the okay to the caller.

"What time?" Bob asked into the phone. "Okay, that's fine. All we request is that you get it done as fast as possible, and don't make too much of a production out of it....Sure....Yes, we'll see you then."

Bob hung up the phone and announced, "Ten o'clock in the morning. They'll be running on a tight schedule. They want a short interview with Dr. Hightower, too. And they have to get back to Atlanta as soon as they can."

Sarah smiled her triumph but became concerned. "I look...terrible."

Barbara turned back from the window and fixed her daughter with a bemused stare. "Just like a movie star. One day away from near death, and she's worried about how she looks. Well, I'll tell you what: if you think you can sit up a few minutes first thing in the morning, we'll have the hospital beautician come up and see what she can do with your hair. I'll bring some makeup and we'll make you look halfway presentable."

"I'll sit up."

Thursday morning, Dr. Westhead wasn't too happy when he learned at the nurse's post that Sarah, barely thirty-six hours after major surgery, was going to hold court for CNN from her hospital bed. When he entered the room and found her sitting up in bed as the beautician worked with a styling brush and dryer, he sighed and threw up his hands in frustration. "I can tell already, young lady, that you can't go on like—"

He paused when Sarah gestured that she couldn't hear him. He reached over and pulled the dryer cord from the outlet. She projected a comical I'm-in-big-trouble face.

He ignored her theatrics and said sternly as he pointed a threatening finger, "As I was trying to say: I don't care who you are, you are not going to turn this hospital into a circus. Perhaps I'm going to have to put chains on you, so you'll at least have half a chance to get well." He paused and looked around the room at all the plants, flowers, and balloons. He released a long hiss of a sigh through his teeth. "What are you, anyway? Some sort of diva or something?"

Barbara answered for Sarah: "That's only a small portion. I think she's filled every room in the hospital." She pointed to the stack of cards and notes on the table beside the bed. "Each of those represents flowers or balloons that she's rerouted to other patients in the hospital. The last delivery guy said his shop had orders for more that he would deliver later."

The doctor turned back toward Sarah and studied her pensively, making her squirm: "I can see, right now, you and I are going to have a knock-down-drag-out fight before you get out of here. You can't possibly get well going ninety miles an hour the whole time you're here."

"Then maybe...you should send me home," Sarah pouted. She

then grinned mischievously. "Then you won't have me bothering you."

Dr. Westhead turned toward Sarah's visibly embarrassed mother. "When was the last time this child has had a good rear-end paddling?"

Barbara, thankful that the doctor wasn't taking her daughter's charade too seriously, answered, "I really don't know. We only adopted her last week."

"Figures." Dr. Westhead turned back toward Sarah. "Well, young lady, after this fiasco is over, do you think we can settle it down a little? You need all the rest you can get, that is, if you want even a chance of getting out of here in time to go to—where was it?"

"New York," Sarah blurted out, only to clutch her wound. She attempted to smooth over her reaction to the pain like it was an act, then continued: "Do you mean it? Will I be able to go to New York?"

"I don't believe I said that, did I?" He ignored her discomfort as she hoped he would. "I said that you had better get some rest if you want even a chance of going. It takes a lot of time to heal, and if you don't get proper rest, it takes more time. Do you understand that, or do I need to make it more clear?"

Much to Barbara's chagrin, Sarah mused, baiting the doctor, "Do you want my autograph now?" She paused to clear her throat. "Or do you want to wait in line later?"

He threw up his hands in mock defeat. "You win this round, but I don't go down easily." He reached over and plugged in the hair dryer.

"Thanks, Doctor Westhead, *sir*. You're such a good doctor."

The doctor studied her chart, then winked at Barbara, and left the room.

At 9:45, Robert Bruce and the director of *Earth Scope*, Johnny Jeffcoat, along with a cameraman, noisily entered Sarah's room. After the usual pleasantries, Bob and Barbara helped the director and cameraman move many of the plants out into the hall to make room as Robert Bruce, dressed in his usual red plaid logger's shirt, explained to Sarah what he was going to ask. He sat down next to the bed so the cameraman could get a light check. When the cameraman nodded that everything was satisfactory, Bruce smoothed his beard and ruffled his curly hair for that windblown look.

"Okay, Sarah," the director announced when everyone appeared ready. "Don't be concerned about making a mistake. This will be short, so we can retake it if you're uncomfortable with anything you've said.

Okay?"

Sarah, sitting upright in bed, nodded.

"Good," the director smiled. "Now, what we—Hold it. Robert, you're just a hair too low. With Sarah sitting that high, we need...Yeah, that'll do," he said, taking a pillow from the other bed offered by Bob. "Here, try this."

Bruce put the pillow on his chair and sat on top of it.

"Perfect," said the director. He gestured impatiently and said something under his breath to himself. "Sorry folks, I'm just not with it this morning. I nearly forget the most important part." He reached into an equipment satchel and pulled out a special speakerphone. Unplugging the hospital room phone, he replaced it with the speakerphone, just within Sarah's reach. He pressed a button and the dial tone came over the speaker.

"What's that for?" Sarah asked.

"Okay, Sarah. Just when we get into the interview, the phone is going to ring. We've arranged it with the hospital receptionist to put through only the call that we're expecting. When it rings, whatever you or Robert are saying, you say, 'Excuse me,' and press this button, right here. You can then answer without picking up the phone. All of us will be able to hear what the caller says through the speaker. Okay?"

"Okay, but, who—?"

"It's going to be a good surprise, I promise."

Sarah frowned her distrust at the director, then pointed a threatening finger. "No tricks, right?"

"No tricks, Sarah. Promise. But we won't be able to retake the phone part, so just act like you always do. Just be yourself and everything will work out fine."

Sarah looked to her mom and dad for help. She could tell they were just as confused. She looked back toward the director and waited patiently, her heart raced as it always did when she was before the camera.

The director looked at his watch and said, "We'd better get started. Bruce, you ready? Sarah?" After he received quick nods from both, he ordered, "Okay, Jim, roll it when ready."

"I'm coming to you, now, from Sarah McPhee's room at Breckenridge Hospital in Cibolo Falls, Texas." The cameraman gradually adjusted the lens to take in both Bruce and Sarah. "And here we have, once again, Sarah McPhee."

Bruce turned toward Sarah and continued: "Sarah, it's good to see you again, but this is under different circumstances than our last meeting. How are you feeling, now that a day and a half has passed since being shot?"

"I'm feeling better…all the time," Sarah answered with a graveled voice, then put her fist over her mouth to stifle an unwelcome cough. She flinched.

"A lot has happened since our program last week. I'm sure you are aware of the enthusiasm shown around the country, as well as the world, for what you're trying to do. We've just shown our viewing audience the tapes that we've collected from the world over, of kids, and even adults, using your Earth Salute to remind themselves and others of their place in the scheme of things. We've also had reports that many of these same people are joining you in taking fifteen minutes out of each day to help clean up or improve the earth."

"Good. Everybody…needs to help. Governments and businesses, Before…uugh…it's too late."

"Sarah, you okay?"

"Yes, go ahead."

"Two days ago, you and another person were shot. Do you think that it had anything to do with the work you're doing or with your beliefs that you are God?"

"That we are *all* God," Sarah corrected, her eyes suddenly sad. "I don't understand. Mr. Holland was…is my friend. I don't understand why he would shoot—"

The ring of the speakerphone interrupted Sarah. She looked puzzled as she glanced first to Bruce, then her mom and dad. Bob gestured for her to answer it.

"Uh...excuse me." She pushed the speaker button and said a tentative, "Hello?"

"Hello, Sarah," came a strange voice over the speaker. "This is President Oakley, calling from the White House."

After initial wide-eyed surprise, Sarah composed herself and beamed a wide smile. Adrenaline kicked in and caused her heart to race. She forgot about the camera filming her.

"Talk to him," Bob silently mouthed with an urgent gesture of his hands and nod of his head.

"Mr. Oakley—I mean, Mr. President," Sarah replied meekly as she looked directly at the speakerphone. "I can't believe...I'm glad you called."

"It's good to hear your voice, Sarah. The First Lady, Sandra, my daughter, April, and I watched you last week on *Earth Scope.* Yesterday, when we heard that you had been hurt while demonstrating for what you believe, we decided to call and see how you're doing."

"I'm doing good. Thank you for calling," Sarah responded much more forcefully. "I hope, since you watch *Earth Scope,* you want to protect the Earth, too, I've heard that a lot of the...uh...people in our government don't care about that."

"Sarah, it's our intention to do whatever we can to protect our precious resources for you and your children. Since I have you on the phone, Sarah, maybe you have some advice that I can give to all the senators and congressmen here in Washington on what we can or should be doing to help protect the Earth's environment and resources."

"Yes, sir. I do have a little something that will help you and the senators. If I had just one thing to ask of you, it would be: in each law you pass, please put your interest in the Earth first. If the law doesn't protect the Earth, don't pass it."

"Well, now, Sarah. That's sound advice. I'm certainly going to keep it in mind when I sign or veto future laws. Now, Sarah, they tell me that you're going to come to the World Environmental Symposium in New York City in a few weeks. I am going, also, as a representative of the United States. I wonder if you'd do me a big favor?"

"Yes, sir. I'll do whatever you want, if I can."

"Good. I wonder if you could arrange to come by the White House on your way to New York and have lunch with Sandra, April, and me? We would love to have you visit our home."

Sarah didn't answer as she was awestruck over what the President had asked. Barbara waved her arms to get her daughter's attention and then exaggerated a nod.

Sarah collected herself and smiled, "I would like that, Mr. President, and I want to meet April. She would probably like to help us."

"Oh, I know she would, Sarah, and she wants to meet you too. Okay, now. It's a date. You get well, so you'll be able to come. We'll be looking forward to seeing you at the White House."

"I can't wait, Mr. President, and thank you for calling."

"It has been my pleasure, Sarah. My secretary will be calling you to set up a date. Bye-bye."

"Good-bye, Mr. President." Sarah was jarred back into her hospital room. She pushed the button to hang up the phone and smiled at Bruce. "Did you know he was—?"

"Yes, the President knew we were coming to talk to you, so he asked if he could call while we were here. Are you going to be well enough to go to the symposium and have lunch with the President, Sarah?"

Sarah grinned, "My doctor is Dr. Westhead. He says that he'll make sure I'm well enough to go…because he's such a good doctor."

"Well, Sarah, we at *Earth Scope* and people all over the world are pulling for you to get well fast. We'll be watching to see what you do next to help the Earth."

Sarah flashed a smile. "Thank you for coming back." She raised her right hand, palm toward the camera, and then closed it into a fist.

"Okay, that's it," the director announced. "Beautiful, Sarah. We couldn't have rehearsed it any better." He gestured toward the cameraman to pack it up. "Let's move it. We've got to have a word with this Hightower guy and get some crowd pictures at the image before we leave."

Robert nodded at Sarah and patted her on the shoulder. "We ought to do this more often. We work well together."

"I work cheap. At least that's what Dad thinks. I barely get minimum wage," she mused as Bob and Barbara joined them.

"That certainly was a surprise," Barbara commented.

Bruce laughed. "The President knows free publicity when he sees it. Yesterday, CNN's White House correspondent called Atlanta on other business, and relayed that the President had mentioned that he was considering calling Sarah. One thing led to another and here we are."

"President Oakley's been receiving a lot of flak over offshore drilling and negligence of what forests are left," added the director. "So, he's been trying to find a way to win back environmentalists. Since Sarah is riding the ecological wave right now, he jumped at the chance to get on it, too."

"We can't complain," Bruce chimed in. "I guess CNN has hopped on Sarah's wagon, too." He winked at Sarah. "If you're going to make any headlines anytime soon, give me a call ahead of time, okay?"

Before her evening meal, Sarah was finally allowed to receive her first visitors from GARBAGE. Steve didn't seem to care that Sarah requested a private visit with Ralph before Steve or any of the others.

Ralph stuck his head through the door not knowing what to expect. Sarah saw a faint shadow on the wall near the door. "Ralph, that you?"

He came grinning into view. "Hey, Sarah! You look great!"

Sarah laughed, the pain cutting it short. "What did you expect? Blood on the sheets?"

"Well, I don't know. Last time I saw you, you were leaking all over the parking lot." He came over and touched the bulge over her left chest, causing her to flinch. "Oh, sorry. You hurt?"

"Only when I laugh...or move...or breathe."

"Ah, man. I'm sorry. I don't want you to hurt."

"Ralph, you don't need to be sorry about anything. Mom made me a tape of the CNN news. I saw it. You saved my life. That make's you a hero, at least to me."

Ralph flipped a hand indifferently. "You gotta do what you gotta do."

"Well, you did it, and you will never live it down. I'm going to remind you everyday. And when you're mad at me, I'll say it's all your fault for saving my life."

"Well, I've got news for you," Ralph countered. "Spook had a hand in it, too. When I was leaving Holland's office, he told me to go back and look at the book. That's when I realized that Holland was in on the *Beelzebub* stuff."

"Really, Ralph. That's cool. So Spook was helping. I thought that he deserted me." Sarah reached up and ran her hand through her newly coiffed hair and let it drop back in place. "Has he talked to you since?"

"Naw, I guess it was a one-time deal." Ralph walked slowly around the room, checking out the flowers, balloons, and other gifts. "Umm, looks like you cleaned up."

"Isn't it crazy?" She pointed to the ever-growing stack of cards. "And stuff came with all those, too. We don't have room for any more. She watched Ralph pick up a few of the cards and read them. "So, how's it going?"

"Kind of dull without your dirty face. When you getting outa here?"

"Don't know yet."

"Your mom said you talked to the Prez. That's tight."

"Yeah, I nearly dropped dead when I heard his voice. I can't wait to see the program."

They looked at each other, neither wishing to say anything else. The silence got to Sarah. "Thanks again, Ralph. Can I give you a kiss?"

Ralph's face felt warm as a blush-like shadow ran over his cheeks. At a loss for response, he ducked his head. "I think I'll get Steve." He waved half-heartedly, "Later," and retreated out the door.

A moment later Steve rapped on the door. It was somehow awkward for both of them. They managed some small talk about the shooting before he finally got around to kissing her—more of a peck on the check, she thought. She watched him sitting in the chair next to the bed, obviously uncomfortable. She knew something was wrong.

"So, what's the deal?" she asked impatiently. "You got a problem?"

"Not really."

"Come on, Steve. What's up?"

Steve got up, walked around the room, and stopped to look out the window. "There's just too much going on with you. We never have time for just us."

"I don't think I planned on getting shot, Steve."

"It's not just that. It's the whole deal—meetings, demonstrations, you're always planning something. JB and Ralph are always hanging around. We're never alone. It's never just us."

Sarah flinched, not only at the words but the tone in which they were said. *Why is he saying these things and why didn't I know before now?* "I don't understand, Steve. You know I have to do all this. I don't have a choice. And you knew this when we hooked-up. I thought I had your support—and love?"

"You do. You know that," he stammered. "It's just that everything is always you. It's Sarah this and Sarah that. That's all I hear."

Sarah's dismay grew by the second. She didn't know how to respond. She didn't want to lose Steve, but she couldn't stop being who she had become in the last few months, for Steve or anybody else.

"What do you want, Steve? What do you want me to do?" she heard herself ask, as if in a fog.

"Just give it up," Steve blurted as he continued to look out the window. "We can't keep going on like this. I can't take it. Football's going to start soon, and I won't have time—we won't have time if both of us are doing different stuff."

Heartbroken, Sarah could only stare at Steve, bewildered. She felt tears welling up in her eyes and willed them to stop. They didn't; a lone hot tear trickled down her cheek.

"I don't know why you had to do this now, Steve. But what do you care? Why don't you just leave?" she choked, trying to hold her emotions in check.

Steve turned away from the window and headed for the door, not saying a word or looking at her. Sarah yielded to her grief and cried, ignoring the pain each new sob caused in her chest.

When Steve walked stone-faced past JB and Ralph, they knew it wasn't good. They quickly entered Sarah's room. Each with a hand on Sarah, they silently comforted her, knowing words would be useless.

Later Sarah attempted to compose herself and was already planning on what she called life after Steve. Through the lingering tears she sadly sifted through the box of get-well notes from the rest of the group and pictures of the candlelight vigil. Awkwardly, Ralph displayed the Thursday edition of the *Gazette* with his *GARBAGE Notes* article, edited by the new reporter, Jeff Broom.

The three of them visited about thirty minutes more while Sarah picked at her dinner, rehashed the shooting, the group's vigil outside the hospital, and the call from the President. Barbara and Bob returned from dinner and were shocked about the bad news from Steve, particularly his timing. They then gathered with the kids to watch the short segment on *Earth Scope*. After the program, they suggested it was time for JB and Ralph to leave.

"What happened, sweetheart? Did you have a fight?"

The tears returned, "I don't know. He just said that the stuff I'm doing is going to interfere with football. He wants me to quit so we can be together."

"Whoa, wait a minute," Bob barked. "You're kidding, aren't you?"

"That's what he said, Dad."

"So, what are you going to do?" Barbara asked.

"I won't quit for Steve. I can't. It's just not fair that he's even asking. I thought that I knew him, but I guess I don't. I just don't understand why he waited until now, just when I needed him most. I guess he's just a jerk."

Barbara studied her daughter and recalled the time when her first boyfriend dumped her. She remembered her friends told her he wasn't good enough for her, and she would find someone better. She still hurt, but she later healed—only to get hurt again. "Sarah, I'm sure Steve feels guilty that he didn't protect you—to keep you from getting hurt. He probably feels like he let you down and just being around you reminds him that he failed. Maybe he isn't mature enough to deal with these feelings."

Sarah didn't comment, and Barbara knew it would take time for Sarah to sort through her feelings for Steve. There wasn't anything she or anyone else could say to ease her pain. Bob and Barbara bid Sarah good night after they made sure she was comfortable.

As night approached it slowly darkened the window, then turned it into a large mirror of the lighted room, Sarah was glad everyone had left and the day was nearly over. The emotions she experienced over Steve's exit had only added to her fatigue. She was well aware that she had extended herself more than she should have and promised that, beginning now, she would rest as Dr. Westhead suggested, so she would heal in time to make the trip to New York and the White House.

She pulled the chain on her bed lamp, pointed the remote at the TV, and turned it off. The room was thrust into darkness except for a stream of light coming under the door. She wondered if hospital rooms were ever completely dark. With her right hand she pulled the sheet up under her chin and tried to find a comfortable position.

She closed her eyes and tried to put Steve out of her mind, fully expecting a visit from Spook. He soon came through, much more clearly than usual:

"With Steve as well as the universe, acknowledge that the circumstances you have been presented are a tool, a challenge, for you to learn, to experience, to teach, to change, and to love. Although you have experienced pain and frustration, always remember, there is a grand design of the universe based on harmony, and you are playing a precious part of that design.

"You have a lot to give. You have a lot to teach. You have a lot to say to others about this harmony. Because of your experience, they want to listen to you. Do not hesitate to use this opportunity, born of your pain,

to teach others. There is no time to be wasted. Lead those that will now gladly follow, down the path to a renewed love and respect of the earth, all its resources and all its creatures."

"Spook?"

"Yes, I understand your question. You are wondering why Steve chose now to hurt you, and why he is so selfish—why he didn't wait until you are well to end your relationship. You must remember that Steve has his own issues to experience. And with this issue, you chose to be involved. It appears that it is a bad experience, but it is not. You both will be better for it."

"I still think he's an asshole."

"Goodnight, little one. This has been another great day for the universe."

"Yeah, right, that's easy for you to say."

Journal Note

"You should listen to the inner guidance that is always with you. Do not ever put another's thoughts ahead of yours, no matter how powerful they may seem or what high position of authority they may occupy. This is very important. If their thoughts and beliefs do not agree with your own, you must never blindly follow them. Always listen to your own inner guidance. Listen with confidence. You, little one, are always your own best counsel."

CHAPTER 20

"What was it she…yeah, I know: *unda frie hongos otro partes.* Mom said I should go fry my mushrooms somewhere else. She told me two weeks ago Pinky wasn't any good, because her rooster chased him out of the yard when he came to visit. She said the same about Steve."

Sarah laughed with very little chest pain. "JB, you're full of it. Because her rooster ran him off, he's no good?"

"The rooster was right. Pinky called me after Steve split up with you. He said he didn't want to go with me anymore. So, I said, 'Hey, *stupido,* I don't understand. All we did was hang out with the guys. You never even asked me on a date; now you don't want to go with me anymore? What kind of deal is that?'"

"What did he say?"

"He thought, since we held hands and kissed a couple of times, we were hooked-up," JB mused. "I laughed at him, and he didn't like it. He got all hyper when I told him that he and Steve were just alike—they would make a great couple."

"I love it," Sarah replied. "I wish I could've seen it."

"There's more, sweetie. He wanted to know if I was accusing him of being gay. I said, 'Hey, dude, any guy that doesn't want to latch onto a hottie like me has to be gay.' That's when he really got his jockeys in a twist. He said that he was going to tell Steve what I said about them being gay."

"He didn't say that? Really?"

"He said it, Sarah. Can you believe it? And you're gonna love this, child. I said, 'Oh no, Pinky. Anything but that. Please don't tell Steve what I said. My world will end.'"

Sarah and JB laughed so hard that Sarah's chest did hurt this time. JB watched her closely. "You all right?"

"Yeah, I'm okay, except for my broken heart. But Mom says I'll live to have many more broken hearts. That doesn't sound like too much fun."

JB noticed Sarah's eyes tear over. "You miss him, don't you?"

"Yeah. He was kind of a doofus sometimes, but I liked the way he smelled, the way I felt when he touched me…kissed me. I really liked the—aw what difference does it make, anyway? I'm better off without him."

"Would you take him back if he begged?"

"That's a big no. One, he dumped me the day after I got shot. Nobody does me that way, *guido*. Two, we don't…we aren't right for each other, even though he made me feel really, really good. But guess what? I'll get over it."

"Go, girl."

Saturday marked four days since the shooting and Sarah was already roaming the third floor hallway of Breckenridge Hospital in her blue robe and Houston Astros baseball cap. She walked with only a little pain, however slowly and cautiously. The only badge of her injury was a dark blue arm sling used to immobilize her left shoulder. She had learned the names of most of the patients on her floor and took time to visit each on her tours. However, she hadn't ventured to any of the other floors yet. Although dreading it, she felt an urge to take a visit to the fourth floor—Dr. Mark Hightower.

At the insistence of the third floor head nurse, Dr. Westhead had limited the number of Sarah's youthful visitors to three in the morning, three in the afternoon and a like number in the evening. On Friday, countless kids had attempted to visit Sarah, clogging elevators, the halls, and Sarah's small room. Ralph had a lottery to choose who could visit, other than himself, JB, Donnie, and Smiley. She was due to check out Tuesday or Wednesday, so only a handful would get to pay her a visit. The others would have to wait.

The nurses ejected the last of her afternoon visitors and Sarah was off to the fourth floor for her dreaded visit. When the elevator door opened, Sarah held back, not quite ready to meet Hightower face-to-face. She pushed the Close Door button, then the button for floor five and the hospital cafeteria.

The cafeteria was empty except for two employees cleaning up after the noon lunch crowd. She purchased a small fountain Pepsi and found a table in a dark corner. It was nice to be alone where no one could bother her. Her body ached more than usual with the anticipation of what lay ahead. *Maybe I should just give up and go back to my room. I can put this off for another time. Yeah, when? Do I want to meet him at his office at the church? No. Well, just get it over with, so I don't have to worry about it any longer*. She had forgotten that she was never without Spook. It startled her when he spoke:

Good afternoon, little one. I can see your reluctance to meet Hightower. You must change your feeling from that of fear to that of love. As you know from our previous talks, fear closes you off from him; love opens you up to him. Your love, as God, toward this person will produce nothing but good for the both of you and, above all, the universe."

That's easy for you to say, Sarah projected her thoughts to Spook. She took a long slow draw on her straw. I'm the one that has to talk to him. I remember what you said about not putting his thoughts ahead of mine, but still he knows more about things than I do. He always says the right thing and I don't.

"You cannot and will not go wrong if you remember to see God and love in every event. Everything is God. So, approach everything that happens as a God situation."

With that, Spook was gone. Unfortunately, she wasn't any less fearful than before. She sighed her disappointment and studied a painting of a girl on a bicycle hanging on a nearby wall. She wondered when she would be able to bike again. She slurped up the last of the soda and stood up. She couldn't put this meeting off any longer.

Getting off the elevator at the fourth floor, she waved to two nurses at their station as she walked slowly by. She paused at the open door of room 414 for a peak. *Maybe he isn't in. Maybe he's checked out already.* She could see feet sticking up under the sheets at the foot of the bed. She reluctantly knocked on the door.

"Yes?" came the deep confident voice, so familiar and so threatening. "Come in."

She encouraged herself not to be afraid and walked a few steps to meet her nemesis face-to-face—to meet her life-saver. He sat before her, propped up in bed. She smiled but said nothing. No fear, she reminded herself.

"Well, well, if it isn't the famous Sarah McPhee!" Hightower boomed when he recovered from his initial surprise. Sarah watched as he ran his hand through his hair. "I must say, this is a pleasant surprise. Please, please have a seat," he said as he gestured toward two chairs. "You certainly do look chipper, considering what you've been through. Are you feeling okay?"

Sarah sat down in the chair closest to the bed. When she was firmly, however uncomfortably settled, she replied more meekly than she would have liked, "I'm doing good, thanks to you. How are you? Are you going to be able to leave here anytime soon?"

"Unlike you, my injury is on the walking end, so, they say I can't get up for another day or so, then I can go home, that is, if I promise to stay in bed for a while." He studied Sarah, making her more uncomfortable, then resumed with a compassion unfamiliar to Sarah. "I'm so glad you came by. We could use a little visit, just you and I, don't you think?"

Sarah projected all the love she could at the man in front of her as she adjusted the baseball cap. "I probably wouldn't be here for a chat," she said, a little more confident and easy, "if you hadn't risked your life to protect me. That's why I'm here—to thank you."

Hightower flashed a brilliant smile. "Yes, that was rather daring of me. I don't know what came over me. Being a hero isn't something you plan on doing, particularly if your life is at stake." He fixed Sarah with an amused stare. "I have to tell you, however, I had a bit of help.

It appears that your…you know, the voice you…the one I believe you call Spook gave me some timely advice. It certainly helped, just when I needed guidance the most."

Hightower watched Sarah's eyes widen in surprise. "Spook talked to you?"

"When I arrived at your demonstration, before I got out of the car, Spook identified himself and said I should be aware that danger awaited me. He urged me to go quickly with caution. As I was nearing you on my way to talk to Joyce Brown, Spook urged me to look back. That's when I saw Mr. Holland with the gun pointed at you. I would have never had the chance to foil his shot if it wasn't for Spook. The rest is all history."

"Wow, that's neat. Spook also talked to my dad when Immanuel…uh…Mr. Holland was shooting at him at the fairgrounds. And he also told Ralph about the book, at John Holland's office."

"Yes, I heard about Ralph and the book. You know, the real hero of this whole story is Ralph. I'm told he saved both of us. Police Chief Sheck said Holland would've emptied his gun on us if Ralph hadn't intervened."

After a moment of uneasy silence, Sarah spoke: "I saw your interview with Bruce on *Earth Scope* the other night. You came across very well...uh...positively. In the past, I hadn't felt it, but on the program I felt love coming from you. Real love."

Hightower studied Sarah. "You know, I guess we all forget the part that love plays in our lives. I need to practice loving each and everyone more."

"Some of my friends also said they saw love coming from you, and that you were very...They thought you were cool." Sarah smiled hesitantly, somewhat surprised at what she said, however more confident in the conversation. As she looked around the room, she noticed that Hightower also had a ton of flowers. She realized that, although they had different beliefs, he was a man that was loved and respected by many, and admired him for that.

"Cool, huh? Well now, that's a first. I was rather cool, wasn't I? At least it was favorable for a change, despite the fact that I was once again upstaged by you. I guess my legacy, in this instance, will probably be limited to being the guy who saved Sarah McPhee—not the guy who saves souls."

"Well, saving my life was pretty important," Sarah smiled as she felt more and more that the man in front of her wasn't so scary after all. "Where would I be if you hadn't saved Sarah McPhee? And isn't saving a life as important as saving a soul? After all, now I can continue talking about what *you* don't believe." The minister didn't respond. "Just think, if I get everyone to believing that they are God, it'll be because of you," she added, feigning innocence.

Hightower ignored the hint of flippancy, or so she thought. He leaned out over his bed and looked out the door to make sure no one was within listening distance. With squinted eyes and a mischievous grin, he pointed at Sarah and asked, "Did anyone ever tell you you're a little smartass?"

Sarah giggled, then folded her good arm over her chest to quell the pain. "Not this week," she answered, all remaining tension vanished.

The minister frowned. "You sure you're okay? Looks like you're having quite a bit of pain."

"Only when I laugh."

"Damn, I wish I could get all the attention from the media that you're getting. What is it with you, that everyone wants to hear what you have to say?"

"Must be my magnetic personality."

Hightower looked up and pleaded, "Ah, charisma, lovely charisma. God, it would be so grand if you would favor me with just a tad more of that dynamic *specialness,* to set me apart from the masses, just as you have done for this mere child sitting before me."

Sarah laughed at Hightower's theatrics, renewing the pain in her chest and shoulder. She adjusted herself as she searched for a more comfortable position as he watched. "Maybe you already have that *specialness* to set you apart. It's the message that needs to be changed."

"Right," he answered with a tight grin. "And I suppose the message would be the same one you've been delivering."

"Why not?" Sarah answered innocently. "Just like yours, it's all about God."

The minister's eyes narrowed. "Tell me, now that it's just you and me. Do you really believe that 'I am God,' stuff you're putting out or is it just a way to get attention?"

Sarah shot back, "Of course I do. Now, you tell me something. Do you believe all that stuff you preach, or is it just a way of getting attention?"

Hightower burst into loud guffaws that echoed down the hall. He continued to laugh until tears came to his eyes. He wiped the tears with the edge of the sheet. "You know, I think you and I could make a great team. If I had the publicity you're getting, I could set the world on fire."

"Yes, I bet you could," Sarah answered, amused at his enthusiastic reaction. "I suppose I could invite you along if you have a bicycle, but I don't think people would go for that, do you?"

"I suppose not." He wiped the few remaining tears. "Your explanation of God is a little too easy and logical to understand. You've got it all too simply laid out for the people. And you have no control that way."

"You left out how you remind them where they're going, if they don't do right—if they sin," Sarah followed.

Hightower pointed a finger of agreement at Sarah. "Right you are. You have to have some fear and, perhaps, a good dose of mysticism. He pointed the same finger to make a point, jabbing it rhythmically as he spoke: "And you know what? That's what most of them want. You, Sarah, are trying to get them to take responsibility for all their actions. Well, with my religion they don't have to take responsibility. All they have to do is follow my lead. You see, I make it easy for them."

"And what about you? Do you believe all that?"

"Let me say this, before I answer your question. Perhaps I shouldn't be telling you what I think and believe because it wouldn't, shall I say, sound right to the people I serve. They would lose confidence in me and in my ability to lead them. So, if you happen to divulge what I say or have said here to others, I may have to deny saying anything of the sort. Do you understand that?"

Sarah nodded that she understood, wondering all along if she even wanted to hear more than she had already. "I won't tell anyone what we've talked about today, if that's what you want. Nobody would believe me, anyway, if it's about you."

"Fine," he said, building a house of fingers in front of him. "I'm going to be honest with you because of what we've been through together, and believe it or not, I have come to respect you and honor your beliefs, even if they are contrary to mine." He collapsed the house of fingers and pointed one at Sarah for emphasis. "Now, does it really make a difference what I believe? It's what *they* believe that counts. That's what keeps them going, and that's what keeps *me* going."

He noticed Sarah starring at him, frowning. "It's just you and me, Sarah," he coaxed. "You may never get a chance to ask again."

"All that stuff you were saying about me in the newspapers and on TV; you don't really believe it, do you? It was all show, wasn't it?"

He lightly scratched his chin. "That's the name of the game, isn't it, Sarah? I have nothing against you. As I said, privately I honor your beliefs. But, publicly, if your beliefs start interfering with what I have going, then it's another story entirely."

As Sarah considered what he said, she realized that he had more color and looked better now than he did when she came in. She figured it was because he had been bored with no one to talk to—he needed some mental activity. "If that's true, it seems by what you were saying about me, you think I was interfering?"

"No, not yet, but if your beliefs catch on, sometime in the future you might interfere. Let's just say I was doing a little bit of preventative maintenance—like nipping you in the bud. But it looks like just the opposite happened. You and your beliefs look better now than they did before I got on your case.

"Nonetheless, I'm no dummy, and neither are most of the leaders of organized religion. If they see that you're a threat, then they will do all within their power to shut you up. We like to use the word 'cult' for those like you. It puts you in a little box and causes people to distrust and fear you. Whenever they fear you, they come running back to us. That's another slant on that fear factor we were talking about."

"You said, 'not yet.' Do you think I might interfere with your religion?"

"Perhaps. I can see that what you're saying intrigues some people. It could, in the future, be a problem." *Man, this kid has all the questions and most of the answers.* "But, then again, if I lose even one of my flock to you, that's not good."

"If what I say intrigues the people, there must be something to it. Why don't you change your beliefs? Like you said, it's so logical, what I believe."

The minister answered with a reserved confidence, "Can't do it, Sarah. You don't understand. I have my own thing going. Let me say it another way. I know the game and I play it for my own benefit. Plenty of religious leaders all over the world do the same. It's been going on for centuries. Now, this is very important. There are many, many great religious leaders who follow the teaching of the Bible, the Koran, the Torah, and other holy books. They will never open their minds to believe anything else, particularly that they are God. They will follow their book, because they believe it to be true. You have to honor this because they may be right."

The minister waited for Sarah's reply. When none came, he continued:

"Buddhists have a similar belief to yours, that we're all a part of God, but most other organized religions won't budge from their belief that we are separate from God. Believing anything else is demonstrating a lack of faith and risking going to hell. They just won't do it—because they believe it. And, again, I have to tell you, they may be right—and you may be wrong."

Sarah felt the need to move on. "Are you still going to bad mouth me?"

"Of course, Sarah," he replied. He then smiled compassionately. "However, you must always remember, I don't hold any ill feelings or animosity toward you. You should always remember that, because if you continue this, there's going to be a lot more out there as bad or even worse than me. Don't let me or them get to you emotionally. If you do, then we have you right where we want you. We'll finish you off, just like that." He snapped his fingers.

The minister scratched at the bandage over his wound through the sheet. "Damn, how do you get rid of the itch? It drives me crazy. Well, where was…That's one of the first things I noticed about you. When I couldn't get you to back down right away, I knew I was in for a fight. I guess, your not backing down and my pushing even harder were instrumental in getting us both shot."

Sarah looked dismally at the man on the bed in front of her. She sighed and said, hardly above a whisper, "That's nice to know."

Bob received the call at Pizza Shack early on Monday morning from the organizers of the World Environmental Symposium. They wanted Sarah to speak for forty minutes on Tuesday, July 27, at 2 P.M.

They were even more anxious for her to speak now, since the attempt on her life had gained worldwide attention.

Although Bob didn't know what Dr. Westhead's decision would be, he got the vital information and promised that Sarah would be there Monday evening. Hotel arrangements had already been made by the symposium staff, and they promised airport limousine service if Bob would notify them of her flight number and arrival time.

Bob relayed the message to Barbara at the hospital. It brought initial elation from Sarah, followed by renewed panic at the thought of having to make a forty-minute speech to environmental leaders of the world.

Later in the morning Sarah received calls from the morning shows of the three major television networks, *The O'Reilly Factor* on the Fox News Network, and CNN's *Larry King Live*. They all requested that Sarah appear on their show while she was in New York, each preferring the earliest time available. Barbara made no commitment but promised consideration when Sarah's schedule was organized.

The President's personal secretary also called to renew the invitation to have lunch with President Oakley and his wife Sandra, and daughter April at the White House. Monday at one o'clock was suggested, so that Sarah and her mom could stop over on their way to New York City. Barbara accepted, and called an agent to work out the travel details to both Washington, D.C., and New York on Monday, and the return to San Antonio on Thursday.

On Tuesday morning, when Dr. Westhead released Sarah from the hospital, he was well aware of the commitment made to the symposium. He wasn't too happy about it, but gave his okay for Sarah to attend, as if at that point he had a choice.

Sarah had hardly settled at home when Ralph and JB arrived. They reported that excitement was high among the hundreds of kids attending the morning GARBAGE meeting. A big send-off was already planned for Sunday afternoon on the Pizza Shack parking lot. And a GARBAGE member had volunteered his sound equipment from his western band, so Sarah could practice her speech on the group. Smiley's mom had talked to the production manager of the symposium and was assured that her Powerpoint program would work fine with their production equipment. She promised Sarah that she would have the program ready in time for several days of practice and a trial run at the send-off.

Later in the afternoon, Bob and Barbara slipped away from the Pizza Shack and came home to help Sarah and the kids work on the first draft of the speech. Prompted by ABC's *Good Morning America* producer, Joyce Brown called to see if, as a favor to her, she could persuade Sarah to appear on *Good Morning America* on Tuesday, her first morning in New York City. Bob answered the call and quickly agreed in exchange for Joyce's help in working with Sarah on her speaking skills and delivery. As this favor to ABC could result in a promotion, she was quick to volunteer. She agreed to meet with Sarah Friday and Saturday and even offered to help refine the speech itself. That way Sarah would have almost a week to practice.

On Friday, three days before the New York trip, Police Chief Sheck sat behind his desk across from Bob and Barbara. "I bet she is going to come home with New York and the world in her pocket. She's got that little unknown something that turns her up a notch when the occasion calls for it. In sports, these people are called gamers. They rise to the occasion—find a way to win. She'll come home just the way she's leaving—a winner."

"That's comforting for you to say that," Barbara replied. "But still, she's just a child. I think she'll handle the television interviews okay, but meeting the President and making that speech will be a nightmare. Can you imagine standing before five thousand people from all kinds of different countries, each waiting to be entertained for forty minutes?"

"How is she taking it so far?"

"Initially she was terrified. Now, either she is covering up her emotions, or she has accepted the fact that she has to do it and is determined it isn't going to bother her."

"Well, so much for Sarah's future problems," Bob said, anxious to hear about John Holland. "What about the object of her past?"

Sheck nodded. "What I tell you here today must be kept in complete confidence. I don't think the DA will be too happy with me if I divulge what he has leaked to me. And I know the judge would—well, he wouldn't appreciate it if this information got out prior to Holland's day in court. So hold it close to your vest, if you know what I mean."

Receiving nods of agreement from the McPhees, Sheck resumed, "We appear to have a true nutcase on our hands. As the shrinks say, Holland is someone our society has neglected, leading him to this dastardly deed. That's only my opinion, of course.

"The judge called in two doctors to evaluate Mr. Holland. I'm told they interviewed him and ran tests. They also contacted his sister who still lives in the house where they grew up. She was happy to make the trip here to help her brother. The doctors gleaned some valuable information from her.

"They then came together and combined their findings into one diagnosis. Because they're continuing their evaluation, this report is only preliminary. Their final report will be in more detail. If they had any differences of opinion, they listed them separately.

"We have to live with what they decide—at least the judge does. He will base his decision about having a trial on the mutual opinion of these two doctors. If they feel Holland is sane, the judge will set a trail date. If he's ruled insane, the judge will send him to a hospital. At a later date he is reevaluated to see what is to be done in his case. It could go on forever."

Sheck rubbed the back of his neck as he gazed at the statuette of his grandfather. He glanced at Barbara with a trace of a smile.

"No mules, huh?" Barbara asked, bringing a full smile from the lawman.

"Okay, according to his sister and the doctors, John Holland was raised over in East Texas, in the little town of Palestine. His father was a charismatic, money-grabbing, publicity-seeking minister of a local church. Highly sensitive to how the public viewed his family, he was never satisfied with their behavior.

"Despite how they acted, Holland's father usually found some fault with him, his mother, and his younger sister. He took to beating them on a daily basis, while telling them God was also sure to punish them. In spite of his profession, he turned into a monster at home. So his actions wouldn't get back to the parishioners, he threatened his family with his own wrath, as well as God's, if they ever told anyone of his abusing them. As far as the church people were concerned, the good minister's wife and children certainly had a lot of little accidents to account for their bruises."

"Holland's father sounds like a real choice character," Bob interjected.

"Kinda like Hightower," added Barbara.

"Right. Well, eventually, the good minister left his wife, John, and his sister, and ran off with a parishioner, a woman of some means. Their mother accused the kids of driving their father away, and they soon were receiving the same brutality from her. She said that God would also punish them.

"John tried to please his father and, later, his mother, but after the frustration of repeated failure and humiliation, he developed a deep un-vented anger and resentment toward his parents, and for God and the church. This anger intensified as he got older. Anyone professing to be God-fearing, or even religious, gained his automatic distrust and even hate."

Sheck rose from his chair and stretched his lower back. "I had a little run in with a bull, yesterday. The bull won."

Bob took the opportunity to stand. He walked over and leaned on the window seal, looking out onto the station lawn. "Maybe you should quit your part-time job?"

"I've considered that, but I'd probably be miserable." Sheck forced his aching back into the chair. "Okay, you people still with me?"

"Yes, I can see where he's headed with Hightower, but I'm curious how Sarah fits into this. Let's hear the rest," Barbara encouraged him to continue.

"John's deep resentment about God and the church finally came to a boiling point, first with Hightower, then with Sarah. They both became a threat to him. Sarah because she spoiled his big effort at notoriety when she proved that his facts were wrong in the devil-worshiping article he wrote. On top of that, she said that she was God. That turned on that old failure, then resentment cycle. When he was the one chosen to cover the news she was making, that rubbed it in even more. He had to write favorably about someone that was associated with God, or perhaps, was actually God.

"In John's eyes Hightower is the epitome of his father, only on a much grander scale. He's a charismatic man of God that everyone reveres. He controls a great deal of money and has the same particular thirst for publicity that his father had. Unfortunately, for several years now, John has had to quench Hightower's thirst by writing about him and his achievements, thus fueling his own silent anger. He really burned inside when Hightower supposedly referred to him as a liar in front of all those people and that woman reporter from San Antonio. This was his father all over again, and he was either unable or afraid to publicly strike back."

Sheck paused as he adjusted his back to a more comfortable position in the chair. "Say, you folks like some coffee or a soda maybe?"

"Coffee, black," Barbara answered. "Soda. Any kind," was Bob's choice.

Sheck called to an aide over the intercom for the refreshments, then continued:

"Because of Sarah and Hightower's continual onslaught of his basic aversion to those associated with God or the church, John's awareness of basic reality was diminished. He also lost his ability to take events and interpret them realistically, which, say the doctors, led to his loss of emotional control—a form of paranoiac schizophrenia.

"So, when he was forced to deal directly with Sarah and Dr. Hightower, whose beliefs were contrary to his own, his protective mechanism was to retreat into his own little world, ironically, the Son of God. He became God, or Immanuel, whom he called the messenger of God, hence the supreme judge and jury. Drawing upon his studies of Milton, he used—"

Sheck waited as an officer served the drinks. He sipped his coffee, then blew into the cup to cool it a bit.

"As I was saying, because of his studies of Milton, Holland used Immanuel as an alter ego, protected from any type of punishment or retaliation. He could vent his own anger through Immanuel, threatening to send anyone to hell whom he connected in any way with his father. Ironically, however, when he became Immanuel, he was somehow under the control of his father. He carried around a portrait recently identified by his sister as that of his father. Holland was shackled by that photo because as Immanuel, if he did not please his father, he went to hell.

"In this state he lost all objective reality. The phone calls merely vented his frustration at having to deal with both Sarah and Hightower. When you called him out to meet you at Fair Park, you forced his hand—either put up or shut up. He went deeper into his protective state of Immanuel, thus losing all connection to reality."

Sheck looked up as Bob, standing at the window, lowered his gaze in confusion. He waited for Bob to speak.

"Which means I sent him over the edge?"

"Probably, but remember, sooner or later it would've happened anyway."

Sheck took a sip of coffee. "During the last few weeks and, particularly, the last few hours before the shooting, he went in and out of his schizophrenic state repeatedly, only to finally lose out to Immanuel. To please his father, Immanuel became the final judge of Hightower and Sarah. And you know the rest." He folded his hands on the desk in front of him.

"Bottom line, what do you think about it" Bob asked.

Sheck thought before answering. "You know, I suppose that you can go back into anyone's past and find some little something to blame present behavior on. We're all victims in some way. We're all from some kind of dysfunctional family. That doesn't give us license to go out and screw up, whether it be killing someone or robbing a neighbor. John's was a criminal act and should be treated as such. Hell, anyone that kills another human being has to be crazy. If you're going to send John Holland to the hospital, all murderers should be sent to the hospital. Where do you draw the line?"

Because Sarah and Barbara's flight was scheduled to leave San Antonio International Airport at 6 A.M., Bob had them up and on their way by three on Monday morning. Their luncheon with the President was scheduled for one o'clock, so they had plenty of spare time for possible airline delays.

Sarah's schedule was set for her special appearances. Monday night was to be with *Larry King Live* on CNN; this after a long hectic day of travel and lunch with the President. ABC garnered the first activity Tuesday for Sarah on *Good Morning America,* followed by the two o'clock symposium speech, then an appearance on *The O'Reilly Factor* on Fox News Network that evening. *This Morning* on CBS was scheduled for Wednesday morning. The remainder of Wednesday would be free for Sarah and Barbara to attend other symposium events or just rest. Before their flight home on Thursday, Sarah was due to be interviewed on NBC's *Today.*

Mrs. Schultz put together an excellent Powerpoint presentation and Joyce Brown's speech coaching was invaluable. Sarah felt comfortable with the computer and confident about her speech. For the send-off party on Sunday afternoon, Smiley and a group of older kids built a makeshift stage and lectern so that Sarah would be higher than the large audience in the parking lot, and a twenty-four inch monitor was rented to show the Powerpoint presentation. Sarah's practice speech came across without a hitch.

Ralph had arranged for Mayor Rayford Johnson to introduce her to the crowd. In his introduction he announced that he had taken a poll among council members and found that GARBAGE's requested ordinance for garbage recycling would pass the final vote. This meant Sarah could include the news on her speech as an accomplishment of GARBAGE.

After Sarah's practice speech, Police Chief Sheck arrived with the emergency lights of his blue and white squad car flashing. As the crowd parted, he came to a halt in front of the small stage. To everyone's surprise, out stepped none other than the Reverend Dr. Mark Hightower on crutches. After a short speech that wished Sarah good-luck, he and Chief Sheck presented Ralph with a plaque of commendation for his heroics at the shooting. As he accepted the award, for once Ralph was speechless.

Sarah thanked both Sheck and Hightower, and embarrassed Hightower by kissing him on the cheek in front of the *Gazette* reporter's camera. "Every little bit of publicity helps," she whispered, much to the minister's chagrin. He shook his head and replied, "Upstaged again."

After the send-off was over, Sarah and Barbara went home. They were in bed by dark, anticipating their two o'clock wake-up time and three days of tight scheduling. Sarah didn't sleep very well, and by the time they reached the airport in San Antonio, she could hardly contain her excitement. Barbara, a bundle of nerves, worried that perhaps she had forgotten something or that the plane would have a problem, making them late at the White House. Bob let them off for curbside check-in and bid them good luck, glad he wasn't going. It was sure to be a hectic three days.

They boarded the plane, located their seats, and Barbara assisted Sarah in putting her carry-on bag in the overhead storage. It would be quite some time before Sarah could remove the sling and use her left arm. Nearby, a small boy about twelve-years-old recognized Sarah and held up his hand in the Earth Salute. "Hi, Sarah," he called out, drawing attention from others close by.

Sarah nodded and winked at the boy. Several other passengers greeted Sarah and asked how she was feeling. She assured them she was doing well and was looking forward to the trip.

She and Barbara soon settled in. Despite the excitement, the lack of sleep began taking its toll and Sarah felt very tired. She buckled up and laid her head back against the chair as the flight attendant presented her usual safety talk. A moment later the plane began to move backward. The plane stopped for an instant, then moved forward in its taxi toward the runway. The brakes squeaked as the plane came to a halt. At the same instant, the engines began to roar and when the brakes were released the plane thrust forward to pick up enough speed for takeoff, the wheels popping against the seams of the runway. There was a slight tilt up, pushing Sarah back against her seat, bringing a slight pain in her chest, then smoothness brought on by flight, followed by an inner rumble of the wheels being retracted. They were airborne.

Sarah released a long tired sigh and closed her eyes just as she heard the signal indicating safety belts were no longer necessary. She longed to be back home, enjoying a carefree lazy summer like the year before, with no particular worries about speeches, television appearances, and, most of all, lunch with the President of the United States. *I wonder what JB and Ralph are going to do today? It would be so neat if I could just put in my fifteen minutes of Earth cleanup, maybe a shift at the Pizza Shack, then spend an afternoon at the river with the guys.*

That empty, white, hazy cloud crept across her mind. Thanks, Spook, she projected. I need help. I don't know if I can handle the next few days, or the next few hours for that matter. She waited for an answer to her concerns.

Spook's voice, as usual, was deep and resonant. *"You must remember, little one, you are here to learn by experience, to teach, and to love. And to really learn, sometimes you have to sacrifice something else that might seem important to you. There will always be a price to pay in learning and loving. You are certainly paying that price.*

"You are being presented with an opportunity to influence a very important man. He is a man who can move mountains with the stroke of the pen. He has the power to change the world. However, he needs to be convinced, to be motivated. Recent events have put you, little one, into

a position to influence this man. You can enlist the help of the wife and daughter of this powerful man, to remind him of what he already knows deep within himself: that the future of the Earth is now in jeopardy.

"Today could be a historic day in the life of Earth, when the energy of four women combine in a united spark of undefeatable love, bringing this man to realize politics must be thrust aside before it's too late, and his power used to save Earth."

Spook was gone. Tears came to Sarah's closed eyes as she thought over what he said, and she knew that there was no way she could give up her fight. Yes, she knew that there would always be a problem presented for her to help solve. Also, the bigger the problem she was able to handle, the bigger the problems would become. She had just as well accept them as a challenge and solve them to the best of her ability in a happy, loving, confident manner.

Sarah opened her eyes and wiped the tears with a tissue from her purse. She glanced over at her mom to find her asleep. Touching her lightly on the arm, Barbara's eyes opened.

"What's wrong, Sarah? Sweetheart, what's the matter?"

"Mom," Sarah asked, disregarding her tears, "can you tell me anything about the President's wife and daughter?"

Journal Note

"Great trip, little one. You are a superstar. The universe is cheering."

EPILOGUE

After the noon rush, Sarah sat next to her dad and across from her mom in a booth. Bob slipped the *Gazette* out of its plastic wrapper and laid it to the side. He poured Ranch dressing on his salad from the buffet, and stabbed at a cherry tomato. It disappeared into his mouth.

Barbara skimmed a spoonful of noodle soup and blew it before slurping it up. "Yum...not bad for a change. I think we should stick with this recipe." She watched Sarah as she sipped on her Coke. For the first time in weeks Sarah appeared to be relaxed and rested. Barbara was happy Sarah had agreed to spend at least a week resting following the New York trip, even to the point of temporarily relinquishing her leadership role in GARBAGE. Her group activity had been her daily litter work and standing on the sideline during Tuesday's meeting. She opted out of the lone supermarket demonstration.

There had been several calls from various news outlets and other organizations pressing for an audience with Sarah, but her parents told them she would be unavailable for another week. They took all the information so she could return their calls in the middle of August. They did agree that Sarah, starting in September, could spend six hours per week for research at Dr. Pauley's Central Texas

Parapsychology Institute.

As Sarah took a hefty bite out of a slice of pepperoni pizza, she watched her mom unwrap a packet of crackers and nibble on one. She could tell she was about to say something by the curious look on her face:

"I've heard that restaurants, motels, service stations, and other tourist related businesses aren't too happy with Spook removing your image from the Guadalupe."

Sarah swallowed the bite of pizza. "Last night he said that it was very hard for him to keep the image there. Since it had served its purpose, there was no point in leaving it any longer."

Bob slid his salad bowl aside and unfolded the newspaper. "Well, it was fun while it lasted, but Chief Sheck is happy it's gone. He said the traffic and crowd control was an ongoing headache—Hey, look here!" he exclaimed, tapping an article on the front page. "Looks like you ladies made a huge impression on the president of these United States." He held up the paper so Sarah and Barbara could see the headline, "President dumps environmental bill."

"Listen to this: 'President Oakley shocked Congress when he refused to sign a long-awaited, admittedly soft environmental protection bill he had strongly supported and personally pushed through the legislative process. In returning the bill to the surprised legislators, he informed them it had to be completely reworked, despite the long hours of debate it had endured. He maintained the bill was not near stringent enough, had too many loopholes, and too heavily favored special interest groups.

"'President Oakley's bewildered advisors and congressional supporters could give no reason for his about-face, suddenly taking a hard-line stance in protecting the environment.'"

"Yes!" Sarah shouted, causing the few remaining customers to turn and see what was all the commotion. "We did it, Mom! We made the President change his mind!"

Barbara beamed her pleasure at her daughter's success. "Yes, you did. I never thought it possible."

Sarah slid out of the booth and skipped to get a refill on her Coke. Bob looked across at Barbara and grinned. "Perhaps she really can rule the Earth."

"Yeah, maybe we'd better make friends with her, to remind her we're on her team—lest we get pushed aside."

"Pushed aside…where?" Sarah asked as she returned.

"Oh, nothing," Barbara answered with an amused sidelong glance at Bob. She watched Sarah take a long gulp from the Coke and wondered just how many her daughter drank each day.

"Whoa, you've got to be kidding," Bob announced as he read a second page article. "Get this: 'On Tuesday, the Reverend Dr. Mark Hightower, having just returned from a week's vacation, abruptly resigned his position at Hill Country Chapel of God. The shocked members of the board reluctantly accepted his resignation.

"'One of the board members reported that Dr. Hightower, while on vacation in Taos, New Mexico, was offered and accepted a pastor's position with the new Unity Church. Attempts to contact Dr. Hightower for comment were unsuccessful.'" Bob laid the newspaper aside and noticed a curious look masking Sarah's face. "What do you think?"

"He believes it. I knew he did when I talked to him at the hospital. He believes like we do—that we're all God."

Barbara studied her daughter before her reply, "So, he's giving up the money and fame to start a new church that teaches about spirituality."

"My daughter. First she conquers the President of the United States, then the most reverend and powerful Dr. Mark Hightower. I'm impressed," Bob added.

Sarah beamed a radiant smile. All of a sudden, all the trouble was worth it.

Lying on the bed, Sarah waited in the dark for Spook to appear as she studied the designs on the ceiling made by the street light filtering through the blinds. Aside from the first day of her trip to New York, all the good news had made this her best day in weeks. She knew she would have a hard time sleeping, but she didn't care—she wanted to bask in her success.

"Yes, It has been a good day, little one. The universe is, indeed, cheering," came Spook's voice, loud and clear."

"You were right, Spook. I can make a difference. It's so neat about Dr. Hightower. I bet you had something to do with that, didn't you?"

"We've had a conversation or two, he and I."

"Wow, you're talking to the Rev. That's cool. What's the deal? Why's he going to Taos? What happened?"

"Well, it appears that he was encouraged to seek out this spiritual lady, and—"

Sarah laughed, interrupting Spook. "You mean *you* got him to talk to a psychic?"

Sarah heard Spook chuckle. *"Well, I might have had a hand in it. You see, they needed to meet each other. They had an instant liking for one another. Each can teach the other a lot...and many other people need their guidance. She has the wisdom to show him the spiritual way and he has the ability to get the message to those who are ready to listen."*

"You said they like each other. How much?"

"Some."

Sarah giggled. "Like, are they hooked-up? Are they lovers or what?"

"You will find out in due time, little one. I will say at this time, she is much like you, only an adult version."

"Oh, really. That's neat. How will I find out?"

"Because, when they get their church started, they want you to come speak about GARBAGE."

"Really? Wow, that's cool. Was that your idea?"

"No, Hightower's. You were responsible for his change. Now, he wants to honor you in return."

"That'll be fun. Now, what's next for GARBAGE?"

"The demands on your time will increase dramatically in the near future. Your message is being accepted all over the world and the people want to hear more—to learn more. You, Ralph, JB, and GARBAGE have much to do.

"Also, if you choose, you will be contacted by a gentleman that's wants to publish the journal in book form. If that's your wish, we will have to spend many hours making it complete. The people need to see the journal. It will be an excellent spiritual guide."

"Yes," Sarah beamed. "That's a great idea. Let's get started right away."

"First, you need a few more days of rest. It has been a long but fruitful journey for you, your parents and the group. Soon, you will have many more opportunities to help protect the Earth."

"And many new bad problems, huh?" Before Spook could answer, Sarah added, "I know, I know. Problems are only bad if you think they are."

"Granted."
"I love you, Spook."
"And the universe is shouting its love for you, little one."

THE END

Please send your comments about this novel to the publisher's address below or to www.omapublishing.com. Enclose your e-mail address for news of forthcoming books on the continuing saga of Sarah McPhee, including her complete journal of information from Spook.

Oma Publishing Company
325 River Springs Drive, Suite 100
Seguin, Texas 78155-0179

Would you like to order additional copies of

GARBAGE Angel (Sarah's Story)

for your friends? Please visit our website at www.omapublishing.com.

To order by mail, use the form below and send to:

Oma Publishing Company
325 River Springs Drive, Suite 100
Seguin, Texas 78155-0179

Please send:
___ copies of *GARGAGE Angel (Sarah's Story)*
at $24 each U.S. (Canada $32) $________

Subtotal $________

Tax (Texas residents only - 8% or $1.92 per book) $________

Postage and handling - $3.25 for first book
and $1.00 for each additional book $________

TOTAL DUE $_____

Name ______________________________

Address ______________________________

City/State/ZIP ______________________________

Phone ______________ E-mail address ______________

__ Check enclosed. Bill my: __VISA __MasterCard __Am Exp

Name on card ______________________________

Account No. ______________ Expiration date ___________

Signature of card holder ______________________________

Make checks payable to Oma Publishing Company (Send to above address)

USUALLY SHIP ORDERS WITHIN 24 HOURS